THE HUGO WINNERS
VOLUME ONE
1962-1967

Edited by Isaac Asimov

ISAAC ASIMOV has been one of the
most prolific and widely read authors in
the field of popular science for the last
twenty years. Over a hundred of his books
have been published and they range from
science fiction and pure science to history,
religion, literature and geography. His
work is read with equal enthusiasm by
SF fans, academics and students. Dr.
Asimov currently lives in New York City,
devoting the greater part of his time to
writing.

THE HUGO WINNERS
VOLUME ONE
1962-1967

Edited by Isaac Asimov

To the memory of Hugo Gernsback
the grandfather of us all.

The Hugo Winners
Volume One
1962-1967

Edited by Isaac Asimov

SPHERE BOOKS LIMITED
30/32 Gray's Inn Road, London, WC1X 8JL

First published in Great Britain in 1973 by Sphere Books Ltd.
© Isaac Asimov, 1971

Printed in Great Britain by
Hazell Watson & Viney Ltd,
Aylesbury, Bucks

ACKNOWLEDGEMENTS

"The Dragon Masters," by Jack Vance, copyright © 1962 by Galaxy Publishing Corporation. Reprinted by permission of the author and the author's agent, Scott Meredith Literary Agency, Inc.

"No Truce With Kings," by Poul Anderson, copyright © 1963 by Mercury Press, Inc. Reprinted by permission of the author and the author's agent, Scott Meredith Literary Agency, Inc.

"Soldier, Ask Not," by Gordon R. Dickson, copyright © 1964 by Galaxy Publishing Corporation. Reprinted by permission of the author and the author's agent, Robert P. Mills, Ltd.

" 'Repent, Harlequin!' said the Ticktockman," by Harlan Ellison, copyright © 1965 by Galaxy Publishing Corporation. All rights reassigned, 1966, to the author. Reprinted by permission of the author and the author's agent, Robert P. Mills, Ltd.

"The Last Castle," by Jack Vance, copyright © 1966 by Galaxy Publishing Corporation. Reprinted by permission of the author and the author's agent, Scott Meredith Literary Agency, Inc.

"Neutron Star," by Larry Niven, copyright © 1966 by Galaxy Publishing Corporation. Reprinted by permission of the author and the author's agent, Robert P. Mills, Ltd.

CONTENTS

Some nine years ago, it had seemed necessary to prepare an anthology of those science fiction novelettes and short stories that had won Hugos—the awards handed out for the best-of-the-year at the World Science Fiction Conventions held each Labor Day weekend in various cities.

Needed as editor of such an anthology was someone who was a person of note, sane and rational, fearless and intrepid, witty and forceful and, above all, devilishly handsome. In addition, he had to be someone who (through some grotesque miscarriage of justice) had never won a Hugo.

Since I (Isaac Asimov) had at that time never won a Hugo and since all the required adjectives were quite notoriously applicable to myself, I was at once chosen as editor by that estimable publishing house, Doubleday and Co., Inc.

The anthology was published in 1962 under the title of *The Hugo Winners* and was an enormous success, partly by the nature of the excellent prize-winning stories it contained and partly by that indefinable cachet I lent it as editor. (Do not bother to volunteer definitions, please!)

Once it was published, though, I faced a dilemma:

(a) The stories in *The Hugo Winners* included only those prize-winning items up to and including the 19th Convention in 1961—but Hugo awards would continue to be made. This meant that sooner or later a second anthology would have to be prepared. Naturally, I wanted to be editor of the second anthology, too, but in order to do that I had to maintain my qualification as the very best science fiction writer in the world never to have won a Hugo. (Or to have won a Hugo, either, but I'm too modest to say that.)

(b) On the other hand, I wanted to win a Hugo.

These two, you see, are mutually exclusive. As a logician would say: if *a*, then *not-b*; and if *b*, then *not-a*. Either way I would be unhappy.

Since I am sane and rational, I sat down and figured out the chances. On the one hand, everybody was going to read *The Hugo Winners* and, in particular, read the introduction in which I movingly described the injustice inflicted on me in the matter of the Hugos. Clearly, one and all would dissolve in tears. Obviously, every fan club in the United States would decide that as soon as they were in a position to run a World Convention they would see to it that one of my sterling science fiction stories would be awarded the Hugo it so richly and automatically deserved.

On the other hand, since 1958, I had written hardly any science fiction aside from an occasional slight short-short, so there was nothing to give me a Hugo *for*.

A weighing of these two propositions proved clearly that I would have to get a Hugo for nothing. It seemed an odd thing to arrange, but I am far too fine a person to disappoint a fan club. If they wanted to give me a Hugo for nothing, I would take it—or even grab it, if they hesitated.

The year 1962 passed with a convention in Chicago which was erratic in the way of Hugos and did not hand an individual award in the short story division but granted one to Brian Aldiss's "Hothouse" series as a whole—five stories which, taken together, are virtually a novel and therefore cannot be included within the purview of an anthology of shorter pieces. (Besides I don't travel very long distances and everyone knew I wouldn't be in Chicago.)

But then came 1963 and Washington, D.C., was going to run the convention that year, and I can go as far as Washington. In plenty of time, George Scithers, who was handling the details, called me to ask if I would come down and be part of a panel-discussion.

With pretended casualness, I asked, "Don't you want me as master of ceremonies?"

You see, usually when I attend a convention, I am master of

ceremonies because of my graceful wit and charming presence, and that means I hand out the Hugos—to other people. Here was George Scithers, going to considerable lengths to make sure I would be there at the convention and yet he was not asking me to be master of ceremonies.

"No," he said, just as casually, "Ted Sturgeon is going to be master of ceremonies."

Ordinarily, I would have kicked and screamed and then gone into a prolonged pout. This time, though, I merely chuckled. "Sure, George," I said, "I'll be there."

You see, my keen analytical mind told me that Sturgeon was going to be master of ceremonies so he could give me a Hugo. I couldn't very well be master of ceremonies myself and give myself a Hugo, could I? I'm far too modest, as anyone can tell.

But then, just about a week before the convention, with my hotel room reserved, my car tuned up, and everything, George called again. "Isaac," he said, "Ted can't make it after all because of family complications. I know this is short notice, but can you be master of ceremonies, after all?"

I had to say, yes, but my heart sank. No Hugo after all!

I went to Washington in pensive mood. I greeted George curtly and occupied my seat at the head table during the banquet sullenly, occasionally eying the audience in a markedly morose manner.

Eventually, I had to give up and begin reading off the list of nominees in the various categories and then read the winner in each and then hand out the Hugo.

There was only one thing to do and I did it. I handed out those Hugos savagely, snarling at each winner as he came up to get the object. When Fred Pohl, a friend of my childhood, approached to pick up one on behalf of a winner, I cried out as he came bounding up, "Break a leg, friend of my childhood!" (But he didn't. Nobody would do the least little thing to oblige me.)

I grew more and more eloquent as Hugo after Hugo was awarded and when only one was left, I hit the peak of invective. With the closed envelope still in my hand, I asked the audience to take note of the fact that no Hugo was ever awarded me, and I told them why. I raised a fist high to heaven and said, "It's anti-Semitic prejudice, that's what it is. You're all a bunch of Nazis."

And with that cold, unimpassioned statement, I opened the envelope and it said, "For putting the science in science fiction —Isaac Asimov."

I had really gotten my Hugo for nothing after all. The original plan had indeed been to have Ted Sturgeon hand me a Hugo, as I had thought. He had really had to stay away against his will and George Scithers had said, "Oh, well, let Isaac give it to himself. It'll make it all the funnier and he's the only writer in science fiction who can give himself a Hugo and not be embarrassed."

A lot he cared that I stood there for ten minutes, trying to accept my Hugo with an air of modest surprise, while the audience laughed itself silly. And he still hasn't explained what he meant by saying that I was the only writer in science fiction who could give himself a Hugo and not be embarrassed. I don't get that at all.

Clearly, though, this was a Hugo for nothing, and would not disqualify me from editing further volumes of Hugo winners. At least, I intended to argue the point in this fashion.

But then came 1966 and the 24th Convention in Cleveland. Again I was invited and again I was to be master of ceremonies. This time though, a new and unprecedented category was offered for the Hugos. It was to be that of a "novel series"; that is, an interconnected group of three or more novels.

Naturally, such an award would be the most impressive one ever offered, since a Hugo is coveted more for a long item than for a short one, and this was the longest item possible. Besides it was the only category which asked for a vote on best-of-all-time, rather than merely best-of-the-year.

I won't stretch this out. When the best novel-series award came up, I was shoved to one side and little Harlan Ellison ran up to make the announcement, and the winner (however did you guess?) was Isaac Asimov for "The Foundation Series."

This time I had a Hugo for something, and the biggest single Hugo ever handed out. Recognition at last, but this time—good-bye anthology.

Came 1970.

Lawrence P. Ashmead, Doubleday's most genial and lovable editor, said, "Isaac, it's time we did *The Hugo Winners, Volume Two.*"

I said sadly, "So it is. Whom ought we to get as the editor?"

"Why, you, of course," said Larry.

"Impossible," I said, "I've won two Hugos."

"That may well be so," said Larry, "but we still need a person of note, sane and rational, fearless and intrepid, witty and forceful, and, above all, devilishly handsome, and is there any science fiction writer but yourself who can possibly fill these qualifications?"

You know, that had never occurred to me!

Larry was obviously right, so, with that modest smile that is the hallmark of my personality, I said, "Larry, you're perfectly correct, and I should have seen that for myself."

Here I am again then, and here is *The Hugo Winners, Volume Two.*

PUBLISHER'S NOTE

THE HUGO WINNERS, volume two originally appeared in America as a single, giant book. In order to offer this excellent collection at a reasonable price on the UK market it was necessary to divide the book into two sections running from 1963–1967 and from 1968–1970.

1963
21st CONVENTION
WASHINGTON

I have a certain system for introducing prize-winnings stories, and the core of it is that I never talk about the stories.

Why should I, after all? They are prize-winners and therefore may be accepted as good stories. It may be that you, as a particular reader, will disagree with the consensus—but only you can tell that, and I wouldn't argue you out of your opinion just by telling you loudly that the story is great. Besides, the story is right here and surely you would rather read it than listen to me talk about it.

So what do I do? Easy! I talk about the authors.

The world of the science fiction writer is a tight one and a friendly one. We're in a minority. All writers are, anyway, because we are misunderstood by normal people. Our charming eccentricities are dismissed as evidence of serious neurotic disorders. Our habit of sitting in a chair and carefully working out intricate and thoughtful story lines with our eyes closed is dismissed as a disgusting sign of feckless sloth, just because we snore a little in the process.

Even among writers generally, the science fiction writer stands out as peculiar. Writers may get ideas, but science fiction writers get *crazy* ideas.

But we like one another, and we meet at conventions and sometimes in between conventions; and we talk, and laugh, and eat and drink, and sometimes just huddle together for security against a world that considers us queer because we have that rare and frightening characteristic—sanity.

All right, then. You don't know these queer people and I do —so I'll tell you about them.

At least, I'll tell you about all of them except those few, those very few, whom I've never met and with whom I've never corresponded. The chances of one of those just happening to come up is laughably small, so let's all laugh because here comes that chance.

I have never met Jack Vance, nor have I ever corresponded with him. But don't worry! I'll get another crack at him later in the anthology and I will think of something!

THE DRAGON MASTERS

I

The apartments of Joaz Banbeck, carved deep from the heart of a limestone crag, consisted of five principal chambers, on five different levels. At the top were the reliquarium and a formal council chamber: the first a room of somber magnificence housing the various archives, trophies and mementos of the Banbecks; the second a long narrow hall, with dark wainscoting chest-high and a white plaster vault above, extending the entire width of the crag, so that balconies overlooked Banbeck Vale at one end and Kergan's Way at the other.

Below were Joaz Banbeck's private quarters: a parlor and bed-chamber, then next his study and finally, at the bottom, a work-room where Joaz permitted none but himself.

Entry to the apartments was through the study, a large L-shaped room with an elaborate groined ceiling, from which depended four garnet-encrusted chandeliers. These were now dark. Into the room came only a watery gray light from four honed-glass plates on which, in the manner of a *camera obscura*, were focused views across Banbeck Vale. The walls were paneled with lignified reed. A rug patterned in angles, squares and circles of maroon, brown and black covered the floor.

In the middle of the study stood a naked man.

His only covering was the long, fine, brown hair which flowed down his back, the golden torc which clasped his neck. His features were sharp and angular, his body thin. He appeared to be listening or perhaps meditating. Occasionally he glanced at a yellow marble globe on a nearby shelf, whereupon his lips would move, as if he were committing to memory some phrase or sequence of ideas.

At the far end of the study a heavy door eased open.

A flower-faced young woman peered through, her expression mischievous, arch. At the sight of the naked man, she clapped her hands to her mouth, stifling a gasp. The naked man turned —but the heavy door had already swung shut.

For a moment he stood deep in frowning reflection, then slowly went to the wall on the inside leg of the L. He swung out a section of the bookcase and passed through the opening. Behind him the bookcase thudded shut. Descending a spiral staircase he came out into a chamber rough-hewn from the rock: Joaz Banbeck's private work-room. A bench supported tools, metal shapes and fragments, a bank of electromotive cells, oddments of circuitry: the current objects of Joaz Banbeck's curiosity.

The naked man glanced at the bench. He picked up one of the devices and inspected it with something like condescension, though his gaze was as clear and wondering as that of a child.

Muffled voices from the study penetrated to the work room. The naked man raised his head to listen, then stooped under the bench. He lifted a block of stone, slipped through the gap into a dark void. Replacing the stone, he took up a luminous wand, and set off down a narrow tunnel, which presently dipped to join a natural cavern. At irregular intervals luminous tubes exuded a wan light, barely enough to pierce the murk.

The naked man jogged forward swiftly, the silken hair flowing like a nimbus behind him.

Back in the study the minstrel-maiden Phade and an elderly seneschal were at odds. "Indeed I saw him!" Phade insisted. "With these two eyes of mine, one of the sacerdotes, standing thus and so, as I have described." She tugged angrily at his elbow. "Do you think me bereft of my wits, or hysterical?"

Rife the seneschal shrugged, committing himself neither one way nor the other. "I do not see him now." He climbed the staircase, peered into the sleeping parlor. "Empty. The doors above are bolted." He peered owlishly at Phade. "And I sat at my post in the entry."

"You sat sleeping. Even when I came past you snored!"

"You are mistaken; I did but cough."

"With your eyes closed, your head lolling back?"

Rife shrugged once more. "Asleep or awake, it is all the same. Admitting that the creature gained access, how did he leave? I was wakeful after you summoned me, as you must agree."

"Then remain on guard, while I find Joaz Banbeck." Phade ran down the passage which presently joined Bird Walk, so called for the series of fabulous birds of lapis, gold, cinnabar, malachite and marcasite inlaid into the marble. Through an arcade of green and gray jade in spiral columns she passed out into Kergan's Way, a natural defile which formed the main thoroughfare of Banbeck Village. Reaching the portal, she summoned a pair of lads from the fields. "Run to the brooder, find Joaz Banbeck! Hasten, bring him here; I must speak with him."

The boys ran off toward a low cylinder of black brick a mile to the north.

Phade waited. With the sun Skene at its nooning, the air was warm. The fields of vetch, bellegarde and spharganum gave off a pleasant odor. Phade went to lean against a fence. Now she began to wonder about the urgency of her news, even its basic reality. "No!" she told herself fiercely. "I saw! I saw!"

At either side tall white cliffs rose to Banbeck Verge, with mountains and crags beyond, and, spanning all, the dark sky flecked with feathers of cirrus. Skene glittered dazzling bright, a miniscule flake of brilliance.

Phade sighed, half-convinced of her own mistake. Once more, less vehemently, she reassured herself. Never before had she seen a sacerdote; why should she imagine one now?

The boys, reaching the brooder, had disappeared into the dust of the exercise pens. Scales gleamed and winked; grooms, dragon-masters, armorers in black leather moved about their work.

After a moment Joaz Banbeck came into view.

He mounted a tall thin-legged Spider, urged it to the full extent of its head-jerking lope, pounded down the track toward Banbeck Village. Phade's uncertainty grew. Might Joaz become exasperated, would he dismiss her news with an unbelieving stare? Uneasily she watched his approach. Coming to Banbeck Vale only a month before, she still felt unsure of her status. Her preceptors had trained her diligently in the barren little valley to the south where she had been born, but the disparity between teaching and practical reality at times bewildered her. She had learned that all men obeyed a small and identical group of behaviors. Joaz Banbeck, however, observed no such limits, and Phade found him completely unpredictable. She knew him to be a relatively young man, though his appearance provided no guide to his age. He had a pale austere face in which gray eyes shone like crystals, a long thin mouth which suggested flexibility, yet never curved far from a straight line. He moved languidly; his voice carried no vehemence; he made no pretense of skill with either saber or pistol; he seemed deliberately to shun any gesture which might win the admiration or affection of his subjects. Yet he had both.

Phade originally had thought him cold, but presently changed her mind. He was, so she decided, a man bored and lonely, with a quiet humor which at times seemed rather grim. But he treated her without discourtesy, and Phade, testing him with all her hundred and one coquetries, not infrequently thought to detect a spark of response.

Joaz Banbeck dismounted from the Spider, ordered it back to its quarters. Phade came diffidently forward, and Joaz turned her a quizzical look. "What requires so urgent a summons? Have you remembered the nineteenth location?"

Phade flushed in confusion. Artlessly she had described the painstaking rigors of her training; Joaz now referred to an item in one of the classifications which had slipped her mind.

Phade spoke rapidly, excited once more. "I opened the door into your study, softly, gently. And what did I see? A sacerdote, naked in his hair! He did not hear me. I shut the door, I

23

ran to fetch Rife. When we returned—the chamber was empty!"

Joaz's eyebrows contracted a trifle; he looked up the valley. "Odd." After a moment he asked, "You are sure that he saw nothing of you?"

"No. I think not. Yet, when I returned with stupid old Rife he had disappeared! Is it true that they know magic?"

"As to that, I cannot say," replied Joaz.

They returned up Kergan's Way, traversed tunnels and rock-walled corridors, finally came to the entry chamber.

Rife once more dozed at his desk. Joaz signaled Phade back and, going quietly forward, thrust aside the door to his study. He glanced here and there, nostrils twitching.

The room was empty.

He climbed the stairs, investigated the sleeping-parlor, returned to the study. Unless magic were indeed involved, the sacerdote had provided himself a secret entrance. With this thought in mind, he swung back the bookcase door, descended to the workshop and again tested the air for the sour-sweet odor of the sacerdotes. A trace? Possibly.

Joaz examined the room inch by inch, peering from every angle. At last, along the wall below the bench, he discovered a barely perceptible crack, marking out an oblong.

Joaz nodded with dour satisfaction. He rose to his feet and returned to his study. He considered his shelves: what was here to interest a sacerdote? Books, folios, pamphlets? Had they even mastered the art of reading? When next I meet a sacerdote I must inquire, thought Joaz vaguely; at least he will tell me the truth. On second thought, he knew the question to be ludicrous; the sacerdotes, for all their nakedness, were by no means barbarians, and in fact had provided him his four vision-panes—a technical engineering feat of no small skill.

He inspected the yellowed marble globe which he considered his most valued possession: a representation of mythical Eden. Apparently it had not been disturbed. Another shelf displayed models of the Banbeck dragons: the rust-red Termagant; the

Long-horned Murderer and its cousin the Striding Murderer; the Blue Horror; the Fiend, low to the ground, immensely strong, tail tipped with a steel barbell; the ponderous Jugger, skullcap polished and white as an egg. A little apart stood the progenitor of the entire group: a pearl-pallid creature upright on two legs, with two versatile central members, a pair of multi-articulated brachs at the neck.

Beautifully detailed though these models might be, why should they pique the curiosity of a sacerdote? No reason whatever, when most of the originals could be studied daily without hindrance.

What of the workshop, then? Joaz rubbed his long pale chin. He had no illusions about the value of his work. It was idle tinkering and no more. Joaz put aside conjecture. Most likely the sacerdote had come upon no specific mission, the visit perhaps being part of a continued inspection? But why?

A pounding at the door: old Rife's irreverent fist. Joaz opened to him.

"Joaz Banbeck, a notice from Ervis Carcolo of Happy Valley. He wishes to confer with you, and at this moment awaits your response on Banbeck Verge."

"Very well," said Joaz. "I will confer with Ervis Carcolo."

"Here? Or on Banbeck Verge?"

"On the Verge, in half an hour."

II

Ten miles from Banbeck Vale, across the wind-scoured wilderness of ridges, crags, spines of stone, amazing crevasses, barren fells and fields of tumbled boulders, lay Happy Valley. As wide as Banbeck Vale but only half as long and half as deep, its bed of wind-deposited soil was only half as thick and correspondingly less productive.

The Chief Councillor of Happy Valley was Ervis Carcolo, a thick-bodied short legged man with a vehement face, a heavy mouth, a disposition by turns jocose and wrathful. Unlike Joaz Banbeck, Carcolo enjoyed nothing more than his visits to the dragon barracks, where he treated dragon-masters, grooms and dragons alike to a spate of bawled invective.

Ervis Carcolo was an energetic man, intent upon restoring Happy Valley to the ascendancy it had enjoyed some twelve generations before. During those harsh times, before the advent of the dragons, men fought their own battles. The men of Happy Valley had been notably daring, deft and ruthless. Banbeck Vale, the Great Northern Rift, Clewhaven, Sadro Valley, Phosphor Gulch: all acknowledged the authority of the Carcolos.

Then down from space came a ship of the Basics, or grephs, as they were known at that time. The ship killed or took prisoner the entire population of Clewhaven. It attempted as much in the Great Northern Rift, but only partially succeeded; then bombarded the remaining settlements with explosive pellets.

When the survivors crept back to their devastated valleys, the dominance of Happy Valley was a fiction. A generation later, during the Age of Wet Iron, even the fiction collapsed. In a climactic battle Goss Carcolo was captured by Kergan Banbeck and forced to emasculate himself with his own knife.

Five years of peace elapsed, and then the Basics returned. After depopulating Sadro Valley, the great black ship landed in Banbeck Vale, but the inhabitants had taken warning and had fled into the mountains. Toward nightfall twenty-three of the Basics sallied forth behind their precisely trained warriors: several platoons of Heavy Troops, a squad of Weaponeers—these hardly distinguishable from the men of Aerlith—and a squad of Trackers: these emphatically different. The sunset storm broke over the Vale, rendering the flyers from the ship useless, which allowed Kergan Banbeck to perform the amazing feat which made his name a legend on Aerlith. Rather than joining the terrified flight of his people to the High Jambles, he assembled sixty warriors and shamed them to courage with jeers and taunts.

It was a suicidal venture—fitting the circumstances.

Leaping from ambush they hacked to pieces one platoon of

the Heavy Troops, routed the others, and captured the twenty-three Basics almost before they realized that anything was amiss. The Weaponeers stood back, frantic with frustration, unable to use their weapons for fear of destroying their masters. The Heavy Troopers blundered forward to attack, halting only when Kergan Banbeck performed an unmistakable pantomime to make it clear that the Basics would be the first to die.

Confused, the Heavy Troopers drew back. Kergan Banbeck, his men and the twenty-three captives escaped into the darkness.

The long Aerlith night passed. The dawn storm swept out of the east, thundered overhead, retreated majestically into the west; Skene rose like a blazing atom.

Three men emerged from a Basic ship: a Weaponeer and a pair of Trackers. They climbed the cliffs to Banbeck Verge, while above flitted a small Basic flyer, no more than a bouyant platform, diving and veering in the wind like a poorly balanced kite. The three men trudged south toward the High Jambles, a region of chaotic shadows and lights, splintered rock and fallen crags, boulders heaped on boulders. It was the traditional refuge of hunted men.

Halting in front of the Jambles, the Weaponeer called out for Kergan Banbeck, asking him to parley.

Kergan Banbeck came forth. There ensued the strangest colloquy in the history of Aerlith. The Weaponeer spoke the language of men with difficulty, his lips, tongue and glottal passages more adapted to the language of the Basics.

"You are restraining twenty-three of our Revered. It is necessary that you usher them forth, in all humility." He spoke soberly, with an air of gentle melancholy, neither asserting, commanding nor urging. As his linguistic habits had been shaped to Basic patterns, so had his mental processes.

Kergan Banbeck, a tall spare man with varnished black eyebrows, black hair shaped and varnished into a crest of five tall spikes, gave a bark of humorless laughter. "What of the Aerlith folk killed, what of the folk seized aboard your ship?"

The Weaponeer bent forward earnestly, himself an impressive man with a noble aquiline head. He was hairless except for small rolls of wispy yellow fleece. His skin shone as if burnished. His ears, where he differed most noticeably from the unadapted men of Aerlith, were small, fragile flaps. He wore a simple garment of dark blue and white, carried no weapons save a small multi-purpose ejector. With complete poise and quiet reasonableness he responded to Kergan Banbeck's question: "The Aerlith folk who have been killed are dead. Those aboard the ship will be merged into the understratum, where the infusion of fresh blood is of value."

Kergan Banbeck inspected the Weaponeer with contemptuous deliberation. In some respects, thought Kergan Banbeck, this modified and carefully inbred man resembled the sacerdotes of his own planet, notably in the clear fair skin, the strongly modeled features, the long legs and arms.

Perhaps telepathy was at work, or perhaps a trace of the characteristic sour-sweet odor had been carried to him: turning his head he noticed a sacerdote standing among the rocks not fifty feet away—a man naked except for his golden torc and long brown hair blowing behind him like a pennant. By the ancient etiquette, Kergan Banbeck looked through him, pretended that he had no existence. The Weaponeer after a swift glance did likewise.

"I demand that you release the folk of Aerlith from your ship," said Kergan Banbeck in a flat voice.

The Weaponeer smilingly shook his head, bent his best efforts to the task of making himself intelligible. "These persons are not under discussion. Their"—he paused, seeking words—"their destiny is . . . parceled, quantum-type, ordained. Established. Nothing can be said more."

Kergan Banbeck's smile became a cynical grimace. He stood aloof and silent while the Weaponeer croaked on. The sacerdote came slowly forward, a few steps at a time. "You will

28

understand," said the Weaponeer, "that a pattern for events exists. It is the function of such as myself to shape events so that they will fit the pattern." He bent, with a graceful sweep of arm, and seized a small jagged pebble. "Just as I can grind this bit of rock to fit a round aperture."

Kergan Banbeck reached forward, took the pebble, tossed it high over the tumbled boulders. "That bit of rock you shall never shape to fit a round hole."

The Weaponeer shook his head in mild deprecation. "There is always more rock."

"And there are always more holes," declared Kergan Banbeck.

"To business then," said the Weaponeer. "I propose to shape this situation to its correct arrangement."

"What do you offer in exchange for the twenty-three grephs?"

The Weaponeer gave his shoulder an uneasy shake. The ideas of this man were as wild, barbaric and arbitrary as the varnished spikes on his hair-dress. "If you desire I will give you instruction and advice, so that—"

Kergan Banbeck made a sudden sharp gesture. "I make three conditions." The sacerdote now stood only ten feet away, face blind, gaze vague. "First," said Kergan Banbeck, "a guarantee against future attacks upon the men of Aerlith. Five grephs must always remain in our custody as hostages. Second —further to secure the perpetual validity of the guarantee— you must deliver me a space-ship, equipped, energized and armed. And you must instruct me in its use."

The Weaponeer threw back his head and made a series of bleating sounds through his nose.

"Third," continued Kergan Banbeck, "you must release all the men and women presently aboard your ship."

The Weaponeer blinked, spoke rapid hoarse words of amazement to the Trackers. They stirred, uneasy and impatient, watching Kergan Banbeck sidelong as if he were not only savage, but mad. Overhead hovered the flyer; the Weaponeer looked up and seemed to derive encouragement from the sight.

Turning back to Kergan Banbeck with a firm fresh attitude, he spoke as if the previous interchange had never occurred. "I have come to instruct you that the twenty-three Revered must be instantly released."

Kergan Banbeck repeated his own demands. "You must furnish me a space-ship, you must raid no more, you must release the captives. Do you agree, yes or no?"

The Weaponeer seemed confused. "This is a peculiar situation—indefinite, unquantizable."

"Can you not understand me?" barked Kergan Banbeck in exasperation. He glanced at the sacerdote, an act of questionable decorum, then performed in manner completely unconventional: "Sacerdote, how can I deal with this blockhead? He does not seem to hear me."

The sacerdote moved a step nearer, his face as bland and blank as before. Living by a doctrine which proscribed active or intentional interference in the affairs of other men, he could make to any question only a specific and limited answer. "He hears you, but there is no meeting of ideas between you. His thought structure is derived from that of his masters. It is incommensurable with yours. As to how you must deal with him, I cannot say."

Kergan Banbeck looked back to the Weaponeer. "Have you heard what I asked of you? Did you understand my conditions for the release of the grephs?"

"I heard you distinctly," replied the Weaponeer. "Your words have no meaning, they are absurdities, paradoxes. Listen to me carefully. It is ordained, complete, a quantum of destiny, that you deliver to us the Revered. It is irregular, it is not ordainment that you should have a ship, or that your other demands be met."

Kergan Banbeck's face became red. He half-turned toward his men but, restraining his anger, spoke slowly and with careful clarity. "I have something you want. You have something I want. Let us trade."

For twenty seconds the two men stared eye to eye. Then the

Weaponeer drew a deep breath. "I will explain in your words, so that you will comprehend. Certainties—no, not certainties: definites . . . Definites exist. These are units of certainty, quanta of necessity and order. Existence is the steady succession of these units, one after the other. The activity of the universe can be expressed by reference to these units. Irregularity, absurdity—these are like—half of a man, with half of a brain, half of a heart, half of all his vital organs. Neither are allowed to exist. That you hold twenty-three Revered as captives is such an absurdity: an outrage to the rational flow of the universe."

Kergan Banbeck threw up his hands, turned once more to the sacerdote. "How can I halt his nonsense? How can I make him see reason?"

The sacerdote reflected. "He speaks not nonsense, but rather a language you fail to understand. You can make him understand your language by erasing all knowledge and training from his mind, and replacing it with patterns of your own."

Kergan Banbeck fought back an unsettling sense of frustration and unreality. In order to elicit exact answers from a sacerdote, an exact question was required; indeed it was remarkable that this sacerdote stayed to be questioned. Thinking carefully, he asked, "How do you suggest that I deal with this man?"

"Release the twenty-three grephs." The sacerdote touched the twin knobs at the front of his golden torc: a ritual gesture indicating that, no matter how reluctantly, he had performed an act which conceivably might alter the course of the future. Again he tapped his torc and intoned, "Release the grephs; he will then depart."

Kergan Banbeck cried out in unrestrained anger. "Who then do you serve? Man or greph? Let us have the truth! Speak!"

"By my faith, by my creed, by the truth of my *tand*, I serve no one but myself." The sacerdote turned his face toward the great crag of Mount Gethron and moved slowly off. The wind blew his long fine hair to the side.

Kergan Banbeck watched him go, then with cold decisiveness turned back to the Weaponeer. "Your discussion of certainties and absurdities is interesting. I feel that you have confused the two. Here is certainty from my viewpoint: I will not release the twenty-three grephs unless you meet my terms. If you attack us further, I will cut them in half, to illustrate and realize your figure of speech, and perhaps convince you that absurdities are possible. I say no more."

The Weaponeer shook his head slowly, pityingly. "Listen, I will explain. Certain conditions are unthinkable. They are un-quantized, un-destined—"

"Go," thundered Kergan Banbeck. "Otherwise you will join your twenty-three revered grephs, and I will teach you how real the unthinkable can become!"

The Weaponeer and the two Trackers, croaking and muttering, turned, retreated from the Jambles to Banbeck Verge, descended into the valley. Over them the flyer fluttered like a falling leaf.

Watching from their retreat among the crags, the men of Banbeck Vale presently witnessed a remarkable scene. Half an hour after the Weaponeer had returned to the ship, he came leaping forth once again: dancing, carvorting. Others followed him—Weaponeers, Trackers, Heavy Troopers and eight more grephs—all jerking, jumping, running back and forth in distracted steps. The ports of the ship flashed lights of various colors, and there came a slow rising sound of tortured machinery.

"They have gone mad!" muttered Kergan Banbeck. He hesitated an instant, then gave an order. "Assemble every man! We attack while they are helpless!"

Down from the High Jambles rushed the men of Banbeck Vale. As they descended the cliffs, a few of the captured men and women from Sadro Valley came timidly forth from the ship, and meeting no restraint fled to freedom across Banbeck Vale. Others followed—and now the Banbeck warriors reached the valley floor.

Besides the ship the insanity had quieted. The out-worlders

huddled quietly beside the hull. There came a sudden mind-shattering explosion: a blankness of yellow and white fire. The ship disintegrated. A great crater marred the valley floor; fragments of metal began to fall among the attacking Banbeck Warriors.

Kergan Banbeck stared at the scene of destruction.

Slowly, his shoulders sagging, he summoned his people and led them back to their ruined valley. At the rear, marching single-file, tied together with ropes, came the twenty-three grephs, dull eyed, pliant, already remote from their previous existence.

The texture of Destiny was inevitable. The present circumstances could not apply to twenty-three of the Revered. The mechanism must therefore adjust to insure the halcyon progression of events. The twenty-three, hence, were something other than the Revered: a different order of creature entirely.

If this were true, what were they? Asking each other the question in sad, croaking undertones, they marched down the cliff into Banbeck Vale.

III

Across the long Aerlith years the fortunes of Happy Valley and Banbeck Vale fluctuated with the capabilities of the opposing Carcolos and Banbecks. Golden Banbeck, Joaz's grandfather, was forced to release Happy Valley from client-ship when Uttern Carcolo, an accomplished dragon-breeder, produced the first Fiends. Golden Banbeck, in his turn, developed the Juggers, but allowed an uneasy truce to continue.

Further years passed. Ilden Banbeck, the son of Golden, a frail ineffectual man, was killed in a fall from a mutinous Spider. With Joaz yet an ailing child, Grode Carcolo decided to try his chances against Banbeck Vale. He failed to reckon with old Handel Banbeck, grand-uncle to Joaz and Chief Dragon-master.

The Happy Valley forces were routed on Starbreak Fell. Grode Carcolo was killed and young Ervis gored by a Murderer. For various reasons, including Handel's age and Joaz's youth, the Banbeck army failed to press to a decisive advantage. Ervis Carcolo, though exhausted by loss of blood and pain, withdrew in some degree of order, and for further years a suspicious truce held between the neighboring valleys.

Joaz matured into a saturnine young man who, if he excited no enthusiastic affection from his people, at least aroused no violent dislike. He and Ervis Carcolo were united in a mutual contempt. At the mention of Joaz's study, with its books, scrolls, models and plans, its complicated viewing-system across Banbeck Vale (the optics furnished, it was rumored, by the sacerdotes), Carcolo would throw up his hands in disgust. "Learning? Pah! What avails all this rolling in bygone vomit? Where does it lead? He should have been born a sacerdote. He is the same sort of sour-mouthed cloud-minded weakling!"

An itinerant named Dae Alvonso, who combined the trades of minstrel, child-buyer, psychiatrist and chiropractor, reported Carcolo's obloquies to Joaz, who shrugged. "Ervis Carcolo should breed himself to one of his own Juggers," said Joaz. "He would thereby produce an impregnable creature with the Jugger's armor and his own unflinching stupidity."

The remark in due course returned to Ervis Carcolo, and by coincidence touched him in a particularly sore spot. Secretly he had been attempting an innovation at his brooders: a dragon almost as massive as the Jugger, with the savage intelligence and agility of the Blue Horror. But Ervis Carcolo worked with an intuitive and over-optimistic approach, ignoring the advice of Bast Givven, his Chief Dragon-master.

The eggs hatched; a dozen spratlings survived. Ervis Carcolo nurtured them with alternate doses of tenderness and objurgation. Eventually the dragons matured.

Carcolo's hoped-for combination of fury and impregnability was realized in four sluggish, irritable creatures, with bloated torsos, spindly legs, insatiable appetites. ("As if one can breed a dragon by commanding it: 'Exist!'" sneered Bast Givven to his helpers, and advised them: "Be wary of the beasts; they are competent only at luring you within reach of their brachs.")

The time, effort, facilities and provender wasted upon the useless hybrid had weakened Carcolo's army. Of the fecund Termagants he had no lack. There was a sufficiency of Long-horned Murderers and Striding Murderers; but the heavier and more specialized types, especially Juggers, were far from adequate to his plans.

The memory of Happy Valley's ancient glory haunted his dreams. First he would subdue Banbeck Vale; and often he planned the ceremony whereby he would reduce Joaz Banbeck to the office of apprentice barracks-boy.

Ervis Carcolo's ambitions were complicated by a set of basic difficulties. Happy Valley's population had doubled but, rather than extending the city by breaching new pinnacles or driving tunnels, Carcolo constructed three new dragon brooders, a dozen barracks and an enormous training compound. The folk of the valley could choose either to cram the fetid existing tunnels or build ramshackle dwellings along the base of the cliff. Brooders, barracks, training compound and huts encroached on Happy Valley's already inadequate fields. Water was diverted from the pond to maintain the brooders. Enormous quantities of produce went to feed the dragons. The folk of Happy Valley, under-nourished, sickly, miserable, shared none of Carcolo's aspirations, and their lack of enthusiasm infuriated him.

In any event, when the itinerant Dae Alvonso repeated Joaz Banbeck's recommendation that Ervis Carcolo breed himself to a Jugger, Carcolo seethed with choler. "Bah! What does Joaz Banbeck know about dragon-breeding? I doubt if he understands his own dragon-talk." He referred to the means by which orders and instructions were transmitted to the dragons: a secret jargon distinctive to every army. To learn an opponent's dragon-talk was the prime goal of every Dragon-master, for he thereby gained a degree of control over his enemies' forces. "I am a practical man, worth two of him," Carcolo went on. "Can he design, nurture, rear and teach dragons? Can he impose discipline, teach ferocity? No. He leaves all this to his Dragon-masters, while he lolls on a couch eating sweetmeats, campaigning only against the patience of his minstrel-maidens. They say that by astrological divination he predicts the return of the Basics, that he walks with his neck cocked, watching the sky. Is such a man deserving of power and a prosperous life? I say no! Is Ervis Carcolo of Happy Valley such a man? I say yes, and this I will demonstrate!"

Dae Alvonso judiciously held up his hand. "Not so fast. He is more alert than you think. His dragons are in prime condition; he visits them often. And as for the Basics—"

"Do not speak to me of Basics," stormed Carcolo. "I am no child to be frightened by bugbears!"

Again Dae Alvonso held up his hand. "Listen, I am serious, and you can profit by my news. Joaz Banbeck took me into his private study—"

"The famous study, indeed!"

"From a cabinet he brought out a ball of crystal mounted on a black box."

"Aha!" jeered Carcolo. "A crystal ball!"

Dae Alvonso went on placidly, ignoring the interruption. "I examined this globe, and indeed it seemed to hold all of space. Within it floated stars and planets, all the bodies of the cluster. 'Look well,' said Joaz Banbeck, 'you will never see the like of this anywhere. It was built by the olden men and brought to Aerlith when our people first arrived.'

" 'Indeed,' I said. 'And what is this object?'

" 'It is a celestial armamentarium,' said Joaz. 'It depicts all the nearby stars, and their positions at any time I choose to specify. Now'—here he pointed—'see this white dot? This is our sun. See this red star? In the old almanacs it is named Coralyne. It swings near us at irregular intervals, for such is the flow of stars in this cluster. These intervals have always coincided with the attacks of the Basics.' Here I expressed astonishment; Joaz assured me regarding the matter. 'The

36

history of men on Aerlith records six attacks by the Basics, or grephs as they were originally known. Apparently as Coralyne swings through space the Basics scour nearby worlds for hidden dens of humanity. The last of these was long ago during the time of Kergan Banbeck, with the results you know about. At that time Coralyne passed close in the heavens. For the first time since then, Coralyne is once more close at hand.' This," Alvonso told Carcolo, "is what Joaz Banbeck told me, and this is what I saw."

Carcolo was impressed in spite of himself. "Do you mean to tell me," demanded Carcolo, "that within this globe swim all the stars of space?"

"As to that, I cannot vouch," replied Dae Alvonso. "The globe is set in a black box, and I suspect that an inner mechanism projects images or perhaps luminous spots which simulate the stars. Either way it is a marvelous device, one which I would be proud to own. I offered Joaz several precious objects in exchange. But he would have none of them."

Carcolo curled his lip in disgust. "You and your stolen children. Have you no shame?"

"No more than my customers," said Dae Alvonso stoutly. "As I recall, I have dealt profitably with you on several occasions."

Ervis Carcolo turned away, pretended to watch a pair of Termagants exercising with wooden scimitars. The two men stood by a stone fence, behind which scores of dragons practiced evolutions, dueled with spears and swords, strengthened their muscles. Scales flashed. Dust rose up under splayed stamping feet. The acrid odor of dragon-sweat permeated the air.

Carcolo muttered. "He is crafty, that Joaz. He knew you would report to me in detail."

Dae Alvonso nodded. "Precisely. His words were—but perhaps I should be discreet." He glanced slyly toward Carcolo from under shaggy white eyebrows.

"Speak," said Ervis Carcolo gruffly.

"Very well. Mind you, I quote Joaz Banbeck. 'Tell blundering old Carcolo that he is in great danger. If the Basics return to Aerlith, as well they may, Happy Valley is absolutely vulnerable and will be ruined. Where can his people hide? They will be herded into the black ship and transported to a cold new planet. If Carcolo is not completely heartless he will drive new tunnels, prepare hidden avenues. Otherwise—' "

"Otherwise what?" demanded Carcolo.

" 'Otherwise there will be no more Happy Valley, and no more Ervis Carcolo.' "

"Bah," said Carcolo in a subdued voice. "The young jackanapes barks in shrill tones."

"Perhaps he extends an honest warning. His further words —but I fear to offend Your Dignity."

"Continue! Speak!"

"These are his words—but no. I dare not repeat them. Essentially he considers your efforts to create an army ludicrous. He contrasts your intelligence unfavourably to his own. He predicts—"

"Enough," roared Ervis Carcolo, waving his fists. "He is a subtle adversary, but why do you lend yourself to his tricks?"

Dae Alvonso shook his frosty old head. "I merely repeat, with reluctance, that which you demand to hear. Now then, since you have wrung me dry, do me some profit. Will you buy drugs, elixirs, wambles or potions? I have here a salve of eternal youth which I stole from the Demie Sacerdote's personal coffer. In my train are both boy and girl children, obsequious and handsome, at a fair price. I will listen to your woes, cure your lisp, guarantee a placidity of disposition. Or perhaps you would buy dragon eggs?"

"I need none of those," grunted Carcolo. "Especially dragon's eggs which hatch to lizards. As for children, Happy Valley seethes with them. Bring me a dozen sound Juggers and you may depart with a hundred children of your choice."

Dae Alvonso shook his head sadly and lurched away. Carcolo slumped against the fence, staring across the dragon pens.

The sun hung low over the crags of Mount Despoire. Evening was close at hand.

This was the most pleasant time of the Aerlith day, when the winds ceased, leaving a vast velvet quiet. Skene's blaze softened to a smoky yellow, with a bronze aureole. The clouds of the approaching evening storm gathered, rose, fell, shifted, swirled; glowing and changing in every tone of gold, orange-brown, gold-brown and dusty violet.

Skene sank; the golds and oranges became oak-brown and purple. Lightning threaded the clouds, and the rain fell in a black curtain. In the barracks men moved with vigilance, for now the dragons became unpredictable, by turns watchful, torpid, quarrelsome. With the passing of the rain, evening became night, and a cool quiet breeze drifted through the valleys. The dark sky began to burn and dazzle with the stars of the cluster. One of the most effulgent twinkled red, green, white, red, green.

Ervis Carcolo studied this star thoughtfully. One idea led to another, and presently to a course of action which seemed to dissolve the entire tangle of uncertainties and dissatisfactions which marred his life.

Carcolo twisted his mouth into a sour grimace. He must make overtures to that popinjay Joaz Banbeck. But, if this were unavoidable so be it!

Hence, the following morning, shortly after Phade the minstrel-maiden discovered the sacerdote in Joaz's study, a messenger appeared in the Vale, inviting Joaz Banbeck up to Banbeck Verge for a conference with Ervis Carcolo.

IV

Ervis Carcolo waited on Banbeck Verge with Chief Dragonmaster Bast Givven and a pair of young fuglemen. Behind, in a row, stood their mounts: four glistening Spiders, brachs folded, legs splayed at exactly identical angles.

These were Carcolo's newest breed. He was immoderately proud of them. The barbs surrounding the horny visages were clasped with cinnabar cabochons; a round target enameled black and studded with a central spike covered each chest. The men wore the traditional black leather breeches, with short maroon cloaks and black leather helmets, with long flaps slanting back across the ears and down to the shoulders.

The four men waited, patient or restless as their natures dictated, surveying the well-tended length of Banbeck Vale. To the south stretched fields of various food-stuffs: vetch, bellegarde, moss-cake, a loquat grove. Directly opposite, near the mouth of Clybourne Crevasse, the shape of the crater created by the explosion of the Basic ship could still be seen. North lay more fields, then the dragon compounds, consisting of black-brick barracks, a brooder, an exercise field. Beyond lay Banbeck Jambles—an area of wasteland, where ages previously a section of the cliff had fallen, creating a wilderness of tumbled rock, similar to the High Jambles under Mount Gethron, but smaller in compass.

One of the young fuglemen rather tactlessly commented upon the evident prosperity of Banbeck Vale. Ervis Carcolo listened glumly a moment or two, then turned a haughty stare toward the offender.

"Notice the dam," said the fugleman. "We waste half our water in seepage."

"True," said the other. "The rock facing is a good idea. I wonder why we don't do something similar."

Carcolo started to speak, but thought better of it. With a growling sound in his throat, he turned away. Bast Givven made a sign: the fuglemen hastily fell silent.

A few moments later Givven announced: "Joaz Banbeck has set forth."

Carcolo peered down toward Kergan's Way. "Where is his company? Does he choose to ride alone?"

"So it seems."

A few minutes later Joaz Banbeck appeared on Banbeck Verge riding a Spider caparisoned in gray and red velvet. Joaz wore a loose lounge cloak of soft brown cloth over a gray shirt and gray trousers, with a long-billed hat of blue velvet. He held up his hand in casual greeting.

Brusquely Ervis Carcolo returned the salute, and with a jerk of his head sent Givven and the fuglemen off out of ear-shot.

Carcolo said gruffly, "You sent me a message by old Alvonso."

Joaz nodded. "I trust he rendered my remarks accurately?"

Carcolo grinned wolfishly. "At times he felt obliged to paraphrase."

"Tactful old Dae Alvonso."

"I am given to understand," said Carcolo, "that you consider me rash, ineffectual, callous to the best interests of Happy Valley. Alvonso admitted that you used the word 'blunderer' in reference to me."

Joaz smiled politely. "Sentiments of this sort are best transmitted through intermediaries."

Carcolo made a great show of dignified forbearance. "Apparently you feel that another Basic attack is imminent."

"Just so," agreed Joaz, "if my theory, which puts their home by the star Coralyne, is correct. In which case, as I pointed out to Alvonso, Happy Valley is seriously vulnerable."

"And why not Banbeck Vale as well?" barked Carcolo.

Joaz stared at him in surprise. "Is it not obvious? I have taken precautions. My people are housed in tunnels, rather than huts. We have several escape routes, should this prove necessary, both to the High Jambles and to Banbeck Jambles."

"Very interesting." Carcolo made an effort to soften his voice. "If your theory is accurate—and I pass no immediate judgment—then perhaps I would be wise to take similar measures. But I think in different terms. I prefer attack to passive defense."

"Admirable," said Joaz Banbeck. "Important deeds are done by men such as you."

Carcolo became a trifle pink in the face. "This is neither here nor there," he said. "I have come to propose a joint project. It

41

is entirely novel, but carefully thought out. I have considered various aspects of this matter for several years."

"I attend you with great interest," said Joaz.

Carcolo blew out his cheeks. "You know the legends as well as I, perhaps better. Our people came to Aerlith as exiles during the War of the Ten Stars. The Nightmare Coalition apparently had defeated the Old Rule, but how the war ended" —he threw up his hands—"who can say?"

"There is a significant indication," said Joaz. "The Basics revisit Aerlith and ravage us at their pleasure. We have seen no men visiting except those who serve the Basics."

"Men?" Carcolo demanded scornfully. "I call them something else. Nevertheless, this is no more than a deduction, and we are ignorant as to the course of history. Perhaps Basics rule the cluster; perhaps they plague us only because we are weak and weaponless. Perhaps we are the last men. Perhaps the Old Rule is resurgent. And never forget that many years have elapsed since the Basics last appeared on Aerlith."

"Many years have elapsed since Aerlith and Coralyne were in such convenient apposition."

Carcolo made an impatient gesture. "A supposition, which may or may not be relevant. Let me explain the basic axiom of my proposal. It is simple enough. I feel that Banbeck Vale and Happy Valley are too small a compass for men such as ourselves. We deserve larger scope."

Joaz agreed. "I wish it were possible to ignore the practical difficulties involved."

"I am able to suggest a method to counter these difficulties," asserted Carcolo.

"In that case," said Joaz, "power, glory and wealth are as good as ours."

Carcolo glanced at him sharply, slapped his breeches with the gold-beaded tassel to his scabbard. "Reflect," he said. "The sacerdotes inhabited Aerlith before us. How long no one can say. It is a mystery. In fact, what do we know of the sacerdotes? Next to nothing. They trade their metal and glass for our food. They live in deep caverns. Their creed is disassociation, reverie, detachment, whatever one may wish to call it—totally incomprehensible to one such as myself." He challenged Joaz with a look; Joaz merely fingered his long chin. "They put themselves forward as simple metaphysical cultists. Actually they are a very mysterious people. Has anyone yet seen a sacerdote woman? What of the blue lights? What of the lightning towers, what of the sacerdote magic? What of weird comings and goings by night, what of strange shapes moving across the sky, perhaps to other planets?"

"The tales exist, certainly," said Joaz. "As to the degree of credence to be placed in them—"

"Now we reach the meat of my proposal!" declared Ervis Carcolo. "The creed of the sacerdotes apparently forbids shame or regard for consequence. Hence, they are forced to answer any question put to them. Nevertheless, creed or no creed, they completely befog any information an assiduous man is able to wheedle from them."

Joaz inspected him curiously. "Evidently you have made the attempt."

Ervis Carcolo nodded. "Why should I deny it? I have questioned three sacerdotes with determination and persistence. They answered all my questions with gravity and calm reflection, but told me nothing." He shook his head in vexation. "Therefore, I suggest that we apply coercion."

"You are a brave man."

Carcolo shook his head modestly. "I would dare no direct measures. But they must eat. If Banbeck Vale and Happy Valley cooperate, we can apply the very cogent persuasion of hunger. Presently their words may be more to the point."

Joaz considered a moment or two. Ervis Carcolo twitched his scabbard tassel. "Your plan," said Joaz at last, "is not a frivolous one, and is ingenious—at least at first glance. What sort of information do you hope to secure? In short, what are your ultimate aims?"

Carcolo sidled close, prodded Joaz with his forefinger. "We

43

know nothing of the outer worlds. We are marooned on this miserable planet of stone and wind while life passes us by. You assume that Basics rule the cluster. But suppose you are wrong? Suppose the Old Rule has returned? Think of the rich cities, the gay resorts, the palaces, the pleasure-islands! Look up into the night sky. Ponder the bounties which might be ours! You ask how can we implement these desires? I respond, the process may be so simple that the sacerdotes will reveal it without reluctance."

"You mean—"

"Communication with the worlds of men! Deliverance from this lonely little world at the edge of the universe!"

Joaz Banbeck nodded dubiously. "A fine vision. But the evidence suggests a situation far different, namely the destruction of man and the Human Empire."

Carcolo held out his hands in a gesture of open-minded tolerance. "Perhaps you are right. But why should we not make inquiries of the sacerdotes? Concretely I propose as follows: that you and I agree to the mutual cause I have outlined. Next, we request an audience with the Demie Sacerdote. We put our questions. If he responds freely, well and good. If he evades, then we act together. No more food to the sacerdotes until they tell us plainly what we want to hear."

"Other valleys exist," said Joaz thoughtfully.

Carcolo made a brisk gesture. "We can deter any such trade by persuasion or by the power of our dragons."

"The essence of your idea appeals to me," said Joaz. "But I fear that all is not so simple."

Carcolo rapped his thigh smartly with the tassel. "And why not?"

"In the first place, Coralyne shines bright in the sky. This is our first concern. Should Coralyne pass and the Basics not attack—then is the time to pursue this matter. Again—and perhaps more to the point—I doubt that we can starve the sacerdotes into submission. In fact, I consider it impossible."

Carcolo blinked. "In what wise?"

"They walk naked through sleet and storm; do you think

they fear hunger? And there is wild lichen to be gathered. How could we forbid this? You might dare some sort of coercion, but not I. The tales told of the sacerdotes may be superstition—or they may be understatement."

Ervis Carcolo heaved a deep disgusted sigh. "Joaz Banbeck, I took you for a man of decision. But you merely pick flaws."

"These are not flaws. They are major errors which would lead to disaster."

"Well then. Do you have any suggestions of your own?"

Joaz fingered his chin. "If Coralyne recedes and we are still on Aerlith—rather than in the hold of the Basic ship—then let us plan to plunder the secrets of the sacerdotes. In the meantime I strongly recommend that you prepare Happy Valley against a new raid. You are over-extended, with your new brooders and barracks. Let them rest, while you dig yourself secure tunnels!"

Ervis Carcolo stared straight across Banbeck Vale. "I am not a man to defend. I attack!"

"You will attack heat-beams and ion-rays with your dragons?"

Ervis Carcolo turned his gaze back to Joaz Banbeck. "Can I consider us allies in the plan I have proposed?"

"In its broadest principles, certainly. However I don't care to cooperate in starving or otherwise coercing the sacerdotes. It might be dangerous, as well as futile."

For an instant Carcolo could not control his detestation of Joaz Banbeck. His lip curled, his hands clenched. "Danger? Pah! What danger from a handful of naked pacifists?"

"We do not know that they are pacifists. We do know that they are men."

Carcolo once more became brightly cordial. "Perhaps you are right. But essentially at least we are allies."

"To a degree."

"Good. I suggest that in the case of the attack you fear, we act together, with a common strategy."

Joaz nodded distantly. "This might be effective."

45

"Let us coordinate our plans. Let us assume that the Basics drop down into Banbeck Vale. I suggest that your folk take refuge in Happy Valley, while the Happy Valley army joins with yours to cover their retreat. And likewise, should they attack Happy Valley, my people will take temporary refuge with you in Banbeck Vale."

Joaz laughed in sheer amusement. "Ervis Carcolo, what sort of lunatic do you take me for? Return to your valley, put aside your foolish grandiosities, dig yourself protection. And fast! Coralyne is bright!"

Carcolo stood stiffly. "Do I understand that you reject my offer of alliance?"

"Not at all. But I cannot undertake to protect you and your people if you will not help yourselves. Meet my requirements, satisfy me that you are a fit ally—then we shall speak further of alliance."

Ervis Carcolo whirled on his heel, signaled to Bast Givven and the two young fuglemen. With no further word or glance he mounted his splendid Spider, goaded him into a sudden leaping run across the Verge and up the slope toward Starbreak Fell. His men followed, somewhat less precipitously.

Joaz watched them go, shaking his head in sad wonder. Then, mounting his own Spider, he returned down the trail to the floor of Banbeck Vale.

V

The long Aerlith day, equivalent to six of the old Diurnal Units, passed.

In Happy Valley there was grim activity, a sense of purpose and impending decision. The dragons exercised in tighter formation. The fuglemen and cornets called orders with harsher voices. In the armory bullets were cast, powder was mixed, swords were ground and honed.

Ervis Carcolo drove himself with dramatic bravado, wearing out Spider after Spider as he sent his dragons through various evolutions. In the case of the Happy Valley forces, these were for the most part Termagants—small active dragons with rust-red scales, narrow darting heads, chisel-sharp fangs. Their brachs were strong and well-developed. They used lance, cutlass or mace with equal skill. A man pitted against a Termagant stood no chance, for the scales warded off bullets as well as any blow the man might have strength enough to deal. On the other hand a single slash of fang, the rip of a scythe-like claw, meant death to the man.

The Termagants were fecund and hardy and throve even under the conditions which existed in the Happy Valley brooders; hence their predominance in Carcolo's army. This was a situation not to the liking of Bast Givven, Chief Dragon-master, a spare wiry man with a flat crooked-nosed face, eyes black and blank as drops of ink on a plate. Habitually terse and tight-lipped, he waxed almost eloquent in opposition to the attack upon Banbeck Vale. "Look you, Ervis Carcolo. We are able to deploy a horde of Termagants, with sufficient Striding Murderers and Long-horned Murderers. But Blue Horrors, Fiends and Juggers—no! We are lost if they trap us on the fells!"

"I do not plan to fight on the fells," said Carcolo. "I will force battle upon Joaz Banbeck. His Juggers and Fiends are useless on the cliffs. And in the matter of Blue Horrors we are almost his equal."

"You overlook a single difficulty," said Bast Givven.

"And what is this?"

"The improbability that Joaz Banbeck plans to permit all this. I allow him greater intelligence than that."

"Show me evidence!" charged Carcolo. "What I know of him suggests vacillation and stupidity! So we will strike—hard!" Carcolo smacked fist into palm. "Thus we will finish the haughty Banbecks!"

Bast Givven turned to go. Carcolo wrathfully called him back. "You show no enthusiasm for this campaign!"

"I know what our army can do and what it cannot do," said Givven bluntly. "If Joaz Banbeck is the man you think he is, we

47

might succeed. If he has even the sagacity of a pair of grooms I listened to ten minutes ago, we face disaster."

In a voice thick with rage, Carcolo said, "Return to your Fiends and Juggers. I want them quick as Termagants."

Bast Givven went his way. Carcolo jumped on a nearby Spider, kicked it with his heels. The creature sprang forward, halted sharply, twisted its long neck about to look Carcolo in the face. Carcolo cried, "Hust, hust! Forward at speed, smartly now! Show these louts what snap and spirit mean!" The Spider jumped ahead with such vehemence that Carcolo tumbled over backward, landing on his neck, where he lay groaning.

Grooms came running and assisted him to a bench where he sat cursing in a steady low voice. A surgeon examined, pressed, prodded, recommended that Carcolo take to his couch and administered a sedative potion.

Carcolo was carried to his apartments beneath the west wall of Happy Valley and placed under the care of his wives. He slept for twenty hours. When he awoke the day was half gone.

He wished to arise, but found himself too stiff to move and, groaning, lay back. Presently he called for Bast Givven, who appeared and listened without comment to Carcolo's adjurations.

Evening arrived. The dragons returned to the barracks. There was nothing to do now but wait for daybreak.

During the long night Carcolo underwent a variety of treatments: massage, hot baths, infusions and poultices. He exercised with diligence, and as the night reached its end he declared himself fit. Overhead the star Coralyne vibrated poisonous colors—red, green, white—by far the brightest star of the cluster. Carcolo refused to look up at the star, but its radiance struck through the corners of his eyes whenever he walked on the valley floor.

Dawn approached. Carcolo planned to march at the earliest moment the dragons were manageable. A flickering to the east told of the oncoming dawn storm, still invisible across the horizon. With great caution the dragons were mustered from their barracks and ordered into a marching column. There were almost three hundred Termagants; eighty-five Striding Murderers, as many Long-horned Murderers; a hundred Blue Horrors; fifty-two squat, immensely powerful Fiends, their tails tipped with spiked steel balls; eighteen Juggers. They growled and muttered evilly among themselves, watching an opportunity to kick each other or to snip a leg from an unwary groom. Darkness stimulated their latent hatred for humanity —though they had been taught nothing of their past, nor the circumstances by which they had become enslaved.

The dawn lightning blazed, outlining the vertical steeples and astonishing peaks of the Malheur Mountains. Overhead passed the storm, with wailing gusts of wind and thrashing banks of rain, moving on toward Banbeck Vale. The east glowed with a gray-green pallor, and Carcolo gave the signal to march.

Still stiff and sore he hobbled to his Spider, mounted, ordered the creature into a special and dramatic curvet. Carcolo had miscalculated. Malice of the night still gripped the mind of the dragon. It ended its curvet with a lash of the neck which once again dashed Carcolo to the ground, where he lay half-mad with pain and frustration.

He tried to rise; collapsed; tried again; fainted.

Five minutes he lay unconscious, then seemed to rouse himself by sheer force of will. "Lift me," he whispered huskily. "Tie me into the saddle. We must march." This being manifestly impossible, no one made a move. Carcolo raged, finally called hoarsely for Bast Givven. "Proceed; we cannot stop now. You must lead the troops."

Givven nodded glumly. This was an honor for which he had no stomach.

"You know the battle-plan," wheezed Carcolo. "Circle north of the Fang, cross the Skanse with all speed, swing north around Blue Crevasse, then south along Banbeck Verge. There Joaz Banbeck may be expected to discover you. You must deploy so that when he brings up his Juggers you can topple them back with Fiends. Avoid committing our Juggers. Harry him with Termagants; reserve the Murderers to strike wherever he reaches the edge. Do you understand me?"

"As you explain it, victory is certain," muttered Bast Givven.

"And so it is, unless you blunder grievously. Ah, my back! I can't move. While the great battle rages I must sit by the brooder and watch eggs hatch! Now go! Strike hard for Happy Valley!"

Givven gave an order. The troops set forth.

Termagants darted into the lead, followed by silken Striding Murderers and the heavier Long-horned Murderers, their fantastic chest-spikes tipped with steel. Behind came the ponderous Juggers, grunting, gurgling, teeth clashing together with the vibration of their steps. Flanking the Juggers marched the Fiends, carrying heavy cutlasses, flourishing their terminal steel balls as a scorpion carries his sting. Then at the rear came the Blue Horrors, who were both massive and quick, good climbers, no less intelligent than the Termagants. To the flanks rode a hundred men: dragon-masters, knights, fuglemen and cornets. They were armed with swords, pistols and large-bore blunderbusses.

Carcolo watched from a stretcher till the last of his forces had passed from view, then commanded himself carried back to the portal which led into the Happy Valley caves.

Never before had the caves seemed so dingy and shallow. Sourly he eyed the straggle of huts along the cliff, built of rock, slabs of resin-impregnated lichen, canes bound with tar. With the Banbeck campaign at an end, he would set about cutting new chambers and halls into the cliff. The splendid decorations of Banbeck Village were well-known. Happy Valley would be even more magnificent. The halls would glow with opal and nacre, silver and gold . . . And yet, to what end? If events went as planned, there was his great dream in prospect. And then, what consequence a few paltry decorations in the tunnels of Happy Valley?

Groaning, he allowed himself to be laid on his couch and

entertained himself picturing the progress of his troops. By now they should be working down from Dangle Ridge, circling the mile-high Fang.

He tentatively stretched his arms, worked his legs. His muscles protested. Pain shot back and forth along his body— but it seemed as if the injuries were less than before . . . By now the army would be mounting the ramparts which rimmed that wide area of upland fell known as the Skanse . . . The surgeon brought Carcolo a potion. He drank and slept, to awake with a start. What was the time? His troops might well have joined battle!

He ordered himself carried to the outer portal; then, still dissatisfied, commanded his servants to transport him across the valley to the new dragon brooder, the walkway of which commanded a view up and down the valley. Despite the protests of his wives, here he was conveyed, and made as comfortable as bruises and sprains permitted.

He settled himself for an indeterminate wait. But news was not long in coming.

Down the North Trail came a cornet on a foam-bearded Spider. Carcolo sent a groom to intercept him and, heedless of aches and pains, raised himself from his couch. The cornet threw himself off his mount, staggered up the ramp, sagged exhausted against the rail.

"Ambush!" he panted. "Bloody disaster!"

"Ambush?" groaned Carcolo in a hollow voice. "Where?"

"As we mounted the Skanse Ramparts. They waited till our Termagants and Murderers were over, then charged with Horrors, Fiends and Juggers. They cut us apart, drove us back, then rolled boulders on our Juggers! Our army is broken!"

Carcolo sank back on the couch, lay staring at the sky. "How many are lost?"

"I do not know. Givven called the retreat. We withdrew in the best style possible."

Carcolo lay as if comatose. The cornet flung himself down on a bench.

A column of dust appeared to the north, which presently dissolved and separated to reveal a number of Happy Valley dragons. All were wounded. They marched, hopped, limped, dragged themselves at random, croaking, glaring, bugling. First came a group of Termagants, darting ugly heads from side to side; then a pair of Blue Horrors, brachs twisting and clasping almost like human arms; then a Jugger, massive, toad-like, legs splayed out in weariness. Even as it neared the barracks it toppled, fell with a thud and lay still, legs and talons jutting into the air.

Down from the North Trail rode Bast Givven, dust-stained and haggard. He dismounted from his drooping Spider, mounted the ramp. With a wrenching effort, Carcolo once more raised himself on the couch.

Givven reported in a voice so even and light as to seem careless, but even the insensitive Carcolo was not deceived. He asked in puzzlement: "Exactly where did the ambush occur?"

"We mounted the Ramparts by way of Chloris Ravine. Where the Skanse falls off into the ravine a porphyry outcrop juts up and over. Here they awaited us."

Carcolo hissed through his teeth. "Amazing."

Bast Givven gave the faintest of nods.

Carcolo said, "Assume that Joaz Banbeck set forth during the dawn-storm, an hour earlier than I would think possible. Assume that he forced his troops at a run. How could he reach the Skanse Ramparts before us even so?"

"By my reckoning," said Givven, "ambush was no threat until we had crossed the Skanse. I had planned to patrol Barchback, all the way down Blue Fell and across Blue Crevasse."

Carcolo gave somber agreement. "How then did Joaz Banbeck bring his troops to the Ramparts so soon?"

Givven turned, looked up the valley, where wounded dragons and men still straggled down the North Trail. "I have no idea."

"A drug?" puzzled Carcolo. "A potion to pacify the dragons? Could he have made bivouac on the Skanse the whole night long?"

"The last is possible," admitted Givven grudgingly. "Under

Barch Spike are empty caves. If he quartered his troops here during the night, then he had only to march across the Skanse to waylay us."

Carcolo grunted. "Perhaps we have underestimated Joaz Banbeck." He sank back on his couch with a groan. "Well, then, what are our losses?"

The reckoning made dreary news. Of the already inadequate squad of Juggers, only six remained. From a force of fifty-two Fiends, forty survived and of these five were sorely wounded. Termagants, Blue Horrors and Murderers had suffered greatly. A large number had been torn apart in the first onslaught. Many others had been toppled down the Ramparts to strew their armored husks through the detritus. Of the hundred men, twelve had been killed by bullets, another fourteen by dragon attack. A score more were wounded in various degree.

Carcolo lay back, his eyes closed and his mouth working feebly.

"The terrain alone saved us," said Givven. "Joaz Banbeck refused to commit his troops to the ravine. If there were any tactical error on either side, it was his. He brought an insufficiency of Termagants and Blue Horrors."

"Small comfort," growled Carcolo. "Where is the balance of the army?"

"We have good position on Dangle Ridge. We have seen none of Banbeck's scouts, either man or Termagant. He may conceivably believe we have retreated to the valley. In any event his main forces were still collected on the Skanse."

Carcolo, by an enormous effort, raised himself to his feet.

He tottered across the walkway to look down into the dispensary. Five Fiends crouched in vats of balsam, muttering and sighing. A Blue Horror hung in a sling, whining as surgeons cut broken fragments of armor from its gray flesh. As Carcolo watched, one of the Fiends raised itself high on its anterior legs, foam gushing from its gills. It cried out in a peculiar, poignant tone and fell back dead into the vat of balsam.

Carcolo turned back to Givven. "This is what you must do.

Joaz Banbeck surely has sent forth patrols. Retire along Dangle Ridge. Then, taking all concealment from the patrols, swing up into one of the Despoire Cols. Tourmaline Col will serve. This is my reasoning. Banbeck will assume that you are retiring to Happy Valley, so he will hurry south behind the Fang, to attack as you come down off Dangle Ridge. As he passes below Tourmaline Col, you have the advantage. You may well destroy Joaz Banbeck there with all his troops."

Bast Givven shook his head decisively. "What if his patrols locate us in spite of our precautions? He need only follow our tracks to bottle us into Tourmaline Col, with no escape except over Mount Despoire or out on Starbreak Fell. And if we venture out on Starbreak Fell his Juggers will destroy us in minutes."

Ervis Carcolo sagged back down upon the couch. "Bring the troops back to Happy Valley. We will regroup and await another occasion."

VI

Cut into the cliff south of the crag which housed Joaz's apartments was a large chamber known as Kergan's Hall. The proportions of the room, the simplicity and lack of ornament, the massive antique furniture contributed to the sense of lingering personality, as well as an odor unique to the room. This odor exhaled from naked stone walls, the petrified moss parquetry, old wood—a rough ripe redolence which Joaz had always disliked, together with every other aspect of the room. The dimensions seemed arrogant in their extent. The lack of ornament impressed him as rude, if not brutal. One day it occurred to Joaz that he disliked not the room but Kergan Banbeck himself, together with the entire system of overblown legends which surrounded him.

The room nevertheless in many respects was pleasant. Three tall groined windows overlooked the vale. The casements were set with small square panes of green-blue glass in muntins of black ironwood. The ceiling likewise was paneled in wood, and here a certain amount of the typical Banbeck intricacy had been permitted. There were mock pilaster capitals with gargoyle heads, a frieze carved with conventionalized fern-fronds. The furniture consisted of three pieces: two tall carved chairs and a massive table, all polished dark wood, all of enormous antiquity.

Joaz had found a use for the room. The table supported a carefully detailed relief map of the district, on a scale of three inches to the mile. At the center was Banbeck Vale, on the right hand Happy Valley, separated by a turmoil of crags and chasms, cliffs, spikes, walls and five titanic peaks: Mount Gethron to the south, Mount Despoire in the center, Barch Spike, the Fang and Mount Halcyon to the north.

At the front of Mount Gethron lay the High Jambles, then Starbreak Fell extended to Mount Despoire and Barch Spike. Beyond Mount Despoire, between the Skanse Ramparts and Barchback, the Skanse reached all the way to the tormented basalt ravines and bluffs at the foot of Mount Halcyon.

As Joaz stood studying the map, into the room came Phade. She was mischievously quiet. But Joaz sensed her nearness by the scent of incense, in the smoke of which she had steeped herself before seeking out Joaz. She wore a traditional holiday costume of Banbeck maidens: a tight-fitting sheath of dragon intestine, with muffs of brown fur at neck, elbows and knees. A tall cylindrical hat, notched around the upper edge, perched on her rich brown curls, and from the top of this hat soared a red plume.

Joaz feigned unconsciousness of her presence. She came up behind him to tickle his neck with the fur of her neck-piece. Joaz pretended stolid indifference. Phade, not at all deceived, put on a face of woeful concern. "Must we all be slain? How goes the war?"

"For Banbeck Vale the war goes well. For poor Ervis Carcolo and Happy Valley the war goes ill indeed."

"You plan his destruction," Phade intoned a voice of hushed accusation. "You will kill him! Poor Ervis Carcolo!"

"He deserves no better."

55

"But what will befall Happy Valley?"

Joaz Banbeck shrugged idly. "Changes for the better."

"Will you seek to rule?"

"Not I."

"Think!" whispered Phade. "Joaz Banbeck, Tyrant of Banbeck Vale, Happy Valley, Phosphor Gulch, Glore, the Tarn, Clewhaven and the Great Northern Rift."

"Not I," said Joaz. "Perhaps you would rule in my stead?"

"Oh! Indeed! What changes there would be! I'd dress the sacerdotes in red and yellow ribbons. I'd order them to sing and dance and drink May wine. The dragons I'd send south to Arcady, except for a few gentle Termagants to nursemaid the children. And no more of these furious battles. I'd burn the armor and break the swords; I'd—"

"My dear little flutterbug," said Joaz with a laugh. "What a swift reign you'd have indeed!"

"Why swift? Why not forever? If men had no means to fight—"

"And when the Basics came down—you'd throw garlands around their necks?"

"Pah. They shall never be seen again. What do they gain by molesting a few remote valleys?"

"Who knows what they gain? We are free men. Perhaps the last free men in the universe. Who knows? And will they be back? Coralyne is bright in the sky!"

Phade became suddenly interested in the relief map. "And your current war—dreadful. Will you attack, will you defend?"

"This depends on Ervis Carcolo," said Joaz. "I need only wait till he exposes himself." Looking down at the map he added thoughtfully, "He is clever enough to do me damage, unless I move with care."

"And what if the Basics come while you bicker with Carcolo?"

Joaz smiled. "Perhaps we shall all flee to the Jambles. Perhaps we shall all fight."

"I will fight beside you," declared Phade, striking a brave

attitude. "We will attack the great Basic space-ship, braving the heat-rays, fending off the power-bolts. We will storm to the very portal. We will pull the nose of the first marauder who shows himself!"

"At one point your otherwise sage strategy falls short," said Joaz. "How does one find the nose of a Basic?"

"In that case," said Phade, "we shall seize their—" She turned her head at a sound in the hall. Joaz strode across the room, flung back the door. Old Rife the porter sidled forward. "You told me to call when the bottle either overturned or broke. Well, it's done both."

Joaz pushed past Rife, ran down the corridor. "What means this?" demanded Phade. "Rife, what have you said to disturb him?"

Rife shook his head fretfully. "I am as perplexed as you. A bottle is pointed out to me. 'Watch this bottle day and night' —so I am commanded. And also, 'When the bottle breaks or tips, call me at once.' I tell myself that here in all truth is a sinecure. And I wonder, does Joaz consider me so senile that I will rest content with a make-work task such as watching a bottle? I am old, my jaws tremble, but I am not witless. To my surprise the bottle breaks! The explanation admittedly is simple. It fell to the floor. Nevertheless, without knowledge of what it all means, I obey orders and notify Joaz Banbeck."

Phade had been squirming impatiently. "Where then is this bottle?"

"In the studio of Joaz Banbeck."

Phade ran off as swiftly as the tight sheath about her thighs permitted: through a transverse tunnel, across Kergan's Way by a covered bridge, then up at a slant toward Joaz's apartments.

Down the long hall ran Phade, through the anteroom where a bottle lay shattered on the floor, into the studio, where she halted in astonishment. No one was to be seen. She noticed a section of shelving which stood at an angle. Quietly, timorously, she stole across the room, peered down into the workshop.

The scene was an odd one. Joaz stood negligently, smiling a cool smile, as across the room a naked sacerdote gravely sought to shift a barrier which had sprung down across an area of the wall. But the gate was cunningly locked in place, and the sacerdote's efforts were to no avail.

He turned, glanced briefly at Joaz, then started for the exit into the studio.

Phade sucked in her breath and backed away.

The sacerdote came out into the studio, started for the door.

"Just a moment," said Joaz. "I wish to speak to you."

The sacerdote paused, turned his head in mild inquiry. He was a young man, his face bland, blank, almost beautiful. Fine transparent skin stretched over his pale bones. His eyes—wide, blue, innocent—seemed to stare without focus. He was delicate of frame and sparsely fleshed. His hands were thin, with fingers trembling in some kind of nervous imbalance. Down his back, almost to his waist, hung the mane of long light-brown hair.

Joaz seated himself with ostentatious deliberation, never taking his eyes from the sacerdote. Presently he spoke in a voice pitched at an ominous level. "I find your conduct far from ingratiating." This was a declaration requiring no response, and the sacerdote made none.

"Please sit," said Joaz. He indicated a bench. "You have a great deal of explaining to do."

Was it Phade's imagination? Or did a spark of something like wild amusement flicker and die almost instantaneously in the sacerdote's eyes? But again he made no response. Joaz, adapting to the peculiar rules by which communication with the sacerdotes must be conducted, asked, "Do you care to sit?"

"It is immaterial," said the sacerdote. "Since I am standing now, I will stand."

Joaz rose to his feet and performed an act without precedent. He pushed the bench behind the sacerdote, rapped the back of the knobbly knees, thrust the sacerdote firmly down upon the bench. "Since you are sitting now," said Joaz, "you might as well sit."

With gentle dignity the sacerdote regained his feet. "I shall stand."

Joaz shrugged. "As you wish. I intend to ask you some questions. I hope that you will cooperate and answer with precision."

The sacerdote blinked owlishly.

"Will you do so?"

"Certainly. I prefer, however, to return the way I came."

Joaz ignored the remark. "First," he asked, "why do you come to my study?"

The sacerdote spoke carefully, in the voice of one talking to a child. "Your language is vague. I am confused and must not respond, since I am vowed to give only truth to anyone who requires it."

Joaz settled himself in his chair. "There is no hurry. I am ready for a long discussion. Let me ask you then: did you have impulses which you can explain to me, which persuaded or impelled you to come to my studio?"

"Yes."

"How many of these impulses did you recognize?"

"I don't know."

"More than one?"

"Perhaps."

"Less than ten?"

"I don't know."

"Hmm . . . Why are you uncertain?"

"I am not uncertain."

"Then why can't you specify the number as I requested?"

"There is no such number."

"I see . . . You mean, possibly, that there are several elements of a single motive which directed your brain to signal your muscles in order that they might carry you here?"

"Possibly."

Joaz's thin lips twisted in a faint smile of triumph. "Can you describe an element of the eventual motive?"

"Yes."

"Do so, then."

There was an imperative, against which the sacerdote was proof. Any form of coercion known to Joaz—fire, sword, thirst, mutilation—these to a sacerdote were no more than inconveniences; he ignored them as if they did not exist. His personal inner world was the single world of reality. Either acting upon or reacting against the affairs of the Utter Men demeaned him. Absolute passivity and absolute candor were his necessary courses of action. Understanding something of this, Joaz rephrased his command: "Can you think of an element of the motive which impelled you to come here?"

"Yes."

"What is it?"

"A desire to wander about."

"Can you think of another?"

"Yes."

"What is it?"

"A desire to exercise myself by walking."

"I see . . . Incidentally, are you trying to evade answering my question?"

"I answer such questions as you put to me. So long as I do so, so long as I open my mind to all who seek knowledge—for this is our creed—there can be no question of evasion."

"So you say. However, you have not provided me an answer that I find satisfactory."

The sacerdote's reply to the comment was an almost imperceptible widening of the pupils.

"Very well then," said Joaz Banbeck. "Can you think of another element to this complex motive we have been discussing?"

"Yes."

"What is it?"

"I am interested in antiques. I came to your study to admire your relics of the old worlds."

"Indeed?" Joaz raised his eyebrows. "I am lucky to possess

such fascinating treasures. Which of my antiques interests you particularly?"

"Your books. Your maps. Your great globe of the Arch-world."

"The Arch-world? Eden?"

"This is one of its names."

Joaz pursed his lips. "So you come here to study my antiques. Well then, what other elements to this motive exist?"

The sacerdote hesitated an instant. "It was suggested to me that I come here."

"By whom?"

"By the Demie."

"Why did he so suggest?"

"I am uncertain."

"Can you conjecture?"

"Yes."

"What are these conjectures?"

The sacerdote made a small bland gesture with the fingers of one hand. "The Demie might wish to become an Utter Man, and so seeks to learn the principles of your existence. Or the Demie might wish to change the trade articles. The Demie might be fascinated by my description of your antiques. Or the Demie might be curious regarding the focus of your vision-panels. Or—"

"Enough. Which of these conjectures, and of other conjectures you have not yet divulged, do you consider most probable?"

"None."

Joaz raised his eyebrows once more. "How do you justify this?"

"Since any desired number of conjectures can be formed, the denominator of any probability-ratio is variable and the entire concept becomes arithmetically meaningless."

Joaz grinned wearily. "Of the conjectures which to this moment have occurred to you, which do you regard as the most likely?"

"I suspect that the Demie might think it desirable that I come here to stand."

"What do you achieve by standing?"

"Nothing."

"Then the Demie does not send you here to stand."

To Joaz's assertion, the sacerdote made no comment.

Joaz framed a question with great care. "What do you believe that the Demie hopes you will achieve by coming here to stand?"

"I believe that he wishes me to learn how Utter Men think."

"And you learn how I think by coming here?"

"I am learning a great deal."

"How does it help you?"

"I don't know."

"How many times have you visited my study?"

"Seven times."

"Why were you chosen specially to come?"

"The synod has approved my *tand*. I may well be the next Demie."

Joaz spoke over his shoulder to Phade. "Brew tea." He turned back to the sacerdote. "What is a *tand*?"

The sacerdote took a deep breath. "My *tand* is the representation of my soul."

"Hmm. What does it look like?"

The sacerdote's expression was unfathomable. "It cannot be described."

"Do I have one?"

"No."

Joaz shrugged. "Then you can read my thoughts."

Silence.

"Can you read my thoughts?"

"Not well."

"Why should you wish to read my thoughts?"

"We are alive in the universe together. Since we are not permitted to act, we are obliged to know."

Joaz smiled skeptically. "How does knowledge help you, if you will not act upon it?"

"Events follow the Rationale, as water drains into a hollom and forms a pool."

"Bah!" said Joaz, in sudden irritation. "Your doctrine commits you to non-interference in our affairs, nevertheless you allow your 'Rationale' to create conditions by which events are influenced. Is this correct?"

"I am not sure. We are a passive people."

"Still, your Demie must have had a plan in mind when he sent you here. Is this not correct?"

"I cannot say."

Joaz veered to a new line of questioning. "Where does the tunnel behind my workshop lead?"

"Into a cavern."

Phade set a silver pot before Joaz. He poured and sipped reflectively. Of contests there were numberless varieties. He and the sacerdote were engaged in a hide-and-seek game of words and ideas. The sacerdote was schooled in patience and supple evasions, to counter which Joaz could bring pride and determination. The sacerdote was handicapped by an innate necessity to speak truth. Joaz, on the other hand, must grope like a man blindfolded, unacquainted with the goal he sought, ignorant of the prize to be won. Very well, thought Joaz, let us continue. We shall see whose nerves fray first. He offered tea to the sacerdote, who refused with a shake of the head so quick and of such small compass as to seem a shudder.

Joaz made a gesture signifying it was all the same to him. "Should you desire sustenance or drink," he said, "please let it be known. I enjoy our conversation so inordinately that I fear I may prolong it to the limits of your patience. Surely you would prefer to sit?"

"No."

"As you wish. Well, then, back to our discussion. This cavern you mentioned: is it inhabited by sacerdotes?"

"I fail to understand your question."

"Do sacerdotes use the cavern?"

"Yes."

Eventually, fragment by fragment, Joaz extracted the information that the cavern connected with a series of chambers, in which the sacerdotes smelted metal, boiled glass, ate, slept, performed their rituals. At one time there had been an opening into Banbeck Vale, but long ago this had been blocked. Why? There were wars throughout the cluster; bands of defeated men were taking refuge upon Aerlith, settling in rifts and valleys. The sacerdotes preferred a detached existence and had shut their caverns away from sight. Where was this opening? The sacerdote seemed vague. To the north end of the valley. Behind Banbeck Jambles? Possibly. But trading between men and sacerdotes was conducted at a cave entrance below Mount Gethron. Why? A matter of usage, declared the sacerdote. In addition this location was more readily accessible to Happy Valley and Phosphor Gulch. How many sacerdotes lived in these caves? Uncertainty. Some might have died, others might have been born. Approximately how many this morning? Perhaps five hundred.

At this juncture the sacerdote was swaying and Joaz was hoarse. "Back to your motive—or the elements of your motives —for coming to my studio. Are they connected in any manner with the star Coralyne, and a possible new coming of the Basics, or the grephs, as they were formerly called?"

Again the sacerdote seemed to hesitate. Then: "Yes."

"Will the sacerdotes help us against the Basics, should they come?"

"No." This answer was terse and definite.

"But I assume that the sacerdotes wish the Basics driven off?" No answer.

Joaz rephrased his words. "Do the sacerdotes wish the Basics repelled from Aerlith?"

"The Rationale bids us stand aloof from affairs of men and non-men alike."

Joaz curled his lip. "Suppose the Basics invaded your cave and dragged you off to the Coralyne planet. Then what?"

The sacerdote almost seemed to laugh. "The question cannot be answered."

"Would you resist the Basics if they made the attempt?"

"I cannot answer your question."

Joaz laughed. "But the answer is not no?"

The sacerdote assented.

"Do you have weapons, then?"

The sacerdote's mild blue eyes seemed to droop. Secrecy? Fatigue? Joaz repeated the question.

"Yes," said the sacerdote. His knees sagged, but he snapped them tight.

"What kind of weapons?"

"Numberless varieties. Projectiles, such as rocks. Piercing weapons, such as broken sticks. Cutting and slashing weapons, such as cooking utensils." His voice began to fade as if he were moving away. "Poisons: arsenic, sulfur, triventidum, acid, black-spore. Burning weapons, such as torches and lenses to focus the sunlight. Weapons to suffocate: ropes, nooses, slings and cords. Cisterns, to drown the enemy . . ."

"Sit down. Rest," Joaz urged him. "Your inventory interests me, but its total effect seems inadequate. Have you other weapons which might decisively repel the Basics should they attack you?"

The question, by design or chance, was never answered. The sacerdote sank to his knees, slowly, as if praying. He fell forward on his face, then sprawled to the side. Joaz sprang forward, yanked up the drooping head by its hair. The eyes, half-open, revealed a hideous white expanse. "Speak!" croaked Joaz. "Answer my last question! Do you have weapons—or a weapon—to repel a Basic attack?"

The pallid lips moved. "I don't know."

Joaz frowned, peered into the waxen face, drew back in bewilderment. "The man is dead," he whispered.

VII

Phade looked up from drowsing on a couch, face pink, hair tossed. "You have killed him!" she cried in a voice of hushed horror.

"No. He has died—or caused himself to die."

Phade staggered blinking across the room, sidled close to Joaz, who pushed her absently away. Phade scowled, shrugged and then, as Joaz paid her no heed, marched from the room.

Joaz sat back, staring at the limp body. "He did not tire," muttered Joaz, "until I verged upon secrets."

Presently he jumped to his feet, went to the entry hall, sent Rife to fetch a barber. An hour later the corpse, stripped of hair, lay on a wooden pallet covered by a sheet, and Joaz held in his hands a rude wig fashioned from the long hair.

The barber departed. Servants carried away the corpse. Joaz stood alone in his studio, tense and light-headed. He removed his garments, to stand naked as the sacerdote. Gingerly he drew the wig across his scalp and examined himself in a mirror. To a casual eye, where the difference? Something was lacking: the torc. Joaz fitted it about his neck. Once more he examined his reflection, with dubious satisfaction.

He entered the workshop, hesitated, disengaged the trap, cautiously pulled away the stone slab. On hands and knees he peered into the tunnel and, since it was dark, held forward a glass vial of luminescent algae. In the faint light the tunnel seemed empty.

Irrevocably putting down his fears, Joaz clambered through the opening. The tunnel was narrow and low. Joaz moved forward tentatively, nerves thrilling with wariness. He stopped often to listen, but heard nothing but the whisper of his own pulse.

After perhaps a hundred yards the tunnel broke out into a natural cavern. Joaz stopped and stood indecisively straining his ears through the gloom. Luminescent vials fixed to the walls at irregular intervals provided a measure of light, enough to delineate the direction of the cavern. It seemed to be north, parallel to the length of the valley. Joaz set forth once again, halting to listen every few yards.

To the best of his knowledge the sacerdotes were a mild unaggressive folk, but they were also intensely secretive. How would they respond to the presence of an interloper? Joaz could not be sure, and proceeded with great caution.

The cavern rose, fell, widened, narrowed. Joaz presently came upon evidences of use: small cubicles, hollowed into the walls, lit by candelabra holding tall vials of luminous stuff. In two of the cubicles Joaz came upon sacerdotes, the first asleep on a reed rug, the second sitting crosslegged, gazing fixedly at a contrivance of twisted metal rods. They gave Joaz no attention; he continued with a more confident step.

The cave sloped downwards, widened like a cornucopia and suddenly broke into a cavern so enormous that Joaz thought for a startled instant that he had stepped out into the starless night.

The ceiling reached beyond the flicker of the myriad lamps, fires and glowing vials. Ahead and to the left smelters and forges were in operation; then a twist in the cavern wall obscured something of the view. Joaz glimpsed a tiered, tubular construction which seemed to be some sort of workshop, for a large number of sacerdotes were occupied at complicated tasks. To the right was a stack of bales, a row of bins containing goods of unknown nature.

Joaz for the first time saw sacerdote women: neither the nymphs nor the half-human witches of popular legend. Like the men they seemed pallid and frail, with sharply defined features; like the men they moved with care and deliberation; like the men they wore only their waist-long hair. There was little conversation and no laughter. Rather there was an atmosphere of not unhappy placidity and concentration. The cavern exuded a sense of time, use and custom. The stone floor was polished by endless padding of bare feet. The exhalations of many generations had stained the walls.

No one heeded Joaz.

He moved slowly forward, keeping to the shadows, and paused under the stack of bales. To the right the cavern dwindled by irregular proportions into a vast horizontal funnel, receding, twisting, telescoping, losing all reality in the dim light.

Joaz searched the entire sweep of vast cavern. Where would be the armory, with the weapons whose existence the sacerdote, by the very act of dying, had promised him? Joaz turned his attention once more to the left, straining to see detail in the odd tiered workshop which rose fifty feet from the stone floor. A strange edifice, thought Joaz, craning his neck; one whose nature he could not entirely comprehend. But every aspect of the great cavern—so close beside Banbeck Vale, and so remote—was strange and marvelous. Weapons? They might be anywhere. Certainly he dared seek no further for them.

There was nothing more he could learn without risk of discovery. He turned back the way he had come: up the dim passage, past the occasional side cubicles, where the two sacerdotes remained as he had found them before: the one asleep, the other intent on the contrivance of twisted metal. He plodded on and on.

Had he come so far? Where was the fissure which led to his own apartments? Had he passed it by, must he search? Panic rose in his throat, but he continued, watching carefully. There, he had not gone wrong. There it opened to his right, a fissure almost dear and familiar. He plunged into it, walked with long loping strides, like a man under water, holding his luminous tube ahead.

An apparition rose before him, a tall white shape.

Joaz stood rigid. The gaunt figure bore down upon him. Joaz pressed against the wall. The figure stalked forward, and suddenly shrank to human scale. It was the young sacerdote whom Joaz had shorn and left for dead. He confronted Joaz, mild blue eyes bright with reproach and contempt. "Give me my torc."

With numb fingers Joaz removed the golden collar. The sacerdote took it, but made no move to clasp it upon himself. He looked at the hair which weighed heavily upon Joaz's scalp. With a foolish grimace Joaz doffed the disheveled wig, proffered it. The sacerdote sprang back as if Joaz had become a cave-goblin. Sidling past, as far from Joaz as the wall of the passage allowed, he paced swiftly off down the tunnel, Joaz dropped the wig to the floor, stared down at the unkempt pile of hair. He turned and looked after the sacerdote, a pallid figure which soon became one with the murk. Slowly Joaz continued up the tunnel.

There. An oblong blank of light, the opening to his workshop. He crawled through, back to the real world. Savagely, with all his strength, he thrust the slab back in the hole and slammed down the gate which originally had trapped the sacerdote.

Joaz's garments lay where he had tossed them. Wrapping himself in a cloak, he went to the outer door and looked forth into the anteroom, where Rife sat dozing. Joaz snapped his fingers. "Fetch masons, with mortar, steel and stone."

Joaz bathed with diligence, rubbing himself time after time with emulsion, rinsing and rerinsing himself. Emerging from the bath he took the waiting masons into his workshop and ordered the sealing of the hole.

Then he took himself to his couch. Sipping a cup of wine, he let his mind rove and wander . . .

Recollection became reverie. Reverie became dream. Joaz once again traversed the tunnel, on feet light as thistledown, down the long cavern, and the sacerdotes in their cubicles now raised their heads to look after him. At last he stood in the entrance to the great underground void, and once more looked right and left in awe. Now he drifted across the floor, past sacerdotes laboring earnestly over fires and anvils. Sparks rose from retorts, blue gas flickered above melting metal.

Joaz moved beyond to a small chamber cut into the stone. Here sat an old man, thin as a pole, his waist-long mane of hair snow-white. The man examined Joaz with fathomless blue eyes, and spoke, but his voice was muffled, inaudible. He spoke again; the words rang loud in Joaz's mind.

"I bring you here to caution you, lest you do us harm, and with no profit to yourself. The weapon you seek is both non-existent and beyond your imagination. Put it outside your ambition."

By great effort Joaz managed to stammer, "The young sacerdote made no denial. This weapon must exist!"

"Only with the narrow limits of special interpretation. The lad can speak no more than the literal truth, nor can he act with other than grace. How can you wonder why we hold ourselves apart? You Utter folk find purity incomprehensible; you thought to advantage yourself, but achieved nothing but an exercise in rat-like stealth. Lest you try again with greater boldness I must abase myself to set matters correct. I assure you, this so-called weapon is absolutely beyond your control."

First shame, then indignation came over Joaz. He cried out, "You do not understand my urgencies! Why should I act differently. Coralyne is close; the Basics are at hand. Are you not men? Why will you not help us defend the planet?"

The Demie shook his head, and the white hair rippled with hypnotic slowness. "I quote you the Rationale: passivity, complete and absolute. This implies solitude, sanctity, quiescence, peace. Can you imagine the anguish I risk in speaking to you? I intervene, I interfere, at vast pain of the spirit. Let there be an end to it. We have made free with your studio, doing you no harm, offering you no indignity. You have paid a visit to our hall, demeaning a noble young man in the process. Let us be quits! Let there be no further spying on either side. Do you agree?"

Joaz heard his voice respond, quite without his conscious prompting. It sounded more nasal and shrill than he liked. "You offer this agreement now when you have learned your fill of my secrets, but I know none of yours."

The Demie's face seemed to recede and quiver. Joaz read contempt, and in his sleep he tossed and twitched. He made an effort to speak in a voice of calm reason: "Come, we are men together. Why should we be at odds? Let us share our secrets, let each help the other. Examine my archives at your leisure, and then allow me to study this existent but non-existent weapon. I swear it shall be used only against the Basics, for the protection of both of us."

The Demie's eyes sparkled. "No."

"Why not?" argued Joaz. "Surely you wish us no harm?"

"We are detached and passionless. We await your extinction. You are the Utter men, the last of humanity. And when you are gone, your dark thoughts and grim plots will be gone. Murder and pain and malice will be gone."

"I cannot believe this," said Joaz. "There may be no men in the cluster, but what of the universe? The Old Rule reached far! Sooner or later men will return to Aerlith."

The Demie's voice became plangent. "Do you think we speak only from faith? Do you doubt our knowledge?"

"The universe is large. The Old Rule reached far."

"The last men dwell on Aerlith," said the Demie. "The Utter men and the Sacerdotes. You shall pass; we will carry forth the Rationale like a banner of glory, through all the worlds of the sky."

"And how will you transport yourselves on this mission?" Joaz asked cunningly. "Can you fly to the stars as naked as you walk the fells?"

"There will be a means. Time is long."

"For your purposes, Time needs to be long. Even on the Coralyne planets there are men. Enslaved, reshaped in body and mind, but men. What of them? It seems that you are wrong, that you are guided by faith indeed."

The Demie fell silent. His face seemed to stiffen.

"Are these not facts?" asked Joaz. "How do you reconcile them with your faith?"

The Demie said mildly, "Facts can never be reconciled with faith. By our faith, these men, if they exist, will also pass. Time is long. O the worlds of brightness: they await us!"

"It is clear," said Joaz, "that you ally yourselves with the Basics and hope for our destruction. This can only change our attitudes toward you. I fear that Ervis Carcolo was right and I wrong."

"We remain passive," said the Demie. His face wavered, seemed to swim with mottled colors. "Without emotion, we

71

will stand witness to the passing of the Utter men, neither helping nor hindering."

Joaz spoke in fury. "Your faith, your Rationale—whatever you call it—misleads you. I make you this threat: if you fail to help us, you will suffer as we suffer."

"We are passive. We are indifferent."

"What of your children? The Basics make no difference between us. They will herd you to their pens as readily as they do us. Why should we fight to protect you?"

The Demie's face faded, became splotched with transparent mist. His eyes glowed like rotten meat. "We need no protection," he howled. "We are secure."

"You will suffer our fate," cried Joaz, "I promise you this!"

The Demie collapsed suddenly into a small dry husk, like a dead mosquito. With incredible speed, Joaz fled back through the caves, the tunnels, up through his work-room, his studio, into his bed chamber where now he jerked upright, eyes starting, throat distended, mouth dry.

The door opened; Rife's head appeared. "Did you call, sir?"

Joaz raised himself on his elbows and looked around the room. "No. I did not call."

Rife withdrew. Joaz settled back on the couch, lay staring at the ceiling.

He had dreamed a most peculiar dream. Dream? A synthesis of his own imaginings? Or, in all verity, a confrontation and exchange between two minds? Impossible to decide, and perhaps irrelevant. The event carried its own conviction.

Joaz swung his legs over the side of the couch and blinked at the floor. Dream or colloquy, it was all the same. He rose to his feet, donned sandals and a robe of yellow fur, limped morosely up to the Council Room and stepped out on a sunny balcony.

The day was two-thirds over. Shadows hung dense along the western cliffs. Right and left stretched Banbeck Vale. Never had it seemed more prosperous or more fruitful, and never before unreal: as if he were a stranger to the planet. He looked north along the great bulwark of stone which rose sheer to

Banbeck Verge. This too was unreal, a façade behind which lived the sacerdotes. He gauged the rock face, superimposing a mental projection of the great cavern. The cliff toward the north end of the vale must be scarcely more than a shell!

Joaz turned his attention to the exercise field, where Juggers were thudding briskly through defensive evolutions. How strange was the quality of life, which had produced Basic and Jugger, sacerdote and himself. He thought of Ervis Carcolo, and wrestled with sudden exasperation. Carcolo was a distraction most unwelcome at the present time. There would be no tolerance when Carcolo was finally brought to account.

A light step behind him, the pressure of fur, the touch of gay hands, the scent of incense. Joaz's tensions melted.

If there were no such creatures as minstrel-maidens, it would be necessary to invent them.

Deep under Banbeck Scarp, in a cubicle lit by a twelve-vial candelabra, a naked white-haired man sat quietly. On a pedestal at the level of his eyes rested his *tand*, an intricate construction of gold rods and silver wire, woven and bent seemingly at random. The fortuitousness of the design, however, was only apparent. Each curve symbolized an aspect of Final Sentience. The shadow cast upon the wall represented the Rationale, ever-shifting, always the same. The object was sacred to the sacerdotes, and served as a source of revelation.

There was never an end to the study of the *tand*. New intuitions were continually derived from some heretofore-overlooked relationship of angle and curve. The nomenclature was elaborate: each part, juncture, sweep and twist had its name; each aspect of the relationships between the various parts was likewise categorized. Such was the cult of the *tand*: abstruse, exacting, without compromise. At his puberty rites the young sacerdote might study the original *tand* for as long as he chose. Then each must construct a duplicate *tand*, relying upon memory alone. Then occurred the most significant event of his lifetime: the viewing of his *tand* by a synod of elders.

In awesome stillness, for hours at a time they would ponder his creation, weigh the infinitesimal variations of proportion, radius, sweep and angle. So they would infer the initiate's quality, judge his personal attributes, determine his understanding of Final Sentience, the Rationale and the Basis.

Occasionally the testimony of the *tand* revealed a character so tainted as to be reckoned intolerable. The vile *tand* would be cast into a furnace, the molten metal consigned to a latrine, the unlucky initiate expelled to the face of the planet, to live on his own terms.

The naked white-haired Demie, contemplating his own beautiful *tand*, sighed, moved restlessly. He had been visited by an influence so ardent, so passionate, so simultaneously cruel and tender, that his mind was oppressed. Unbidden, into his mind, came a dark seep of doubt.

Can it be, he asked himself, that we have insensibly wandered from the true Rationale? Do we study our *tands* with blinded eyes? . . . How to know, oh how to know! All is relative ease and facility in orthodoxy, yet how can it be denied that good is in itself undeniable? Absolutes are the most uncertain of all formulations, while the uncertainties are the most real.

Twenty miles over the mountains, in the long pale light of the Aerlith afternoon, Ervis Carcolo planned his own plans. "By daring, by striking hard, by cutting deep can I defeat him! In resolve, courage and endurance, I am more than his equal. Not again will he trick me, to slaughter my dragons and kill my men! Oh, Joaz Banbeck, how I will pay you for your deceit!" He raised his arms in wrath. "Oh Joaz Banbeck, you whey-faced sheep!" Carcolo smote the air with his fist. "I will crush you like a clod of dry moss!"

He frowned and rubbed his round red chin. But how? Where? He had every advantage! Carcolo pondered his possible stratagems. "He will expect me to strike. So much is certain. Doubtless he will again wait in ambush. So I will patrol every inch, but this too he will expect and so be wary lest I thunder upon him from above. Will he hide behind Despoire, or along Northguard, to catch me as I cross the Skanse? If so, I must approach by another route—through Maudlin Pass and under Mount Gethron? Then, if he is tardy in his march I will meet him on Banbeck Verge. And if he is early, I stalk him through the peaks and chasms . . ."

VIII

With the cold rain of dawn pelting down upon them, with the trail illuminated only by lightning-glare, Ervis Carcolo, his dragons and his men set forth. When the first sparkle of sunlight struck Mount Despoire, they had already traversed Maudlin Pass.

So far, so good, exulted Ervis Carcolo. He stood high in his stirrups to scan Starbreak Fell. No sign of the Banbeck forces. He waited, scanning the far edge of Northguard Ridge, black against the sky. A minute passed. Two minutes. The men beat their hands together, the dragons rumbled and muttered fretfully.

Impatience began to prickle along Carcolo's ribs. He fidgeted and cursed. Could not the simplest of plans be carried through without mistake? But now the flicker of a heliograph from Barch Spike, and another to the southeast from the slopes of Mount Gethron. Carcolo waved forward his army; the way lay clear across Starbreak Fell. Down from Maudlin Pass surged the Happy Valley army: first the Long-horned Murderers, steel-spiked and crested with steel prongs; then the rolling red seethe of the Termagants, darting their heads as they ran; and, behind, the balance of the forces.

Starbreak Fell spread wide before them, a rolling slope strewn with flinty meteoric fragments which glinted like flowers on the gray-green moss. To all sides rose majestic peaks, snow blazing white in the clear morning light: Mount Gethron, Mount Despoire, Barch Spike and, far to the south, Clew Taw.

The scouts converged from left and right. They brought

identical reports: no sign of Joaz Banbeck or his troops. Carcolo began to toy with a new possibility. Perhaps Joaz Banbeck had not deigned to take the field. The idea enraged him and filled him with a great joy: if so, Joaz would pay dearly for his neglect.

Halfway across Starbreak Fell they came upon a pen occupied by two hundred of Joaz Banbeck's spratling Fiends. Two old men and a boy tended the pen, and watched the Happy Valley horde advance with manifest terror.

But Carcolo rode past leaving the pen unmolested. If he won the day, it would become part of his spoils. If he lost, the spratling Fiends could do him no harm.

The old men and the boy stood on the roof of their turf hut, watching Carcolo and his troops pass: the men in black uniforms and black peaked caps with back-slanting ear-flaps; the dragons bounding, crawling, loping, plodding, according to their kind, scales glinting: the dull red and maroon of Termagants; the poisonous shine of the Blue Horrors; the black-green Fiends; the gray and brown Juggers and Murderers. Ervis Carcolo rode on the right flank, Bast Givven rode to the rear. And now Carcolo hastened the pace, haunted by the anxiety that Joaz Banbeck might bring his Fiends and Juggers up Banbeck Scarp before he arrived to thrust him back—assuming that Joaz Banbeck had been caught napping.

But Carcolo reached Banbeck Verge without challenge.

He shouted out in triumph, waved his cap high. "Joaz Banbeck the sluggard! Let him try now the ascent of Banbeck Scarp!" And Ervis Carcolo surveyed Banbeck Vale with the eye of a conqueror.

Bast Givven seemed to share none of Carcolo's triumph, and kept an uneasy watch to north and south and to the rear.

Carcolo observed him peevishly from the corner of his eye and presently called out, "Ho, ho, then! What's amiss?"

"Perhaps much. Perhaps nothing," said Bast Givven, searching the landscape.

Carcolo blew out his mustaches. Givven went on, in the cool

voice which so completely irritated Carcolo. "Joaz Banbeck seems to be tricking us as before."

"Why do you say this?"

"Judge for yourself. Would he allow us advantage without claiming a miser's price?"

"Nonsense!" muttered Carcolo. "The sluggard is fat with his last victory." But he rubbed his chin and peered uneasily down into Banbeck Vale. From here it seemed curiously quiet. There was a strange inactivity in the fields and barracks. A chill began to grip Carcolo's heart—then he cried out. "Look at the brooder: there are the Banbeck dragons!"

Givven squinted down into the vale, glanced sidewise at Carcolo. "Three Termagants, in egg." He straightened, abandoned all interest in the vale and scrutinized the peaks and ridges to the north and east. "Assume that Joaz Banbeck set out before dawn, came up to the Verge, by the Slickenslides, crossed Blue Fell in strength—"

"What of Blue Crevasse?"

"He avoids Blue Crevasse to the north, comes over Barchback, steals across the Skanse and around Barch Spike . . ."

Carcolo studied Northguard Ridge with new and startled awareness. A quiver of movement, the glint of scales?

"Retreat!" roared Carcolo. "Make for Barch Spike! They're behind us!"

Startled, his army broke ranks, fled across Banbeck Verge, up into the harsh spurs of Barch Spike. Joaz, his strategy discovered, launched squads of Murderers to intercept the Happy Valley army, to engage and delay and, if possible, deny them the broken slopes of Barch Spike.

Carcolo calculated swiftly. His own Murderers he considered his finest troops, and held them in great pride. Purposely now he delayed, hoping to engage the Banbeck skirmishers, quickly destroy them and still gain the protection of the Barch declivities.

The Banbeck Murderers, however, refused to close, and scrambled for height up Barch Spike. Carcolo sent forward his Termagants and Blue Horrors.

With a horrid snarling the two lines met. The Banbeck Termagants rushed up, to be met by Carcolo's Striding Murderers and forced into humping pounding flight.

The main body of Carcolo's troops, excited at the sight of retreating foes, could not be restrained. They veered off from Barch Spike, plunged down upon Starbreak Fell. The striding Murderers overtook the Banbeck Termagants, climbed up their backs, toppled them over squealing and kicking, then knifed open the exposed pink bellies.

Banbeck's Long-horned Murderers came circling, struck from the flank into Carcolo's Striding Murderers, goring with steel-tipped horns, impaling on lances.

Somehow they overlooked Carcolo's Blue Horrors who sprang down upon them. With axes and maces they laid the Murderers low, performing the rather grisly entertainment of clambering on a subdued Murderer, seizing the horn, stripping back horn, skin and scales, from head to tail. So Joaz Banbeck lost thirty Termagants and perhaps two dozen Murderers. Nevertheless, the attack served its purpose, allowing him to bring his knights, Fiends and Juggers down from Northguard before Carcolo could gain the heights of Barch Spike.

Carcolo retreated in a slantwise line up the pocked slopes, and meanwhile sent six men across the fell to the pen where the spratling Fiends milled in fear at the battle. The men broke the gates, struck down the two old men, herded the young Fiends across the fell toward the Banbeck troops. The hysterical spratlings obeyed their instincts. They clasped themselves to the neck of whatever dragon they first encountered, which thereupon became sorely hampered, for its own instincts prevented it from detaching the spratling by force.

This ruse, a brilliant improvisation, created enormous disorder among the Banbeck troops. Ervis Carcolo now charged with all his power directly into the Banbeck center. Two squads of Termagants fanned out to harass the men. His Murderers—the only category in which he outnumbered Joaz Banbeck—were sent to engage Fiends, while Carcolo's own

Fiends, pampered, strong, glistening with oily strength, snaked in toward the Juggers. Under the great brown hulks they darted, lashing the fifty-pound steel ball at the tip of their tails against the inner side of the Jugger's legs.

A roaring melee ensued. Battle-lines were uncertain. Both men and dragons were crushed, torn apart, hacked to bits. The air sang with bullets, whistled with steel, reverberated to trumpeting, whistles, shouts, screams and bellows.

The reckless abandon of Carcolo's tactics achieved results out of proportion to his numbers. His Fiends burrowed ever deeper into the crazed and almost helpless Banbeck Juggers, while the Carcolo Murderers and Blue Horrors held back the Banbeck Fiends. Joaz Banbeck himself, assailed by Termagants, escaped with his life only by fleeing around behind the battle, where he picked up the support of a squad of Blue Horrors. In a fury he blew a withdrawal signal, and his army backed off down the slopes, leaving the ground littered with struggling and kicking bodies.

Carcolo, throwing aside all restraint, rose in his saddle and signaled to commit his own Juggers, which so far he had treasured like his own children.

Shrilling, hiccuping, they lumbered down into the seethe, tearing away great mouthfuls of flesh to right and left, ripping apart lesser dragons with their brachs, treading on Termagants, seizing Blue Horrors and Murderers, flinging them wailing and clawing through the air. Six Banbeck knights sought to stem the charge, firing their muskets point-blank into the demoniac faces; they went down and were seen no more.

Down on Starbreak Fell tumbled the battle. The nucleus of the fighting became less concentrated, the Happy Valley advantage dissipated. Carcolo hesitated, a long heady instant.

He and his troops alike were afire; the intoxication of unexpected success tingled in their brains—but here on Starbreak Fell, could they counter the odds posed by the greater Banbeck forces? Caution dictated that Carcolo withdraw up Barch Spike, to make the most of his limited victory. Already a strong platoon of Fiends had grouped and were maneuvering to charge his meager force of Juggers. Bast Givven approached, clearly expecting the word to retreat. But Carcolo still waited, reveling in the havoc being wrought by his paltry six Juggers.

Bast Givven's saturnine face was stern. "Withdraw, withdraw! It's annihilation when their flanks bear in on us!"

Carcolo seized his elbow. "Look! See where those Fiends gather, see where Joaz Banbeck rides! As soon as they charge, send six Striding Murderers from either side; close in on him, kill him!"

Givven opened his mouth to protest, looked where Carcolo pointed, rode to obey the orders.

Here came the Banbeck Fiends, moving with stealthy certainty toward the Happy Valley Juggers. Joaz, raising in his saddle, watched their progress. Suddenly from either side the Striding Murderers were on him. Four of his knights and six young cornets, screaming alarm, dashed back to protect him; there was clanging of steel on steel and steel on scale. The Murderers fought with sword and mace. The knights, their muskets useless, countered with cutlasses, one by one going under.

Rearing on hind legs the Murderer corporal hacked down at Joaz, who desperately fended off the blow. The Murderer raised sword and mace together—and from fifty yards a musket pellet smashed into its ear. Crazy with pain, it dropped its weapons, fell forward upon Joaz, writhing and kicking. Banbeck Blue Horrors came to attack; the Murderers darted back and forth over the thrashing corporal, stabbing down at Joaz, kicking at him, finally fleeing the Blue Horrors.

Ervis Carcolo groaned in disappointment. By a half-second only had he fallen short of victory. Joaz Banbeck, bruised, mauled, perhaps wounded, had escaped with his life.

Over the crest of the hill came a rider: an unarmed youth whipping a staggering Spider. Bast Givven pointed him out to Carcolo. "A messenger from the Valley, in urgency."

The lad careened down the fell toward Carcolo, shouting

ahead, but his message was lost in the din of battle. At last he drew close. "The Basics, the Basics!"

Carcolo slumped like a half-empty bladder. "Where?"

"A great black ship, half the valley wide. I was up on the heath, I managed to escape." He pointed, whimpered.

"Speak, boy!" husked Carcolo. "What do they do?"

"I did not see; I ran to you."

Carcolo gazed across the battle-field; the Banbeck Fiends had almost reached his Juggers, who were backing slowly, with heads lowered, fangs fully extended.

Carcolo threw up his hands in despair. He ordered Givven, "Blow a retreat, break clear!"

Waving a white kerchief he rode around the battle to where Joaz Banbeck still lay on the ground, the quivering Murderer only just now being lifted from his legs. Joaz stared up, his face white as Carcolo's kerchief. At the sight of Carcolo his eyes grew wide and dark, his mouth became still.

Carcolo blurted, "The Basics have come once more; they have dropped into Happy Valley, they are destroying my people."

Joaz Banbeck, assisted by his knights, gained his feet. He stood swaying, arms limp, looking silently into Carcolo's face.

Carcolo spoke once more. "We must call truce. This battle is waste! With all our forces let us march to Happy Valley and attack the monsters before they destroy all of us! Ah, think what we could have achieved with the weapons of the sacerdotes!"

Joaz stood silent. Another ten seconds passed. Carcolo cried angrily, "Come now, what do you say?"

In a hoarse voice Joaz spoke, "I say no truce. You rejected my warning. You thought to loot Banbeck Vale. I will show you no mercy."

Carcolo gaped, his mouth a red hole under the sweep of his mustaches. "But the Basics—"

"Return to your troops. You as well as the Basics are my

enemy. Why should I choose between you? Prepare to fight for your life; I give you no truce."

Carcolo drew back a face as pale as Joaz's own. "Never shall you rest! Even though you win this battle here on Starbreak Fell, yet you shall never know victory. I will persecute you until you cry for relief."

Banbeck motioned to his knights. "Whip this dog back to his own."

Carcolo backed his Spider from the threatening flails, turned, loped away.

The tide of battle had turned. The Banbeck Fiends now had broken past his Blue Horrors. One of his Juggers was gone; another, facing three sidling Fiends, snapped its great jaws, waved its monstrous sword. The Fiends flicked and feinted with their steel balls, scuttled forward. The Jugger chopped, shattered its sword on the rock-hard armor of the Fiends; they were underneath, slamming their steel balls into the monstrous legs. It tried to hop clear, toppled majestically. The Fiends slit its belly, and now Carcolo had only five Juggers left.

"Back!" he cried. "Disengage!"

Up Barch Spike toiled his troops, the battle-front a roaring seethe of scales, armor, flickering metal. Luckily for Carcolo his rear was to the high ground, and after ten terrible minutes he was able to establish an orderly retreat.

Two more Juggers had fallen. The three remaining scrambled free. Seizing boulders, they hurled them down into the attackers, who, after a series of sallies and lunges, were well content to break clear. In any event Joaz, after hearing Carcolo's news, was of no disposition to spend further troops.

Carcolo, waving his sword in desperate defiance, led his troops back around Barch Spike, presently down across the dreary Skanse. Joaz turned back to Banbeck Vale. The news of the Basic raid had spread to all ears. The men rode sober and quiet, looking behind and overhead. Even the dragons seemed infected, and muttered restlessly among themselves.

As they crossed Blue Fell the almost omnipresent wind died. The stillness added to the oppression.

Termagants, like the men, began to watch the sky. Joaz wondered, how could they know, how could they sense the Basics? He himself searched the sky, and as his army passed down over the scarp he thought to see high over Mount Gethron, a fitting little black rectangle, which presently disappeared behind a crag.

IX

Ervis Carcolo and the remnants of his army raced pell-mell down from the Skanse, through the wilderness of ravines and gulches at the base of Mount Despoire, out on the barrens to the west of Happy Valley. All pretense of military precision had been abandoned.

Carcolo led the way, his Spider sobbing with fatigue. Behind in disarray pounded first Murderers and Blue Horrors, with Termagants hurrying along behind. Then the Fiends, racing low to the ground, steel balls grinding on rocks, sending up sparks. Far in the rear lumbered the Juggers and their attendants.

Down to the verge of Happy Valley plunged the army and pulled up short, stamping and squealing. Carcolo jumped from his Spider, ran to the brink, stood looking down into the valley.

He had expected to see the ship, yet the actuality of the thing was so immediate and intense as to shock him. It was a tapered cylinder, glossy and black, resting in a field of legumes not far from ramshackle Happy Town. Polished metal disks at either end shimmered and glistened with fleeting films of color. There were three entrance ports—forward, central and aft—and from the central port a ramp had been extended to the ground.

The Basics had worked with ferocious efficiency. From the town straggled a line of people, herded by Heavy Troopers. Approaching the ship they passed through an inspection apparatus controlled by a pair of Basics. A series of instruments and the eyes of the Basics appraised each man, woman and child, classified them by some system not instantly obvious, whereupon the captives were either hustled up the ramp into the ship or prodded into a nearby booth.

Peculiarly, no matter how many persons entered, the booth never seemed to fill.

Carcolo rubbed his forehead with trembling fingers, turned his eyes to the ground. When once more he looked up, Bast Givven stood beside him, and together they stared down into the valley.

From behind came a cry of alarm. Starting around, Carcolo saw a black rectangular flyer sliding silently down from above Mount Gethron.

Waving his arms Carcolo ran for the rocks, bellowing orders to take cover. Dragons and men scuttled up the gulch. Overhead slid the flyer. A hatch opened, releasing a load of explosive pellets. They struck with a great rattling volley, and up into the air flew pebbles, rock splinters, fragments of bone, scales, skin and flesh. All who failed to reach cover were shredded.

The Termagants fared relatively well. The Fiends, though battered and scraped, had all survived. Two of the Juggers had been blinded, and could fight no more till they had grown new eyes.

The flyer slid back once more. Several of the men fired their muskets—an act of apparently futile defiance, but the flyer was struck and damaged. It twisted, veered, soared up in a roaring curve, swooped over its back, plunged toward the mountainside, crashed in a brilliant orange gush of fire. Carcolo shouted in maniac glee, jumped up and down, ran to the verge of the cliff, shook his fist at the ship below. He quickly quieted, to stand glum and shivering.

Then, turning to the ragged cluster of men and dragons who once more had crept down from the gulch, Carcolo cried hoarsely, "What do you say? Shall we fight? Shall we charge down upon them?"

There was silence.

Bast Givven replied in a colorless voice, "We are helpless. We can accomplish nothing. Why commit suicide?"

Carcolo turned away, heart too full for words. Givven spoke the obvious truth. They would either be killed or dragged aboard the ship; and then, on a world too strange for imagining, be put to uses too dismal to be borne.

Carcolo clenched his fists and looked westward with bitter hatred. "Joaz Banbeck, you brought me to this! When I might yet have fought for my people you detained me!"

"The Basics were here already," said Givven with unwelcome rationality. "We could have done nothing since we had nothing to do with."

"We could have fought!" bellowed Carcolo. "We might have swept down the Crotch and come upon them with all force! A hundred warriors and four hundred dragons—are these to be despised?"

Bast Givven judged further argument to be pointless. He pointed. "They now examine our brooders."

Carcolo turned to look, gave a wild laugh. "They are astonished! They are awed! And well have they a right to be."

Givven agreed. "I imagine the sight of a Fiend or a Blue Horror—not to mention a Jugger—gives them pause for reflection."

Down in the valley the grim business had ended. The Heavy Troopers marched back into the ship. A pair of enormous men twelve feet high came forth, lifted the booth, carried it up the ramp into the ship. Carcolo and his men watched with protruding eyes. "Giants!"

Bast Givven chuckled dryly. "The Basics stare at our Juggers, we ponder their Giants."

The Basics presently returned to the ship. The ramp was drawn up, the ports closed. From a turret in the bow came a shaft of energy, touching each of the three brooders in succession, and each exploded with great eruption of black bricks.

Carcolo moaned softly under his breath, but said nothing.

The ship trembled, floated. Carcolo bellowed an order; men and dragons rushed for cover. Flattened behind boulders they watched the black cylinder rise from the valley, drift to the west. "They make for Banbeck Vale," said Bast Givven.

Carcolo laughed, a cackle of mirthless glee. Bast Givven looked at him sidelong. Had Ervis Carcolo become addled? He turned away. A matter of no great moment.

Carcolo came to a sudden resolve. He stalked to one of the Spiders, mounted, swung around to face his men. "I ride to Banbeck Vale. Joaz Banbeck has done his best to despoil me; I shall do my best against him. I give no orders: come or stay as you wish. Only remember! Joaz Banbeck would not allow us to fight the Basics!"

He rode off. The men stared into the plundered valley, turned to look after Carcolo. The black ship was just now slipping over Mount Despoire. There was nothing for them in the valley. Grumbling and muttering, they summoned the bone-tired dragons and set off up the dreary mountainside.

Ervis Carcolo rode his Spider at a plunging run across the Skanse. Tremendous crags soared to either side, the blazing sun hung halfway up the black sky. Behind, the Skanse Ramparts; ahead, Barchback, Barch Spike and Northguard Ridge.

Oblivious to the fatigue of his Spider, Carcolo whipped it on. Gray-green moss pounded back from its wild feet, the narrow head hung low, foam trailed from its gill-vents. Carcolo cared nothing. His mind was empty of all but hate—for the Basics, for Joaz Banbeck, for Aerlith, for man, for human history.

Approaching Northguard the Spider staggered and fell. It lay moaning, neck outstretched, legs trailing back. Carcolo dismounted in disgust. He looked back down the long rolling slope of the Skanse to see how many of his troops had followed him. A man riding a Spider at a modest lope turned out to be Bast Givven, who presently came up beside him and inspected the fallen Spider. "Loosen the surcingle. He will recover the sooner." Carcolo glared, thinking to hear a new note in Givven's voice. Nevertheless he bent over the foundered dragon and slipped loose the broad bronze buckle. Givven dismounted, stretched his arms, massaged his thin legs. He pointed. "The Basic ship descends into Banbeck Vale."

Carcolo nodded grimly. "I would be an audience to the landing." He kicked the Spider. "Come, get up, have you not rested enough? Do you wish me to walk?"

The Spider whimpered its fatigue, but nevertheless struggled to its feet. Carcolo started to mount, but Bast Givven laid a restraining hand on his shoulder. Carcolo looked back in outrage: here was impertinence! Givven said calmly, "Tighten the surcingle, otherwise you will fall on the rocks and once more break your bones."

Uttering a spiteful phrase under his breath, Carcolo clasped the buckle back into position. The Spider cried out in despair. Paying no heed, Carcolo mounted, and the Spider moved off with trembling steps.

Barch Spike rose ahead like the prow of a white ship, dividing Northguard Ridge from Barchback. Carcolo paused to consider the landscape, tugging his mustaches.

Givven was tactfully silent. Carcolo looked down the Skanse to the listless straggle of his army, then set off to the left.

Passing close under Mount Gethron, skirting the High Jambles, they descended an ancient water-course to Banbeck Verge. Though perforce they had come without great speed, the Basic ship had moved no faster. It had only started to settle into the vale, the disks at bow and stern swirling with furious colors.

Carcolo grunted bitterly. "Trust Joaz Banbeck to scratch his own itch. Not a soul in sight! He's taken to his tunnels, dragons and all." Pursing his mouth he rendered a mincing parody of Joaz's voice: " 'Ervis Carcolo, my dear friend, there is but one answer to attack: dig tunnels!' And I replied to him, 'Am I a sacerdote to live underground? Burrow and delve, Joaz Banbeck, do as you will. I am but an old-time man; I go under the cliffs only when I must.' "

Givven gave the faintest of shrugs.

Carcolo went on, "Tunnels or not, they'll winkle him out.

If need be they'll blast open the entire valley. They've no lack of tricks."

Givven grinned sardonically. "Joaz Banbeck knows a trick or two—as we know to our sorrow."

"Let him capture two dozen Basics today," snapped Carcolo. "Then I'll concede him a clever man." He stalked away to the very brink of the cliff, standing in full view of the Basic ship. Givven watched without expression.

Carcolo pointed. "Aha! Look there!"

"Not I," said Givven. "I respect the Basic weapons too greatly."

"Pah!" spat Carcolo. Nevertheless he moved a trifle back from the brink. "There are dragons in Kergan's Way. For all Joaz Banbeck's talk of tunnels." He gazed north along the valley a moment or two, then threw up his hands in frustration. "Joaz Banbeck will not come up here to me. There is nothing I can do. Unless I walk down into the village, seek him out and strike him down, he will escape me."

"Unless the Basics captured the two of you and confined you in the same pen," said Givven.

"Bah!" muttered Carcolo, and moved off to one side.

X

The vision-plates which allowed Joaz Banbeck to observe the length and breadth of Banbeck Vale for the first time were being put to practical use.

He had evolved the scheme while playing with a set of old lenses, and dismissed it as quickly. Then one day, while trading with the sacerdotes in the cavern under Mount Gethron, he had proposed that they design and supply the optics for such a system.

The blind old sacerdote who conducted the trading gave an ambiguous reply. The possibility of such a project, under certain circumstances, might well deserve consideration. Three months passed. The scheme receded to the back of Joaz Banbeck's mind. Then the sacerdote in the trading-cave inquired if Joaz still planned to install the viewing system. If so he might take immediate delivery of the optics.

Joaz agreed to the barter price, returned to Banbeck Vale with four heavy crates. He ordered the necessary tunnels driven, installed the lenses, and found that with the study darkened he could command all quarters of Banbeck Vale.

Now, with the Basic ship darkening the sky, Joaz Banbeck stood in his study, watching the descent of the great black hulk.

At the back of the chamber maroon portieres parted. Clutching the cloth with taut fingers stood the minstrel-maiden Phade. Her face was pale, her eyes bright as opals. In a husky voice she called, "The ship of death. It has come to gather souls!"

Joaz turned her a stony glance and turned back to the honed-glass screen. "The ship is clearly visible."

Phade ran forward, clasped Joaz's arm, swung around to look into his face. "Let us try to escape into the High Jambles. Don't let them take us so soon!"

"No one deters you," said Joaz indifferently. "Escape in any direction you choose."

Phade stared at him blankly, then turned her head and watched the screen. The great black ship sank with sinister deliberation, the disks at bow and stern now shimmering mother-of-pearl. Phade looked back to Joaz, licked her lips. "Are you not afraid?"

Joaz smiled thinly. "What good to run? Their Trackers are swifter than Murderers, more vicious than Termagants. They can smell you a mile away, take you from the very center of the Jambles."

Phade shivered with superstitious horror. She whispered, "Let them take me dead, then. I can't go with them alive."

Joaz suddenly cursed. "Look where they land! In our best field of bellegarde!"

"What is the difference?"

" 'Difference?' Must we stop eating because they pay their visit?"

89

Phade looked at him in a daze, beyond comprehension. She sank slowly to her knees and began to perform the ritual gestures of the Theurgic cult. Hands palm down to either side, slowly up till the back of the hand touched the ears, and the simultaneous protrusion of the tongue; over and over again, eyes staring with hypnotic intensity into emptiness.

Joaz ignored the gesticulations, until Phade, her face screwed up into a fantastic mask, began to sigh and whimper. Then he swung the flaps of his jacket into her face. "Give over your folly!"

Phade collapsed moaning to the floor. Joaz's lips twitched in annoyance. Impatiently he hoisted her erect. "Look you, these Basics are neither ghouls nor angels of death. They are no more than pallid Termagants, the basic stock of our dragons. So now, give over your idiocy, or I'll have Rife take you away."

"Why do you not make ready? You watch and do nothing."

"There is nothing more that I can do."

Phade drew a deep shuddering sigh, stared dully at the screen. "Will you fight them?"

"Naturally."

"How can you hope to counter such miraculous power?"

"We will do what we can. They have not yet met our dragons."

The ship came to rest in a purple and green vine-field across the valley, near the mouth of Clybourne Crevasse. The port slid back and a ramp rolled forth. "Look," said Joaz, "there you see them."

Phade stared at the queer pale shapes who had come tentatively out on the ramp. "They seem strange and twisted, like silver puzzles for children."

"They are the Basics. From their eggs came our dragons. They have done as well with men: look, here are their Heavy Troops."

Down the ramp, four abreast, in exact cadence, marched the Heavy Troops, to half fifty yards in front of the ship. There were three squads of twenty: short squat men with massive shoulders, thick necks and stern, down-drawn faces. They

90

wore armor fashioned from overlapping scales of black and blue metal, a wide belt slung with pistol and sword. Black epaulets, extending past their shoulders, supported a short ceremonial flap of black cloth ranging down their backs. Their helmets bore a crest of sharp spikes. Their knee-high boots were armed with kick-knives.

A number of Basics now rode forth. Their mounts were creatures only remotely resembling men. They ran on hands and feet, backs high off the ground. Their heads were long and hairless, with quivering loose lips. The Basics controlled them with negligent touches of a quirt, and once on the ground set them cantering smartly through the bellegarde. Meanwhile a team of Heavy Troopers rolled a three-wheeled mechanism down the ramp, directed its complex snout toward the village.

"Never before have they prepared so carefully," muttered Joaz. "Here come the Trackers." He counted. "Only two dozen? Perhaps they are hard to breed. Generations pass slowly with men; dragons lay a clutch of eggs every year . . ."

The Trackers moved to the side and stood in a loose restless group: gaunt creatures seven feet tall, with bulging black eyes, beaked noses, small undershot mouths pursed as if for kissing. From narrow shoulders long arms dangled and swung like ropes. As they waited they flexed their knees, staring sharply up and down the valley, in constant restless motion. After them came a group of Weaponeers—unmodified men wearing loose cloth smocks and cloth hats of green and yellow. They brought with them two more three-wheeled contrivances which they at once began to adjust and test.

The entire group became still and tense.

The Heavy Troopers stepped forward with a stumping, heavy-legged gait, hands ready at pistols and swords. "Here they come," said Joaz. Phade made a quiet desperate sound, knelt and once more began to perform Theurgic gesticulations. Joaz in disgust ordered her from the study. He went to a panel equipped with a bank of six direct-wire communications, the construction of which he had personally supervised. He spoke into three of the telephones, assuring himself that his defenses were alert, then returned the honed-glass screens.

Across the field of bellegarde came the Heavy Troopers, faces heavy, hard, marked with down-veering creases. Upon either flank the Weaponeers trundled their three-wheeled mechanisms, but the Trackers waited beside the ship. About a dozen Basics rode behind the Heavy Troopers, carrying bulbous weapons on their backs.

A hundred yards from the portal into Kergan's Way, beyond the range of the Banbeck muskets, the invaders halted. A Heavy Trooper ran to one of the Weaponeers' carts, thrust his shoulders under a harness and stood erect. He now carried a gray machine, from which extended a pair of black globes. The Trooper scuttled toward the village like an enormous rat, while from the black globes streamed a flux, intended to interfere with the neural currents of the Banbeck defenders, and so immobilize them.

Explosions sounded. Puffs of smoke appeared from nooks and vantages through the crags. Bullets spat into the ground beside the Trooper. Several caromed off his armor.

At once heat-beams from the ship stabbed against the cliff walls. In his study Joaz Banbeck smiled. The smoke puffs were decoys. The actual shots came from other areas. The Trooper, dodging and jerking, avoided a rain of bullets and ran under the portal, above which two men waited. Affected by the flux, they tottered, stiffened, but nevertheless dropped a great stone which struck the Trooper where the neck joined his shoulders and hurled him to the ground.

He thrashed his arms and legs up and down, rolled over and over. Then, bouncing to his feet, he raced back into the valley, soaring and bounding, finally to stumble, plunge headlong to the ground and lay kicking and quivering.

The Basic army watched with no apparent concern or interest.

There was a moment of inactivity. Then from the ship came

an invisible field of vibration, traveling across the face of the cliff.

Where the focus struck, puffs of dust arose and loose rock became dislodged. A man, lying on a ledge, sprang to his feet, dancing and twisting, plunged two hundred feet to his death. Passing across one of Joaz Banbeck's spy-holes, the vibration was carried into the study where it set up a nerve-grinding howl. The vibration passed along the cliff. Joaz rubbed his aching head.

Meanwhile the Weaponeers discharged one of their instruments. First there came a muffled explosion, then through the air curved a wobbling gray sphere. Inaccurately aimed, it struck the cliff and burst in a great gush of yellow-white gas. The mechanism exploded once more, and this time lobbed the bomb accurately into Kergan's Way—which was now deserted. The bomb produced no effect.

In his study Joaz waited grimly. To now the Basics had taken only tentative, almost playful, steps. More serious efforts would surely follow.

Wind dispersed the gas; the situation remained as before. The casualties so far had been one Heavy Trooper and one Banbeck rifleman.

From the ship now came a stab of red flame, harsh, decisive. The rock at the portal shattered. Slivers sang and spun; the Heavy Troopers jogged forward.

Joaz spoke into his telephone, bidding his captains caution, lest in counter-attacking against a feint they expose themselves to a new gas bomb.

But the Heavy Troopers stormed into Kergan's Way—in Joaz's mind an act of contemptuous recklessness. He gave a curt order.

Out from passages and areas swarmed his dragons: Blue Horrors, Fiends, Termagants.

The squat Troopers stared with sagging jaws. Here were unexpected antagonists! Kergan's Way resounded with their calls and orders. First they fell back, then, with the courage of desperation, fought furiously. Up and down Kergan's Way raged the battle.

Certain relationships quickly became evident. In the narrow defile neither the Trooper pistols nor the steel-weighted tails of the Fiends could be used effectively. Cutlasses were useless against dragon-scale, but the pincers of the Blue Horrors, the Termagant daggers, the axes, swords, fangs and claws of the Fiends, did bloody work against the Heavy Troopers. A single Trooper and a single Termagant were approximately a match; though the Trooper, gripping the dragon with massive arms, tearing away its brachs, breaking back its neck, won more often than the Termagant. But if two or three Termagants confronted a single Trooper, he was doomed. As soon as he committed himself to one, another would crush his legs, blind him or hack open his throat.

So the Troopers fell back to the valley floor, leaving twenty of their fellows dead in Kergan's Way. The Banbeck men once more opened fire, but once more with minor effect.

Joaz watched from his study, wondering as to the next Basic tactic. Enlightenment was not long in coming. The Heavy Troopers regrouped and stood panting, while the Basics rode back and forth receiving information, admonishing, advising, chiding.

From the black ship came a gush of energy, to strike the cliff above Kergan's Way. The study rocked with the concussion.

Joaz backed away from the vision-plates. What if a ray struck one of his collecting lenses? Might not the energy be guided and reflected directly toward him?

He departed his study as it shook to a new explosion.

He ran through a passage, descended a staircase, emerged into one of the central galleries, to find apparent confusion. White-faced women and children, retiring deeper into the mountain, pushed past dragons and men in battle-gear entering one of the new tunnels. Joaz watched for a moment or two to satisfy himself that the confusion held no panic, then joined his warriors in the tunnel leading north.

In some past era an entire section of the cliff at the head of the valley had sloughed off, creating a jungle of piled rock and boulders: the Banbeck Jambles. Here, through a fissure, the new tunnel opened; and here Joaz went with his warriors. Behind them, down the valley, sounded the rumble of explosions as the black ship began to demolish Banbeck Village.

Joaz, peering around a boulder, watched in a fury, as great slabs of rock began to scale away from the cliff.

Then he stared in astonishment, for to the Basic troops had come an extraordinary reinforcement: eight Giants twice an ordinary man's stature—barrel-chested monsters, gnarled of arm and legs, with pale eyes, shocks of tawny hair. They wore brown and red armor with black epaulettes, and carried swords, maces and blast-cannon slung over their backs.

Joaz considered. The presence of the Giants gave him no reason to alter his central strategy, which in any event was vague and intuitive. He must be prepared to suffer losses, and could only hope to inflict greater losses on the Basics. But what did they care for the lives of their troops? Less than he cared for his dragons. And if they destroyed Banbeck Village, ruined the Vale, how could he do corresponding damage to them?

He looked over his shoulder at the tall white cliffs, wondering how closely he had estimated the position of the sacerdote's hall. And now he must act; the time had come.

He signaled to a small boy, one of his own sons, who took a deep breath, hurled himself blindly away from the shelter of the rocks, ran helter-skelter out to the valley floor. A moment later his mother ran forth to snatch him up and dash back into the Jambles.

"Done well," Joaz commended them. "Done well indeed." Cautiously he again looked forth through the rocks. The Basics were gazing intently in his direction.

For a long moment, while Joaz tingled with suspense, it

seemed that they had ignored his ploy. They conferred, came to a decision, flicked the leathery buttocks of their mounts with their quirts. The creatures pranced sidewise, then loped north up the valley. The Trackers fell in behind, then came the Heavy Troopers moving at a humping quick-step. The Weaponeers followed with their three-wheeled mechanisms, and ponderously at the rear came the eight Giants.

Across the fields of bellegarde and vetch, over vines, hedges, beds of berries and stands of oil-pod tramped the raiders, destroying with a certain morose satisfaction.

The Basics prudently halted before the Banbeck Jambles, while the Trackers ran ahead like dogs, clambering over the first boulders, rearing high to test the air for odor, peering, listening, pointing, twittering doubtfully to each other. The Heavy Troopers moved in carefully, and their near presence spurred on the Trackers.

Abandoning caution, they bounded into the heart of the Jambles, emitting squeals of horrified consternation when a dozen Blue Horrors dropped among them. They clawed out heat-guns, in their excitement burning friend and foe alike. With silken ferocity the Blue Horrors ripped them apart. Screaming for aid, kicking, flailing, thrashing, those who were able fled as precipitously as they had come.

Only twelve from the original twenty-four regained the valley floor; and even as they did so, even as they cried out in relief at winning free from death, a squad of Long-horned Murderers burst out upon them, and these surviving Trackers were knocked down, gored, hacked.

The Heavy Troopers charged forward with hoarse calls of rage, aiming pistols, swinging swords; but the Murderers retreated to the shelter of the boulders.

Within the Jambles the Banbeck men had appropriated the heat-guns dropped by the Trackers. Warily coming forward, they tried to burn the Basics. But, unfamiliar with the weapons, the men neglected either to focus or condense the flame. The Basics were no more than mildly singed. Hastily they whipped their mounts back out of range. The Heavy Troopers, halting not a hundred feet in front of the Jambles, sent in a volley of explosive pellets, which killed two of the Banbeck knights and forced the others back.

XI

At a discreet distance the Basics appraised the situation. Weaponeers came up and, while awaiting instructions, conferred in low tones with the mounts.

One of these Weaponeers was now summoned and given orders. He divested himself of all his weapons and holding his empty hands in the air marched forward to the edge of the Jambles. Choosing a gap between a pair of ten-foot boulders, he resolutely entered the rock-maze.

A Banbeck knight escorted him to Joaz. Here, by chance, were also half a dozen Termagants. The Weaponeer paused uncertainly, made a mental readjustment, approached the Termagants. Bowing respectfully he started to speak. The Termagants listened without interest, and presently one of the knights directed him to Joaz.

"Dragons do not rule men on Aerlith," said Joaz dryly. "What is your message?"

The Weaponeer looked dubiously toward the Termagants, then somberly back to Joaz. "You are authorized to act for the entire warren?" He spoke slowly in a dry bland voice, selecting his words with conscientious care.

Joaz repeated shortly, "What is your message?"

"I bring an integration from my masters."

"Integration? I do not understand you."

"An integration of the instantaneous vectors of destiny. An interpretation of the future. They wish the sense conveyed to you in the following terms: 'Do not waste lives, both ours and your own. You are valuable to us and will be given treatment in accordance with this value. Surrender to the Rule. Cease the wasteful destruction of enterprise.' "

Joaz frowned. "Destruction of 'enterprise?' "

"The reference is to the content of your genes. The message

is at its end. I advise you to accede. Why waste your blood, why destroy yourselves? Come forth now with me. All will be for the best."

Joaz gave a brittle laugh. "You are a slave. How can you judge what is best for us?"

The Weaponeer blinked. "What choice is there for you? All residual pockets of disorganized life are to be expunged. The way of facility is best." He inclined his head respectfully toward the Termagants. "If you doubt me, consult your own Revered Ones. They will advise you."

"There are no Revered Ones here," said Joaz. "The dragons fight with us and for us; they are our fellow-warriors. But I have an alternate proposal. Why do not you and your fellows join us? Throw off your slavery, become free men! We will take the ship and go searching for the old worlds of men."

The Weaponeer exhibited only polite interest. " 'Worlds of men?' There are none of them. A few residuals such as yourself remain in the desolate regions. All are to be expunged. Would you not prefer to serve the Rule?"

"Would you not prefer to be a free man?"

The Weaponeer's face showed mild bewilderment. "You do not understand me. If you choose—"

"Listen carefully," said Joaz. "You and your fellows can be your own masters, live among other men."

The Weaponeer frowned. "Who would wish to be a wild savage? To whom would we look for law, control, direction, order?"

Joaz threw up his hands in disgust, but made one last attempt. "I will provide all these; I will undertake such a responsibility. Go back, kill all the Basics—the Revered Ones, as you call them. These are my first orders."

"Kill them?" The Weaponeer's voice was soft with horror.

"Kill them." Joaz spoke as if to a child. "Then we men will possess the ship. We will go to find the worlds where men are powerful—"

"There are no such worlds."

"Ah, but there must be! At one time men roamed every star in the sky."

"No longer."

"What of Eden?"

"I know nothing of it."

Joaz threw up his hands. "Will you join us?"

"What would be the meaning of such an act?" said the Weaponeer gently. "Come then. Lay down your arms, submit to the Rule." He glanced doubtfully toward the Termagants. "Your own Revered Ones will receive fitting treatment. Have no fear on this account."

"You fool! These 'Revered Ones' are slaves, just as you are a slave to the Basics! We breed them to serve us, just as you are bred! Have at least the grace to recognize your own degradation!"

The Weaponeer blinked. "You speak in terms I do not completely understand. You will not surrender then?"

"No. We will kill all of you, if our strength holds out."

The Weaponeer bowed, turned, departed through the rocks. Joaz followed, peered out over the valley floor.

The Weaponeer made his report to the Basics, who listened with characteristic detachment. They gave an order, and the Heavy Troopers, spreading out in a skirmish line, moved slowly in toward the rocks.

Behind lumbered the Giants, blasters slung forward at the ready, and about twenty Trackers, survivors of the first foray. The Heavy Troopers reached the rocks, peered in. The Trackers clambered above, searching for ambushes, and finding none, signaled back. With great caution the Heavy Troopers entered the Jambles, necessarily breaking formation. Twenty feet they advanced, fifty feet, a hundred feet. Emboldened, the vengeful Trackers sprang forward over the rocks . . . and up surged the Termagants.

Screaming and cursing the Trackers scrambled back, pursued by the dragons. The Heavy Troopers recoiled, then swung up their weapons, fired. Two Termagants were struck under the lower armpits, their most vulnerable spot. Floundering, they tumbled down among the rocks. Others, maddened, jumped squarely down upon the Troopers. There was roaring, squealing, cries of shock and pain. The Giants lumbered up, and grinning vastly plucked away the Termagants, wrenched off their heads, flung them high over the rocks. Those Termagants who were able scuttled back, leaving half a dozen Heavy Troopers wounded, two with their throats torn open.

Again the Heavy Troopers moved forward, with the Trackers reconnoitering above, but more warily. The Trackers froze, yelled a warning. The Heavy Troopers stopped short, calling to each other, swinging their guns nervously. Overhead the Trackers scrambled back, and through the rocks, over the rocks, came dozens of Fiends and Blue Horrors.

The Heavy Troopers, grimacing dourly, fired their pistols; and the air reeked with the stench of burning scale, exploded viscera. The dragons surged in upon the men, and now began a terrible battle among the rocks, with the pistols, the maces, even the swords useless for lack of room.

The Giants lumbered forward and in turn were attacked by Fiends. Astonished, the idiotic grins faded from their faces; they hopped awkwardly back from the steel-weighted tails; but among the rocks the Fiends were also at a disadvantage, their steel balls clattering and jarring away from rock more often than flesh.

The Giants, recovering, discharged their chest-projectors into the melée. Fiends were torn apart as well as Blue Horrors and Heavy Troopers, the Giants making no distinction.

Over the rocks came another wave of dragons: Blue Horrors. They slid down on the heads of the Giants, clawing, stabbing, tearing. In a frenzy the Giants tore at the creatures, flung them to the ground, stamped on them, and the Heavy Troopers burnt them with their pistols.

From nowhere, for no reason, there came a lull.

Ten seconds, fifteen seconds passed, with no sound but whimpering and moaning from wounded dragons and men. A sense of imminence weighted the air, and here came the Juggers, looming through the passages.

For a brief period Giants and Juggers looked each other face to face. Then Giants groped for their blast-projectors, while Blue Horrors sprang down once more, grappling the Giant arms. The Juggers stumped quickly forward. Dragon-brachs grappled Giant arms; bludgeons and maces swung, dragon armor and man armor crushed and ground apart. Man and dragon tumbled over and over, ignoring pain, shock, mutilation.

The struggle became quiet. Sobbing and wheezing replaced the roars, and presently eight Juggers, superior in mass and natural armament, staggered away from eight destroyed Giants.

The Troopers meanwhile had drawn together, standing back to back in clots. Step by step, burning with heat-beams the screaming Horrors, Termagants and Fiends who lunged after them, they retreated toward the valley floor, and finally won free of the rocks. The pursuing Fiends, anxious to fight in the open, sprang into their midst, while from the flanks came Long-horned Murderers and Striding Murderers. In a spirit of reckless jubilation, a dozen men riding Spiders, carrying blast-cannon taken from the fallen Giants, charged the Basics and Weaponeers, who waited beside the rather casual emplacement of three-wheeled weapons. The Basics, without shame, jerked their man-mounts around and fled toward the black ship.

The Weaponeers swiveled their mechanisms, aimed, discharged bursts of energy. One man fell, two men, three men—then the others were among the Weaponeers, who were soon hacked to pieces . . . including the persuasive individual who had served as envoy.

Several of the men, whooping and hooting, set out in chase of the Basics. But the human mounts, springing along like monstrous rabbits, carried the Basics as fast as the Spiders carried the men.

From the Jambles came a horn signal. The mounted men

halted, wheeled back; the entire Banbeck force turned and retreated full speed into the Jambles.

The Troopers stumbled a few defiant steps in pursuit, then halted in sheer fatigue.

Of the original three squads, not enough men to make up a single squad survived. The eight Giants had perished, all Weaponeers and almost the entire group of Trackers.

The Banbeck forces gained the Jambles with seconds only to spare. From the black ship came a volley of explosive pellets, to shatter the rocks at the spot where they had disappeared.

On a wind-polished cape of rock above Banbeck Vale Ervis Carcolo and Bast Givven had watched the battle.

The rocks hid the greater part of the fighting. The cries and clangor rose faint and tinny, like insect noise. There would be the glint of dragon scale, glimpses of running men, the shadow and flicker of movement, but not until the mangled forces of the Basics staggered forth did the outcome of the battle reveal itself. Carcolo shook his head in sour bewilderment. "The crafty devel, Joaz Banbeck! He's turned them back. He's slaughtered their best!"

"It would appear," said Bast Givven, "that dragons armed with fangs, swords and steel balls are more effective than men with guns and heat-beams—at least in close quarters."

Carcolo grunted. "I might have done as well myself, under like circumstances." He turned Bast Givven a waspish glance. "Do you not agree?"

"Certainly. Beyond question."

"Of course," Carcolo went on, "I had not the advantage of preparation. The Basics surprised me, but Joaz Banbeck labored under no such handicap." He looked back down into Banbeck Vale, where the Basic ship was bombarding the Jambles, shattering rocks into splinters. "Do they plan to blast the Jambles out of the valley? In which case, of course, Joaz Banbeck would have no further refuge. Their strategy is clear. And as I suspected: reserve forces!"

Another thirty Troopers had marched down the ramp to stand immobile in the trampled field before the ship.

Carcolo pounded his fist into his palm. "Bast Givven, listen now, listen carefully! For it is in our power to do a great deed, to reserve our fortunes! Notice Clyborne Crevasse, how it opens into the Vale, directly behind the Basic ship."

"Your ambition will yet cost us our lives."

Carcolo laughed. "Come, Givven, how many times does a man die? What better way to lose a life than in the pursuit of glory?"

Bast Givven turned, surveyed the meager remnants of the Happy Valley army. "We could win glory by trouncing a dozen sacerdotes. Flinging ourselves upon a Basic ship is hardly needful."

"Nevertheless," said Ervis Carcolo, "that is how it must be. I ride ahead, you marshal the forces and follow. We meet at the head of Clyborne Crevasse, on the west edge of the Vale!"

XII

Stamping his feet, muttering nervous curses, Ervis Carcolo waited at the head of Clyborne Crevasse.

Unlucky chance after chance paraded before his imagination. The Basics might surrender to the difficulties of Banbeck Vale and depart. Joaz Banbeck might attack across the open fields to save Banbeck Village from destruction and so destroy himself. Bast Givven might be unable to control the disheartened men and mutinous dragons of Happy Valley. Any of these situations might occur; any would expunge Carcolo's dreams of glory and leave him a broken man.

Back and forth he paced the scarred granite. Every few seconds he peered down into Banbeck Vale. Every few seconds he turned to scan the bleak skylines for the dark shapes of his dragons, the taller silhouettes of his men.

Beside the Basic ship waited a scanty two squads of Heavy Troopers: those who had survived the original attack and the reserves. They squatted in silent groups, watching the leisurely destruction of Banbeck Village. Fragment by fragment, the spires, towers and cliffs which had housed the Banbeck folk cracked off, slumped down into an ever-growing mound of rubble. An even heavier barrage poured against the Jambles. Boulders broke like eggs. Rock splinters drifted down the valley.

A half hour passed. Ervis Carcolo seated himself glumly on a rock.

A jingle, the pad of feet: Carcolo bounded to his feet. Winding across the sky-line came the sorry remnants of his forces, the men dispirited, the Termagants surly and petulant, a mere handful each of Fiends, Blue Horrors and Murderers.

Carcolo's shoulders sagged. What could be accomplished with a force so futile as this? He took a deep breath. Show a brave front! Never say die! He assumed his bluffest mien. Stepping forward, he cried out, "Men, dragons! Today we have known defeat, but the day is not over. The time of redemption is at hand; we shall revenge ourselves on both the Basics and Joaz Banbeck!"

He searched the faces of his men, hoping for enthusiasm. They looked back at him without interest. The dragons, their understanding less complete, snorted softly, hissed and whispered. "Men and dragons!" bawled Carcolo. "You ask me, how shall we achieve these glories? I answer, follow where I lead! Fight where I fight! What is death to us, with our valley despoiled?"

Again he inspected his troops, once more finding only listlessness and apathy. Carcolo stifled the roar of frustration which rose into his throat, and turned away. "Advance!" he called gruffly over his shoulder. Mounting his drooping Spider, he set off down Clyborne Crevasse.

The Basic ship pounded the Jambles and Banbeck Village with equal vehemence. From a vantage on the west rim of the valley Joaz Banbeck watched the blasting of corridor after familiar corridor. Apartments and halls hewn earnestly from the rock, carved, tooled, polished across the generations—all

104

opened, destroyed, pulverized. Now the target became that spire which contained Joaz Banbeck's private apartments, with his study, his workroom, the Banbeck reliquarium.

Joaz clenched and unclenched his fists, furious at his own helplessness. The goal of the Basics was clear. They intended to destroy Banbeck Vale, to exterminate as completely as possible the men of Aerlith—and what could prevent them?

Joaz studied the Jambles. The old talus had been splintered away almost to the sheer face of the cliff. Where was the opening into the Great Hall of the sacerdotes? His far-fetched hypotheses were diminishing to futility. Another hour would see the utter devastation of Banbeck Village.

Joaz tried to control a sickening sense of frustration. How to stop the destruction? He forced himself to calculate. Clearly, an attack across the valley floor was equivalent to suicide. But behind the black ship opened a ravine similar to that in which Joaz stood concealed: Clybourne Crevasse. The ship's entry gaped wide. Heavy Troopers squatted listlessly to the side. Joaz shook his head with a sour grimace. Inconceivable that the Basics could neglect so obvious a threat.

Still—in their arrogance might they not overlook the possibility of so insolent an act?

Indecision tugged Joaz forward and backward. And now a barrage of explosive pellets split open the spire which housed his apartments. The reliquarium, the ancient trove of the Banbeck's, was about to be destroyed . . . Joaz made a blind gesture, jumped to his feet, called the closest of his dragon-masters.

"Assemble the Murderers, three squads of Termagants, two dozen Blue Horrors, ten Fiends, all the riders. We climb to Banbeck Verge. We descend Clybourne Crevasse. We attack the ship!"

The dragon-master departed. Joaz gave himself to gloomy contemplation. If the Basics intended to draw him into a trap, they were about to succeed.

The dragon-master returned. "The force is assembled."

"We ride."

Up the ravine surged men and dragons, emerging upon Banbeck Verge. Swinging south, they came to the head of Clyborne Crevasse.

A knight at the head of the column suddenly signaled a halt. When Joaz approached he pointed out marks on the floor of the crevasse. "Dragons and men have passed here recently."

Joaz studied the tracks. "Heading down the crevasse."

"Yes."

Joaz dispatched a party of scouts who presently came galloping wildly back. "Ervis Carcolo, with men and dragons, is attacking the ship!"

Joaz wheeled his Spider and plunged headlong down the dim passage, followed by his army.

Outcries and screams of battle reached their ears as they approached the mouth of the crevasse. Bursting out on the valley floor Joaz came upon a scene of desperate carnage, with dragon and Heavy Trooper hacking, stabbing, burning, blasting. Where was Ervis Carcolo? Joaz recklessly rode to look into the entry port. It hung wide! Ervis Carcolo then had forced his way into the ship!

A trap? Or had he effectuated Joaz's own plan of seizing the ship? What of the Heavy Troopers? Would the Basics sacrifice forty warriors to capture a handful of men? Unreasonable—but now the Heavy Troopers were holding their own. They had formed a phalanx, they now concentrated the energy of their weapons on those dragons who yet opposed them. A trap? If so, it was sprung—unless Ervis Carcolo already had captured the ship. Joaz rose in his saddle, signaled his company. "Attack!"

The Heavy Troopers were doomed. Striding Murderers hewed from above, Long-horned Murderers thrust from below, Blue Horrors pinched, clipped, dismembered. The battle was done, but Joaz, with men and Termagants, had already charged up the ramp. From within came the hum and throb of power, and also human sounds—cries and shouts of fury.

The sheer ponderous bulk struck at Joaz. He stopped short,

peered uncertainly into the ship. Behind him his men waited, muttering under their breath.

Joaz asked himself, "Am I as brave as Ervis Carcolo? What is bravery, in any case? I am completely afraid: I dare not enter, I dare not stay outside." He put aside all caution and rushed forward, followed by his men and a horde of scuttling Termagants.

Even as Joaz entered the ship he knew Ervis Carcolo had not succeeded. Above him the guns still sang and hissed. Joaz's apartments splintered apart. Another tremendous volley struck into the Jambles, laying bare the naked stone of cliff, and what was hitherto hidden: the edge of a tall opening.

Joaz, inside the ship, found himself in an ante-chamber. The inner port was closed. He sidled forward, peered through a rectangular pane into what seemed a lobby or staging chamber. Ervis Carcolo and his knights crouched against the far wall, casually guarded by about twenty Weaponeers. A group of Basics rested in an alcove to the side, relaxed, quiet, their attitude one of contemplation.

Carcolo and his men were not completely subdued. As Joaz watched Carcolo lunged furiously forward. A purple crackle of energy punished him, hurled him back against the wall.

From the alcove one of the Basics, staring across the inner chamber, took note of Joaz Banbeck. He flicked out with his brach, touched a rod. An alarm whistle sounded, the outer port slid shut. A trap? An emergency process? The result was the same. Joaz motioned to four men, heavily burdened. They came forward, kneeled, placed on the deck four of the blast cannon which the Giants had carried into the Jambles.

Joaz swung his arm. Cannon belched; metal creaked, melted; acrid odors permeated the room. The hole was still too small. "Again!" The cannon flamed; the inner port vanished.

Into the gap sprang Weaponeers, firing their energy guns. Purple fire cut into the Banbeck ranks. Men curled, twisted, wilted, fell with clenched fingers and contorted faces. Before the cannon could respond, red-scaled shapes scuttled forward: Termagants. Hissing and wailing, they swarmed over the

Weaponeers, on into the staging chamber. In front of the alcove occupied by the Basics they stopped short, as if in astonishment. The men crowding after fell silent. Even Carcolo watched in fascination.

Basic stock confronted its derivative, each seeing in the other its caricature. The Termagants crept forward with sinister deliberation. The Basics waved their brachs, whistled, fluted. The Termagants scuttled forward, sprang into the alcove.

There was a horrid tumbling and croaking. Joaz, sickened at some elementary level, was forced to look away. The struggle was soon over.

There was silence in the alcove. Joaz turned to examine Ervis Carcolo, who stared back, rendered inarticulate by anger, humiliation, pain and fright.

Finally finding his voice Carcolo made an awkward gesture of menace and fury. "Be off with you," he croaked. "I claim this ship. Unless you would lie in your own blood, leave me to my conquest!"

Joaz snorted contemptuously, turned his back on Carcolo, who sucked in his breath, and with a whispered curse, lurched forward. Bast Givven seized him, drew him back. Carcolo struggled. Givven talked earnestly into his ear, and Carcolo at last relaxed, half-weeping.

Joaz meanwhile examined the chamber. The walls were blank, gray; the deck was covered with resilient black foam. There was no obvious illumination, but light was everywhere, exuding from the walls. The air chilled the skin, and smelled unpleasantly acrid: an odor which Joaz had not previously noticed. He coughed. His ear-drums rang.

A frightening suspicion became certainty. On heavy legs he lunged for the port, beckoning to his troops. "Outside, they poison us!" He stumbled out on the ramp, gulped fresh air. His men and Termagants followed, and then in a stumbling rush came Ervis Carcolo and his men. Under the hulk of the great ship the group stood gasping, tottering on limp legs, eyes dim and swimming.

Above them, oblivious or careless of their presence, the ship's guns sent forth another barrage. The spire housing Joaz's apartment tottered, collapsed. The Jambles were no more than a heap of rock splinters drifting into a high arched opening. Inside the opening Joaz glimpsed a dark shape, a glint, a shine, a structure—then he was distracted by an ominous sound at his back. From a port at the other end of the ship, a new force of Heavy Troopers had alighted. Three new squads of twenty men each, accompanied by a dozen Weaponeers with four of the rolling projectors.

Joaz sagged back in dismay.

He glanced along his troops. They were in no condition either to attack or defend. A single alternative remained: flight. "Make for Clybourne Crevasse," he called thickly.

Stumbling, lurching, the remnants of the two armies fled under the brow of the great black ship. Behind them Heavy Troopers swung smartly forward, but without haste.

Rounding the ship, Joaz stopped short. In the mouth of Clybourne Crevasse waited a fourth squad of Heavy Troopers, with another Weaponeer and his weapon.

Joaz looked to right and left, up and down the valley. Which way to run, where to turn? The Jambles? They were non-existent. Motion, slow and ponderous in the opening previously concealed by tumbled rock caught his attention. A dark object moved forth. A shutter drew back, a bright disk glittered. Almost instantly a pencil of milky blue radiance lanced at, into, through the end-disk of the Basic ship.

Within, tortured machinery whined, simultaneously up and down the scale, to inaudibility at either end. The luster of the end-disks vanished. They became gray, dull; the whisper of power and life previously pervading the ship gave way to dead quiet. The ship itself was dead, and its mass, suddenly unsupported, crushed groaning into the ground.

The Heavy Troopers gazed up in consternation at the hulk

which had brought them to Aerlith. Joaz, taking advantage of their indecision, called, "Retreat! North—up the valley!"

The Heavy Troopers doggedly followed. The Weaponeers however cried out an order to halt. They emplaced their weapons, brought them to bear on the cavern behind the Jambles. Within the opening naked shapes moved with frantic haste. There was slow shifting of massive machinery, a change of lights and shadows, and the milky blue shaft of radiance struck forth once more. It flicked down.

Weaponeers, weapons, two-thirds of the Heavy Troopers vanished like moths in a furnace. The surviving Heavy Troopers halted, retreated uncertainly toward the ship.

In the mouth of Clybourne Crevasse waited the remaining squad of Heavy Troopers. The single Weaponeer crouched over his three-wheeled mechanism.

With fateful care he made his adjustments. Within the dark opening the naked sacerdotes worked furiously, thrusting, wedging, the strain of their sinews and hearts and minds communicating itself to every man in the valley. The shaft of milky-blue light sprang forth, but too soon: it melted the rock a hundred yards south of Clybourne Crevasse, and now from the Weaponeer's gun came a splash of orange and green flame. Seconds later the mouth of the sacerdote's cavern erupted. Rocks, bodies, fragments of metal, glass, rubber arched through the air.

The sound of the explosion reverberated through the valley. And the dark object in the cavern was destroyed, was no more than tatters and shreds of metal.

Joaz took three deep breaths, throwing off the effects of the narcotic gas by sheer power of will. He signaled to his Murderers. "Charge! Kill!"

The Murderers loped forward.

The Heavy Troopers threw themselves flat, aimed their weapons, but soon died. In the mouth of Clybourne Crevasse the final squad of Troopers charged wildly forth, to be instantly attacked by Termagants and Blue Horrors who had sidled along the face of the cliff. The Weaponeer was gored by a Murderer. There was no further resistance in the valley, and the ship lay open to attack.

Joaz led the way back up the ramp, through the entry into the now dim staging-chamber. The blast-cannon captured from the Giants lay where his men had dropped them.

Three portals led from the chamber, and these were swifly burned down. The first revealed a spiral ramp. The second, a long empty hall lined with tiers of bunks. The third, a similar hall in which the bunks were occupied. Pale faces peered from the tiers, pallid hands flickered. Up and down the central corridor marched squat matrons in gray gowns. Ervis Carcolo rushed forward, buffeting the matrons to the deck, peering into the bunks. "Outside," he bellowed. "You are rescued, you are saved. Outside, quickly, while there is opportunity."

But there was only meager resistance to overcome from a half-dozen Weaponeers and Trackers, none whatever from twenty Mechanics—these, short thin men with sharp features and dark hair—and none from the sixteen remaining Basics.

All were marched off the ship as prisoners.

XIII

Quiet filled the valley floor, the silence of exhaustion.

Men and dragons sprawled in the trampled fields. The captives stood in a dejected huddle beside the ship. Occasionally an isolated sound came to emphasize the silence: the creak of cooling metal within the ship, the fall of a loose rock from the shattered cliffs; an occasional murmur from the liberated Happy Valley folk, who sat in a group apart from the surviving warriors.

Ervis Carcolo alone seemed restless. For a space he stood with his back to Joaz, slapping his thigh with his scabbard tassel. He contemplated the sky where Skene, a dazzling atom, hung close over the western cliffs, then turned, studied the shattered gap at the north of the valley, filled with the twisted remains of the sacerdote's construction. He gave his thigh a final slap, looked toward Joaz Banbeck, turned to stalk through the huddle of Happy Valley folk, making brusque motions of no particular significance, pausing here and there to harangue or cajole, apparently attempting to instill spirit and purpose into his defeated people.

In this purpose he was unsuccessful. Presently he swung sharply about and marched across the field to where Joaz Banbeck lay outstretched.

Carcolo stared down. "Well, then," he said bluffly. "The battle is over, the ship is won."

Joaz raised himself upon one elbow. "True."

"Let us have no misunderstanding on one point," said Carcolo. "Ship and contents are mine. An ancient rule defines the rights of him who is first to attack. On this rule I base my claim."

Joaz looked up in surprise, and seemed almost amused. "By a rule even more ancient, I have already assumed possession."

"I dispute this assertion," said Carcolo hotly. "Who—"

Joaz held up his hand wearily. "Silence, Carcolo! You are alive now only because I am sick of blood and violence. Do not test my patience!"

Carcolo turned away, twitching his scabbard tassel with restrained fury. He looked up the valley, turned back to Joaz. "Here come the sacerdotes, who in fact demolished the ship. I remind you of my proposal, by which we might have prevented this destruction and slaughter."

Joaz smiled. "You made your proposal only two days ago. Further, the sacerdotes possess no weapons."

Carcolo stared as if Joaz had taken leave of his wits. "Then how did they destroy the ship?"

Joaz shrugged. "I can only make conjectures."

Carcolo asked sarcastically, "And what direction do these conjectures lead?"

"I wonder if they had constructed the frame of a space-ship. I wonder if they turned the propulsion beam against the Basic ship."

Carcolo pursed his mouth dubiously. "Why should the sacerdotes build themselves a space-ship?"

"The Demie approaches. Why do you not put your question to him?"

"I will do so," said Carcolo with dignity.

But the Demie, followed by four younger sacerdotes and walking with the air of a man in a dream, passed without speaking.

Joaz rose to his knees and watched after him. The Demie apparently planned to mount the ramp and enter the ship. Joaz jumped to his feet, followed, barred the way to the ramp.

Politely he asked, "What do you seek, Demie?"

"I seek to board the ship."

"To what end? I ask, of course, from sheer curiosity."

The Demie inspected him a moment without reply. His face was haggard and tight. His eyes gleamed like frost-stars. Finally he replied, in a voice hoarse with emotion. "I wish to determine if the ship can be repaired."

Joaz considered a moment, then spoke in a gentle rational voice. "The information can be of little interest to you. Would the sacerdotes place themselves so completely under my command?"

"We obey no one."

"In that case, I can hardly take you with me when I leave."

The Demie swung around, and for a moment seemed as if he would walk away. His eyes fell on the shattered opening at the end of the vale, and he turned back.

He spoke, not in the measured voice of a sacerdote, but in a burst of grief and fury. "This is your doing! You preen yourself, you count yourself resourceful and clever. You forced us to act, and thereby violate ourselves and our dedication!"

Joaz nodded, with a faint grim smile. "I knew the opening must lie behind the Jambles. I wondered if you might be building a space-ship; I hoped that you might protect yourselves against the Basics, and so serve my purposes. I admit your charges. I used you and your construction as a weapon, to save myself and my people. Did I do wrong?"

"Right or wrong—who can weigh? You wasted our effort across more than eight hundred Aerlith years! You destroyed more than you can ever replace."

"I destroyed nothing Demie. The Basics destroyed your ship. If you had cooperated with us in the defense of Banbeck Vale this disaster would have never occurred. You chose neutrality. You thought yourselves immune from our grief and pain. As you see, such is not the case."

"And meanwhile our labor of eight hundred and twelve years goes to naught," the Demie said.

Joaz asked with feigned innocence, "Why did you need a space-ship? Where do you plan to travel?"

The Demie's eyes burst with flames as intense as those of Skene. "When the race of men is gone, then we go abroad. We move across the galaxy. We re-populate the terrible old worlds, and the new universal history starts from that day, with the past wiped clean as if it never existed. If the grephs destroy you, what is it to us? We await only the death of the last man in the universe."

"Do you not consider yourselves men?"

"We are as you know us—above-men."

At Joaz's shoulder someone laughed coarsely. Joaz turned his head to see Ervis Carcolo. "Overmen?" mocked Carcolo. "Poor naked waifs of the caves! What can you display to prove your superiority?"

The Demie's mouth drooped, the lines of his face deepened. "We have our *tands*. We have our knowledge. We have our strength."

Carcolo turned away with another coarse laugh. Joaz said in a subdued voice, "I feel more pity for you than you ever felt for us."

Carcolo returned. "And where did you learn to build a space-ship? From your own efforts? Or from the work of men before you, men of the old times?"

"We are the ultimate men," said the Demie. "We know all that men have ever thought, spoken or devised. We are the last

114

and the first. And when the under-folk are gone, we shall renew the cosmos as innocent and fresh as rain."

"But men have never gone and will never go," said Joaz. "A setback, yes. But is not the universe wide? Somewhere are the worlds of men. With the help of the Basics and their Mechanics, I will repair the ship and go forth to find these worlds."

"You will seek in vain," said the Demie.

"These worlds do not exist?"

"The Human Empire is dissolved. Men exist only in feeble groups."

"What of Eden, old Eden?"

"A myth, no more."

"My marble globe, what of that?"

"A toy. An imaginative fabrication."

"How can you be sure?" asked Joaz, troubled in spite of himself.

"Have I not said that we know all of history? We can look into our *tands* and see deep into the past, until the recollections are dim and misty, and never do we remember planet Eden."

Joaz shook his head stubbornly. "There must be an original world from which men came. Call it Earth or Tempe or Eden; somewhere it exists."

The Demie started to speak, then in a rare show of irresolution held his tongue. Joaz said, "Perhaps you are right. Perhaps we are the last men. But I shall go forth to look."

"I shall come with you," said Ervis Carcolo.

"You will be fortunate to find yourself alive tomorrow," said Joaz.

Carcolo drew himself up. "Do not dismiss my claim to the ship so carelessly!"

Joaz struggled for words, but could find none. What to do with the unruly Carcolo? He could not find in himself enough harshness to do what he knew should be done. He temporized, turned his back on Carcolo.

"Now you know my plans," he told the Demie. "If you do not interfere with me, I shall not interfere with you."

The Demie moved slowly back. "Go then. We are a passive race. We despise ourselves for our activity of today. Perhaps it was our greatest mistake . . . But go, seek your forgotten world. You will only perish somewhere among the stars. We will wait, as already we have waited." He turned and walked away, followed by the four younger sacerdotes, who had all the time stood gravely to the side.

Joaz called after him. "And if the Basics come again? Will you fight with us? Or against us?"

The Demie made no response, but walked to the north, the long white hair swinging down his thin shoulder-blades.

Joaz watched him a moment, gazed up and down the ruined valley, shook his head in wonder and puzzlement, turned back to study the great black ship.

Skene touched the western cliffs. There was an instant dimming of light, a sudden chill.

Carcolo approached him. "Tonight I shall hold my folk here in Banbeck Vale, and send them home on the morrow. Meanwhile, I suggest that you board the ship with me and make a preliminary survey."

Joaz took a deep breath. Why could it not come easier for him? Carcolo had twice sought his life, and, had positions been reversed, would have shown him no mercy. He forced himself to act. His duty to himself, to his people, to his ultimate goal, was clear.

He called to those of his knights who carried the captured heat-guns. They approached.

Joaz said, "Take Carcolo into Clybourne Crevasse. Execute him at once."

Protesting, bellowing, Carcolo was dragged off. Joaz turned away with a heavy heart, and sought Bast Givven. "I take you for a sensible man."

"I regard myself so."

"I set you in charge of Happy Valley. Take your folk home, before darkness falls."

116

Bast Givven silently went to his people. They stirred, and presently departed Banbeck Vale.

Joaz crossed the valley floor to the tumble of rubble which choked Kergan's Way. He choked with fury as he looked upon the destruction, and for a moment almost wavered in his resolve. Might it not be fit to fly the black ship to Coralyne and take revenge on the Basics? He walked around to stand under the spire which had housed his apartments, and by some strange freak of chance came upon a rounded fragment of yellow marble.

Weighing this in his palm he looked up into the sky where Coralyne already twinkled red, and tried to bring order to his mind.

The Banbeck folk had emerged from the deep tunnels. Phade the minstrel-maiden came to find him. "What a terrible day," she murmured. "What awful events. What a great victory."

Joaz tossed the bit of yellow marble back into the rubble. "I feel much the same way. And where it all ends, no one knows less than I!"

Poul Anderson is of Danish extraction and as that old song from *South Pacific* says, "There is nothing like a Dane." Poul knows the Nordic and Teutonic mythology the way I know the Greek (although, oddly enough, I am not a Greek).

But that is not what I want to talk about.

We science fiction writers are concerned with the present world as well as with the future one, and we have our dis- agreements in outlook on all the great problems that agitate the public generally. Consider the war in Vietnam, for in- stance:

The Vietnam issue has divided the microcosm of the science fiction writer, as it has the United States as a whole. I, myself, for instance, am a liberal and, in connection with Vietnam, I am a dove. I always have been. Practically everyone thinks *now* that getting into an Asian landwar was a mistake, but I thought so even when we were in the process of getting into it and said so loudly.

Naturally, then, when a statement was handed around at a science fiction convention urging immediate withdrawal from Vietnam, a couple of years ago, I signed it at once. That state- ment with a number of names of science fiction personalities attached, was published in a science fiction magazine.

But there are conservatives among us, too, and prominent in that list is Poul Anderson. When he heard of the dove state- ment, he helped prepare a hawk statement in which signers urged the government to remain in Vietnam until its aims were achieved. The competing statement was also published.

Fears were expressed at the time that this would create storms and divisions among science fiction writers and would break up our camaraderie in a tempest of controversy. Well, if the statements have done so, I haven't noticed it. Our mutual identification as fellow science fiction writers persists above and beyond lesser divisions.

To be specific, Poul knows that I am a "fuzzy-minded pinko" and I know that he is a "narrow-minded hardhat" (not that either of us would ever use such terms), but we love each other anyway, and our relations with each other in these last couple of years have not suffered at all.

May I point out that to disagree without rancor and to engage in rational argument without emotional disintegration is a faculty that need not be confined to the science fiction world. It would be great if that large world outside could boast of it as well.

"Song, Charlie! Give's a song!"

"Yay, Charlie!"

The whole mess was drunk, and the junior officers at the far end of the table were only somewhat noisier than their seniors near the colonel. Rugs and hangings could not much muffle the racket, shouts, stamping boots, thump of fists on oak and clash of cups raised aloft, that rang from wall to stony wall. High up among shadows that hid the rafters they hung from, the regimental banners stirred in a draft, as if to join the chaos. Below, the light of bracketed lanterns and bellowing fireplace winked on trophies and weapons.

Autumn comes early on Echo Summit, and it was storming outside, wind-hoot past the watchtowers and rain-rush in the courtyards, an undertone that walked through the buildings and down all corridors, as if the story were true that the unit's dead came out of the cemetery each September Nineteenth night and tried to join the celebration but had forgotten how. No one let it bother him, here or in the enlisted barracks, except maybe the hex major. The Third Division, the Catamounts, was known as the most riotous gang in the Army of the Pacific States of America, and of its regiments the Rolling Stones who held Fort Nakamura were the wildest.

"Go on, boy! Lead off. You've got the closest thing to a voice in the whole goddamn Sierra," Colonel Mackenzie called. He loosened the collar of his black dress tunic and lounged back, legs asprawl, pipe in one hand and beaker of whisky in the other: a thickset man with blue wrinkle-meshed eyes in a battered face, his cropped hair turned gray but his mustache still arrogantly red.

"Charlie is my darlin', my darlin', my darlin'," sang Captain

Hulse. He stopped as the noise abated a little. Young Lieutenant Amadeo got up, grinned, and launched into one they well knew.

"I am a Catamountain, I guard a border pass.
And every time I venture out, the cold will freeze m—"

"Colonel, sir. Begging your pardon."

Mackenzie twisted around and looked into the face of Sergeant Irwin. The man's expression shocked him. "Yes?"

"I am a bloody hero, a decorated vet:
The Order of the Purple Shaft, with pineapple clusters yet!"

"Message just come in, sir. Major Speyer asks to see you right away."

Speyer, who didn't like being drunk, had volunteered for duty tonight; otherwise men drew lots for it on a holiday. Remembering the last word from San Francisco, Mackenzie grew chill.

The mess bawled forth the chorus, not noticing when the colonel knocked out his pipe and rose.

"The guns go boom! Hey, tiddley boom!
The rockets vroom, the arrows zoom.
From slug to slug is damn small room.
Get me out of here and back to the good old womb!
(Hey, doodle dee day!)"

All right-thinking Catamounts maintained that they could operate better with the booze sloshing up to their eardrums than any other outfit cold sober. Mackenzie ignored the tingle in his veins; forgot it. He walked a straight line to the door, automatically taking his sidearm off the rack as he passed by. The song pursued him into the hall.

"For maggots in the rations, we hardly ever lack.
You bite into a sandwich and the sandwich bites right back.

The coffee is the finest grade of Sacramento mud.
The ketchup's good in combat, though, for simulating blood.
(Cho-orus!)

> *The drums go bump! Ah-tumpty-tump!*
> *The bugles make like Gabri'l's trump—"*

Lanterns were far apart in the passage. Portraits of former commanders watched the colonel and the sergeant from eyes that were hidden in grotesque darknesses. Footfalls clattered too loudly here.

> *"I've got an arrow in my rump.*
> *Right about and rearward, heroes, on the jump!*
> *(Hey, doodle dee day!)"*

Mackenzie went between a pair of fieldpieces flanking a stairway—they had been captured at Rock Springs during the Wyoming War, a generation ago—and upward. There was more distance between places in this keep than his legs liked at their present age. But it was old, had been added to decade by decade; and it needed to be massive, chiseled and mortared from Sierra granite, for it guarded a key to the nation. More than one army had broken against its revetments, before the Nevada marches were pacified, and more young men than Mackenzie wished to think about had gone from this base to die among angry strangers.

But she's never been attacked from the west. God, or whatever you are, you can spare her that, can't you?

The command office was lonesome at this hour. The room where Sergeant Irwin had his desk lay so silent: no clerks pushing pens, no messengers going in or out, no wives making a splash of color with their dresses as they waited to see the colonel about some problem down in the Village. When he opened the door to the inner room, though, Mackenzie heard the wind shriek around the angle of the wall. Rain slashed at the black windowpane and ran down in streams which the lanterns turned molten.

"Here the colonel is, sir," Irwin said in an uneven voice. He gulped and closed the door behind Mackenzie.

Speyer stood by the commander's desk. It was a beat-up old object with little upon it: an inkwell, a letter basket, an interphone, a photograph of Nora, faded in these dozen years since her death. The major was a tall and gaunt man, hook-nosed, going bald on top. His uniform always looked unpressed, somehow. But he had the sharpest brain in the Cats, Mackenzie thought; and Christ, how could any man read as many books as Phil did! Officially he was the adjutant, in practice the chief adviser.

"Well?" Mackenzie said. The alcohol did not seem to numb him, rather make him too acutely aware of things: how the lanterns smelled hot (when would they get a big enough generator to run electric lights?), and the floor was hard under his feet, and a crack went through the plaster of the north wall, and the stove wasn't driving out much of the chill. He forced bravado, stuck thumbs in belt and rocked back on his heels. "Well, Phil, what's wrong now?"

"Wire from Frisco," Speyer said. He had been folding and unfolding a piece of paper, which he handed over.

"Huh? Why not a radio call?"

"Telegram's less likely to be intercepted. This one's in code, at that. Irwin decoded it for me."

"What the hell kind of nonsense is this?"

"Have a look, Jimbo, and you'll find out. It's for you, anyway. Direct from GHQ."

Mackenzie focused on Irwin's scrawl. The usual formalities of an order; then:

You are hereby notified that the Pacific States Senate has passed a bill of impeachment against Owen Brodsky, formerly Judge of the Pacific States of America, and deprived him of office. As of 2000 hours this date, former Vice Humphrey Fallon is Judge of the PSA in accordance with the Law of Suc-

cession. The existence of dissident elements constituting a public danger has made it necessary for Judge Fallon to put the entire nation under martial law, effective at 2100 hours this date. You are therefore issued the following instructions:

1. The above intelligence is to be held strictly confidential until an official proclamation is made. No person who has received knowledge in the course of transmitting this message shall divulge same to any other person whatsoever. Violators of this section and anyone thereby receiving information shall be placed immediately in solitary confinement to await court-martial.

2. You will sequestrate all arms and ammunition except for ten percent of available stock, and keep same under heavy guard.

3. You will keep all men in the Fort Nakamura area until you are relieved. Your relief is Colonel Simon Hollis, who will start from San Francisco tomorrow morning with one battalion. They are expected to arrive at Fort Nakamura in five days, at which time you will surrender your command to him. Colonel Hollis will designate those officers and enlisted men who are to be replaced by members of his battalion, which will be integrated into the regiment. You will lead the men replaced back to San Francisco and report to Brigadier General Mendoza at New Fort Baker. To avoid provocations, these men will be disarmed except for officers' side arms.

4. For your private information, Captain Thomas Danielis has been appointed senior aide to Colonel Hollis.

5. You are again reminded that the Pacific States of America are under martial law because of a national emergency. Complete loyalty to the legal government is required. Any mutinous talk must be severely punished. Anyone giving aid or comfort to the Brodsky faction is guilty of treason and will be dealt with accordingly.

Gerald O'Donnell, Gen. APSA, CINC

Thunder went off in the mountains like artillery. It was a while before Mackenzie stirred, and then merely to lay the paper on his desk. He could only summon feeling slowly, up into a hollowness that filled his skin.

"They dared," Speyer said without tone. "They really did."

"Huh?" Mackenzie swiveled eyes around to the major's face. Speyer didn't meet that stare. He was concentrating his own gaze on his hands, which were now rolling a cigarette. But the words jerked from him, harsh and quick:

"I can guess what happened. The warhawks have been hollering for impeachment ever since Brodsky compromised the border dispute with West Canada. And Fallon, yeah, he's got ambitions of his own. But his partisans are a minority and he knows it. Electing him Vice helped soothe the warhawks some, but he'd never make Judge the regular way, because Brodsky isn't going to die of old age before Fallon does, and anyhow more than fifty percent of the Senate are sober, satisfied bossmen who don't agree that the PSA has a divine mandate to reunify the continent. I don't see how an impeachment could get through an honestly convened Senate. More likely they'd vote out Fallon."

"But a Senate had been called," Mackenzie said. The words sounded to him like someone else talking. "The newscasts told us."

"Sure. Called for yesterday 'to debate ratification of the treaty with West Canada.' But the bossmen are scattered up and down the country, each at his own Station. They have to *get* to San Francisco. A couple of arranged delays—hell, if a bridge just happened to be blown on the Boise railroad, a round dozen of Brodsky's staunchest supporters wouldn't arrive on time—so the Senate has a quorum, all right, but every one of Fallon's supporters are there, and so many of the rest are missing that the warhawks have a clear majority. Then they meet on a holiday, when no cityman is paying attention. Presto, impeachment and a new Judge!" Speyer finished his cigarette and stuck it between his lips while he fumbled for a match. A muscle twitched in his jaw.

"You sure?" Mackenzie mumbled. He thought dimly that this moment was like one time he'd visited Puget City and been invited for a sail on the Guardian's yacht, and a fog had closed in. Everything was cold and blind, with nothing you could catch in your hands.

"Of course I'm not sure!" Speyer snarled. "Nobody will be sure till it's too late." The matchbox shook in his grasp.

"They, uh, they got a new Cinc too, I noticed."

"Uh-huh. They'd want to replace everybody they can't trust, as fast as possible, and De Barros was a Brodsky appointee." The match flared with a hellish *scrit*. Speyer inhaled till his cheeks collapsed. "You and me included, naturally. The regiment reduced to minimum armament so that nobody will get ideas about resistance when the new colonel arrives. You'll note he's coming with a battalion at his heels just the same, just in case. Otherwise he could take a plane and be here tomorrow."

"Why not a train?" Mackenzie caught a whiff of smoke and felt for his pipe. The bowl was hot in his tunic pocket.

"Probably all rolling stock has to head north. Get troops among the bossmen there to forestall a revolt. The valleys are safe enough, peaceful ranchers and Esper colonies. None of them'll pot-shot Fallonite soldiers marching to garrison Echo and Donner outposts." A dreadful scorn weighted Speyer's words.

"What are we going to do?"

"I assume Fallon's take-over followed legal forms; that there was a quorum," Speyer said. "Nobody will ever agree whether it was really Constitutional. . . . I've been reading this damned message over and over since Irwin decoded it. There's a lot between the lines. I think Brodsky's at large, for instance. If he were under arrest this would've said as much, and there'd have been less worry about rebellion. Maybe some of his household troops smuggled him away in time. He'll be hunted like a jack-rabbit, of course."

Mackenzie took out his pipe but forgot he had done so. "Tom's coming with our replacements," he said thinly.

"Yeah. Your son-in-law. That was a smart touch, wasn't it? A kind of hostage for your good behavior, but also a backhand

128

promise that you and yours won't suffer if you report in as ordered. Tom's a good kid. He'll stand by his own."

"This is his regiment too," Mackenzie said. He squared his shoulders. "He wanted to fight West Canada, sure. Young and . . . and a lot of Pacificans did get killed in the Idaho Panhandle during the skirmishes. Women and kids among 'em."

"Well," Speyer said, "you're the colonel, Jimbo. What should we do?"

"Oh, Jesus, I don't know. I'm nothing but a soldier." The pipestem broke in Mackenzie's fingers. "But we're not some bossman's personal militia here. We swore to support the Constitution."

"*I* can't see where Brodsky's yielding some of our claims in Idaho is grounds for impeachment. I think he was right."

"Well—"

"A *coup d'état* by any other name would stink as bad. You may not be much of a student of current events, Jimbo, but you know as well as I do what Fallon's Judgeship will mean. War with West Canada is almost the least of it. Fallon also stands for a strong central government. He'll find ways to grind down the old bossman families. A lot of their heads and scions will die in the front lines; that stunt goes back to David and Uriah. Others will be accused of collusion with the Brodsky people— not altogether falsely—and impoverished by fines. Esper communities will get nice big land grants, so their economic competition can bankrupt still other estates. Later wars will keep bossmen away for years at a time, unable to supervise their own affairs, which will therefore go to the devil. And thus we march toward the glorious goal of Reunification."

"If Esper Central favors him, what can we do? I've heard enough about psi blasts. I can't ask my men to face them."

"You could ask your men to face the Hellbomb itself, Jimbo, and they would. A Mackenzie has commanded the Rolling Stones for over fifty years."

"Yes. I thought Tom, someday—"

"We've watched this brewing for a long time. Remember the talk we had about it last week?"

"Uh-huh."

"I might also remind you that the Constitution was written explicitly 'to confirm the separate regions in their ancient liberties.' "

"Let me alone!" Mackenzie shouted. "I don't know what's right or wrong, I tell you! Let me alone!"

Speyer fell silent, watching him through a screen of foul smoke. Mackenzie walked back and forth a while, boots slamming the floor like drumbeats. Finally he threw the broken pipe across the room so it shattered.

"Okay." He must ram each word past the tension in his throat. "Irwin's a good man who can keep his lip buttoned. Send him out to cut the telegraph line a few miles downhill. Make it look as if the storm did it. The wire breaks often enough, heaven knows. Officially, then, we never got GHQ's message. That gives us a few days to contact Sierra Command HQ. I won't go against General Cruikshank . . . but I'm pretty sure which way he'll go if he sees a chance. Tomorrow we prepare for action. It'll be no trick to throw back Hollis' battalion, and they'll need a while to bring some real strength against us. Before then the first snow should be along, and we'll be shut off for the winter. Only we can use skis and snowshoes, ourselves, to keep in touch with the other units and organize something. By spring—we'll see what happens."

"Thanks, Jimbo." The wind almost drowned Speyer's words.

"I'd . . . I'd better go tell Laura."

"Yeah." Speyer squeezed Mackenzie's shoulder. There were tears in the major's eyes.

Mackenzie went out with parade-ground steps, ignoring Irwin: down the hall, down a stairway at its other end, past guarded doors where he returned salutes without really noticing, and so to his own quarters in the south wing.

His daughter had gone to sleep already. He took a lantern off its hook in his bleak little parlor, and entered her room. She had come back here while her husband was in San Francisco.

For a moment Mackenzie couldn't quite remember why he

130

had sent Tom there. He passed a hand over his stubbly scalp, as if to squeeze something out . . . oh, yes, ostensibly to arrange for a new issue of uniforms; actually to get the boy out of the way until the political crisis had blown over. Tom was too honest for his own good, an admirer of Fallon and the Esper movement. His outspokenness had led to friction with his brother officers. They were mostly of bossman stock or from well-to-do protectee families. The existing social order had been good to them. But Tom Danielis began as a fisher lad in a poverty-stricken village on the Mendocino coast. In spare moments he'd learned the three R's from a local Esper; once literate, he joined the Army and earned a commission by sheer guts and brains. He had never forgotten that the Espers helped the poor and that Fallon promised to help the Espers. . . . Then, too, battle, glory, Reunification, Federal Democracy, those were heady dreams when you were young.

Laura's room was little changed since she left it to get married last year. And she had only been seventeen then. Objects survived which had belonged to a small person with pigtails and starched frocks—a teddy bear loved to shapelessness, a doll house her father had built, her mother's picture drawn by a corporal who stopped a bullet at Salt Lake. Oh, God, how much she had come to look like her mother.

Dark hair streamed over a pillow turned gold by the light. Mackenzie shook her as gently as he was able. She awoke instantly, and he saw the terror within her.

"Dad! Anything about Tom?"

"He's okay." Mackenzie set the lantern on the floor and himself on the edge of the bed. Her fingers were cold where they caught at his hand.

"He isn't," she said. "I know you too well."

"He's not been hurt yet. I hope he won't be."

Mackenzie braced himself. Because she was a soldier's daughter, he told her the truth in a few words; but he was not strong enough to look at her while he did. When he had finished, he sat dully listening to the rain.

"You're going to revolt," she whispered.

"I'm going to consult with SCHQ and follow my commanding officer's orders," Mackenzie said.

"You know what they'll be . . . once he knows you'll back him."

Mackenzie shrugged. His head had begun to ache. Hangover started already? He'd need a good deal more booze before he could sleep tonight. No, no time for sleep—yes, there would be. Tomorrow would do to assemble the regiment in the courtyard and address them from the breech of Black Hepzibah, as a Mackenzie of the Rolling Stones always addressed his men, and—. He found himself ludicrously recalling a day when he and Nora and this girl here had gone rowing on Lake Tahoe. The water was the color of Nora's eyes, green and blue and with sunlight flimmering across the surface, but so clear you could see the rocks on the bottom; and Laura's own little bottom had stuck straight in the air as she trailed her hands astern.

She sat thinking for a space before saying flatly: "I suppose you can't be talked out of it." He shook his head. "Well, can I leave tomorrow early, then?"

"Yes. I'll get you a coach."

"T-t-to hell with that. I'm better in the saddle than you are."

"Okay. A couple of men to escort you, though." Mackenzie drew a long breath. "Maybe you can persuade Tom—"

"No. I can't. Please don't ask me to, Dad."

He gave her the last gift he could: "I wouldn't want you to stay. That'd be shirking your own duty. Tell Tom I still think he's the right man for you. Goodnight, duck." It came out too fast, but he dared not delay. When she began to cry he must unfold her arms from his neck and depart the room.

"But I had not expected so much killing!"

"Nor I . . . at this stage of things. There will be more yet, I am afraid, before the immediate purpose is achieved."

"You told me—"

"I told you our hopes, Mwyr. You know as well as I that the

Great Science is only exact on the broadest scale of history. Individual events are subject to statistical fluctuation."

"That is an easy way, is it not, to describe sentient beings dying in the mud?"

"You are new here. Theory is one thing, adjustment to practical necessities is another. Do you think it does not hurt me to see that happen which I myself have helped plan?"

"Oh, I know, I know. Which makes it no easier to live with my guilt."

"To live with your responsibilities, you mean."

"Your phrase."

"No, this is not semantic trickery. The distinction is real. You have read reports and seen films, but I was here with the first expedition. And here I have been for more than two centuries. Their agony is no abstraction to me."

"But it was different when we first discovered them. The aftermath of their nuclear wars was still so horribly present. That was when they needed us—the poor starveling anarchs —and we, we did nothing but observe."

"Now you are hysterical. Could we come in blindly, ignorant of every last fact about them, and expect to be anything but one more disruptive element? An element whose effects we ourselves would not have been able to predict. That would have been criminal indeed, like a surgeon who started to operate as soon as he met the patient, without so much as taking a case history. We had to let them go their own way while we studied in secret. You have no idea how desperately hard we worked to gain information and understanding. That work goes on. It was only seventy years ago that we felt enough assurance to introduce the first new factor into this one selected society. As we continue to learn more, the plan will be adjusted. It may take us a thousand years to complete our mission."

"But meanwhile they have pulled themselves back out of the wreckage. They are finding their own answers to their problems. What right have we to—"

"I begin to wonder, Mwyr, what right you have to claim

even the title of apprentice psychodynamician. Consider what their 'answers' actually amount to. Most of the planet is still in a state of barbarism. This continent has come farthest toward recovery, because of having the widest distribution of technical skills and equipment, before the destruction. But what social structure has evolved? A jumble of quarrelsome successor states. A feudalism where the balance of political, military, and economic power lies with a landed aristocracy, of all archaic things. A score of languages and subcultures developing along their own incompatible lines. A blind technology worship inherited from the ancestral society that, unchecked, will lead them in the end back to a machine civilization as demoniac as the one that tore itself apart three centuries ago. Are you distressed that a few hundred men have been killed because our agents promoted a revolution which did not come off quite so smoothly as we hoped? Well, you have the word of the Great Science itself that, without our guidance, the totaled misery of this race through the next five thousand years would outweigh by three orders of magnitude whatever pain we are forced to inflict."

"Yes. Of course. I realize I am being emotional. It is difficult not to be at first, I suppose."

"You should be thankful that your initial exposure to the hard necessities of the plan was so mild. There is worse to come."

"So I have been told."

"In abstract terms. But consider the reality. A government ambitious to restore the old nation will act aggressively, thus embroiling itself in prolonged wars with powerful neighbors. Both directly and indirectly, through the operation of economic factors they are too naïve to control, the aristocrats and freeholders will be eroded away by those wars. Anomic democracy will replace their system, first dominated by a corrupt capitalism and later by sheer force of whoever holds the central government. But there will be no place for the vast displaced proletariat, the one-time landowners and the foreigners incorporated by conquest. They will offer fertile soil to any demagogue. The empire will undergo endless up-heaval, civil strife, despotism, decay, and outside invasion. Oh, we will have much to answer for before we are done!"

"Do you think . . . when we see the final result . . . will the blood wash off us?"

"No. We pay the heaviest price of all."

Spring in the high Sierra is cold, wet, snowbanks melting away from forest floor and giant rocks, rivers in spate until their canyons clang, a breeze ruffling puddles in the road. The first green breath across the aspen seems infinitely tender against pine and spruce, which gloom into a brilliant sky. A raven swoops low, gruk, gruk, look out for that damn hawk! But then you cross timber line and the world becomes tumbled blue-gray immensity, with the sun ablaze on what snows remain and the wind sounding hollow in your ears.

Captain Thomas Danielis, Field Artillery, Loyalist Army of the Pacific States, turned his horse aside. He was a dark young man, slender and snub-nosed. Behind him a squad slipped and cursed, dripping mud from feet to helmets, trying to get a gun carrier unstuck. Its alcohol motor was too feeble to do more than spin the wheels. The infantry squelched on past, stoop-shouldered, worn down by altitude and a wet bivouac and pounds of mire on each boot. Their line snaked from around a prowlike crag, up the twisted road and over the ridge ahead. A gust brought the smell of sweat to Danielis.

But they were good joes, he thought. Dirty, dogged, they did their profane best. His own company, at least, was going to get hot food tonight, if he had to cook the quartermaster sergeant.

The horse's hoofs banged on a block of ancient concrete jutting from the muck. If this had been the old days . . . but wishes weren't bullets. Beyond this part of the range lay lands mostly desert, claimed by the Saints, who were no longer a menace but with whom there was scant commerce. So the mountain highways had never been considered worth repaving, and the railroad ended at Hangtown. Therefore the expeditionary force to the Tahoe area must slog through unpeopled forests and icy uplands. God help the poor bastards.

God help them in Nakamura, too, Danielis thought. His mouth drew taut, he slapped his hands together and spurred the horse with needless violence. Sparks shot from iron shoes as the beast clattered off the road toward the highest point of the ridge. The man's saber banged his leg.

Reining in, he unlimbered his field glasses. From here he could look across a jumbled sweep of mountainscape, where cloud shadows sailed over cliffs and boulders, down into the gloom of a canyon and across to the other side. A few tufts of grass, thrust out beneath him, mummy brown, and a marmot wakened early from winter sleep whistled somewhere in the stone confusion. He still couldn't see the castle. Nor had he expected to, as yet. He knew this country . . . how well he did!

There might be a glimpse of hostile activity, though. It had been eerie to march this far with no sign of the enemy, of anyone else whatsoever; to send out patrols in search of rebel units that could not be found; to ride with shoulder muscles tense against the sniper's arrow that never came. Old Jimbo Mackenzie was not one to sit passive behind walls, and the Rolling Stones had not been given their nicknames in jest.

If Jimbo is alive. How do I know he is? That buzzard yonder may be the very one which hacked out his eyes.

Danielis bit his lip and made himself look steadily through the glasses. Don't think about Mackenzie, how he outroared and outdrank and outlaughed you and you never minded, how he sat knotting his brows over the chessboard where you could mop him up ten times out of ten and *he* never cared, how proud and happy he stood at the wedding. . . . Nor think about Laura, who tried to keep you from knowing how often she wept at night, who now bore a grandchild beneath her heart and woke alone in the San Francisco house from the evil dreams of pregnancy. Every one of those dogfaces plodding toward the castle which has killed every army ever sent against it—every one of them has somebody at home and hell rejoices

136

at how many have somebody on the rebel side. Better look for hostile spoor and let it go at that.

Wait! Danielis stiffened. A rider— He focused. *One of our own.* Fallon's army added a blue band to the uniform. *Returning scout.* A tingle went along his spine. He decided to hear the report firsthand. But the fellow was still a mile off, perforce riding slowly over the hugger-mugger terrain. There was no hurry about intercepting him. Danielis continued to survey the land.

A reconnaissance plane appeared, an ungainly dragonfly with sunlight flashing off a propeller head. Its drone bumbled among rock walls, where echoes threw the noise back and forth. Doubtless an auxiliary to the scouts, employing two-way radio communication. Later the plane would work as a spotter for artillery. There was no use making a bomber of it; Fort Nakamura was proof against anything that today's puny aircraft could drop, and might well shoot the thing down.

A shoe scraped behind Danielis. Horse and man whirled as one. His pistol jumped into his hand.

It lowered. "Oh. Excuse me, Philosopher."

The man in the blue robe nodded. A smile softened his stern face. He must be around sixty years old, hair white and skin lined, but he walked these heights like a wild goat. The Yang and Yin symbol burned gold on his breast.

"You're needlessly on edge, son," he said. A trace of Texas accent stretched out his words. The Espers obeyed the laws wherever they lived, but acknowledged no country their own: nothing less than mankind, perhaps ultimately all life through the space-time universe. Nevertheless, the Pacific States had gained enormously in prestige and influence when the Order's unenterable Central was established in San Francisco at the time when the city was being rebuilt in earnest. There had been no objection—on the contrary—to the Grand Seeker's desire that Philosopher Woodworth accompany the expedition as an observer. Not even from the chaplains; the churches had finally gotten it straight that the Esper teachings were neutral with respect to religion.

137

Danielis managed a grin. "Can you blame me?"

"No blame. But advice. Your attitude isn't useful. Does nothin' but wear you out. You've been fightin' a battle for weeks before it began."

Danielis remembered the apostle who had visited his home in San Francisco—by invitation, in the hope that Laura might learn some peace. His simile had been still homelier: "You only need to wash one dish at a time." The memory brought a smart to Danielis' eyes, so that he said roughly:

"I might relax if you'd use your powers to tell me what's waiting for us."

"I'm no adept, son. Too much in the material world, I'm afraid. Somebody's got to do the practical work of the Order, and someday I'll get the chance to retire and explore the frontier inside me. But you need to start early, and stick to it a lifetime, to develop your full powers." Woodworth looked across the peaks, seemed almost to merge himself with their loneliness.

Danielis hesitated to break into that meditation. He wondered what practical purpose the Philosopher was serving on this trip. To bring back a report, more accurate than untrained senses and undisciplined emotions could prepare? Yes, that must be it. The Espers might yet decide to take a hand in this war. However reluctantly, Central had allowed the awesome psi powers to be released now and again, when the Order was seriously threatened; and Judge Fallon was a better friend to them than Brodsky or the earlier Senate of Bossmen and House of People's Deputies had been.

The horse stamped and blew out its breath in a snort. Woodworth glanced back at the rider. "If you ask me, though," he said. "I don't reckon you'll find much doin' around here. I was in the Rangers myself, back home, before I saw the Way. This country feels empty."

"If we could know!" Danielis exploded. "They've had the whole winter to do what they liked in the mountains, while the snow kept us out. What scouts we could get in reported a beehive—as late as two weeks ago. What have they planned?"

Woodworth made no reply.

It flooded from Danielis, he couldn't stop, he had to cover the recollection of Laura bidding him good-bye on his second expedition against her father, six months after the first one came home in bloody fragments:

"If we had the resources! A few wretched little railroads and motor cars; a handful of aircraft; most of our supply trains drawn by mules—what kind of mobility does that give us? And what really drives me crazy . . . we know how to make what they had in the old days. We've got the books, the information. More, maybe, than the ancestors. I've watched the electrosmith at Fort Nakamura turn out transistor units with enough bandwidth to carry television, no bigger than my fist. I've seen the scientific journals, the research labs, biology, chemistry, astronomy, mathematics. And all useless!"

"Not so," Woodworth answered mildly. "Like my own Order, the community of scholarship's becomin' supranational. Printin' presses, radiophones, telescribes—"

"I say useless. Useless to stop men killing each other because there's no authority strong enough to make them behave. Useless to take a farmer's hands off a horse-drawn plow and put them on the wheel of a tractor. We've got the knowledge, but we can't apply it."

"You do apply it, son, where too much power and industrial plant isn't required. Remember, the world's a lot poorer in natural resources than it was before the Hellbombs. I've seen the Black Lands myself, where the firestorm passed over the Texas oilfields." Woodworth's serenity cracked a little. He turned his eyes back to the peaks.

"There's oil elsewhere," Danielis insisted. "And coal, iron, uranium, everything we need. But the world hasn't got the organization to get at it. Not in any quantity. So we fill the Central Valley with crops that'll yield alcohol, to keep a few motors turning; and we import a dribble of other stuff along an unbelievably inefficient chain of middlemen; and most of it's eaten by the armies." He jerked his head toward that part of the sky which the handmade airplane had crossed. "That's one reason we've got to have Reunification. So we can rebuild."

"And the other?" Woodworth asked softly.

"Democracy—universal suffrage—" Danielis swallowed. "And so fathers and sons won't have to fight each other again."

"Those are better reasons," Woodworth said. "Good enough for the Espers to support. But as for that machinery you want—" He shook his head. "No, you're wrong there. That's no way for men to live."

"Maybe not," Danielis said. "Though my own father wouldn't have been crippled by overwork if he'd had some machines to help him. . . . Oh, I don't know. First things first. Let's get this war over with and argue later." He remembered the scout, now gone from view. "Pardon me, Philosopher, I've got an errand."

The Esper raised his hand in token of peace. Danielis cantered off.

Splashing along the roadside, he saw the man he wanted, halted by Major Jacobsen. The latter, who must have sent him out, sat mounted near the infantry line. The scout was a Klamath Indian, stocky in buckskins, a bow on his shoulder. Arrows were favored over guns by many of the men from the northern districts: cheaper than bullets, no noise, less range, but as much firepower as a bolt-action rifle. In the bad old days before the Pacific States had formed their union, archers along forest trails had saved many a town from conquest; they still helped keep that union loose.

"Ah, Captain Danielis," Jacobsen hailed. "You're just in time. Lieutenant Smith was about to report what his detachment found out."

"And the plane," said Smith imperturbably. "What the pilot told us he'd seen from the air gave us the guts to go there and check for ourselves."

"Well?"

"Nobody around."

"What?"

"Fort's been evacuated. So's the settlement. Not a soul."

"But—but—" Jacobsen collected himself. "Go on."

"We studied the signs as best's we could. Looks like non-combatants left some time ago. By sledge and ski, I'd guess, maybe north to some strong point. I suppose the men shifted their own stuff at the same time, gradual-like, what they couldn't carry with 'em at the last. Because the regiment and its support units, even field artillery, pulled out just three-four days ago. Ground's all tore up. They headed downslope, sort of west by northwest, far's we could tell from what we saw."

Jacobsen choked. "Where are they bound?"

A flow of wind struck Danielis in the face and ruffled the horses' manes. At his back he heard the slow plop and squish of boots, groan of wheels, chuff of motors, rattle of wood and metal, yells and whipcracks of muleskinners. But it seemed very remote. A map grew before him, blotting out the world.

The Loyalist Army had had savage fighting the whole winter, from the Trinity Alps to Puget Sound—for Brodsky had managed to reach Mount Rainier, whose lord had furnished broadcasting facilities, and Rainier was too well fortified to take at once. The bossmen and the autonomous tribes rose in arms, persuaded that a usurper threatened their damned little local privileges. Their protectees fought beside them, if only because no rustic had been taught any higher loyalty than to his patron. West Canada, fearful of what Fallon might do when he got the chance, lent the rebels aid that was scarcely even clandestine.

Nonetheless, the national army was stronger: more matériel, better organization, above everything an ideal of the future. Cinc O'Donnell had outlined a strategy—concentrate the loyal forces at a few points, overwhelm resistance, restore order and establish bases in the region, then proceed to the next place—which worked. The government now controlled the entire coast, with naval units to keep an eye on the Canadians in Vancouver and guard the important Hawaii trade routes; the northern half of Washington almost to the Idaho line; the Columbia Valley; central California as far north as Redding. The remaining rebellious Stations and towns were isolated from each other in mountains, forests, deserts. Bossdom after bossdom fell as the loyalists pressed on, defeating the enemy in detail, cutting him off from supplies and hope. The only real worry had been Cruikshank's Sierra Command, an army in its own right rather than a levy of yokels and citymen, big and tough and expertly led. This expedition against Fort Nakamura was only a small part of what had looked like a difficult campaign.

But now the Rolling Stones had pulled out. Offered no fight whatsoever. Which meant that their brother Catamounts must also have evacuated. You don't give up one anchor of a line you intend to hold. So?

"Down into the valleys," Danielis said; and there sounded in his ears, crazily, the voice of Laura as she used to sing. *Down in the valley, valley so low.*

"Judas!" the major exclaimed. Even the Indian grunted as if he had taken a belly blow. "No, they couldn't. We'd have known."

Hang your head over, hear the wind blow. It hooted across cold rocks.

"There are plenty of forest trails," Danielis said. "Infantry and cavalry could use them, if they're accustomed to such country. And the Cats are. Vehicles, wagons, big guns, that's slower and harder. But they only need to outflank us, then they can get back onto Forty and Fifty—and cut us to pieces if we attempt pursuit. I'm afraid they've got us boxed."

"The eastern slope—," said Jacobsen helplessly.

"What for? Want to occupy a lot of sagebrush? No, we're trapped here till they deploy in the flatlands." Danielis closed a hand on his saddlehorn so that the knuckles went bloodless. "I miss my guess if this isn't Colonel Mackenzie's idea. It's his style, for sure."

"But then they're between us and Frisco! With damn near our whole strength in the north—"

Between me and Laura, Danielis thought.

He said aloud: "I suggest, Major, we get hold of the C.O. at once. And then we better get on the radio." From some well he drew the power to raise his head. The wind lashed his eyes.

"This needn't be a disaster. They'll be easier to beat out in the open, actually, once we come to grips."

Roses love sunshine, violets love dew,
Angels in heaven know I love you.

The rains which fill the winter of the California lowlands were about ended. Northward along a highway whose pavement clopped under hoofs, Mackenzie rode through a tremendous greenness. Eucalyptus and live oak, flanking the road, exploded with new leaves. Beyond them on either side stretched a checkerboard of fields and vineyards, intricately hued, until the distant hills on the right and the higher, nearer ones on the left made walls. The freeholder houses that had been scattered across the land a ways back were no longer to be seen. This end of the Napa Valley belonged to the Esper community at St. Helena. Clouds banked like white mountains over the western ridge. The breeze bore to Mackenzie a smell of growth and turned earth.

Behind him it rumbled with men. The Rolling Stones were on the move. The regiment proper kept to the highway, three thousand boots slamming down at once with an earthquake noise, and so did the guns and wagons. There was no immediate danger of attack. But the cavalrymen attached to the force must needs spread out. The sun flashed off their helmets and lance heads.

Mackenzie's attention was directed forward. Amber walls and red tile roofs could be seen among plum trees that were a surf of pink and white blossoms. The community was big, several thousand people. The muscles tightened in his abdomen. "Think we can trust them?" he asked, not for the first time. "We've only got a radio agreement to a parley."

Speyer, riding beside him, nodded. "I expect they'll be honest. Particularly with our boys right outside. Espers believe in non-violence anyway."

"Yeah, but if it did come to fighting—I know there aren't very many adepts so far. The Order hasn't been around long enough for that. But when you get this many Espers together, there's bound to be a few who've gotten somewhere with

143

their damned psionics. I don't want my men blasted, or lifted in the air and dropped, or any such nasty thing."

Speyer threw him a sidelong glance. "Are you scared of them, Jimbo?" he murmured.

"Hell, no!" Mackenzie wondered if he was a liar or not. "But I don't like 'em."

"They do a lot of good. Among the poor, especially."

"Sure, sure. Though any decent bossman looks after his own protectees, and we've got things like churches and hospices as well. I don't see where just being charitable—and they can afford it, with the profits they make on their holdings—I don't see where that gives any right to raise the orphans and pauper kids they take in, the way they do; so's to make the poor tikes unfit for life anywhere outside."

"The object of that, as you well know, is to orient them toward the so-called interior frontier. Which American civilization as a whole is not much interested in. Frankly, quite apart from the remarkable powers some Espers have developed, I often envy them."

"You, Phil?" Mackenzie goggled at his friend.

The lines drew deep in Speyer's face. "This winter I've helped shoot a lot of my fellow countrymen," he said low. "My mother and wife and kids are crowded with the rest of the Village in the Mount Lassen fort, and when we said good-by we knew it was quite possibly permanent. And in the past I've helped shoot a lot of other men who never did me any personal harm." He sighed. "I've often wondered what it's like to know peace, inside as well as outside."

Mackenzie sent Laura and Tom out of his head.

"Of course," Speyer went on, "the fundamental reason you —and I, for that matter—distrust the Espers is that they do represent something alien to us. Something that may eventually choke out the whole concept of life that we grew up with. You know, a couple weeks back in Sacramento I dropped in at the University research lab to see what was going on. Incredible! The ordinary soldier would swear it was witchwork. It was certainly more weird than . . . than simply reading minds

144

or moving objects by thinking at them. But to you or me it's a shiny new marvel. We'll wallow in it."

"Now why's that? Because the lab is scientific. Those men work with chemicals, electronics, subviral particles. That fits into the educated American's world-view. But the mystic unity of creation . . . no, not our cup of tea. The only way we can hope to achieve Oneness is to renounce everything we've ever believed in. At your age or mine, Jimbo, a man is seldom ready to tear down his whole life and start from scratch."

"Maybe so." Mackenzie lost interest. The settlement was quite near now.

He turned around to Captain Hulse, riding a few paces behind. "Here we go," he said. "Give my compliments to Lieutenant Colonel Yamaguchi and tell him he's in charge till we get back. If anything seems suspicious, he's to act at his own discretion."

"Yes, sir." Hulse saluted and wheeled smartly about. There had been no practical need for Mackenzie to repeat what had long been agreed on; but he knew the value of ritual. He clicked his big sorrel gelding into a trot. At his back he heard bugles sound orders and sergeants howl at their platoons.

Speyer kept pace. Mackenzie had insisted on bringing an extra man to the discussion. His own wits were probably no match for a high-level Esper, but Phil's might be.

Not that there's any question of diplomacy or whatever. I hope. To ease himself, he concentrated on what was real and present—hoofbeats, the rise and fall of the saddle beneath him, the horse's muscles rippling between his thighs, the creak and jingle of his saber belt, the clean odor of the animal —and suddenly remembered this was the sort of trick the Espers recommended.

None of their communities was walled, as most towns and every Bossman's Station was. The officers turned off the highway and went down a street between colonnaded buildings. Side streets ran off in both directions. The settlement covered no great area, though, being composed of groups that lived together, sodalities or superfamilies or whatever you wanted to call them. Some hostility toward the Order and a great many dirty jokes stemmed from that practice. But Speyer, who should know, said there was no more sexual swapping around than in the outside world. The idea was simply to get away from possessiveness, thee versus me, and to raise children as part of a whole rather than an insular clan.

The kids were out, staring round-eyed from the porticoes, hundreds of them. They looked healthy and, underneath a natural fear of the invaders, happy enough. But pretty solemn, Mackenzie thought; and all in the same blue garb. Adults stood among them, expressionless. Everybody had come in from the fields as the regiment neared. The silence was like barricades. Mackenzie felt sweat begin to trickle down his ribs. When he emerged on the central square, he let out his breath in a near gasp.

A fountain, the basin carved into a lotus, tinkled in the middle of the plaza. Flowering trees stood around it. The square was defined on three sides by massive buildings that must be for storage. On the fourth side rose a smaller temple-like structure with a graceful cupola, obviously headquarters and meeting house. On its lowest step were ranked half a dozen blue-robed men, five of them husky youths. The sixth was middle-aged, the Yang and Yin on his breast. His features, ordinary in themselves, held an implacable calm.

Mackenzie and Speyer drew reign. The colonel flipped a soft salute. "Philosopher Gaines? I'm Mackenzie, here's Major Speyer." He swore at himself for being so awkward about it and wondered what to do with his hands. The young fellows he understood, more or less; they watched him with badly concealed hostility. But he had some trouble meeting Gaines' eyes.

The settlement leader inclined his head. "Welcome, gentlemen. Won't you come in?"

Mackenzie dismounted, hitched his horse to a post and removed his helmet. His worn reddish-brown uniform felt shabbier yet in these surroundings. "Thanks. Uh, I'll have to make this quick."

"To be sure. Follow me, please."

Stiff-backed, the young men trailed after their elders, through an entry chamber and down a short hall. Speyer looked around at the mosaics. "Why, this is lovely," he murmured.

"Thank you," said Gaines. "Here's my office." He opened a door of superbly grained walnut and gestured the visitors through. When he closed it behind himself, the acolytes waited outside.

The room was austere, whitewashed walls enclosing little more than a desk, a shelf of books, and some backless chairs. A window opened on a garden. Gaines sat down, Mackenzie and Speyer followed suit, uncomfortable on this furniture.

"We'd better get right to business," the colonel blurted.

Gaines said nothing. At last Mackenzie must plow ahead:

"Here's the situation. Our force is to occupy Calistoga, with detachments on either side of the hills. That way we'll control both the Napa Valley and the Valley of the Moon . . . from the northern ends, at least. The best place to station our eastern wing is here. We plan to establish a fortified camp in the field yonder. I'm sorry about the damage to your crops, but you'll be compensated once the proper government has been restored. And food, medicine—you understand this army has to requisition such items, but we won't let anybody suffer undue hardship and we'll give receipts. Uh, as a precaution we'll need to quarter a few men in this community, to sort of keep an eye on things. They'll interfere as little as possible. Okay?"

"The charter of the Order guarantees exemption from military requirements," Gaines answered evenly. "In fact, no armed man is supposed to cross the boundary of any land held by an Esper settlement. I cannot be party to a violation of the law, Colonel."

"If you want to split legal hairs, Philosopher," Speyer said, "then I'll remind you that both Fallon and Judge Brodsky have declared martial law. Ordinary rules are suspended."

Gaines smiled. "Since only one government can be legitimate," he said, "the proclamations of the other are necessarily null and void. To a disinterested observer, it would appear

147

that Judge Fallon's title is the stronger, especially when his side controls a large continuous area rather than some scattered bossdoms."

"Not any more, it doesn't," Mackenzie snapped.

Speyer gestured him back. "Perhaps you haven't followed the developments of the last few weeks, Philosopher," he said. "Allow me to recapitulate. The Sierra Command stole a march on the Fallonites and came down out of the mountains. There was almost nothing left in the middle part of California to oppose us, so we took over rapidly. By occupying Sacramento, we control river and rail traffic. Our bases extend south below Bakersfield, with Yosemite and King's Canyon not far away to provide sites for extremely strong positions. When we're consolidated this northern end of our gains, the Fallonite forces around Redding will be trapped between us and the powerful bossmen who still hold out in the Trinity, Shasta, and Lassen regions. The very fact of our being here has forced the enemy to evacuate the Columbia Valley, so that San Francisco may be defended. It's an open question which side today has the last word in the larger territory."

"What about the army that went into the Sierra against you?" Gaines inquired shrewdly. "Have you contained them?"

Mackenzie scowled. "No. That's no secret. They got out through the Mother Lode country and went around us. They're down in Los Angeles and San Diego now."

"A formidable host. Do you expect to stand them off indefinitely?"

"We're going to make a hell of a good try," Mackenzie said. "Where we are, we've got the advantage of interior communications. And most of the freeholders are glad to slip us word about whatever they observe. We can concentrate at any point the enemy starts to attack."

"Pity that this rich land must also be torn apart by war."

"Yeah. Isn't it?"

"Our strategic objective is obvious enough," Speyer said. "We have cut enemy communications across the middle, except by sea, which is not very satisfactory for troops operating far

148

inland. We deny him access to a good part of his food and manufactured supplies, and most especially to the bulk of his fuel alcohol. The backbone of our own side is the bossdoms, which are almost self-contained economic and social units. Before long they'll be in better shape than the rootless army they face. I think Judge Brodsky will be back in San Francisco before fall."

"If your plans succeed," Gaines said.

"That's our worry." Mackenzie leaned forward, one fist doubled on his knee. "Okay, Philosopher. I know you'd rather see Fallon come out on top, but I expect you've got more sense than to sign up in a lost cause. Will you cooperate with us?"

"The Order takes no part in political affairs, Colonel, except when its own existence is endangered."

"Oh, pipe down. By 'cooperate' I don't mean anything but keeping out from under our feet."

"I am afraid that would still count as cooperation. We cannot have military establishments on our lands."

Mackenzie stared at Gaines face, which had set into granite lines, and wondered if he had heard aright. "Are you ordering us off?" a stranger asked with his voice.

"Yes," the Philosopher said.

"With our artillery zeroed in on your town?"

"Would you really shell women and children, Colonel?"

O Nora— "We don't need to. Our men can walk right in."

"Against psi blasts? I beg you not to have those poor boys destroyed." Gaines paused, then: "I might also point out that by losing your regiment you imperil your whole cause. You are free to march around our holdings and proceed to Calistoga."

Leaving a Fallonite nest at my back, spang across my communications southward. The teeth grated together in Mackenzie's mouth.

Gaines rose. "The discussion is at an end, gentlemen," he said. "You have one hour to get off our lands."

Mackenzie and Speyer stood up too. "We're not done yet,"

the major said. Sweat studded his forehead and the long nose. "I want to make some further explanations."

Gaines crossed the room and opened the door. "Show these gentlemen out," he said to the five acolytes.

"No, by God!" Mackenzie shouted. He clapped a hand to his sidearm.

"Inform the adepts," Gaines said.

One of the young men turned. Mackenzie heard the slap-slap of his sandals, running down the hall. Gaines nodded. "I think you had better go," he said.

Speyer grew rigid. His eyes shut. They flew open and he breathed. "*Inform* the adepts?"

Mackenzie saw the stiffness break in Gaines' countenance. There was no time for more than a second's bewilderment. His body acted for him. The gun clanked from his holster simultaneously with Speyer's.

"Get that messenger, Jimbo," the major rapped. "I'll keep these birds covered."

As he plunged forward, Mackenzie found himself worrying about the regimental honor. Was it right to open hostilities when you had come on a parley? But Gaines had cut the talk off himself—

"Stop him!" Gaines yelled.

The four remaining acolytes sprang into action. Two of them barred the doorway, the other two moved in on either side. "Hold it or I'll shoot!" Speyer cried, and was ignored.

Mackenzie couldn't bring himself to fire on unarmed men. He gave the youngster before him the pistol barrel in his teeth. Bloody-faced, the Esper lurched back. Mackenzie stiff-armed the one coming in from the left. The third tried to fill the doorway. Mackenzie put a foot behind his ankles and pushed. As he went down, Mackenzie kicked him in the temple, hard enough to stun, and jumped over him.

The fourth was on his back. Mackenzie writhed about to face the man. Those arms that hugged him, pinioning his gun, were bear strong. Mackenzie put the butt of his free left hand under the fellow's nose, and pushed. The acolyte must let go.

150

Mackenzie gave him a knee in the stomach, whirled, and ran.

There was not much further commotion behind him. Phil must have them under control. Mackenzie pelted along the hall, into the entry chamber. Where had that goddamn runner gone? He looked out the open entrance, onto the square. Sunlight hurt his eyes. His breath came in painful gulps, there was a stitch in his side, yeah, he was getting old.

Blue robes fluttered from a street. Mackenzie recognized the messenger. The youth pointed at this building. A gabble of his words drifted faintly through Mackenzie's pulse. There were seven or eight men with him—older men, nothing to mark their clothes . . . but Mackenzie knew a high-ranking officer when he saw one. The acolyte was dismissed. Those whom he had summoned crossed the square with long strides.

Terror knotted Mackenzie's bowels. He put it down. A Catamount didn't stampede, even from somebody who could turn him inside out with a look. He could do nothing about the wretchedness that followed, though. *If they clobber me, so much the better. I won't lie awake nights wondering how Laura is.*

The adepts were almost to the steps. Mackenzie trod forth. He swept his revolver in an arc. "Halt!" His voice sounded tiny in the stillness that brooded over the town.

They jarred to a stop and stood there in a group. He saw them enforce a catlike relaxation, and their faces became blank visors. None spoke. Finally Mackenzie was unable to keep silent.

"This place is hereby occupied under the laws of war," he said. "Go back to your quarters."

"What have you done with our leader?" asked a tall man. His voice was even but deeply resonant.

"Read my mind and find out," Mackenzie gibed. *No, you're being childish.* "He's okay, long's he keeps his nose clean. You too. Beat it."

"We do not wish to pervert psionics to violence," said the tall man. "Please do not force us."

"Your chief sent for you before we'd done anything," Mac-

151

kenzie retorted. "Looks like violence was what he had in mind. On your way."

The Espers exchanged glances. The tall man nodded. His companions walked slowly off. "I would like to see Philosopher Gaines," the tall man said.

"You will pretty soon."

"Am I to understand that he is being held a prisoner?"

"Understand what you like." The other Espers were rounding the corner of the building. "I don't want to shoot. Go on back before I have to."

"An impasse of sorts," the tall man said. "Neither of us wishes to injure one whom he considers defenseless. Allow me to conduct you off these grounds."

Mackenzie wet his lips. Weather had chapped them rough. "If you can put a hex on me, go ahead," he challenged. "Otherwise scram."

"Well, I shall not hinder you from rejoining your men. It seems the easiest way of getting you to leave. But I most solemnly warn that any armed force which tries to enter will be annihilated."

Guess I had better go get the boys, at that. Phil can't mount guard on those guys forever.

The tall man went over to the hitching post. "Which of these horses is yours?" he asked blandly.

Almighty eager to get rid of me, isn't he—Holy hellfire! There must be a rear door!

Mackenzie spun on his heel. The Esper shouted. Mackenzie dashed back through the entry chamber. His boots threw echoes at him. No, not to the left, there's only the office that way. Right . . . around this corner—

A long hall stretched before him. A stairway curved from the middle. The other Espers were already on it.

"Halt!" Mackenzie called. "Stop or I'll shoot!"

The two men in the lead sped onward. The rest turned and headed down again, toward him.

He fired with care, to disable rather than kill. The hall reverberated with the explosions. One after another they dropped, a bullet in leg or hip or shoulder. With such small targets, Mackenzie missed some shots. As the tall man, the last of them, closed in from behind, the hammer clicked on an empty chamber.

Mackenzie drew his saber and gave him the flat of it alongside the head. The Esper lurched. Mackenzie got past and bounded up the stair. It wound like something in a nightmare. He thought his heart was going to go to pieces.

At the end, an iron door opened on a landing. One man was fumbling with the lock. The other blue-robe attacked.

Mackenzie stuck his sword between the Esper's legs. As his opponent stumbled, the colonel threw a left hook to the jaw. The man sagged against the wall. Mackenzie grabbed the robe of the other and hurled him to the floor. "Get out," he rattled.

They pulled themselves together and glared at him. He thrust air with his blade. "From now on I am to kill," he said.

"Get help, Dave," said the one who had been opening the door. "I'll watch him." The other went unevenly down the stairs. The first man stood out of saber reach. "Do you want to be destroyed?" he asked.

Mackenzie turned the knob at his back, but the door was still locked. "I don't think you can do it," he said. "Not without what's here."

The Esper struggled for self-control. They waited through minutes that stretched. Then a noise began below. The Esper pointed. "We have nothing but agricultural implements," he said, "but you have only that blade. Will you surrender?"

Mackenzie spat on the floor. The Esper went on down. Presently the attackers came into view. There might be a hundred, judging from the hubbub behind them, but because of the curve Mackenzie could see no more than ten or fifteen —burly fieldhands, their robes tucked high and sharp tools aloft. The landing was too wide for defense. He advanced to the stairway, where they could only come at him two at a time.

A couple of sawtoothed hay knives led the assault. Mackenzie parried one blow and chopped. His edge went into meat and struck bone. Blood ran out, impossibly red, even in the dim light here. The man fell to all fours with a shriek. Mackenzie dodged a cut from the companion. Metal clashed on metal. The weapons locked. Mackenzie's arm was forced back. He looked into a broad suntanned face. The side of his hand smote the young man's larynx. The Esper fell against the one behind and they went down together. It took a while to clear the tangle and resume action.

A pitchfork thrust for the colonel's belly. He managed to grab it with his left hand, divert the tines, and chop at the fingers on the shaft. A scythe gashed his right side. He saw his own blood but wasn't aware of pain. A flesh wound, no more. He swept his saber back and forth. The forefront retreated from its whistling menace. *But God, my knees are like rubber, I can't hold out another five minutes.*

A bugle sounded. There was a spatter of gunfire. The mob on the staircase congealed. Someone screamed.

Hoofs banged across the ground floor. A voice rasped: "Hold everything, there! Drop those weapons and come on down. First man tries anything gets shot."

Mackenzie leaned on his saber and fought for air. He hardly noticed the Espers melt away.

When he felt a little better, he went to one of the small windows and looked out. Horsemen were in the plaza. Not yet in sight, but nearing, he heard infantry.

Speyer arrived, followed by a sergeant of engineers and several privates. The major hurried to Mackenzie. "You okay, Jimbo? You been hurt!"

"A scratch," Mackenzie said. He was getting back his strength, though no sense of victory accompanied it, only the knowledge of aloneness. The injury began to sting. "Not worth a fuss. Look."

"Yes, I suppose you'll live. Okay, men, get that door open."

The engineers took forth their tools and assailed the lock with a vigor that must spring half from fear. "How'd you guys show up so soon?" Mackenzie asked.

"I thought there'd be trouble," Speyer said, "so when I

heard shots I jumped through the window and ran around to my horse. That was just before those clodhoppers attacked you; I saw them gathering as I rode out. Our cavalry got in almost at once, of course, and the dogfaces weren't far behind."

"Any resistance?"

"No, not after we fired a few rounds in the air." Speyer glanced outside. "We're in full possession now."

Mackenzie regarded the door. "Well," he said, "I feel better about our having pulled guns on them in the office. Looks like their adepts really depend on plain old weapons, huh? And Esper communities aren't supposed to have arms. Their charters say so. . . . That was a damn good guess of yours, Phil. How'd you do it?"

"I sort of wondered why the chief had to send a runner to fetch guys that claim to be telepaths. There we go!"

The lock jingled apart. The sergeant opened the door. Mackenzie and Speyer went into the great room under the dome. They walked around for a long time, wordless, among shapes of metal and less identifiable substances. Nothing was familiar. Mackenzie paused at last before a helix which projected from a transparent cube. Formless darknesses swirled within the box, sparked as if with tiny stars.

"I figured maybe the Espers had found a cache of old-time stuff, from just before the Hellbombs," he said in a muffled voice. "Ultra-secret weapons that never got a chance to be used. But this doesn't look like it. Think so?"

"No," Speyer said. "It doesn't look to me as if these things were made by human beings at all."

"But do you not understand? They occupied a settlement! That proves to the world that Espers are not invulnerable. And to complete the catastrophe, they seized its arsenal."

"Have no fears about that. No untrained person can activate those instruments. The circuits are locked except in the presence of certain encephalic rhythms which result from conditioning. That same conditioning makes it impossible for the

155

so-called adepts to reveal any of their knowledge to the un-initiated, no matter what may be done to them."

"Yes, I know that much. But it is not what I had in mind. What frightens me is the fact that the revelation will spread. Everyone will know the Esper adepts do not plumb unknown depths of the psyche after all, but merely have access to an advanced physical science. Not only will this lift rebel spirits, but worse, it will cause many, perhaps most of the Order's members to break away in disillusionment."

"Not at once. News travels slowly under present conditions. Also, Mwyr, you underestimate the ability of the human mind to ignore data which conflict with cherished beliefs."

"But—"

"Well, let us assume the worst. Let us suppose that faith is lost and the Order disintegrates. That will be a serious setback to the plan, but not a fatal one. Psionics was merely one bit of folklore we found potent enough to serve as the motivator of a new orientation toward life. There are others, for example the widespread belief in magic among the less educated classes. We can begin again on a different basis, if we must. The exact form of the creed is not important. It is only scaffolding for the real structure: a communal, anti-materialistic social group, to which more and more people will turn for sheer lack of anything else, as the coming empire breaks up. In the end, the new culture can and will discard whatever superstitions gave it the initial impetus."

"A hundred-year setback, at least."

"True. It would be much more difficult to introduce a radical alien element now, when the autochthonous society has developed strong institutions of its own, than it was in the past. I merely wish to reassure you that the task is not impossible. I do not actually propose to let matters go that far. The Espers can be salvaged."

"How?"

"We must intervene directly."

"Has that been computed as being unavoidable?"

"Yes. The matrix yields an unambiguous answer. I do not

like it any better than you. But direct action occurs oftener than we tell neophytes in the schools. The most elegant procedure would of course be to establish such initial conditions in a society that its evolution along desired lines becomes automatic. Furthermore, that would let us close our minds to the distressing fact of our own blood guilt. Unfortunately, the Great Science does not extend down to the details of day-to-day practicality.

"In the present instance, we shall help to smash the reactionaries. The government will then proceed so harshly against its conquered opponents that many of those who accept the story about what was found at St. Helena will not live to spread the tale. The rest . . . well, they will be discredited by their own defeat. Admittedly, the story will linger for lifetimes, whispered here and there. But what of that? Those who believe in the Way will, as a rule, simply be strengthened in their faith, by the very process of denying such ugly rumors. As more and more persons, common citizens as well as Espers, reject materialism, the legend will seem more and more fantastic. It will seem obvious that certain ancients invented the tale to account for a fact that they in their ignorance were unable to comprehend."

"I see. . . ."

"You are not happy here, are you, Mwyr?"

"I cannot quite say. Everything is so distorted."

"Be glad you were not sent to one of the really alien planets."

"I might almost prefer that. There would be a hostile environment to think about. One could forget how far it is to home."

"Three years' travel."

"You say that so glibly. As if three shipboard years were not equal to fifty in cosmic time. As if we could expect a relief vessel daily, not once in a century. And . . . as if the region that our ships have explored amounts to one chip out of this one galaxy!"

"That region will grow until someday it engulfs the galaxy."

157

"Yes, yes, yes. I know. Why do you think I chose to become a psychodynamician? Why am I here, learning how to meddle with the destiny of a world where I do not belong? 'To create the union of sentient beings, each member species a step toward life's mastery of the universe.' Brave slogan! But in practice, it seems, only a chosen few races are to be allowed the freedom of that universe."

"Not so, Mwyr. Consider these ones with whom we are, as you say, meddling. Consider what use they made of nuclear energy when they had it. At the rate they are going, they will have it again within a century or two. Not long after that they will be building spaceships. Even granted that time lag attenuates the effects of interstellar contact, those effects are cumulative. So do you wish such a band of carnivores turned loose on the galaxy?

"No, let them become inwardly civilized first; then we shall see if they can be trusted. If not, they will at least be happy on their own planet, in a mode of life designed for them by the Great Science. Remember, they have an immemorial aspiration toward peace on earth; but that is something they will never achieve by themselves. I do not pretend to be a very good person, Mwyr. Yet this work that we are doing makes me feel not altogether useless in the cosmos."

Promotion was fast that year, casualties being so high. Captain Thomas Danielis was raised to major for his conspicuous part in putting down the revolt of the Los Angeles citymen. Soon after occurred the Battle of Maricopa, when the loyalists failed bloodily to break the stranglehold of the Sierran rebels on the San Joaquin Valley, and he was brevetted lieutenant colonel. The army was ordered northward and moved warily under the coast ranges, half expecting attack from the east. But the Brodskyites seemed too busy consolidating their latest gains. The trouble came from guerrillas and the hedgehog resistance of bossman Stations. After one particularly stiff clash, they stopped near Pinnacles for a breather.

Danielis made his way through camp, where tents stood in

tight rows between the guns and men lay about dozing, talking, gambling, staring at the blank blue sky. The air was hot, pungent with cookfire smoke, horses, mules, dung, sweat, boot oil; the green of the hills that lifted around the site was dulling toward summer brown. He was idle until time for the conference the general had called, but restlessness drove him. *By now I'm a father*, he thought, *and I've never seen my kid.*

At that, I'm lucky, he reminded himself. *I've got my life and limbs.* He remembered Jacobsen dying in his arms at Maricopa. You wouldn't have thought the human body could hold so much blood. Though maybe one was no longer human, when the pain was so great that one could do nothing but shriek until the darkness came.

And I used to think war was glamorous. Hunger, thirst, exhaustion, terror, mutilation, death, and forever the sameness, boredom grinding you down to an ox. . . . I've had it. I'm going into business after the war. Economic integration, as the bossman system breaks up, yes, there'll be a lot of ways for a man to get ahead, but decently, without a weapon in his hand— Danielis realized he was repeating thoughts that were months old. What the hell else was there to think about, though?

The large tent where prisoners were interrogated lay near his path. A couple of privates were conducting a man inside. The fellow was blond, burly, and sullen. He wore a sergeant's stripes, but otherwise his only item of uniform was the badge of Warden Echevarry, bossman in this part of the coastal mountains. A lumberjack in peacetime, Danielis guessed from the look of him; a soldier in a private army whenever the interests of Echevarry were threatened; captured in yesterday's engagement.

On impulse, Danielis followed. He got into the tent as Captain Lambert, chubby behind a portable desk, finished the preliminaries, and blinked in the sudden gloom.

"Oh." The intelligence officer started to rise. "Yes, sir?"

"At ease," Danielis said. "Just thought I'd listen in."

"Well, I'll try to put on a good show for you." Lambert reseated himself and looked at the prisoner, who stood with

159

hunched shoulders and widespread legs between his guards. "Now, sergeant, we'd like to know a few things."

"I don't have to say nothing except name, rank, and home town," the man growled. "You got those."

"Um-m-m, that's questionable. You aren't a foreign soldier, you're in rebellion against the government of your own country."

"The hell I am! I'm an Echevarry man."

"So what?"

"So my Judge is whoever Echevarry says. He says Brodsky. That makes you the rebel."

"The law's been changed."

"Yur mucking Fallon got no right to change any laws. Especially part of the Constitution. I'm no hillrunner, Captain. I went to school some. And every year our Warden reads his people the Constitution."

"Times have changed since it was drawn," Lambert said. His tone sharpened. "But I'm not going to argue with you. How many riflemen and how many archers in your company?"

Silence.

"We can make things a lot easier for you," Lambert said. "I'm not asking you to do anything treasonable. All I want is to confirm some information I've already got."

The man shook his head angrily.

Lambert gestured. One of the privates stepped behind the captive, took his arm, and twisted a little.

"Echevarry wouldn't do that to me," he said through white lips.

"Of course not," Lambert said. "You're his man."

"Think I wanna be just a number on some list in Frisco? Damn right I'm my bossman's man!"

Lambert gestured again. The private twisted harder.

"Hold on, there," Danielis barked. "Stop that!"

The private let go, looking surprised. The prisoner drew a sobbing breath.

"I'm amazed at you, Captain Lambert," Danielis said. He

160

felt his own face reddening. "If this has been your usual practice, there's going to be a court-martial."

"No, sir," Lambert said in a small voice. "Honest. Only . . . they don't talk. Hardly any of them. What'm I supposed to do?"

"Follow the rules of war."

"With rebels?"

"Take that man away," Danielis ordered. The privates made haste to do so.

"Sorry, sir," Lambert muttered. "I guess . . . I guess I've lost too many buddies. I hate to lose more, simply for lack of information."

"Me too." A compassion rose in Danielis. He sat down on the table edge and began to roll a cigarette. "But you see, we aren't in a regular war. And so, by a curious paradox, we have to follow the conventions more carefully than ever before."

"I don't quite understand, sir."

Danielis finished the cigarette and gave it to Lambert: olive branch or something. He started another for himself. "The rebels aren't rebels by their own lights," he said. "They're being loyal to a tradition that we're trying to curb, eventually to destroy. Let's face it, the average bossman is a fairly good leader. He may be descended from some thug who grabbed power by strong-arm methods during the chaos, but by now his family's integrated itself with the region he rules. He knows it, and its people, inside out. He's there in the flesh, a symbol of the community and its achievements, its folkways and essential independence. If you're in trouble, you don't have to work through some impersonal bureaucracy, you go direct to your bossman. His duties are as clearly defined as your own, and a good deal more demanding, to balance his privileges. He leads you in battle and in the ceremonies that give color and meaning to life. Your fathers and his have worked and played together for two or three hundred years. The land is alive with the memories of them. You and he *belong*.

"Well, that has to be swept away, so we can go on to a higher level. But we won't reach that level by alienating every-

161

one. We're not a conquering army; we're more like the House-holder Guard putting down a riot in some city. The opposition is part and parcel of our own society."

Lambert struck a match for him. He inhaled and finished: "On a practical plane, I might also remind you, Captain, that the federal armed forces, Fallonite and Brodskyite together, are none too large. Little more than a cadre, in fact. We're a bunch of younger sons, countrymen who failed, poor citymen, adventurers, people who look to their regiment for that sense of wholeness they've grown up to expect and can't find in civilian life."

"You're too deep for me, sir, I'm afraid," Lambert said.

"Never mind," Danielis sighed. "Just bear in mind, there are a good many more fighting men outside the opposing armies than in. If the bossmen could establish a unified command, that'd be the end of the Fallon government. Luckily, there's too much provincial pride and too much geography between them for this to happen—unless we outrage them beyond endurance. What we want the ordinary freeholder, and even the ordinary bossman, to think, is: 'Well, those Fallonites aren't such bad guys, and if I keep on the right side of them I don't stand to lose much, and should even be able to gain something at the expense of those who fight them to a finish.' You see?"

"Y-yes. I guess so."

"You're a smart fellow, Lambert. You don't have to beat information out of prisoners. Trick it out."

"I'll try, sir."

"Good." Danielis glanced at the watch that had been given him as per tradition, together with a sidearm, when he was first commissioned. (Such items were much too expensive for the common man. They had not been so in the age of mass production; and perhaps in the coming age—) "I have to go. See you around."

He left the tent feeling somewhat more cheerful than before. *No doubt I am a natural-born preacher*, he admitted, *and I never could quite join in the horseplay at mess, and a lot of jokes go completely by me; but if I can get even a few ideas across where they count, that's pleasure enough.* A strain of music came to him, some men and a banjo under a tree, and he found himself whistling along. It was good that this much morale remained, after Maricopa and a northward march whose purpose had not been divulged to anybody.

The conference tent was big enough to be called a pavilion. Two sentries stood at the entrance. Danielis was nearly the last to arrive, and found himself at the end of the table, opposite Brigadier General Perez. Smoke hazed the air and there was a muted buzz of conversation, but faces were taut.

When the blue-robed figure with a Yang and Yin on the breast entered, silence fell like a curtain. Danielis was astonished to recognize Philosopher Woodworth. He'd last seen the man in Los Angeles, and assumed he would stay at the Esper center there. Must have come here by special conveyance, under special orders. . . .

Perez introduced him. Both remained standing, under the eyes of the officers. "I have some important news for you, gentlemen," Perez said most quietly. "You may consider it an honor to be here. It means that in my judgment you can be trusted, first, to keep absolute silence about what you are going to hear, and second, to execute a vital operation of extreme difficulty." Danielis was made shockingly aware that several men were not present whose rank indicated they should be.

"I repeat," Perez said, "any breach of secrecy and the whole plan is ruined. In that case, the war will drag on for months or years. You know how bad our position is. You also know it will grow still worse as our stocks of those supplies the enemy now denies us are consumed. We could even be beaten. I'm not defeatist to say that, only realistic. We could lose the war.

"On the other hand, if this new scheme pans out, we may break the enemy's back this very month."

He paused to let that sink in before continuing:

"The plan was worked out by GHQ in conjunction with

163

Esper Central in San Francisco some weeks ago. It's the reason we are headed north—" He let the gasp subside that ran through the stifling air. "Yes, you know that the Esper Order is neutral in political disputes. But you also know that it defends itself when attacked. And you probably know that an attack was made on it by the rebels. They seized the Napa Valley settlement and have been spreading malicious rumors about the Order since then. Would you like to comment on that, Philosopher Woodworth?"

The man in blue nodded and said coolly: "We've our own ways of findin' out things—intelligence service, you might say —so I can give y'all a report of the facts. St. Helena was assaulted at a time when most of its adepts were away, helpin' a new community get started out in Montana." *How did they travel so fast?* Danielis wondered. *Teleport, or what?* "I don't know, myself, if the enemy knew about that or were just lucky. Anyhow, when the two or three adepts that were left came and warned them off, fightin' broke out and the adepts were killed before they could act." He smiled. "We don't claim to be immortal, except the way every livin' thing is immortal. Nor infallible, either. So now St. Helena's occupied. We don't figure to take any immediate steps about that, because a lot of people in the community might get hurt.

"As for the yarns the enemy command's been handin' out, well, I reckon I'd do the same, if I had a chance like that. Everybody knows an adept can do things that nobody else can. Troops that realize they've done wrong to the Order are goin' to be scared of supernatural revenge. You're educated men here, and know there's nothin' supernatural involved, just a way to use the powers latent in most of us. You also know the Order doesn't believe in revenge. But the ordinary foot soldier doesn't think your way. His officers have got to restore his spirit somehow. So they fake some equipment and tell him that's what the adepts were really usin'—an advanced technology, sure, but only a set of machines that can be put out of action if you're brave, same as any other machine. That's what happened.

"Still, it is a threat to the Order; and we can't let an attack on our people go unpunished, either. So Esper Central has decided to help out your side. The sooner this war's over, the better for everybody."

A sigh gusted around the table, and a few exultant oaths. The hair stirred on Danielis' neck. Perez lifted a hand.

"Not too fast, please," the general said. "The adepts are not going to go around blasting your opponents for you. It was one hell of a tough decision for them to do as much as they agreed to. I, uh, understand that the, uh, personal development of every Esper will be set back many years by this much violence. They're making a big sacrifice.

"By their charter, they can use psionics to defend an establishment against attack. Okay . . . an assault on San Francisco will be construed as one on Central, their world headquarters."

The realization of what was to come was blinding to Danielis. He scarcely heard Perez' carefully dry continuation:

"Let's review the strategic picture. By now the enemy holds more than half of California, all of Oregon and Idaho, and a good deal of Washington. We, this army, we're using the last land access to San Francisco that we've got. The enemy hasn't tried to pinch that off yet, because the troops we pulled out of the north—those that aren't in the field at present—make a strong city garrison that'd sally out. He's collecting too much profit elsewhere to accept the cost.

"Nor can he invest the city with any hope of success. We still hold Puget Sound and the southern California ports. Our ships bring in ample food and munitions. His own sea power is much inferior to ours: chiefly schooners donated by coastal bossmen, operating out of Portland. He might overwhelm an occasional convoy, but he hasn't tried that so far because it isn't worth his trouble; there would be others, more heavily escorted. And of course he can't enter the Bay, with artillery and rocket emplacements on both sides of the Golden Gate. No, about all he can do is maintain some water communication with Hawaii and Alaska.

"Nevertheless, his ultimate object is San Francisco. It has

to be—the seat of government and industry, the heart of the nation.

"Well, then, here's the plan. Our army is to engage the Sierra Command and its militia auxiliaries again, striking out of San Jose. That's a perfectly logical maneuver. Successful, it would cut his California forces in two. We know, in fact, that he is already concentrating men in anticipation of precisely such an attempt.

"We aren't going to succeed. We'll give him a good stiff battle and be thrown back. That's the hardest part: to feign a serious defeat, even convincing our own troops, and still maintain good order. We'll have a lot of details to thresh out about that.

"We'll retreat northward, up the Peninsula toward Frisco. The enemy is bound to pursue. It will look like a God-given chance to destroy us and get to the city walls.

"When he is well into the Peninsula, with the ocean on his left and the Bay on his right, we will outflank him and attack from the rear. The Esper adepts will be there to help. Suddenly he'll be caught, between us and the capital's land defenses. What the adepts don't wipe out, we will. Nothing will remain of the Sierra Command but a few garrisons. The rest of the war will be a mopping-up operation.

"It's a brilliant piece of strategy. Like all such, it's damn difficult to execute. Are you prepared to do the job?"

Danielis didn't raise his voice with the others. He was thinking too hard of Laura.

Northward and to the right there was some fighting. Cannon spoke occasionally, or a drumfire of rifles; smoke lay thin over the grass and the wind-gnarled live oaks which covered those hills. But down along the seacoast was only surf, blowing air, a hiss of sand across the dunes.

Mackenzie rode on the beach, where the footing was easiest and the view widest. Most of his regiment were inland. But that was a wilderness: rough ground, woods, the snags of ancient homes, making travel slow and hard. Once this area

166

had been densely peopled, but the firestorm after the Hellbomb scrubbed it clean and today's reduced population could not make a go on such infertile soil. There didn't even seem to be any foemen near this left wing of the army.

The Rolling Stones had certainly not been given it for that reason. They could have borne the brunt at the center as well as those outfits which actually were there, driving the enemy back toward San Francisco. They had been blooded often enough in this war, when they operated out of Calistoga to help expel the Fallonites from northern California. So thoroughly had that job been done that now only a skeleton force need remain in charge. Nearly the whole Sierra Command had gathered at Modesto, met the northward-moving opposition army that struck at them out of San Jose, and sent it in a shooting retreat. Another day or so, and the white city should appear before their eyes.

And there the enemy will be sure to make a stand, Mackenzie thought, *with the garrison to reinforce him. And his positions will have to be shelled; maybe we'll have to take the place street by street. Laura, kid, will you be alive at the end?*

Of course, maybe it won't happen that way. Maybe my scheme'll work and we'll win easy— What a horrible word "maybe" is! He slapped his hands together with a pistol sound.

Speyer threw him a glance. The major's people were safe; he'd even been able to visit them at Mount Lassen, after the northern campaign was over. "Rough," he said.

"Rough on everybody," Mackenzie said with a thick anger. "This is a filthy war."

Speyer shrugged. "No different from most, except that this time Pacificans are on the receiving as well as the giving end."

"You know damn well I never liked the business, anyplace."

"What man in his right mind does?"

"When I want a sermon I'll ask for one."

"Sorry," said Speyer, and meant it.

"I'm sorry too," said Mackenzie, instantly contrite. "Nerves on edge. Damnation! I could almost wish for some action."

"Wouldn't be surprised if we got some. This whole affair smells wrong to me."

Mackenzie looked around him. On the right the horizon was bounded by hills, beyond which the low but massive San Bruno range lifted. Here and there he spied one of his own squads, afoot or ahorse. Overhead sputtered a plane. But there was plenty of concealment for a redoubt. Hell could erupt at any minute . . . though necessarily a small hell, quickly reduced by howitzer or bayonet, casualties light. (Huh! Every one of those light casualties was a man dead, with women and children to weep for him, or a man staring at the fragment of his arm, or a man with eyes and face gone in a burst of shot, and what kind of unsoldierly thoughts were these?)

Seeking comfort, Mackenzie glanced left. The ocean rolled greenish-gray, glittering far out, rising and breaking in a roar of white combers closer to land. He smelled salt and kelp. A few gulls mewed above dazzling sands. There was no sail or smoke-puff—only emptiness. The convoys from Puget Sound to San Francisco and the lean swift ships of the coastal bossmen were miles beyond the curve of the world.

Which was as it should be. Maybe things were working out okay on the high waters. One could only try, and hope. And . . . it had been his suggestion, James Mackenzie speaking at the conference General Cruikshank held between the battles of Mariposa and San Jose; the same James Mackenzie who had first proposed that the Sierra Command come down out of the mountains, and who had exposed the gigantic fraud of Esperdom, and succeeded in playing down for his men the fact that behind the fraud lay a mystery one hardly dared think about. He would endure in the chronicles, that colonel, they would sing ballads about him for half a thousand years.

Only it didn't feel that way. James Mackenzie knew he was not much more than average bright under the best of conditions, now dull-minded with weariness and terrified of his daughter's fate. For himself he was haunted by the fear of certain crippling wounds. Often he had to drink himself to sleep. He was shaved, because an officer must maintain appearances, but realized very well that if he hadn't had an orderly to do the job for him he would be as shaggy as any buck private. His uniform was faded and threadbare, his body stank and itched, his mouth yearned for tobacco but there had been some trouble in the commissariat and they were lucky to eat. His achievements amounted to patchwork jobs carried out in utter confusion, or to slogging like this and wishing only for an end to the whole mess. One day, win or lose, his body would give out on him—he could feel the machinery wearing to pieces, arthritic twinges, shortness of breath, dozing off in the middle of things—and the termination of himself would be as undignified and lonely as that of every other human slob. Hero? What an all-time laugh!

He yanked his mind back to the immediate situation. Behind him a core of the regiment accompanied the artillery along the beach, a thousand men with motorized gun carriages, caissons, mule-drawn wagons, a few trucks, one precious armored car. They were a dun mass topped with helmets, in loose formation, rifles or bows to hand. The sand deadened their footfalls, so that only the surf and the wind could be heard. But whenever the wind sank, Mackenzie caught the tune of the hex corps: a dozen leathery older men, mostly Indians, carrying the wands of power and whistling together the Song Against Witches. He took no stock in magic himself, yet when that sound came to him the skin crawled along his backbone.

Everything's in good order, he insisted. *We're doing fine.*

Then: *But Phil's right. This is a screwball business. The enemy should have fought through to a southward line of retreat, not let themselves be boxed.*

Captain Hulse galloped close. Sand spurted when he checked his horse. "Patrol report, sir."

"Well?" Mackenzie realized he had almost shouted. "Go ahead."

"Considerable activity observed about five miles northeast. Looks like a troop headed our way."

Mackenzie stiffened. "Haven't you anything more definite than that?"

"Not so far, with the ground so broken."

"Get some aerial reconnaissance there, for Pete's sake!"

"Yes, sir. I'll throw out more scouts, too."

"Carry on here, Phil." Mackenzie headed toward the radio truck. He carried a minicom in his saddlebag, of course, but San Francisco had been continuously jamming on all bands and you needed a powerful set to punch a signal even a few miles. Patrols must communicate by messenger.

He noticed that the firing inland had slacked off. There were decent roads in the interior Peninsula a ways further north, where some resettlement had taken place. The enemy, still in possession of that area, could use them to effect rapid movements.

If they withdrew their center and hit our flanks, where we're weakest—

A voice from field HQ, barely audible through the squeals and buzzes, took his report and gave back what had been seen elsewhere. Large maneuvers right and left, yes, it did seem as if the Fallonites were going to try a breakthrough. Could be a feint, though. The main body of the Sierrans must remain where it was until the situation became clearer. The Rolling Stones must hold out a while on their own.

"Will do." Mackenzie returned to the head of his columns. Speyer nodded grimly at the word.

"Better get prepared, hadn't we?"

"Uh-huh." Mackenzie lost himself in a welter of commands, as officer after officer rode to him. The outlying sections were to be pulled in. The beach was to be defended, with the high ground immediately above.

Men scurried, horses neighed, guns trundled about. The scout plane returned, flying low enough to get a transmission through: yes, definitely an attack on the way; hard to tell how big a force, through the damned tree cover and down in the damned arroyos, but it might well be at brigade strength.

Mackenzie established himself on a hilltop with his staff

and runners. A line of artillery stretched beneath him, across the strand. Cavalry waited behind them, lances agleam, an infantry company for support. Otherwise the foot soldiers had faded into the landscape. The sea boomed its own cannonade, and gulls began to gather as if they knew there would be meat before long.

"Think we can hold them?" Speyer asked.

"Sure," Mackenzie said. "If they come down the beach, we'll enfilade them, as well as shooting up their front. If they come higher, well, that's a textbook example of defensible terrain. 'Course, if another troop punches through the lines further inland, we'll be cut off, but that isn't our worry right now."

"They must hope to get around our army and attack our rear."

"Guess so. Not too smart of them, though. We can approach Frisco just as easily fighting backwards as forwards."

"Unless the city garrison makes a sally."

"Even then. Total numerical strengths are about equal, and we've got more ammo and alky. Also a lot of bossman militia for auxiliaries, who're used to disorganized warfare in hilly ground."

"If we do whip them—" Speyer shut his lips together.

"Go on," Mackenzie said.

"Nothing."

"The hell it is. You were about to remind me of the next step: how do we take the city without too high a cost to both sides? Well, I happen to know we've got a hole card to play there, which might help."

Speyer turned pitying eyes away from Mackenzie. Silence fell on the hilltop.

It was an unconscionably long time before the enemy came in view, first a few outriders far down the dunes, then the body of him, pouring from the ridges and gullies and woods. Reports flickered about Mackenzie—a powerful force, nearly twice as big as ours, but with little artillery; by now badly short of fuel, they must depend far more than we on animals to move their equipment. They were evidently going to charge, accept losses

171

in order to get sabers and bayonets among the Rolling Stones' cannon. Mackenzie issued his directions accordingly.

The hostiles formed up, a mile or so distant. Through his field glasses Mackenzie recognized them, red sashes of the Madera Horse, green and gold pennon of the Dagos, fluttering in the iodine wind. He'd campaigned with both outfits in the past. It was treacherous to remember that Ives favored a blunt wedge formation and use the fact against him. . . . One enemy armored car and some fieldpieces, light horse-drawn ones, gleamed wickedly in the sunlight.

Bugles blew shrill. The Fallonite cavalry laid lance in rest and started trotting. They gathered speed as they went, a canter, a gallop, until the earth trembled with them. Then their infantry got going, flanked by its guns. The car rolled along between the first and second line of foot. Oddly, it had no rocket launcher on top or repeater barrels thrust from the fire slits. Those were good troops, Mackenzie thought, advancing in close order with that ripple down the ranks which bespoke veterans. He hated what must happen.

His defence waited immobile on the sand. Fire crackled from the hillsides where mortar squads and riflemen crouched. A rider toppled, a dogface clutched his belly and went to his knees, their companions behind moved forward to close the lines again. Mackenzie looked to his howitzers. Men stood tensed at sights and lanyards. Let the foe get well in range— There! Yamaguchi, mounted just rearward of the gunners, drew his saber and flashed the blade downward. Cannon bellowed. Fire spurted through smoke, sand gouted up, shrapnel sleeted over the charging force. At once the gun crews fell into the rhythm of reloading, relaying, refiring, the steady three rounds per minute which conserved barrels and broke armies. Horses screamed in their own tangled red guts. But not many had been hit. The Madera cavalry continued in full gallop. Their lead was so close now that Mackenzie's glasses picked out a face, red, freckled, a ranch boy turned trooper, his mouth stretched out of shape as he yelled.

The archers behind the defending cannon let go. Arrows

whistled skyward, flight after flight, curved past the gulls and down again. Flame and smoke ran ragged in the wiry hill grass, out of the ragged-leaved live oak copses. Men pitched to the sand, many still hideously astir, like insects that had been stepped on. The fieldpieces on the enemy left flank halted, swiveled about, and spat return fire. Futile . . . but God, their officer had courage! Mackenzie saw the advancing lines waver. An attack by his own horse and foot, down the beach, ought to crumple them. "Get ready to move," he said into his minicom. He saw his men poise. The cannon belched anew.

The oncoming armored car slowed to a halt. Something within it chattered, loud enough to hear through the explosions.

A blue-white sheet ran over the nearest hill. Mackenzie shut half-blinded eyes. When he opened them again, he saw a grass fire through the crazy patterns of after-image. A Rolling Stone burst from cover, howling, his clothes ablaze. The man hit the sand and rolled over. That part of the beach lifted in one monster wave, crested twenty feet high, and smashed across the hill. The burning soldier vanished in the avalanche that buried his comrades.

"*Psi blast!*" someone screamed, thin and horrible, through chaos and ground-shudder. "The Espers—"

Unbelievably, a bugle sounded and the Sierran cavalry lunged forward. Past their own guns, on against the scattering opposition . . . and horses and riders rose into the air, tumbled in a giant's invisible whirligig, crashed bone-breakingly to earth again. The second rank of lancers broke. Mounts reared, pawed the air, wheeled and fled in every direction.

A terrible deep hum filled the sky. Mackenzie saw the world as if through a haze, as if his brain were being dashed back and forth between the walls of his skull. Another glare ran across the hills, higher this time, burning men alive.

"They'll wipe us out," Speyer called, a dim voice that rose and fell on the air tides. "They'll re-form as we stampede—"

"No!" Mackenzie shouted. "The adepts must be in that car. Come on!"

Most of his horse had recoiled on their own artillery, one squealing, trampling wreck. The infantry stood rigid, but about to bolt. A glance thrown to his right showed Mackenzie how the enemy themselves were in confusion, this had been a terrifying surprise to them too, but as soon as they got over the shock they'd advance and there'd be nothing left to stop them. . . . It was as if another man spurred his mount. The animal fought, foam-flecked with panic. He slugged its head around, brutally, and dug in spurs. They rushed down the hill toward the guns.

He needed all his strength to halt the gelding before the cannon mouths. A man slumped dead by his piece, though there was no mark on him. Mackenzie jumped to the ground. His steed bolted.

He hadn't time to worry about that. Where was help? "Come here!" His yell was lost in the riot. But suddenly another man was beside him, Speyer, snatching up a shell and slamming it into the breach. Mackenzie squinted through the telescope, took a bearing by guess and feel. He could see the Esper car where it squatted among dead and hurt. At this distance it looked too small to have blackened acres.

Speyer helped him lay the howitzer. He jerked the lanyard. The gun roared and sprang. The shell burst a few yards short of target, sand spurted and metal fragments whined.

Speyer had the next one loaded. Mackenzie aimed and fired. Overshot this time, but not by much. The car rocked. Concussion might have hurt the Espers inside; at least, the psi blasts had stopped. But it was necessary to strike before the foe got organized again.

He ran toward his own regimental car. The door gaped, the crew had fled. He threw himself into the driver's seat. Speyer clanged the door shut and stuck his face in the hood of the rocket-launcher periscope. Mackenzie raced the machine forward. The banner on its rooftop snapped in the wind.

Speyer aimed the launcher and pressed the firing button. The missile burned across intervening yards and exploded. The other car lurched on its wheels. A hole opened in its side.

If the boys will only rally and advance— Well, if they don't, I'm done for anyway. Mackenzie squealed to a stop, flung open the door and leaped out. Curled, blackened metal framed his entry. He wriggled through, into murk and stenches.

Two Espers lay there. The driver was dead, a chunk of steel through his breast. The other one, the adept, whimpered among his unhuman instruments. His face was hidden by blood. Mackenzie pitched the corpse on its side and pulled off the robe. He snatched a curving tube of metal and tumbled back out.

Speyer was still in the undamaged car, firing repeaters at those hostiles who ventured near. Mackenzie jumped onto the ladder of the disabled machine, climbed to its roof and stood erect. He waved the blue robe in one hand and the weapon he did not understand in the other. "Come on, you sons!" he shouted, tiny against the sea wind. "We've knocked 'em out for you! Want your breakfast in bed too?"

One bullet buzzed past his ear. Nothing else. Most of the enemy, horse and foot, stayed frozen. In that immense stillness he could not tell if he heard surf or the blood in his own veins.

Then a bugle called. The hex corps whistled triumphantly; their tomtoms thuttered. A ragged line of his infantry began to move toward him. More followed. The cavalry joined them, man by man and unit by unit, on their flanks. Soldiers ran down the smoking hillsides.

Mackenzie sprang to sand again and into his car. "Let's get back," he told Speyer. "We got a battle to finish."

"Shut up!" Tom Danielis said.

Philosopher Woodworth stared at him. Fog swirled and dripped in the forest, hiding the land and the brigade, gray nothingness through which came a muffled noise of men and horses and wheels, an isolated and infinitely weary sound. The air was cold, and clothing hung heavy on the skin.

"Sir," protested Major Lescarbault. The eyes were wide and shocked in his gaunted face.

"I dare tell a ranking Esper to stop quacking about a subject of which he's totally ignorant?" Danielis answered. "Well, it's past time that somebody did."

Woodworth recovered his poise. "All I said, son, was that we should consolidate our adepts and strike the Brodskyite center," he reproved. "What's wrong with that?"

Danielis clenched his fists. "Nothing," he said, "except it invites a worse disaster than you've brought on us yet."

"A setback or two," Lescarbault argued. "They did rout us on the west, but we turned their flank here by the Bay."

"With the net result that their main body pivoted, attacked, and split us in half," Danielis snapped. "The Espers have been scant use since then . . . now the rebels know they need vehicles to transport their weapons, and can be killed. Artillery zeroes in on their positions, or bands of woodsmen hit and run, leaving them dead, or the enemy simply goes around any spot where they're known to be. We haven't got enough adepts!"

"That's why I proposed gettin' them in one group, too big to withstand," Woodworth said.

"And too cumbersome to be of any value," Danielis replied. He felt more than a little sickened, knowing how the Order had cheated him his whole life; yes, he thought, that was the real bitterness, not the fact that the adepts had failed to defeat the rebels—by failing, essentially, to break their spirit—but the fact that the adepts were only someone else's cat's paws and every gentle, earnest soul in every Esper community was only someone's dupe.

Wildly he wanted to return to Laura—there'd been no chance thus far to see her—Laura and the kid, the last honest reality this fog-world had left him. He mastered himself and went on more evenly:

"The adepts, what few of them survive, will of course be helpful in defending San Francisco. An army free to move around in the field can deal with them, one way or another, but your . . . your weapons can repel an assault on the city walls. So that's where I'm going to take them."

Probably the best he could do. There was no word from the northern half of the loyalist army. Doubtless they'd withdrawn

176

to the capital, suffering heavy losses en route. Radio jamming continued, hampering friendly and hostile communications alike. He had to take action, either retreat southward or fight his way through to the city. The latter course seemed wisest. He didn't believe that Laura had much to do with his choice.

"I'm no adept myself," Woodworth said. "I can't call them mind to mind."

"You mean you can't use their equivalent of radio," Danielis said brutally. "Well, you've got an adept in attendance. Have him pass the word."

Woodworth flinched. "I hope," he said, "I hope you understand this came as a surprise to me too."

"Oh, yes, certainly, Philosopher," Lescarbault said unbidden.

Woodworth swallowed. "I still hold with the Way and the Order," he said harshly. "There's nothin' else I can do. Is there? The Grand Seeker has promised a full explanation when this is over." He shook his head. "Okay, son, I'll do what I can."

A certain compassion touched Danielis as the blue robe disappeared into the fog. He rapped his orders the more severely.

Slowly his command got going. He was with the Second Brigade; the rest were strewn over the Peninsula in the fragments into which the rebels had knocked them. He hoped the equally scattered adepts, joining him on his march through the San Bruno range, would guide some of those united to him. But most, wandering, demoralized, were sure to surrender to the first rebels they came upon.

He rode near the front, on a muddy road that snaked over the highlands. His helmet was a monstrous weight. The horse stumbled beneath him, exhausted by—how many days?—of march, countermarch, battle, skirmish, thin rations or none, heat and cold and fear, in an empty land. Poor beast, he'd see that it got proper treatment when they reached the city. That all those poor beasts behind him did, after trudging and fighting and trudging again until their eyes were filmed with fatigue.

There'll be chance enough for rest in San Francisco. We're impregnable there, walls and cannon and the Esper machines to landward, the sea that feeds us at our backs. We can recover our strength, regroup our forces, bring fresh troops down from Washington and up from the south by water. The war isn't decided yet . . . God help us.

I wonder if it will ever be.

And then, will Jimbo Mackenzie come to see us, sit by the fire and swap yarns about what we did? Or talk about something else, anything else? If not, that's too high a price for victory.

Maybe not too high a price for what we've learned, though. Strangers on this planet . . . what else could have forged those weapons? The adepts will talk if I myself have to torture them till they do. But Danielis remembered tales muttered in the fisher huts of his boyhood, after dark, when ghosts walked in old men's minds. Before the holocaust there had been legends about the stars, and the legends lived on. He didn't know if he would be able to look again at the night sky without a shiver.

This damned fog—

Hoofs thudded. Danielis half drew his sidearm. But the rider was a scout of his own, who raised a drenched sleeve in salute. "Colonel, an enemy force about ten miles ahead by road. Big."

So we'll have to fight now. "Do they seem aware of us?"

"No, sir. They're proceeding east along the ridge there."

"Probably figure to occupy the Candlestick Park ruins," Danielis murmured. His body was too tired for excitement. "Good stronghold, that. Very well, Corporal." He turned to Lescarbault and issued instructions.

The brigade formed itself in the formlessness. Patrols went out. Information began to flow back, and Danielis sketched a plan that ought to work. He didn't want to try for a decisive engagement, only brush the enemy aside and discourage them from pursuit. His men must be spared, as many as possible, for the city defense and the eventual counteroffensive.

Lescarbault came back. "Sir! The radio jamming's ended!"

"What?" Danielis blinked, not quite comprehending.

"Yes, sir. I've been using a minicom"—Lescarbault lifted the wrist on which his tiny transceiver was strapped—"for very short-range work, passing the battalion commanders their orders. The interference stopped a couple of minutes ago. Clear as daylight."

Danielis pulled the wrist toward his own mouth. "Hello, hello, radio wagon, this is the C.O. You read me?"

"Yes, sir," said the voice.

"They turned off the jammer in the city for a reason. Get me the open military band."

"Yes, sir." Pause, while men mumbled and water runneled unseen in the arroyos. A wraith smoked past Danielis' eyes. Drops coursed off his helmet and down his collar. The horse's mane hung sodden.

Like the scream of an insect:

"—here at once! Every unit in the field, get to San Francisco at once! We're under attack by sea!"

Danielis let go Lescarbault's arm. He stared into emptiness while the voice wailed on and forever on.

"—bombarding Potrero Point. Decks jammed with troops. They must figure to make a landing there—"

Danielis's mind raced ahead of the words. It was as if Esp were no lie, as if he scanned the beloved city himself and felt her wounds in his own flesh. There was no fog around the Gate, of course, or so detailed a description could not have been given. Well, probably some streamers of it rolled in under the rusted remnants of the bridge, themselves like snowbanks against blue-green water and brilliant sky. But most of the Bay stood open to the sun. On the opposite shore lifted the Eastbay hills, green with gardens and agleam with villas; and Marin shouldered heavenward across the strait, looking to the roofs and walls and heights that were San Francisco. The convoy had gone between the coast defenses that could have smashed it, an unusually large convoy and not on time: but still the familiar big-bellied hulls, white sails, occasional fuming stacks, that kept the city fed. There had been an explanation

179

about trouble with commerce raiders; and the fleet was passed on into the Bay, where San Francisco had no walls. Then the gun covers were taken off and the holds vomited armed men.

Yes, they did seize a convoy, those piratical schooners. Used radio jamming of their own; together with ours, that choked off any cry of warning. They threw our supplies overboard and embarked the bossman militia. Some spy or traitor gave them the recognition signals. Now the capital lies open to them, her garrison stripped, hardly an adept left in Esper Central, the Sierrans thrusting against her southern gates, and Laura without me.

"We're coming!" Danielis yelled. His brigade groaned into speed behind him. They struck with a desperate ferocity that carried them deep into enemy positions and then stranded them in separated groups. It became knife and saber in the fog. But Danielis, because he led the charge, had already taken a grenade on his breast.

East and south, in the harbor district and at the wreck of the Peninsula wall, there was still some fighting. As he rode higher, Mackenzie saw how those parts were dimmed by smoke, which the wind scattered to show rubble that had been houses. The sound of firing drifted to him. But otherwise the city shone untouched, roofs and white walls in a web of streets, church spires raking the sky like masts, Federal House on Nob Hill and the Watchtower on Telegraph Hill as he remembered them from childhood visits. The Bay glittered insolently beautiful.

But he had no time for admiring the view, nor for wondering where Laura huddled. The attack on Twin Peaks must be swift, for surely Esper Central would defend itself.

On the avenue climbing the opposite side of those great humps, Speyer led half the Rolling Stones. (Yamaguchi lay dead on a pockmarked beach.) Mackenzie himself was taking this side. Horses clopped along Portola, between blankly shuttered mansions; guns trundled and creaked, boots knocked on pavement, moccasins slithered, weapons rattled, men breathed

180

heavily and the hex corps whistled against unknown demons. But silence overwhelmed the noise, echoes trapped it and let it die. Mackenzie recollected nightmares when he fled down a corridor which had no end. *Even if they don't cut loose at us,* he thought bleakly, *we've got to seize their place before our nerve gives out.*

Twin Peaks Boulevard turned off Portola and wound steeply to the right. The houses ended; wild grasses alone covered the quasi-sacred hills, up to the tops where stood the buildings forbidden to all but adepts. Those two soaring, iridescent, fountainlike skyscrapers had been raised by night, within a matter of weeks. Something like a moan stirred at Mackenzie's back.

"Buglar, sound the advance. On the double!"

A child's jeering, the notes lifted and were lost. Sweat stung Mackenzie's eyes. If he failed and was killed, that didn't matter too much . . . after everything which had happened . . . but the regiment, the regiment—

Flame shot across the street, the color of hell. There went a hiss and a roar. The pavement lay trenched, molten, smoking and reeking. Mackenzie wrestled his horse to a standstill. A *warning only. But if they had enough adepts to handle us, would they bother trying to scare us off?* "Artillery, open fire!"

The field guns bellowed together, not only howitzers but motorized 75s taken along from Alemany Gate's emplacements. Shells went overhead with a locomotive sound. They burst on the walls above and the racket thundered back down the wind.

Mackenzie tensed himself for an Esper blast, but none came. Had they knocked out the final defensive post in their own first barrage? Smoke cleared from the heights and he saw that the colors which played in the tower were dead and that wounds gaped across loveliness, showing unbelievably thin framework. It was like seeing the bones of a woman murdered by his hand.

Quick, though! He issued a string of commands and led the horse and foot on. The battery stayed where it was, firing and firing with hysterical fury. The dry brown grass started to burn, as red-hot fragments scattered across the slope. Through mushroom bursts, Mackenzie saw the building crumble. Whole sheets of facing broke and fell to earth. The skeleton vibrated, took a direct hit and sang in mental agony, slumped and twisted apart.

What was that which stood within?

There were no separate rooms, no floors, nothing but girders, enigmatic machines, here and there a globe still aglow like a minor sun. The structure had enclosed something nearly as tall as itself, a finned and shining column, almost like a rocket shell but impossibly huge and fair.

Their spaceship, Mackenzie thought in the clamor. *Yes, of course, the ancients had begun making spaceships, and we always figured we would again someday. This, thought—!*

The archers lifted a tribal screech. The riflemen and cavalry took it up, crazy, jubilant, the howl of a beast of prey. By Satan, we've whipped the stars themselves! As they burst onto the hillcrest, the shelling stopped, and their yells overrode the wind. Smoke was acrid as blood smell in their nostrils.

A few dead blue-robes could be seen in the debris. Some half-dozen survivors milled toward the ship. A bowman let fly. His arrow glanced off the landing gear but brought the Espers to a halt. Troopers poured over the shards to capture them.

Mackenzie reined in. Something that was not human lay crushed near a machine. Its blood was deep violet color. *When the people have seen this, that's the end of the Order.* He felt no triumph. At St. Helena he had come to appreciate how fundamentally good the believers were.

But this was no moment for regret, or for wondering how harsh the future would be with man taken entirely off the leash. The building on the other peak was still intact. He had to consolidate his position here, then help Phil if need be.

However, the minicom said, "Come on and join me, Jimbo. The fracas is over," before he had completed his task. As he rode alone toward Speyer's place, he saw a Pacific States flag flutter up the mast on that skyscraper's top.

Guards stood awed and nervous at the portal. Mackenzie dismounted and walked inside. The entry chamber was a soaring, shimmering fantasy of colors and arches, through which men moved troll-like. A corporal led him down a hall. Evidently this building had been used for quarters, offices, storage, and less understandable purposes. . . . There was a room whose door had been blown down with dynamite. The fluid abstract murals were stilled, scarred, and sooted. Four ragged troopers pointed guns at the two beings whom Speyer was questioning.

One slumped at something that might answer to a desk. The avian face was buried in seven-fingered hands and the rudimentary wings quivered with sobs. *Are they able to cry, then?* Mackenzie thought, astonished, and had a sudden wish to take the being in his arms and offer what comfort he was able.

The other one stood erect in a robe of woven metal. Great topaz eyes met Speyer's from a seven-foot height, and the voice turned accented English into music.

"—a G-type star some fifty light-years hence. It is barely visible to the naked eye, though not in this hemisphere."

The major's fleshless, bristly countenance jutted forward as if to peck. "When do you expect reinforcements?"

"There will be no other ship for almost a century, and it will only bring personnel. We are isolated by space and time; few can come to work here, to seek to build a bridge of minds across that gulf—"

"Yeah," Speyer nodded prosaically. "The light-speed limit. I thought so. If you're telling the truth."

The being shuddered. "Nothing is left for us but to speak truth, and pray that you will understand and help. Revenge, conquest, any form of mass violence is impossible when so much space and time lies between. Our labor has been done in the mind and heart. It is not too late, even now. The most crucial facts can still be kept hidden—oh, listen to me, for the sake of your unborn!"

Speyer nodded to Mackenzie. "Everything okay?" he said. "We got us a full bag here. About twenty left alive, this fellow the bossman. Seems like they're the only ones on Earth."

"We guessed there couldn't be many," the colonel said. His tone and his feelings were alike ashen. "When we talked it over, you and me, and tried to figure what our clues meant. They'd have to be few, or they'd've operate more openly."

"Listen, listen," the being pleaded. "We came in love. Our dream was to lead you—to make you lead yourselves—toward peace, fulfilment. . . . Oh, yes, we would also gain, gain yet another race with whom we could someday converse as brothers. But there are many races in the universe. It was chiefly for your own tortured sakes that we wished to guide your future."

"That controlled history notion isn't original with you," Speyer grunted. "We've invented it for ourselves now and then on Earth. The last time it led to the Hellbombs. No, thanks!"

"But we *know!* The Great Science predicts with absolute certainty—"

"Predicted this?" Speyer waved a hand at the blackened room.

"There are fluctuations. We are too few to control so many savages in every detail. But do you not wish an end to war, to all your ancient sufferings? I offer you that for your help to-day."

"You succeeded in starting a pretty nasty war yourselves," Speyer said.

The being twisted its fingers together. "That was an error. The plan remains, the only way to lead your people toward peace. I, who have traveled between suns, will get down before your boots and beg you—"

"Stay put!" Speyer flung back. "If you'd come openly, like honest folk, you'd have found some to listen to you. Maybe enough, even. But no, your do-gooding had to be subtle and crafty. You knew what was right for us. We weren't entitled to any say in the matter. God in heaven, I've never heard anything so arrogant!"

The being lifted its head. "Do you tell children the whole truth?"

"As much as they're ready for."

"Your child-culture is not ready to hear these truths."

"Who qualified you to call us children—besides yourselves?"

"How do you know you are adult?"

"By trying adult jobs and finding out if I can handle them. Sure, we make some ghastly blunders, we humans. But they're our own. And we learn from them. You're the ones who won't learn, you and that damned psychological science you were bragging about, that wants to fit every living mind into the one frame it can understand.

"You wanted to re-establish the centralized state, didn't you? Did you ever stop to think that maybe feudalism is what suits man? Some one place to call our own, and belong to, and be part of; a community with traditions and honor; a chance for the individual to make decisions that count; a bulwark for liberty against the central overlords, who'll always want more and more power; a thousand different ways to live. We've always built supercountries, here on Earth, and we've always knocked them apart again. I think maybe the whole idea is wrong. And maybe this time we'll try something better. Why not a world of little states, too well rooted to dissolve in a nation, too small to do much harm—slowly rising above petty jealousies and spite, but keeping their identities—a thousand separate approaches to our problems. Maybe then we can solve a few of them . . . for ourselves!"

"You will never do so," the being said. "You will be torn in pieces all over again."

"That's what you think. I think otherwise. But whichever is right—and I bet this is too big a universe for either of us to predict—we'll have made a free choice on Earth. I'd rather be dead than domesticated.

"The people are going to learn about you as soon as Judge Brodsky's been reinstated. No, sooner. The regiment will hear today, the city tomorrow, just to make sure no one gets ideas about suppressing the truth again. By the time your next spaceship comes, we'll be ready for it: in our own way, whatever that is."

The being drew a fold of robe about its head. Speyer turned to Mackenzie. His face was wet. "Anything . . . you want to say . . . Jimbo?"

"No," Mackenzie mumbled. "Can't think of anything. Let's get our command organized here. I don't expect we'll have to fight any more, though. It seems to be about ended down there."

"Sure." Speyer drew an uneven breath. "The enemy troops elsewhere are bound to capitulate. They've got nothing left to fight for. We can start patching up pretty soon."

There was a house with a patio whose wall was covered by roses. The street outside had not yet come back to life, so that silence dwelt here under the yellow sunset. A maidservant showed Mackenzie through the back door and departed. He walked toward Laura, who sat on a bench beneath a willow. She watched him approach but did not rise. One hand rested on a cradle.

He stopped and knew not what to say. How thin she was.

Presently she told him, so low he could scarcely hear: "Tom's dead."

"Oh, no." Darkness came and went before his eyes.

"I learned the day before yesterday, when a few of his men straggled home. He was killed in the San Bruno."

Mackenzie did not dare join her, but his legs would not up-bear him. He sat down on the flagstones and saw curious patterns in their arrangement. There was nothing else to look at.

Her voice ran on above him, toneless: "Was it worth it? Not only Tom, but so many others, killed for a point of politics?"

"More than that was at stake," he said.

"Yes, I heard on the radio. I still can't understand how it was worth it. I've tried very hard, but I can't."

He had no strength left to defend himself. "Maybe you're right, duck. I wouldn't know."

"I'm not sorry for myself," she said. "I still have Jimmy. But Tom was cheated out of so much."

186

He realized all at once that there was a baby, and he ought to take his grandchild to him and think thoughts about life going on into the future. But he was too empty.

"Tom wanted him named after you," she said.

Did you, Laura? he wondered. Aloud: "What are you going to do now?"

"I'll find something."

He made himself glance at her. The sunset burned on the willow leaves above and on her face, which was now turned toward the infant he could not see. "Come back to Nakamura," he said.

"No. Anywhere else."

"You always loved the mountains," he groped. "We—"

"No." She met his eyes. "It isn't you, Dad. Never you. But Jimmy is not going to grow up a soldier." She hesitated. "I'm sure some of the Espers will keep going, on a new basis, but with the same goals. I think we should join them. He ought to believe in something different from what killed his father, and work for it to become real. Don't you agree?"

Mackenzie climbed to his feet against Earth's hard pull. "I don't know," he said. "Never was a thinker. . . . Can I see him?"

"Oh, Dad—"

He went over and looked down at the small sleeping form. "If you marry again," he said, "and have a daughter, would you call her for her mother?" He saw Laura's head bend downward and her hands clench. Quickly he said, "I'll go now. I'd like to visit you some more, tomorrow or sometime, if you'll have me."

Then she came to his arms and wept. He stroked her hair and murmured, as he had done when she was a child. "You do want to return to the mountains, don't you? They're your country too, your people, where you belong."

"Y-you'll never know how much I want to."

"Then why not?" he cried.

His daughter straightened herself. "I can't," she said. "Your war is ended. Mine has just begun."

Because he had trained that will, he could only say, "I hope you win it."

"Perhaps in a thousand years—" She could not continue.

Night had fallen when he left her. Power was still out in the city, so the street lamps were dark and the stars stood forth above all roofs. The squad that waited to accompany their colonel to barracks looked wolfish by lantern light. They saluted him and rode at his back, rifles ready for trouble; but there was only the iron sound of horseshoes.

Gordon Dickson is, in some ways, a man of heroism. I once received one of his paperback books in the mail with a form-card attached which asked me to read it carefully and write back all the things wrong with the book so that he could improve his writing next time around.

Now that's heroic!

Of course, it's also idiotic and I wouldn't have a thing to do with it. Suppose it set a precedent!

I made my own position quite clear. Anytime anyone reads one of *my* books and spots something wrong with it, I'll thank him to keep it secret. I don't want to know. When *I* ask for criticism, all I want is applause. I hope that's clear!

Then, too, Gordie has the fictional hero's ability to be unaffected by the strong drink that is, on rare occasions, forced upon him by his convivial and loving friends. When that happens, his general glow of benevolence merely glitters more brightly.

It was only last summer when Lester del Rey, one of the bantamweights of our field (in physical proportions only, *not* in talent) looked pretty poorly and I was concerned, for Lester is one of my favorites, even when he's talking, which is all the time.

I said "What's the matter, Lester?"

And he said, "I tried to outdrink Gordie."

"Lester," I said, shocked, "you have only half his volume."

"I almost did," he said.

He almost died, is what he should have said.

But my most poignant memory of Gordie is in connection with the 1959 Convention at Detroit. Robert Bloch was so busily engaged in getting ready to introduce me to some girl I had never met that I suspected something was up. I managed to locate the girl and I must say I was staggered. She was 5′ 11″ tall. She was beautiful and she made Anita Ekberg look like Audrey Hepburn. I saw the plan at once. I was to be introduced and after one goggle-eyed look, I was to fall into a speechless catalepsy, thus utterly ruining my reputation as a dirty old man.

Remaining master of myself only by an eyelash, I approached the young lady with diffidence, introduced myself in a quiver, and humbly asked if she would cooperate with me in a biter-bit routine. Being as good-natured as she was beautiful, she agreed.

So when Bob Bloch introduced me, I calmly walked up to her and snapped my fingers. She put her arm about my waist, swung me back (she was bigger and stronger and had to play the lead) and we kissed. It was the talk of the convention.

With that beautiful head-start, you would think I was all set. Wouldn't you?

Nonsense! Rotten old Gordie Dickson moved in and cut me out, leaving me in the Arctic regions somewhere.

The funny thing is that I forgive him. *He's* lovable, too, you see—in a completely different way.

3

SOLDIER, ASK NOT

Soldier, ask not—now, or ever,
Where to war your banners go . . .

I

As I got off the spaceliner on St. Marie, the little breeze from the higher pressure of the ship's atmosphere at my back was like a hand from the darkness behind me, shoving me into the dark day and the rain. My Newsman's cloak covered me. The wet chill of the day wrapped around me but did not enter me. I was like the naked claymore of my own early ancestors, wrapped and hidden in the plaid—sharpened on a stone—and carried now at last to the meeting for which it had been guarded over three years of waiting.

A meeting in the cold rain of spring. I felt it, cold as old blood on my hands and tasteless on my lips. Above, the sky was low and clouds flowing to the east. The rain fell steadily.

The sound of it was like a rolling of drums as I went down the outside landing stairs, the multitude of raindrops sounding their own end against the unyielding concrete all around. The concrete stretched far from the ship in every direction, hiding the earth, as bare and clean as the last page of an account book before the final entry. At its far edge, the spaceport terminal stood like a single gravestone. The curtains of falling water between it and me thinned and thickened like the smoke of battle, but could not hide it entirely from my sight.

It was the same rain that falls in all places and on all worlds. It had fallen like this on Athens of Old Earth, when I was only a boy, on the dark, unhappy house of the uncle who brought me up after my parents' death, on the ruins of the Parthenon as I saw it from my bedroom window.

I listened to it now as I went down the landing stairs, drumming on the great ship behind me which had shifted me free between the stars—from Old Earth to this second smallest of the worlds, this small terraformed planet under the Procyon suns—and drumming hollowly upon the Credentials case sliding down the conveyor belt beside me. That case now meant nothing to me—neither my papers or the Credentials of Impartiality I had carried six years and worked so long to earn. Now I thought less of these than of the name of the man I should find dispatching groundcars at the edge of the field. If, that was, he was actually the man my Earth informants had named to me. And if they had not lied . . .

". . . Your luggage, sir?"

I woke from my thoughts and the rain. I had reached the concrete. The debarking officer smiled at me. He was older than I, though he looked younger. As he smiled some beads of moisture broke and spilled like tears from the brown visor-edge of his cap onto the tally sheet he held.

"Send it to the Friendly compound," I said. "I'll take the Credentials case."

I took it up from the conveyor belt and turned to walk off. The man standing in a dispatcher's uniform by the first ground-car in line did fit the description.

"Name, sir?" he said. "Business on St. Marie?"

If he had been described to me, I must have been described to him. But I was prepared to humor him.

"Tam Olyn," I said. "Old Earth resident and Interworld News Network representative. I'm here to cover the Friendly-Exotic conflict." I opened my case and gave him my papers.

"Fine, Mr. Olyn." He handed them back to me, damp from the rain. He turned away to open the door of the car beside him and set the automatic pilot. "Follow the highway straight to Joseph's Town. Put it on automatic at the city limits and the car'll take you to the Friendly compound."

"All right," I said. "Just a minute."

He turned back. He had a young, good-looking face with a little mustache and he looked at me with a bright blankness. "Sir?"

"Help me get in the car."

"Oh, I'm sorry, sir." He came quickly over to me. "I didn't realize your leg—"

"Damp stiffens it," I said. He adjusted the seat and I got my left leg in behind the steering column. He started to turn away.

"Wait a minute," I said again. I was out of patience. "You're Walter Imera, aren't you?"

"Yes, sir," he said softly.

"Look at me," I said. "You've got some information for me, haven't you?"

He turned slowly back to face me. His face was still blank. "No, sir."

I waited a long moment, looking at him.

"All right," I said then, reaching for the car door. "I guess you know I'll get the information anyway. And they'll believe you told me."

His little mustache began to look like it was painted on.

"Wait—" he said.

"What for?"

"Look," he said, "you've got to understand. Information like that's not part of your news, is it? I've got a family—"

"And I haven't," I said. I felt nothing for him.

"But you don't understand. They'd kill me. That's the sort of organization the Blue Front is now, here on St. Marie. What d'you want to know about them for? I didn't understand you meant—".

"All right," I said. I reached for the car door.

"Wait—" He held out a hand to me in the rain. "How do I know you can make them leave me alone if I tell you?"

"They may be back in power here some day," I said. "Not even outlawed political groups want to antagonize the Inter-planetary News Network." I started to close the door once more.

"All right—" he said quickly. "All right. You go to New San Marcos. The Wallace Street Jewelers there. It's just beyond Joseph's Town, where the Friendly compound is you're going to." He licked his lips. "You'll tell them about me?"

"I'll tell them." I looked at him. Above the edge of the blue uniform collar on the right side of his neck I could see an inch or two of fine silver chain, bright against winter-pale skin. The crucifix attached to it would be down under his shirt. "The Friendly soldiers have been here two years now. How do people like them?"

He grinned a little. His color was coming back.

"Oh, like anybody," he said. "You just have to understand them. They've got their own ways."

I felt the ache in my stiff leg where the doctors on New Earth had taken the needle from the spring rifle out of it three years before.

"Yes, they have," I said. "Shut the door."

He shut it. I drove off.

There was a St. Christopher's medal on the car's instrument panel. One of the Friendly soldiers would have ripped it off and thrown it away, or refused the car. And so it gave me a particular pleasure to leave it where it was, though it meant no more to me than it would to him. It was, not just because of Dave, my brother-in-law, and the other prisoners they had shot down on New Earth. It was simply because there are some duties that have a small element of pleasure. After the illusions of childhood are gone and there is nothing left but duties, such pleasures are welcome. Fanatics, when all is said and done, are no worse than mad dogs.

But mad dogs have to be destroyed; it is a simple common sense.

And you return to common sense after a while in life, inevitably. When the wild dreams of justice and progress are all dead and buried, when the painful beatings of feeling inside you are finally stilled, then it becomes best to be still, unliving, and unyielding as—the blade of a sword sharpened on a stone.

195

The rain through which such a blade is carried to its using does not stain it, any more than the blood in which it is bathed at last. Rain and blood are alike to sharpened iron.

I drove for half an hour past wooded hills and plowed meadows. The furrows of the fields were black in the rain. I thought it a kinder black than some other shades I had seen; and at last I reached the outskirts of Joseph's Town.

The autopilot of the car threaded me through a small, neat, typical St. Marie City of about a hundred thousand people. We came out on the far side into a cleared area, beyond which lifted the massive, sloping concrete walls of a military compound.

A Friendly non-com stopped my car at the gate with his black spring rifle, and opened the car door at my left.

"Thee have business here?"

His voice was harsh and high in his nose. The cloth tabs of a groupman edged his collar. Above them his forty-year-old face was lean and graven with lines. Both face and hands, the only uncovered parts of him, looked unnaturally white against the black cloth and rifle.

I opened the case beside me and handed him my papers.

"My Credentials," I said. "I'm here to see your acting Commander of Expeditionary Forces, Commandant Jamethon Black."

"Move over, then," he said nasally. "I must drive thee."

I moved.

He got in and took the stick. We drove through the gate and turned down an approach alley. I could see an interior square at the alley's far end. The close concrete walls on either side of us echoed the sound of our passage as we went. I heard drill commands growing louder as we approached the square. When we rolled out into it, soldiers were drawn up in ranks for their mid-day service, in the rain.

The groupman left me and went in the entrance of what seemed to be an office inset in the wall on one side of the square. I looked over the soldiers standing in formation. They

196

stood at present-arms, their position of worship under field conditions; and as I watched, the officer standing facing them, with his back to a wall, led them into the words of their Battle Hymn.

> *Soldier, ask not—now, or ever,*
> *Where to war your banners go.*
> *Anarch's legions all surround us.*
> *Strike! And do not count the blow!*

I sat trying not to listen. There was no musical accompaniment, no religious furniture or symbols except the thin shape of the cross whitewashed on the gray wall behind the officer. The massed male voices rose and fell slowly in the dark, sad hymn that promised them only pain, and suffering, and sorrow. At last, the final line mourned its harsh prayer for a battle death, and they ordered arms.

A groupman dismissed the ranks as the officer walked back past my car without looking at me, and passed in through the entrance where my non-commissioned guide had disappeared. As he passed I saw the officer was young.

A moment later the guide came for me. Limping a little on my stiffened leg, I followed him to an inner room with the lights on above a single desk. The young officer rose and nodded as the door closed behind me. He wore the faded tabs of a commandant on his uniform lapels.

As I handed my credentials across the desk to him, the glare of the light over the desk came full in my eyes, blinding me. I stepped back and blinked at his blurred face. As it came back into focus I saw it for a moment as if it was older, harsher, twisted and engraved with the lines of years of fanaticism.

Then my eyes refocused completely, and I saw him as he actually was. Dark-faced, but thin with the thinness of youth rather than that of self-starvation. He was not the face burned in my memory. His features were regular to the point of being handsome, his eyes tired and shadowed; and I saw the straight, weary line of his mouth above the still, self-controlled stiffness of his body, smaller and slighter than mine.

He held the credentials without looking at them. His mouth quirked a little, dryly and wearily, at the corners. "And no doubt, Mr. Olyn," he said, "you've got another pocket filled with authorities from the Exotic Worlds to interview the mercenary soldiers and officers they've hired from the Dorsai and a dozen other worlds to oppose God's Chosen in War?"

I smiled. Because it was good to find him as strong as that, to add to my pleasure of breaking him.

II

I looked across the ten feet or so of distance that separated us. The Friendly non-com who had killed the prisoners on New Earth had also spoken of God's Chosen.

"If you'll look under the papers directed to you," I said, "you'll find them. The News Network and its people are impartial. We don't take sides."

"Right," said the dark young face opposing me, "take sides."

"Yes, Commandant," I said. "That's right. Only sometimes it's a matter of debate where Right is. You and your troops here now are invaders on the world of a planetary system your ancestors never colonized. And opposing you are mercenary troops hired by two worlds that not only belong under the Procyon suns but have a commitment to defend the smaller worlds of their system—of which St. Marie is one. I'm not sure right *is* on your side."

He shook his head slightly and said, "We expect small understanding from those not Chosen." He transferred his gaze from me to the papers in his hand.

"Mind if I sit down?" I said. "I've got a bad leg."

"By all means." He nodded to a chair beside his desk and, as I sat down, seated himself. I looked across the papers on the desk before him and saw, standing to one side, the solidograph of one of the windowless high-peaked churches the Friendlies build. It was a legitimate token for him to own—but there just happened to be three people, an older man and woman and a young girl of about fourteen, in the foreground of the image. All three of them bore a family resemblance to Jamethon Black. Glancing up from my credentials he saw me looking at them; and his gaze shifted momentarily to the graph and away again, as if he would protect it.

"I'm required, I see," he said, drawing my eyes back to him, "to provide you with cooperation and facilities. We'll find quarters for you here. Do you need a car and driver?"

"Thanks," I said. "That commercial car outside will do. And I'll manage my own driving."

"As you like." He detached the papers directed to him, passed the rest back to me and leaned toward a grill in his desktop. "Groupman."

"Sir," the grill answered promptly.

"Quarters for a single male civilian. Parking assignment for a civilian vehicle, personnel."

"Sir."

The voice from the grill clicked off. Jamethon Black looked across his desk at me. I got the idea he was waiting for my departure.

"Commandant," I said, putting my credentials back in their case, "two years ago your Elders of the United Churches on Harmony and Association found the planetary government of St. Marie in default of certain disputed balances of credit, so they sent an expedition in here to occupy and enforce payment. Of that expedition, how much in the way of men and equipment do you have left?"

"That, Mr. Olyn," he said, "is restricted military information."

"However"—and I closed the case—"you, with the regular rank of commandant, are acting Commander of Forces for that remnant of your expedition. That position calls for someone about five ranks higher than you. Do you expect such an officer to arrive and take charge?"

"I'm afraid you'd have to ask that question of Headquarters on Harmony, Mr. Olyn."

"Do you expect reinforcements of personnel and more supplies?"

"If I did"—his voice was level—"I would have to consider that restricted information, too."

"You know that it's been pretty widely mentioned that your General Staff on Harmony has decided that this expedition to St. Marie is a lost cause? But that to avoid loss of face they prefer you here to be cut up, instead of withdrawing you and your men."

"I see," he said.

"You wouldn't care to comment?"

His dark, young, expressionless face did not change. "Not in the case of rumors, Mr. Olyn."

"One last question then. Do you plan to retreat westward, or surrender when the spring offensive of the Exotic mercenary forces begins to move against you?"

"The Chosen in War never retreat," he said. "Neither do they abandon, or suffer abandonment by, their Brothers in the Lord." He stood up. "I have work I must get back to, Mr. Olyn."

I stood up, too. I was taller than he was, older, and heavier-boned. It was only his almost unnatural composure that enabled him to maintain his appearance of being my equal or better.

"I'll talk to you later, perhaps, when you've got more time," I said.

"Certainly." I heard the office door open behind me. "Groupman," he said, speaking past me, "take care of Mr. Olyn."

The groupman he had turned me over to found me a small concrete cubicle with a single high window, a camp bed and a uniform cabinet. He left me for a moment and returned with a signed pass.

"Thanks," I said as I took it. "Where do I find the Headquarters of the Exotic Forces?"

"Our latest advice, sir," he said, "is that they're ninety kilo-

200

meters east of here. New San Marcos." He was my height, but, like most of them, half a dozen years younger than I, with an innocence that contrasted with the strange air of control they all had.

"San Marcos." I looked at him. "I suppose you enlisted men know your General Headquarters on Harmony has decided against wasting replacements for you?"

"No, sir," he said. I might have commented on the rain for all the reaction he showed. Even these boys were still strong and unbroken. "Is there somewhat else?"

"No," I said. "Thanks."

He went out. And I went out, to get in my car and head ninety kilometers east through the same sort of country to New San Marcos. I reached it in about three-quarters of an hour. But I did not go directly to find the Exotic Field Headquarters. I had other fish to fry.

These took me to the Wallace Street Jewelers. There, three shallow steps down from street level and an opaqued door let me in to a long, dim-lighted room filled with glass cases. There was a small elderly man at the back of the store behind the final case and I saw him eyeing my correspondent's cloak and badge as I got closer.

"Sir?" he said, as I stopped across the case from him. He raised gray, narrow old eyes in a strangely smooth face to look at me.

"I think you know what I represent," I said. "All worlds know the News Services. We're not concerned with local politics."

"Sir?"

"You'll find out how I learned your address anyway." I kept on smiling at him. "So I'll tell you it was from a spaceport auto-dispatcher named Imera. I promised him protection for telling me. We'd appreciate it if he remains well and whole."

"I'm afraid—" He put his hands on the glass top of the case. They were veined with the years. "You wanted to buy something?"

"I'm willing to pay in good will," I said, "for information."

His hands slid off the countertop.

"Sir." He sighed a little. "I'm afraid you're in the wrong store."

"I'm sure I am," I said. "But your store'll have to do. We'll pretend it's the right store and I'm talking to someone who's a member of the Blue Front."

He shook his head slowly and stepped back from the case.

"The Blue Front is illegal," he said. "Good-by, sir."

"In a moment. I've got a few things to say first."

"Then I'm sorry." He retreated toward some drapes covering a doorway. "I can't listen. No one will come into this room with you, sir, as long as you talk like that."

He slipped through the drapes and was gone. I looked around the long, empty room.

"Well," I said, a little more loudly, "I guess I'll have to speak to the walls. I'm sure the walls can hear me."

I paused. There was no sound.

"All right," I said. "I'm a correspondent. All I'm interested in is information. Our assessment of the military situation here on St. Marie"—and here I told the truth—"shows the Friendly Expeditionary Forces abandoned by their home headquarters and certain to be overrun by the Exotic Forces as soon as the ground dries enough for heavy equipment to move."

There was still no answer, but the back of my neck knew they were listening, and watching me.

"As a result," I went on—and here I lied, though they would have no way of knowing—"we consider it inevitable that the Friendly Command here will have got in contact with the Blue Front. Assassination of enemy commanders is expressly in violation of the Mercenaries' Code and the Articles of Civilized Warfare—but civilians could do what soldiers could not."

Still there was no sound or movement beyond the drapes.

"A news representative," I said, "carries Credentials of Impartiality. You know how highly these are held. I only want to ask a few questions. And the answers will be kept confidential . . ."

For a last time I waited, and there was still no answer. I turned and went up the long room and out. It was not until I was well out on to the street that I let the feeling of triumph within spread out and warm me.

They would take the bait. People of their sort always did. I found my car and drove to Exotic Headquarters.

These were outside the town. There a mercenary commandant named Janol Marat took me in charge. He conducted me to the bubble structure of their HQ building. There was a feel of purpose, there, a sure and cheerful air of activity. They were well armed, well trained. After the Friendlies it jumped at me. I said so to Janol.

"We've got a Dorsai Commander and we outnumber the opposition." He grinned at me. He had a deeply tanned, long face that went into deep creases as his lips curved up. "That makes everybody pretty optimistic. Besides, our commander gets promoted if he wins. Back to the Exotics and staff rank—out of field combat for good. It's good business for us to win."

I laughed and he laughed.

"Tell me more, though," I said. "I want reasons I can use in the stories I send back to News Network."

"Well"—he answered the snappy salute of a passing groupman, a Cassidan, by the look of him—"I guess you might mention the usual—the fact our Exotic employers don't permit themselves to use violence and consequently they're always rather generous than otherwise when it comes to paying for men and equipment. And the OutBond—that's the Exotic Ambassador to St. Marie, you know—"

"I know."

"He replaced the former OutBond here three years ago. Anyway, he's something special, even for someone from Mara or Kultis. He's an expert in ontogenic calculations. If that means much to you. It's all over my head." Janol pointed. "Here's the Field Commander's office. He's Kensie Graeme."

"Graeme?" I said, frowning. I had spent a day at the Hague looking up Kensie Graeme before I came, but I wanted Janol's reactions to him. "Sounds familiar." We approached the office building. "Graeme . . ."

"You're probably thinking of another member of the same family." Janol took the bait. "Donal Graeme. A nephew. The one who pulled that wild stunt not long ago, attacking Newton with just a handful of Freiland ships. Kensie is Donal's uncle. Not as spectacular as the young Graeme, but I'll bet you'll like him better than you would the nephew. Kensie's got two men's likeableness." He looked at me, grinning slightly again.

"That supposed to mean something special?" I said.

"That's right," said Janol. "His own likeableness and his twin brother's, too. Meet Ian Graeme sometime when you're in Blauvain. That's where the Exotic Embassy is, east of here. Ian's a dark man."

We walked into the office.

"I can't get used," I said, "to how so many Dorsai seem related."

"Neither can I. Actually, I guess it's because there really aren't so many of them. The Dorsai's a small world, and those that live more than a few years—" Janol stopped by a commandant sitting at a desk. "Can we see the Old Man, Hari? This is a News Network man."

"Why, I guess so." The other looked at his desk signal board. "The OutBond's with him, but he's just leaving now. Go on in."

Janol led me between the desks. A door at the back of the room opened before we reached it and a calm-faced man of middle age wearing a blue robe and close-cropped white hair came out. He looked strange but not ridiculous—particularly after you met his odd, hazel-colored eyes.

He was an Exotic.

I knew of Padma, as I knew the Exotics. I had seen them on their own home worlds of Mara and Kultis. A people committed to non-violence, mystics but very practical mystics, masters of what were known as the "strange sciences"—a dozen wizardic step-children of early psychology, sociology and the humanistic fields of research.

"Sir," said Janol to Padma, "this is—"

"Tam Olyn. I know," said Padma softly. He smiled up at me, and those eyes of his seemed to catch light for a moment and blind me. "I was sorry to learn about your brother-in-law, Tam."

I went quite cool all over. I had been ready to walk on, but now I stood stock-still and looked at him.

"My brother-in-law?" I said.

"The young man who died near Castlemain, on New Earth."

"Oh, yes," I said, between stiff lips. "I'm surprised that you'd know."

"I know because of you, Tam." Once more the hazel eyes of Padma seemed to catch light. "We have a science called ontogenics, by which we calculate the probabilities of human actions in present and future situations. You've been an important factor in those calculations for some time." He smiled. "That's why I was expecting to meet you here, and now. We've calculated you into our present situation here on St. Marie, Tam."

"Have you?" I said. "Have you? That's interesting."

"I thought it would be," said Padma softly. "To you, especially. Someone like a newsman, like yourself, would find it interesting."

"It is," I said. "It sounds like you know more than I do about what I'm going to be doing here."

"We've got calculations," said Padma in his soft voice, "to that effect. Come see me in Blauvain, Tam; and I'll show you."

"I'll do that," I said.

"You'll be very welcome." Padma inclined his head. His blue robe whispered on the floor as he turned, and went out of the room.

"This way," said Janol, touching my elbow. I started as if I had just wakened from a deep sleep. "The commander's in here."

I followed him automatically into a further office. The individual I had come to see stood up as we came through the door. He was a great, lean man in field uniform, with a heavy-boned, but open, smiling face under black, slightly curly hair. A sort of golden warmth of personality—a strange thing in a Dorsai—seemed to flow out from him as he rose to meet me and his long-fingered, powerful hand swallowed mine in a handshake.

"Come on in," he said. "Let me fix you up with a drink. Janol," he added to my mercenary commandant from New Earth, "no need for you to stick around. Go on to chow. And tell the rest of them in the outer office to knock off."

Janol saluted and went. I sat down as Graeme turned to a small bar cabinet behind his desk. And for the first time in three years, under the magic of the unusual fighting man opposite me, a little peace came into my soul. With someone like this on my side, I could not lose.

III

"Credentials?" asked Graeme, as soon as we were settled with drinks of Dorsai whisky—which is a fine whisky—in our hands.

I passed my papers over. He glanced through them, picking out the letters from Sayona, the Bond of Kultis, to *"Commander—St. Marie Field Forces."* He looked these over and put them aside. He handed me back the credentials folder.

"You stopped at Joseph's Town first?" he said.

I nodded. I saw him looking at my face, and his own sobered.

"You don't like the Friendlies," he said.

His words took my breath away. I had come prepared to fence for an opening to tell him. It was too sudden. I looked away.

I did not dare answer right away. I could not. There was either too much or too little to say if I let it come out without thinking. Then I got a grip on myself.

"If I do anything at all with the rest of my life," I said, slowly, "it'll be to do everything in my power to remove the

206

Friendlies and all they stand for from the community of civilized human beings."

I looked back up at him. He was sitting with one massive elbow on his desktop, watching me.

"That's a pretty harsh point of view, isn't it?"

"No harsher than theirs."

"Do you think so?" he said seriously. "I wouldn't say so."

"I thought," I said, "you were the one who was fighting them."

"Why, yes." He smiled a little. "But we're soldiers on both sides."

"I don't think they think that way."

He shook his head a little.

"What makes you say that?" he said.

"I've seen them," I answered. "I got caught up front in the lines on Castlemain on New Earth, three years ago." I tapped my stiff knee. "I got shot and I couldn't navigate. The Cassidans around me began to retreat—they were mercenaries, and the troops opposing them were Friendlies hired out as mercenaries."

I stopped and took a drink of the whisky. When I took the glass away, Graeme had not moved. He sat as if waiting.

"There was young Cassidan, a buck soldier," I said. "I was doing a series on the campaign from an individual point of view. I'd picked him for my individual. It was a natural choice. You see"—I drank again, and emptied the glass—"my younger sister went out on contract as an accountant to Cassida two years before that, and she'd married him. He was my brother-in-law."

Graeme took the glass from my hand and silently replenished it.

"He wasn't actually a military man," I said. "He was studying shift mechanics and he had about three years to go. But he stood low on one of the competitive examinations at a time when Cassida owed a contractual balance of troops to New Earth." I took a deep breath. "Well, to make a long story short,

207

he ended up on New Earth in this same campaign I was covering. Because of the series I was writing, he was assigned to me. We both thought it was a good deal for him, that he'd be safer that way."

I drank some more of the whisky.

"But," I said, "you know, there's always a better story a little deeper in the combat zone. We got caught up front one day when the New Earth troops were retreating. I picked up a needle through the kneecap. The Friendly armor was moving up and things were getting hot. The soldiers around us took off toward the rear in a hurry, but Dave tried to carry me, because he thought the Friendly armor would fry me before they had time to notice I was a non-combatant. Well," I took another deep breath, "the Friendly ground troops caught us. They took us to a sort of clearing where they had a lot of prisoners and kept us there for a while. Then a groupman—one of their fanatic types, a tall, starved-looking soldier about my age— came up with orders they were to reform for a fresh attack."

I stopped and took another drink. But I could not taste it.

"That meant they couldn't spare men to guard the prisoners. They'd have to turn them loose back of the Friendly lines. The Groupman said that wouldn't work. They'd have to make sure the prisoners couldn't endanger them."

Graeme was still watching me.

"I didn't understand. I didn't even catch on when the other Friendlies—none of them were non-coms like the Groupman— objected." I put my glass on the desk beside me and stared at the wall of the office, seeing it all over again, as plainly as if I looked through a window at it. "I remember how the Groupman pulled himself up straight. I saw his eyes. As if he'd been insulted by the others, objecting.

"'Are they Chosen of God?' he shouted at them. 'Are they of the Chosen?'"

I looked across at Kensie Graeme and saw him still motionless, still watching me, his own glass small in one big hand.

"You understand?" I said to him. "As if because the prisoners weren't Friendlies, they weren't quite human. As if

208

they were some lower order it was all right to kill." I shook, suddenly. "And he did it! I sat there against a tree, safe because of my News Correspondent's uniform and watched him shoot them down. All of them. I sat there and looked at Dave, and he looked at me, sitting there, as the Groupman shot him!"

I quit all at once. I hadn't meant to have it all come out like that. It was just that I'd been able to tell no one who would understand how helpless I had been. But something about Graeme had given me the idea he would understand.

"Yes," he said after a moment, and took and filled my glass again. "That sort of thing's very bad. Was the Groupman found and tried under the Mercenaries Code?"

"After it was too late, yes."

He nodded and looked past me at the wall. "They aren't all like that, of course."

"There's enough to give them a reputation for it."

"Unfortunately, yes. Well"—he smiled slightly at me— "we'll try and keep that sort of thing out of this campaign."

"Tell me something," I said, putting my glass down. "Does that sort of thing—as you put it—ever happen to the Friendlies, themselves?"

Something took place then in the atmosphere of the room. There was a little pause before he answered. I felt my heart beat slowly, three times, as I waited for him to speak.

He said at last, "No, it doesn't."

"Why not?" I said.

The feeling in the room became stronger. And I realized I had gone too fast. I had been sitting talking to him as a man and forgetting what else he was. Now I began to forget that he was a man and become conscious of him as a Dorsai—an individual as human as I was, but trained all his life, and bred down the generations to a difference. He did not move or change the tone of his voice, or any such thing; but somehow he seemed to move off some distance from me, up into a higher, colder, stonier land into which I could venture only at my peril.

I remembered what was said about his people from that small, cold stony-mountained world: that if the Dorsai chose to withdraw their fighting men from the services of all the other worlds, and challenge those other worlds, not the combined might of the rest of civilization could stand against them. I had never really believed that before. I had never even really thought much about it. But sitting there just then, because of what was happening in the room, suddenly it became real to me. I could feel the knowledge, cold as a wind blowing on me off a glacier, that it was true; and then he answered my question.

"Because," said Kensie Graeme, "anything like that is specifically prohibited by Article Two of the Mercenaries' Code."

Then he broke out abruptly into a smile and what I had just felt in the room withdrew. I breathed again.

"Well," he said, putting his glass down empty on the desk, "how about joining us in the Officers' Mess for something to eat?"

I had dinner with them and the meal was very pleasant. They wanted to put me up for the night—but I could feel myself being pulled back to that cold, joyless compound near Joseph's Town, where all that waited for me was a sort of cold and bitter satisfaction at being among my enemies.

I went back.

It was about eleven p.m. when I drove through the gate of the compound and parked, just as a figure came out of the entrance to Jamethon's headquarters. The square was dim-lighted with only a few spotlights about the walls, their light lost in the rain-wet pavement. For a moment I did not recognize the figure—and then I saw it was Jamethon.

He would have passed by me at some distance, but I got out of my car and went to meet him. He stopped when I stepped in front of him.

"Mr. Olyn," he said evenly. In the darkness I could not make out the expression of his face.

"I've got a question to ask," I said, smiling in the darkness.

210

"It's late for questions."

"This won't take long." I strained to catch the look on his face, but it was all in shadow. "I've been visiting the Exotic camp. Their commander's a Dorsai. I suppose you know that?"

"Yes." I could barely see the movement of his lips.

"We got to talking. A question came up and I thought I'd ask you, Commandant. Do you ever order your men to kill prisoners?"

An odd, short silence came between us. Then he answered.

"The killing or abuse of prisoners of war," he said without emotion, "is forbidden by Article Two of the Mercenaries' Code."

"But you aren't Mercenaries here, are you? You're native troops in service to your own True Church and Elders."

"Mr. Olyn," he said, while I still strained without success to make out the expression of his shadowed face—and it seemed that the words came slowly, though the tone of the voice that spoke them remained as calm as ever, "My Lord has set me to be His servant and a leader among men of war. In neither of those tasks will I fail Him."

And with that he turned, his face still shadowed and hidden from me, and passed around me and went on.

Alone, I went back inside to my quarters, undressed and lay down on the hard and narrow bed they had given me. The rain outside had stopped at last. Through my open, unglazed window I could see a few stars showing.

I lay there getting ready to sleep and making mental notes on what I would need to do tomorrow. The meeting with Padma the OutBond had jolted me sharply. I took his so-called calculations of human actions with reservation—but I had been shaken to learn of them. I would have to find out more about how much his science of ontogenics knew and could predict. If necessary, from Padma himself. But I would start first with ordinary reference sources.

No one, I thought, would ordinarily entertain the fantastic thought that one man like myself could destroy a culture involving the populations of two worlds. No one, except perhaps a Padma. What I knew, he with his calculations might have discovered. And that was that the Friendly worlds of Harmony and Association were facing a decision that would mean life or death to their way of living. A very small thing could tip the scales they weighed on.

For there was a new wind blowing between the stars.

Four hundred years before we had all been men of Earth— Old Earth, the mother planet which was my native soil. One people.

Then, with the movement out to new worlds, the human race had "splintered," to use an Exotic term. Every small social fragment and psychological type had drawn apart by itself, and joined others like it and progressed toward specialized types. Until we had half a dozen fragments of human types—the warrior on the Dorsai, the philosopher on the Exotic worlds, the hard scientist on Newton, Cassida and Venus, and so forth . . .

Isolation had bred specific types. Then a growing intercommunication between the younger worlds, now established, and an ever-increasing rate of technological advance had forced specialization. The trade between the worlds was the trade of skilled minds. Generals from the Dorsai were worth their exchange rate in psychiatrists from the Exotics. Communications men like myself from Old Earth bought spaceship designers from Cassida. And so it had been for the last hundred years.

But now the worlds were drifting together. Economics was fusing the race into one whole, again. And the struggle on each world was to gain the advantages of that fusion while holding on to as much as possible of their own ways.

Compromise was necessary—and the harsh, stiff-necked Friendly religion forbade compromise and had made many enemies. Already public opinion moved against the Friendlies on other worlds. Discredit them, smear them, publicly here in this campaign and they would not be able to hire out their soldiers. They would lose the balance of trade they needed to hire the skilled specialists trained by the special facilities of other worlds, and which they needed to keep their own two poor-in-natural-resources worlds alive. They would die.

As young Dave had died. Slowly. In the dark.

. . . In the darkness now, as I thought of it, it rose up before me once again. It had been only noon when we were taken prisoner, but by the time the Groupman came with his orders for our guards to move up, the sun was almost down.

After they left, after it was all over and I was left alone, I crawled to the bodies in the clearing. And I found Dave among them; and he was not quite gone.

He was wounded in the body and I could not stop the bleeding.

It would not have helped if I had, they told me afterwards. But then it seemed that it would have. So I tried. But finally I gave up and by that time it was quite dark. I only held him and did not know he was dead until he began to grow cold. And then was when I had begun to change into what my uncle had always tried to make me. I felt myself die inside. Dave and my sister were to have been my family, the only family I had ever had hopes of keeping. Instead, I could only sit there in the darkness, holding him and hearing the blood from his red-soaked clothing, falling drop by drop, slowly on the dead variform oak leaves beneath us.

I lay there now in the Friendly compound, not able to sleep and remembering. And after a while I heard the soldiers marching, forming in the square for midnight service.

I lay on my back, listening to them. Their marching feet stopped at last. The single window of my room was over my bed—high in the wall against which the left side of my cot was set. It was unglazed and the night air with its sounds came freely through it along with the dim light from the square which painted a pale rectangle on the opposite wall of my room. I lay watching that rectangle and listening to the service outside; and I heard the duty officer lead them in a prayer for worthiness. After that they sang their battle hymn again, and I lay hearing it, this time, all the way through.

> Soldier, ask not—now or ever,
> Where to war your banners go.
> Anarch's legions all surround us.
> Strike! And do not count the blow!
>
> Glory, honor—praise and profit,
> Are but toys of tinsel worth.
> Render up your work, unasking,
> Leave the human clay to earth.
>
> Blood and sorrow—pain unending,
> Are the portion of us all.
> Grasp the naked sword, opposing.
> Gladly in the battle fall.
>
> So shall we, anointed soldiers,
> Stand at last before the Throne.
> Baptized in our wounds, red-flowing,
> Sealed unto our Lord—alone!

After that they dispersed to cots no different from mine. I lay there listening to the silence in the square and the measured dripping of a rainspout outside by my window, its slow drops falling after the rain, one by one, uncounted in the darkness.

IV

After the day I landed, there was no more rain. Day by day the fields dried. Soon they would be firm underneath the weight of heavy surface-war equipment, and everyone knew that then the Exotic spring offensive would get under way. Meanwhile both Exotic and Friendly troops were in training.

During the next few weeks, I was busy about my newswork. Mostly feature and small stories on the soldiers and the native people. I had dispatches to send and I sent them faithfully. A correspondent is only as good as his contacts; I made contacts everywhere but among the Friendly troops. These remained aloof, though I talked to many of them. They refused to show fear or doubt.

I had heard these Friendly soldiers were generally under-trained because the suicidal tactics of their officers kept their ranks always filled with green replacements. But the ones here were the remnants of an Expeditionary Force six times their present numbers. They were all veterans, though most of them were in their teens. Only here and there, among the non-coms, and more often among the commissioned officers, I saw the prototype of the non-com who had ordered the prisoners shot on New Earth. Here, the men of this type looked like rabid, gray wolves mixed among polite, well-schooled young dogs just out of puppyhood.

It was a temptation to think that they alone were what I had set out to destroy.

To fight that temptation I told myself that Alexander the Great had led expeditions against the hill tribes and ruled in Pella, capital of Macedonia, and ordered men put to death when he was sixteen. But still the Friendly soldiers looked young to me. I could not help contrasting them with the adult, experienced mercenaries in Kensie Graeme's forces. For the Exotics, in obedience to their principles, would hire no drafted troops or soldiers who were not in uniform of their own free will.

Meanwhile I had heard no word from the Blue Front. But by the time two weeks had gone, I had my own connections in New San Marcos, and at the beginning of the third week one of these brought me word that the jewelers shop in Wallace Street there had closed its door—had pulled its blinds and emptied the long room of stock and fixtures, and moved or gone out of business. That was all I needed to know.

For the next few days, I stayed in the vicinity of Jamethon Black himself, and by the end of the week my watching him paid off.

At ten o'clock that Friday night I was up on a catwalk just above my quarters and under the sentry-walk of the walls, watching as three civilians with Blue Front written all over them drove into the square, got out and went into Jamethon's office.

They stayed a little over an hour. When they left, I went back down to bed. That night I slept soundly.

The next morning I got up early, and there was mail for me. A message had come by spaceliner from the director of News Network back on Earth, personally congratulating me on my dispatches. Once, three years before, this would have meant a great deal to me. Now, I only worried that they would decide I had made the situation here newsworthy enough to require extra people being sent out to help me. I could not risk having other news personnel here now to see what I was doing.

I got in my car and headed east along the highway to New San Marcos and the Exotic Headquarters. The Friendly troops were already out in the field; eighteen kilometers east of Joseph's Town, I was stopped by a squad of five young soldiers with no non-com over them. They recognized me.

"In God's name, Mr. Olyn," said the first one to reach my car, bending down to speak to me through the open window at my left shoulder. "You cannot go through."

"Mind if I ask why?" I said.

He turned and pointed out and down into a little valley between two wooded hills at our left.

"Tactical survey in progress."

I looked. The little valley or meadow was perhaps a hundred yards wide between the wooded slopes, and it wound away from me and curved to disappear to my right. At the edge of the wooded slopes where they met open meadow, there were lilac bushes with blossoms several days old. The meadow itself was green and fair with the young chartreuse grass of early summer and the white and purple of the lilacs, and the variform oaks behind the lilacs were fuzzy in outline, with small, new leaves.

In the middle of all this, in the center of the meadow, were black-clad figures moving about with computing devices, measuring and figuring the possibilities of death from every angle. In the very center of the meadow for some reason they had set up marking stakes—a single stake, then a stake in front of that with two stakes on either side of it, and one more stake in line before these. Farther on was another single stake, down, as if fallen on the grass and discarded.

I looked back up into the lean young face of the soldier.

"Getting ready to defeat the Exotics?" I said.

He took it as if it had been a straightforward question, with no irony in my voice at all.

"Yes sir," he said seriously. I looked at him and at the taut skin and clear eyes of the rest.

"Ever think you might lose?"

"No, Mr. Olyn." He shook his head solemnly. "No man loses who goes to battle for the Lord." He saw that I needed to be convinced, and he went about it earnestly. "He hath set His hand upon His soldiers. And all that is possible to them is victory—or sometimes death. And what is death?"

He looked to his fellow-soldiers and they all nodded.

"What is death?" they echoed.

I looked at them. They stood there asking me and each other what was death as if they were talking about some hard but necessary job.

I had an answer for them, but I did not say it. Death was a Groupman, one of their own kind, giving orders to soldiers just like themselves to assassinate prisoners. That was death.

"Call an officer," I said. "My pass lets me through here."

"I regret, sir," said the one who had been talking to me. "We cannot leave our posts to summon an officer. One will come soon."

I had a hunch what "soon" meant, and I was right. It was high noon before a Force Leader came by to order them to chow and let me through.

As I pulled into Kensie Graeme's Headquarters, the sun was

217

low, patterning the ground with the long shadows of trees. Yet it was as if the camp was just waking up. I did not need experience to see the Exotics were beginning to move at last against Jamethon.

I found Janol Marat, the New Earth commandant.

"I've got to see Field Commander Graeme," I said.

He shook his head, for all that we now knew each other well.

"Not now, Tam. I'm sorry."

"Janol," I said, "this isn't for an interview. It's a matter of life and death. I mean that. I've got to see Kensie."

He stared at me. I stared back.

"Wait here," he said. We were standing just inside the headquarters office. He went out and was gone for perhaps five minutes. I stood, listening to the wall clock ticking away. Then he came back.

"This way," he said.

He led me outside and back between the bubble roundness of the plastic buildings to a small structure half-hidden in some trees. When we stepped through its front entrance, I realized it was Kensie's personal quarters. We passed through a small sitting room into a combination bedroom and bath. Kensie had just stepped out of the shower and was getting into battle clothes. He looked at me curiously, then turned his gaze back on Janol.

"All right, Commandant," he said, "you can get back to your duties, now."

"Sir," said Janol, without looking at me.

He saluted and left.

"All right, Tam," Kensie said, pulling on a pair of uniform slacks. "What is it?"

"I know you're ready to move out," I said.

He looked at me a little humorously as he locked the waistband of his slacks. He had not yet put on his shirt, and in that relatively small room he loomed like a giant, like some irresistible natural force. His body was tanned like dark wood and the muscles lay in flat bands across his chest and shoulders. His belly was hollow and the cords in his arms came and went as he moved them. Once more I felt the particular, special element of the Dorsai in him. It was not just his physical size and strength. It was not even the fact that he was someone trained from birth to war, someone bred for battle. No, it was something living but untouchable—the same quality of difference to be found in the pure Exotic like Padma the OutBond, or in some Newtonian or Cassidan researchist. Something so much above and beyond the common form of man that it was like a serenity, a sense of conviction where his own type of thing was concerned that was so complete it made him beyond all weaknesses, untouchable, unconquerable.

I saw the slight, dark shadow of Jamethon Black in my mind's eye, standing opposed to such a man as this; and the thought of any victory for Jamethon was unthinkable, an impossibility.

But there was always danger.

"All right, I'll tell you what I came about," I said to Kensie. "I've just found out Black's been in touch with the Blue Front, a native terrorist political group with its headquarters in Blauvain. Three of them visited him last night. I saw them."

Kensie picked up his shirt and slid a long arm into one sleeve.

"I know," he said.

I stared at him.

"Don't you understand?" I said. "They're assassins. It's their stock in trade. And the one man they and Jamethon Black both could use out of the way is you."

He put his other arm in a sleeve.

"I know that," he said. "They want the present government here on St. Marie out of the way and themselves in power—which isn't possible with Exotic money hiring us to keep the peace here."

"They haven't had Jamethon Black's help."

"Have they got it now?" he asked, sealing the shirt closure between thumb and forefinger.

"The Friendlies are desperate," I said. "Even if reinforcements arrived tomorrow, Jamethon knows what his chances are with you ready to move. Assassins may be outlawed by the Conventions of War and the Mercenaries' Code, but you and I know the Friendlies."

Kensie looked at me oddly and picked up his jacket.

"Do we?" he said.

I met his eyes. "Don't we?"

"Tam." He put on the jacket and closed it. "I know the men I have to fight. It's my business to know. But what makes you think you know them?"

"They're my business too," I said. "Maybe you'd forgotten. I'm a newsman. People are my business, first, last and always."

"But you've got no use for the Friendlies."

"Should I?" I said. "I've been on all the worlds. I've seen the Cetan entrepreneur—and he wants his margin, but he's a human being. I've seen the Newtonian and the Cassidan with their heads in the clouds, but if you yanked on their sleeves hard enough, you could pull them back to reality. I've seen Exotics like Padma at their mental parlor tricks, and the Freilander up to his ears in his own red tape. I've seen them from my own world of Old Earth, and Coby, and Venus and even from the Dorsai, like you. And I tell you they've all got one thing in common. Underneath it all they're human. Every one of them's human—they've just specialized in some one, valuable way."

"And the Friendlies haven't?"

"Fascinaticism," I said. "Is that valuable? It's just the opposite. What's good—what's even permissible about blind, deaf, dumb, unthinking faith that doesn't let a man reason for himself?"

"How do you know they don't reason?" Kensie asked. He was standing facing me now.

"Maybe some of them do," I said. "Maybe the young ones, before the poison's had time to work in. What good does that do, as long as the culture exists?"

A sudden silence came into the room.

"What are you talking about?" said Kensie.

"I mean you want the assassins," I said. "You don't want the Friendly troops. Prove that Jamethon Black has broken the Conventions of War by arranging with them to kill you; and you can win St. Marie for the Exotics without firing a shot."

"And how would I do that?"

"Use me," I said. "I've got a pipeline to the political group the assassins represent. Let me go to them as your representative and outbid Jamethon. You can offer them recognition by the present government, now. Padma and the present St. Marie government heads would have to back you up if you could clean the planet of Friendlies that easily."

He looked at me with no expression at all.

"And what would I be supposed to buy with this?" he said.

"Sworn testimony they'd been hired to assassinate you. As many of them as needed could testify."

"No Court of Interplanetary Inquiry would believe people like that," Kensie said.

"Ah," I said, and I could not help smiling. "But they'd believe me as a News Network Representative when I backed up every word that was said."

There was a new silence. His face had no expression at all.

"I see," he said.

He walked past me into the salon. I followed him. He went to his phone, put his finger on a stud and spoke into an image-less, gray screen.

"Janol," he said.

He turned away from the screen, crossed the room to an arms cabinet and began putting on his battle harness. He moved deliberately and neither looked nor spoke in my direction. After a few long minutes, the building entrance slid aside and Janol stepped in.

"Sir?" said the Freilander officer.

"Mr. Olyn stays here until further orders."

"Yes sir," said Janol.

Graeme went out.

I stood numb, staring at the entrance through which he had

left. I could not believe that he would violate the Conventions so far himself as not only to disregard me, but to put me essentially under arrest to keep me from doing anything further about the situation.

I turned to Janol. He was looking at me with a sort of wry sympathy on his long, brown face.

"Is the OutBond here in camp?" I asked him.

"No." He came up to me. "He's back in the Exotic Embassy in Blauvain. Be a good fella now and sit down, why don't you? We might as well kill the next few hours pleasantly."

We were standing face to face; I hit him in the stomach.

I had done a little boxing as an undergraduate on the college level. I mention this not to make myself out a sort of muscular hero, but to explain why I had sense enough not to try for his jaw. Graeme could probably have found the knockout point there without even thinking, but I was no Dorsai. The area below a man's breastbone is relatively large, soft, handy and generally just fine for amateurs. And I did know something about how to punch.

For all that, Janol was not knocked out. He went over on the floor and lay there doubled up with his eyes still open. But he was not ready to get up right away. I turned and went quickly out of the building.

The camp was busy. Nobody stopped me. I got back into my car, and five minutes later I was free on the darkening road for Blauvain.

V

From New San Marcos to Blauvain and Padma's Embassy was fourteen hundred kilometers. I should have made it in six hours, but a bridge was washed out and I took fourteen.

It was after eight the following morning when I burst into the half-park, half-building that was the embassy.

"Padma—" I said. "Is he still—"

"Yes, Mr. Olyn," said the girl receptionist. "He's expecting you."

She smiled above her purple robe. I did not mind. I was too busy being glad Padma had not already taken off for the fringe areas of the conflict.

She took me down and around a corner and turned me over to a young male Exotic, who introduced himself as one of Padma's secretaries. He took me a short distance and introduced me to another secretary, a middle-aged man this time, who led me through several rooms and then directed me down a long corridor and around a corner, beyond which he said was the entrance to the office area where Padma worked at the moment. Then he left me.

I followed his direction. But when I stepped through that entrance it was not into a room, but into a further short corridor. And I checked, stopping myself dead. For what I suddenly thought I saw coming at me was Kensie Graeme—Kensie with murder on his mind.

But the man who looked like Kensie merely glanced at me and dismissed me, continuing to come on. Then I knew.

Of course, he was not Kensie. He was Kensie's twin brother, Ian, commander of Garrison Forces for the Exotics, here in Blauvain. He strode on toward me, and I began once more to walk toward him, but the shock stayed with me until we had passed one another.

I do not think anyone could have come on him like that, in my position and not been hit the same way. From Janol, at different times, I had gathered how Ian was the converse of Kensie. Not in a military sense—they were both magnificent specimens of Dorsai officers—but in the matter of their individual natures.

Kensie had had a profound effect on me from the first moment, with his cheerful nature and the warmth of being that at times obscured the very fact that he was a Dorsai. When the pressure of military affairs was not directly on him he seemed all sunshine; you could warm yourself in his presence as you might in the sun. Ian, his physical duplicate, striding toward me, like some two-eyed Odin, was all shadow.

Here at last was the Dorsai legend come to life. Here was

223

the grim man with the iron heart and the dark and solitary soul. In the powerful fortress of his body, what was essentially Ian dwelt as isolated as a hermit on a mountain. He was the fierce and lonely Highlandman of his distant ancestry, come to life again.

Not law, not ethics, but the trust of the given word, clan-loyalty and the duty of the blood feud held sway in Ian. He was a man who would cross hell to pay a debt for good or ill; and in that moment when I saw him coming toward me and recognized him at last, I suddenly thanked whatever gods were left, that he had no debt with me.

Then we had passed each other, and he was gone around a corner.

Rumor had it, I remembered then, that the blackness around him never lightened except in Kensie's presence. That he was truly his twin brother's other half. And that if he should ever lose the light that Kensie's bright presence shed on him, he would be doomed to his own lightlessness forever.

It was a statement I was to remember at a later time, as I was to remember seeing him come toward me in that moment.

But now I forgot him as I went forward through another entrance into what looked like a small conservatory and saw the gentle face and short-cropped white hair of Padma, the OutBond, wearing a pale yellow robe.

"Come in, Mr Olyn," he said, getting up. "And come along with me."

He turned and walked out through an archway of purple clematis blooms. I followed him, and found a small courtyard, all but filled with the elliptical shape of a sedan aircar. Padma was already climbing into one of the seats facing the controls. He held the door for me.

"Where are we going?" I asked as I got in.

He touched the autopilot panel; the ship rose in the air. He left it to its own navigation, and pivoted his chair about to face me.

"To Commander Graeme's headquarters in the field," he answered.

His eyes were a light hazel color, but they seemed to catch and swim with the sunlight striking through the transparent top of the aircar, as we reached altitude and began to move horizontally. I could not read them, or the expression on his face.

"I see," I said. "Of course, I know a call from Graeme's HQ could get to you much faster than I could by groundcar from the same spot. But I hope you aren't thinking of having him kidnap me or something like that. I have Credentials of Impartiality protecting me as a Newsman, as well as authorizations from both the Friendly and the Exotic worlds. And I don't intend to be held responsible for any conclusions drawn by Graeme after the conversation the two of us had earlier this morning—*alone.*"

Padma sat still in his aircar seat, facing me. His hands were folded in his lap together, pale against the yellow robe, but with strong sinews showing under the skin of their backs.

"You're coming with me now by my decision, not Kensie Graeme's."

"I want to know why," I said tensely.

"Because," he said slowly, "you are very dangerous." And he sat still, looking at me with unwavering eyes.

I waited for him to go on, but he did not. "Dangerous?" I said. "Dangerous to who?"

"To the future of all of us."

I stared at him, then I laughed. I was angry.

"Cut it out!" I said.

He shook his head slowly, his eyes never leaving my face. I was baffled by those eyes. Innocent and open as a child's, but I could not see through them into the man himself.

"All right," I said. "Tell me, why am I dangerous?"

"Because you want to destroy a race of people. And you know how."

There was a short silence. The aircar fled on through the skies without a sound.

"Now that's an odd notion," I said slowly and calmly. "I wonder where you got it?"

"From our ontogenic calculations," said Padma, as calmly as I had spoken. "And it's not a notion, Tam. As you know yourself."

"Oh, yes," I said. "Ontogenics. I was going to look that up."

"You did look it up, didn't you, Tam?"

"Did I?" I said. "I guess I did, at that. It didn't seem very clear to me, though, as I remember. Something about evolution."

"Ontogenics," said Padma, "is the study of the effect of evolution upon the interacting forces of human society."

"Am I an interacting force?"

"At the moment and for the past several years, yes," said Padma. "And possibly for some years into the future. But possibly not."

"That sounds almost like a threat."

"In a sense it is." Padma's eyes caught the light as I watched them. "You're capable of destroying yourself as well as others."

"I'd hate to do that."

"Then," said Padma, "you'd better listen to me."

"Why, of course," I said. "That's my business, listening. Tell me all about ontogenics—and myself."

He made an adjustment in the controls, then swung his seat back to face mine once more.

"The human race," said Padma, "broke up in an evolutionary explosion at the moment in history when interstellar colonization became practical." He sat watching me. I kept my face attentive. "This happened for reasons stemming from racial instinct which we haven't completely charted yet, but which was essentially self-protective in nature."

I reached into my jacket pocket.

"Perhaps I'd better take a few notes," I said.

"If you want to," said Padma, unperturbed. "Out of that explosion came cultures individually devoted to single facets of the human personality. The fighting, combative facet became the Dorsai. The facet which surrendered the individual wholly to some faith or other became the Friendly. The philosophical facet created the Exotic culture to which I belong. We call these Splinter Cultures."

"Oh, yes," I said. "I know about Splinter Cultures."

"You know about them, Tam, but you don't know them."

"I don't?"

"No," said Padma, "because you, like all our ancestors, are from Earth. You're old, full-spectrum man. The Splinter peoples are evolutionarily advanced over you."

I felt a little twist of bitter anger knot suddenly inside me.

"Oh? I'm afraid I don't see that."

"Because you don't want to," said Padma. "If you did, you'd have to admit that they were different from you, and had to be judged by different standards."

"Different? How?"

"Different in a sense that all Splinter people, including myself, understand instinctively, but full-spectrum man has to extrapolate to imagine." Padma shifted a little in his seat. "You'll get some idea, Tam, if you imagine a member of a Splinter culture to be a man like yourself, only with a monomania that shoves him wholly toward being one type of person. But with this difference: Instead of all parts of his mental and physical self outside the limits of that monomania being ignored and atrophied as, they would be with you—"

I interrupted, "Why specifically with me?"

"With any full-spectrum man, then," said Padma calmly. "These parts, instead of being atrophied, are altered to agree with and support the monomania, so that we don't have a sick man—but a healthy, different one."

"Healthy?" I said, seeing the Friendly non-com on New Earth again in my mind's eye.

"Healthy as a culture. Not as occasional crippled individuals of that culture. But as a culture."

"Sorry," I said. "I don't believe it."

"But you do, Tam," said Padma, softly. "Unconsciously you do. Because you're planning to take advantage of the weakness such a culture must have to destroy it."

"And what weakness is that?"

"The obvious weakness that's the converse of any strength," said Padma. "The Splinter Cultures are not viable."

I must have blinked. I was honestly bewildered.

"Not viable? You mean they can't live on their own?"

"Of course not," said Padma. "Faced with an expansion into space, the human race reacted to the challenge of a different environment by trying to adapt to it. It adapted by trying out separately all the elements of its personality, to see which could survive best. Now that all elements—the Splinter Cultures—have survived and adapted, it's time for them to breed back into each other again, to produce a more hardy, universe-oriented human."

The aircar began to descend. We were nearing our destination.

"What's that got to do with me?" I said, at last.

"If you frustrate one of the Splinter Cultures, it can't adapt on its own as full-spectrum man would do. It will die. And when the race breeds back to a whole, that valuable element will be lost to the race."

"Maybe it'll be no loss," I said, softly in my turn.

"A vital loss," said Padma. "And I can prove it. You, a full-spectrum man, have in you an element from every Splinter Culture. If you admit this you can identify even with those you want to destroy. I have evidence to show you. Will you look at it?"

The ship touched ground; the door beside me opened. I got out with Padma and found Kensie waiting.

I looked from Padma to Kensie, who stood with us and a head taller than I—two heads taller than OutBond. Kensie looked back down at me with no particular expression. His eyes were not the eyes of his twin brother—but just then, for some reason, I could not meet them.

"I'm a newsman," I said. "Of course my mind is open."

Padma turned and began walking toward the headquarters building. Kensie fell in with us and I think Janol and some of the others came along behind, though I didn't look back to make sure. We went to the inner office where I first met Graeme —just Kensie, Padma and myself. There was a file folder on Graeme's desk. He picked it up, extracted a photocopy of something and handed it to me as I came up to him.

I took it. There was no doubting its authenticity.

It was a memo from Eldest Bright, ranking elder of the joint government of Harmony and Association, to the Friendly War Chief at the Defense X Center, on Harmony. It was dated two months previously. It was on the single-molecule sheet, where the legend cannot be tampered with, or removed once it is on.

Be Informed, in God's Name—
—That since it does seem the Lord's Will that our Brothers on St. Marie make no success, it is ordered that henceforth no more replacements or personnel or supplies be sent them. For if our Captain does intend us the victory, surely we shall conquer without further expenditure. And if it be His will that we conquer not, then surely it would be an impiety to throw away the substance of God's Churches in an attempt to frustrate that Will.
Be it further ordered that our Brothers on St. Marie be spared the knowledge that no further assistance is forthcoming, that they may bear witness to their faith in battle as ever, and God's Churches be undismayed.
Heed this Command, in the Name of the Lord:
By order of he who is called . . .
Bright
Eldest Among The Chosen

I looked up from the memo. Both Graeme and Padma were watching me.

"How'd you get hold of this?" I said. "No, of course, you won't tell me." The palms of my hands were suddenly sweating so that the slick material of the sheet in my fingers was slippery. I held it tightly, and talked fast to keep their eyes on my face. "But what about it? We already knew this, everybody knew Bright had abandoned them. This just proves it. Why even bother showing it to me?"

"I thought," said Padma, "it might move you just a little. Perhaps enough to make you take a different view of things."

I said, "I didn't say that wasn't possible. I tell you a Newsman keeps an open mind at all times. Of course," I picked my words carefully, "if I could study it—"

"I'd hoped you'd take it with you," said Padma.

"Hoped?"

"If you dig into it and really understand what Bright means there, you might understand all the Friendlies differently. You might change your mind about them."

"I don't think so," I said. "But—"

"Let me ask you to do that much," said Padma. "Take the memo with you."

I stood for a moment, with Padma facing me and Kensie looming behind him, then shrugged and put the memo in my pocket.

"All right," I said. "I'll take it back to my quarters and think about it—I've got a groundcar here somewhere, haven't I?" And I looked at Kensie.

"Ten kilometers back," said Kensie. "You wouldn't get through anyway. We're moving up for the assault and the Friendlies are maneuvering to meet us."

"Take my aircar," said Padma. "The Embassy flags on it will help."

"All right," I said.

We went out together toward the aircar. I passed Janol in the outer office and he met my eyes coldly. I did not blame him. We walked to the aircar and I got in.

"You can send the aircar back whenever you're through with it," said Padma, as I stepped in through the entrance section of its top. "It's an Embassy loan to you, Tam. I won't worry about it."

"No," I said. "You needn't worry."

I closed the section and touched the controls.

It was a dream of an aircar. It went up into the air as lightly as thought, and in a second I was two thousand feet up and well away from the spot. I made myself calm down, though, before I reached into my pocket and took the memo out.

I looked at it. My hand still trembled a little as I held it.

Here it was in my grasp at last. What I had been after from the start. And Padma himself had insisted I carry it away with me.

It was the lever, the Archimedes pry-bar which would move not one world but fourteen. And push the Friendly Peoples over the edge to extinction.

VI

They were waiting for me. They converged on the aircar as I landed it in the interior square of the Friendlies compound, all four of them with black rifles at the ready.

They were apparently the only ones left. Black seemed to have turned out every other man of his remnant of a battle unit. And these were all men I recognized, case-hardened veterans. One was the Groupman who had been in the office that first night when I had come back from the Exotic camp and stepped in to speak to Black, asking him if he ever ordered his men to kill prisoners. Another was a forty-year-old Force Leader, the lowest commissioned rank, but acting Major—just as Black, a Commandant, was acting as Expeditionary Field Commander—a position equivalent to Kensie Graeme's. The other two soldiers were non-commissioned, but similar. I knew them all. Ultrafanatics. And they knew me.

We understood each other.

"I have to see the commandant," I said, as I got out, before they could begin to question me.

"On what business?" said the Force Leader. "This aircar hath no business here. Nor thyself."

I said, "I must see Commandant Black immediately. I

wouldn't be here in a car flying the flags of the Exotic Embassy if it wasn't necessary."

They could not take the chance that my reason for seeing Black wasn't important, and I knew it. They argued a little, but I kept insisting I had to see the Commandant. Finally, the Force Leader took me across into the same outer office where I had always waited to see Black.

I faced Jamethon Black alone in the office.

He was putting on his battle harness, as I had seen Graeme putting on his earlier. On Graeme, the harness and the weapons it carried had looked like toys. On Jamethon's slight frame they looked almost too heavy to bear.

"Mr Olyn," he said.

I walked across the room toward him, drawing the memo from my pocket as I came. He turned a little to face me, his fingers sealing the locks on his harness, jingling slightly with his weapons and his harness as he turned.

"You're taking the field against the Exotics," I said.

He nodded. I had never been this close to him before. From across the room I would have believed he was holding his usual stony expression, but standing just a few feet from him now I saw the tired wraith of a smile touch the corners of his straight mouth in that dark, young face, for a second.

"That is my duty, Mr. Olyn."

"Some duty," I said. "When your superiors back on Harmony have already written you off their books."

"I've already told you," he said, calmly. "The Chosen are not betrayed in the Lord, one by another."

"You're sure of that?" I said.

Once more I saw that little ghost of a weary smile.

"It's a subject, Mr. Olyn, on which I am more expert than you."

I looked into his eyes. They were exhausted but calm. I glanced aside at the desk where the picture of the church, the older man and woman and the young girl stood still.

"Your family?" I asked.

"Yes," he said.

"It seems to me you'd think of them in a time like this."

"I think of them quite often."

"But you're going to go out and get yourself killed just the same."

"Just the same," he said.

"Sure!" I said. "You would!" I had come in calm and in control of myself. But now it was as if a cork had been pulled on all that had been inside me since Dave's death. I began to shake. "Because that's the kind of hypocrites you are—all of you Friendlies. You're so lying, so rotten clear through with your own lies, if someone took them away from you there'd be nothing left. Would there? So you'd rather die now than admit committing suicide like this isn't the most glorious thing in the universe. You'd rather die than admit you're just as full of doubts as anyone else, just as afraid."

I stepped right up to him. He did not move.

"Who're you trying to fool?" I said. "Who? I see through you just like the people on all the other worlds do! I know you know what a mumbo-jumbo your United Churches are. I know you know the way of life you sing of through your nose so much isn't what you claim it is. I know your Eldest Bright and his gang of narrow-minded old men are just a gang of world-hungry tyrants that don't give a damn for religion or anything as long as they get what they want. I know you know it—and I'm going to make you admit it!"

And I shoved the memo under his nose.

"Read it!"

He took it from me. I stepped back from him, shaking badly as I watched him.

He studied it for a long minute, while I held my breath. His face did not change. Then handed it back to me.

"Can I give you a ride to meet Graeme?" I said. "We can get across the lines in the OutBond's aircar. You can get the surrender over with before any shooting breaks out."

He shook his head. He was looking at me in a particularly level way, with an expression I could not understand.

"What do you mean—no?"

"You'd better stay here," he said. "Even with ambassadorial flags, that aircar may be shot at over the lines." And he turned as if he would walk away from me, out the door.

"Where're you going?" I shouted at him. I got in front of him and pushed the memo before his eyes again. "That's real. You can't close your eyes to that!"

He stopped and looked at me. Then he reached out and took my wrist and put my arm and hand with the memo aside. His fingers were thin, but much stronger than I thought, so that I let the arm go down in front of him when I hadn't intended to do so.

"I know it's real. I'll have to warn you not to interfere with me any more, Mr. Olyn. I've got to go now." He stepped past me and walked toward the door.

"You're a liar!" I shouted after him. He kept on going. I had to stop him. I grabbed the solidograph from his desk and smashed it on the floor.

He turned like a cat and looked at the broken pieces at my feet.

"That's what you're doing!" I shouted, pointing at them.

He came back without a word and squatted down and carefully gathered up the pieces, one by one. He put them into his pocket and got back to his feet, and raised his face at last to mine. And when I saw his eyes I stopped breathing.

"If my duty," he said, in a low, controlled voice, "were not in this minute to—"

His voice stopped. I saw his eyes staring into me; and slowly I saw them change and the murder that was in them soften into something like wonder.

"Thou"—he said, softly—"Thou hast *no* faith?"

I had opened my mouth to speak. But what he said stopped me. I stood as if punched in the stomach, without the breath for words. He stared at me.

"What made you think," he said, "that that memo would change my mind?"

"You read it!" I said. "Bright wrote you were a losing proposition here, so you weren't to get any more help. And no one was to tell you for fear you might surrender if you knew."

"Is that how you read it?" he said. "Like that?"

"How else? How else can you read it?"

"As it is written." He stood straight facing me now and his eyes never moved from mine. "You have read it without faith, leaving out the Name and the will of the Lord. Eldest Bright wrote not that we were to be abandoned here—but that since our cause was sore tried, we be put in the hands of our Captain and our God. And further he wrote that we should not be told of this, that none here should be tempted to a vain and special seeking of the martyr's crown. Look, Mr. Olyn. It's down there in black and white."

"But that's not what he meant! *That's not what he meant!*"

He shook his head. "Mr. Olyn, I can't leave you in such delusion."

I stared at him, for it was sympathy I saw in his face. For me.

"It's your own blindness that deludes you," he said. "You see nothing, and so believe no man can see. Our Lord is not just a name, but all things. That's why we have no ornament in our churches, scorning any painted screen between us and our God. Listen to me, Mr. Olyn. Those churches themselves are but tabernacles of the earth. Our Elders and Leaders, though they are Chosen and Anointed, are still but mortal men. To none of these things or people do we hearken in our faith, but to the very voice of God within us."

He paused. Somehow I could not speak.

"Suppose it was even as you think," he went on, even more gently. "Suppose that all you say was a fact; and that our Elders were but greedy tyrants, ourselves abandoned here by their selfish will and set to fulfill a false and prideful purpose. No." Jamethon's voice rose. "Let me attest as if it were only for myself. Suppose that you could give me proof that all our Elders lied, that our very Covenant was false. Suppose that you could prove to me"—his face lifted to mine and his voice drove at me—"that all was perversion and falsehood, and nowhere among the Chosen, not even in the house of my father, was there faith or hope! If you could prove to me that no miracle could save me, that no soul stood with me—and that opposed were all the legions of the universe—still I, I *alone*, Mr. Olyn, would go forward as I have been commanded, to the end of the universe, to the culmination of eternity. For without my faith I am but common earth. But with my faith, there is no power can stay me!"

He stopped speaking and turned about. I watched him walk across the room and out the door.

Still I stood there, as if I had been fastened in place—until I heard from outside, in the square of the compound, the sound of a military aircar starting up.

I broke out of my stasis then and ran out of the building.

As I burst into the square, the military aircar was just taking off. I could see Black and his four hard-shell subordinates in it. And I yelled up into the air after them.

"That's all right for you, but what about your men?"

They could not hear me. I knew that. Uncontrollable tears were running down my face, but I screamed up into the air after him anyway—

"You're killing your men to prove your point! Can't you listen? You're murdering helpless men!"

Unheeding, the military aircar dwindled rapidly to the west and south, where the converging battle forces waited. And the heavy concrete walls and buildings about the empty compound threw back my words with a hollow, wild and mocking echo.

VII

I should have gone to the spaceport. Instead, I got back into the aircar and flew back across the lines looking for Graeme's Battle Command Center.

I was as little concerned about my own life just then as a Friendly. I think I was shot at once or twice, in spite of the ambassadorial flags on the aircar, but I don't remember exactly. Eventually I found the Command Center and descended.

Enlisted men surrounded me as I stepped out of the aircar. I showed my credentials and went up to the battle screen, which had been set up in open air at the edge of shadow from some tall variform oaks. Graeme, Padma and his whole staff were grouped around it, watching the movements of their own and the Friendly troops reported on it. A continual low-voiced discussion of the movements went on, and a steady stream of information came from the communications center fifteen feet off.

The sun slanted steeply through the trees. It was almost noon and the day was bright and warm. No one looked at me for a long time; and then Janol, turning away from the screen, caught sight of me standing off at one side by the flat-topped shape of a tactics computer. His face went cold. He went on about what he was doing. But I must have been looking pretty bad, because after a while he came by with a canteen cup and set it down on the computer top.

"Drink that," he said shortly, and went off. I picked it up, found it was Dorsai whisky and swallowed it down. I could not taste it; but evidently it did me some good, because in a few minutes the world began to sort itself out around me and I began to think again.

I went up to Janol. "Thanks."

"All right." He did not look at me, but went on with the papers on the field desk before him.

"Janol," I said. "Tell me what's going on."

"See for yourself," he said, still bent over his papers.

"I can't see for myself. You know that. Look—I'm sorry about what I did. But this is my job, too. Can't you tell me what's going on now and fight with me afterwards?"

"You know I can't brawl with civilians." Then his face relaxed. "All right," he said, straightening up. "Come on."

He led me over to the battle screen, where Padma and

Kensie were standing, and pointed to a sort of small triangle of darkness between two snakelike lines of light. Other spots and shapes of light ringed it about.

"These"—he pointed to the two snakelike lines—"are the Macintok and Sarah Rivers, where they come together—just about ten miles this side of Joseph's Town. It's fairly high ground, hills thick with cover, fairly open between them. Good territory for setting up a stubborn defense, bad area to get trapped in."

"Why?"

He pointed to the two river lines.

"Get backed up in here and you find yourself hung up on high bluffs over the river. There is no easy way across, no cover for retreating troops. It's nearly all open farmland the rest of the way, from the other sides of the rivers to Joseph's Town."

His finger moved back out from the point where the river lines came together, past the small area of darkness and into the surrounding shapes and rings of light.

"On the other hand, the approach to this territory from our position is through open country, too—narrow strips of farmland interspersed with a lot of swamp and marsh. It's a tight situation for either commander, if we commit to a battle here. The first one who has to backpedal will find himself in trouble in a hurry."

"Are you going to commit?"

"It depends. Black sent his light armor forward. Now he's pulling back into the high ground, between the rivers. We're far superior in strength and equipment. There's no reason for us not to go in after him, as long as he's trapped himself—" Janol broke off.

"No reason?" I asked.

"Not from a tactical standpoint." Janol frowned at the screen. "We couldn't get into trouble unless we suddenly had to retreat. And we wouldn't do that unless he suddenly acquired some great tactical advantage that'd make it impossible for us to stay there."

I looked at his profile.

"Such as losing Graeme?" I said.

He transferred his frown to me. "There's no danger of that."

There was a certain change in the movement and the voices of the people around us. We both turned and looked.

Everybody was clustering around a screen. We moved in with the crowd and, looking between the soldiers of two of the officers of Graeme's staff, I saw on the screen the image of a small grassy meadow enclosed by wooded hills. In the center of the meadow, the Friendly flag floated its thin black cross on white background beside a long table on the grass. There were folding chairs on each side of the table, but only one person— a Friendly officer, standing on the table's far side as if waiting. There were the lilac bushes along the edge of the wooded hills where they came down in variform oak and ash to the meadow's edge; and the lavender blossoms were beginning to brown and darken for their season was almost at an end. So much difference had twenty-four hours made. Off to the left of the screen I could see the gray concrete of a highway.

"I know that place—" I started to say, turning to Janol.

"Quiet!" he said, holding up a finger. Around us, everybody else had fallen still. Up near the front of our group a single voice was talking.

"—it's a truce table."

"Have they called?" said the voice of Kensie.

"No, sir."

"Well, let's go see." There was a stir up front. The group began to break up and I saw Kensie and Padma walking off toward the area where the aircars were parked. I shoved myself through the thinning crowd like a process server, running after them.

I heard Janol shout behind me, but I paid no attention. Then I was up to Kensie and Padma, who turned.

"I want to go with you," I said.

"It's all right, Janol," Kensie said, looking past me. "You can leave him with us."

"Yes, sir." I could hear Janol turn and leave.

239

"So you want to come with me, Mr. Olyn?" Kensie said.

"I know that spot," I told him. "I drove by it just earlier today. The Friendlies were taking tactical measurements all over that meadow and the hills on both sides. They weren't setting up truce talks."

Kensie looked at me for a long moment, as if he was taking some tactical measurements himself.

"Come on, then," he said. He turned to Padma. "You'll be staying here?"

"It's a combat zone. I'd better not." Padma turned his unwrinkled face to me. "Good luck, Mr. Olyn," he said, and walked away. I watched his yellow-robed figure glide over the turf for a second, then turned to see Graeme halfway to the nearest military aircar. I hurried after him.

It was a battle car, not luxurious like the OutBond's, and Kensie did not cruise at two thousand feet, but snaked it between the trees just a few feet above ground. The seats were cramped. His big frame overfilled his, crowding me where I sat. I felt the butt-plate of his spring pistol grinding into my side with every movement he made on the controls.

We came at last to the edge of the wooded and hilly triangle occupied by the Friendlies and mounted a slope under the cover of the new-leaved variform oaks.

They were massive enough to have killed off most ground cover. Between their pillar-like trunks the ground was shaded, and padded with the brown shapes of dead leaves. Near the crest of the hill, we came upon a unit of Exotic troops resting and waiting the orders to advance. Kensie got out of the car and returned the Force Leader's salute.

"You've seen these tables the Friendlies set up?" Kensie asked.

"Yes, Commander. That officer they've got is still standing there. If you go just up over the crest of the slope here, you can see him—and the furniture."

"Good," said Kensie. "Keep your men here, Force. The Newsman and I'll go take a look."

He led the way up among the oak trees. At the top of the hill we looked down through about fifty yards more of trees and out into the meadow. It was two hundred yards across, the table right in the middle, the unmoving black figure of the Friendly officer standing on its far side.

"What do you think of it, Mr. Olyn?" asked Kensie, looking down through the trees.

"Why hasn't somebody shot him?" I asked.

He glanced sideways at me.

"There's plenty of time to shoot him," he said, "before he can get back to cover on the far side. If we have to shoot him at all. That wasn't what I wanted to know. You've seen the Friendly commander recently. Did he give you the impression he was ready to surrender?"

"No!" I said.

"I see," said Kensie.

"You don't really think he means to surrender? What makes you think something like that?"

"Truce tables are generally set up for the discussion of terms between opposing forces," he said.

"But he hasn't asked you to meet him?"

"No," Kensie watched the figure of the Friendly officer, motionless in the sunlight. "It might be against his principles to call for a discussion, but not to discuss—if we just happened to find ourselves across a table from one another."

He turned and signaled with his hand. The Force Leader, who had been waiting down the slope behind us, came up.

"Sir?" he said to Kensie.

"Any Friendly strength in those trees across the way?"

"Four men, that's all, sir. Our scopes pick out their body heats clear and sharp. They aren't attempting to hide."

"I see." He paused. "Force."

"Sir?"

"Be good enough to go down there in the meadow and ask that Friendly officer what this is all about."

"Yes, sir."

We stood and watched as the Force Leader went stiff-legging

it down the steep slope between the trees. He crossed the grass
—it seemed very slowly—and came up to the Friendly officer.

They stood facing each other. They were talking but there
was no way to hear their voices. The flag with its thin black
cross whipped in the little breeze that was blowing there. Then
the Force Leader turned and climbed back toward us.

He stopped in front of Kensie, and saluted. "Commander,"
he said, "the Commander of the Chosen Troops of God will
meet with you in the field to discuss a surrender." He stopped
to draw a fresh breath. "If you'll show yourself at the edge of
the opposite woods at the same time; and you can approach
the table together."

"Thank you, Force Leader," said Kensie. He looked past his
officer at the field and the table. "I think I'll go down."

"He doesn't mean it," I said.

"Force Leader," said Kensie. "Form your men ready, just
under the crown of the slope on the back side, here. If he sur-
renders, I'm going to insist he come back with me to this side
immediately."

"Yes, sir."

"All this business without a regular call for parley may be
because he wants to surrender first and break the news of it to
his troops afterwards. So get your men ready. If Black intends
to present his officers with an accomplished fact, we don't
want to let him down."

"He's not going to surrender," I said.

"Mr. Olyn," said Kensie, turning to me. "I suggest you go
back behind the crest of the hill. The Force Leader will see
you're taken care of."

"No," I said. "I'm going down. If it's a truce parley to
discuss surrender terms, there's no combat situation involved
and I've got a perfect right to be there. If it isn't, what're you
doing going down yourself?"

Kensie looked at me strangely for a moment.

"All right," he said. "Come with me."

Kensie and I turned and went down the sharply pitched

slope between the trees. Our boot-soles slipped until our heels dug in, with every step downward. Coming through the lilacs I smelled the faint, sweet scent—almost gone now—of the decaying blossoms.

Across the meadow, directly in line with the table, four figures in black came forward as we came forward. One of them was Jamethon Black.

Kensie and Jamethon saluted each other.

"Commandant Black," said Kensie.

"Yes, Commander Graeme. I am indebted to you for meeting me here," said Jamethon.

"My duty and a pleasure, Commandant."

"I wished to discuss the terms of a surrender."

"I can offer you," said Kensie, "the customary terms extended to troops in your position under the Mercenaries' Code."

"You misunderstand me, sir," said Jamethon. "It was your surrender I came here to discuss."

The flag snapped.

Suddenly I saw the men in black measuring the field here, as I had seen them the day before. They had been right where we were now.

"I'm afraid the misunderstanding is mutual, Commandant," said Kensie. "I am in a superior tactical position and your defeat is normally certain. I have no need to surrender."

"You will not surrender?"

"No," said Kensie strongly.

All at once I saw the five stakes, in the position the Friendly non-coms, officers and Jamethon were now, and the stake up in front of them fallen down.

"Look out!" I shouted at Kensie—but I was far too late.

Things had already begun to happen. The Force Leader had jerked back in front of Jamethon and all five of them were drawing their sidearms. I heard the flag snap again, and the sound of its rolling seemed to go on for a long time.

For the first time then I saw a man of the Dorsai in action.

243

So swift was Kensie's reaction that it was eerily as if he had read Jamethon's mind in the instant before the Friendlies began to reach for their weapons. As their hands touched their sidearms, he was already in movement forward over the table and his spring pistol was in his hand. He seemed to fly directly into the Force Leader and the two of them went down together, but Kensie kept traveling. He rolled on off the Force Leader who now lay still in the grass. He came to his knees, fired, and dived forward, rolling again.

The Groupman on Jamethon's right went down. Jamethon and the remaining two were turned nearly full about now, trying to keep Kensie before them. The two that were left shoved themselves in front of Jamethon, their weapons not yet aimed. Kensie stopped moving as if he had run into a stone wall, came to his feet in a crouch, and fired twice more. The two Friendlies fell apart, one to each side.

Jamethon was facing Kensie now, and Jamethon's pistol was in his hand and aimed. Jamethon fired, and a light blue streak leaped through the air, but Kensie had dropped again. Lying on his side on the grass, propped on one elbow, he pressed the firing button on his spring pistol twice.

Jamethon's sidearm sagged in his hand. He was backed up against the table now, and he put out his free hand to steady himself against the table top. He made another effort to lift his sidearm but he could not. It dropped from his hand. He bore more of his weight on the table, half-turning around, and his face came about to look in my direction. His face was as controlled as it had ever been, but there was something different about his eyes as he looked into mine and recognized me—something oddly like the look a man gives a competitor whom he had just beaten, and who was no real threat to begin with. A little smile touched the corners of his thin lips. Like a smile of inner triumph.

"Mr. Olyn . . ." he whispered. And then the life went out of his face and he fell beside the table.

Nearby explosions shook the ground under my feet. From the crest of the hill behind us the Force Leader whom Kensie had left there was firing smoke bombs between us and the Friendly side of the meadow. A gray wall of smoke was rising between us and the far hillside, to screen us from the enemy. It towered up the blue sky like some impassable barrier, and under the looming height of it, only Kensie and I were standing.

On Jamethon's dead face there was a faint smile.

VIII

In a daze I watched the Friendly troops surrender that same day. It was the one situation in which their officers felt justified in doing so.

Not even their Elders expected subordinates to fight a situation set up by a dead Field Commander for tactical reasons unexplained to his officers. And the live troops remaining were worth more than the indemnity charges for them that the Exotics would make.

I did not wait for the settlements. I had nothing to wait for. One moment the situation on this battlefield had been poised like some great, irresistible wave above all our heads, cresting, curling over and about to break downward with an impact that would reverberate through all the worlds of Man. Now, suddenly, it was no longer above us. There was nothing but a far-flooding silence, already draining away into the records of the past.

There was nothing for me. Nothing.

If Jamethon had succeeded in killing Kensie—even if as a result he had won a practically bloodless surrender of the Exotic troops—I might have done something damaging with the incident of the truce table. But he had only tried; and died, failing. Who could work up emotion against the Friendlies for that?

I took ship back to Earth like a man walking in a dream, asking myself why.

Back on Earth, I told my editors I was not in good shape physically; and they took one look at me and believed me. I took an indefinite leave from my job and sat around the News

Network Center Library, at the Hague, searching blindly through piles of writings and reference material on the Friendlies, the Dorsai and the Exotic worlds. For what? I did not know. I also watched the news dispatches from St. Marie concerning the settlement, and drank too much while I watched.

I had the numb feeling of a soldier sentenced to death for failure on duty. Then in the news dispatches came the information that Jamethon's body would be returned to Harmony for burial; and I realized suddenly it was this I had been waiting for: The unnatural honoring by fanatics of the fanatic who with four henchmen had tried to assassinate the lone enemy commander under a truce flag. Things could still be written.

I shaved, showered, pulled myself together after a fashion and went to see my superiors about being sent to Harmony to cover the burial of Jamethon, as a wrap-up.

The congratulations of the Director of News Network, that had reached me on St. Marie earlier, stood me in good stead. It was still fresh in the minds of the men just over me. I was sent.

Five days later I was on Harmony, in a little town called Remembered-of-the-Lord. The buildings in the town were of concrete and bubble plastic, though evidently they had been up for many years. The thin, stony soil about the town had been tilled as the fields on St. Marie had been tilled when I got to that other world—for Harmony now was just entering the spring of its northern hemisphere. And it was raining as I drove from the spaceport of the town, as it had on St. Marie that first day. But the Friendly fields I saw did not show the rich darkness of the fields of St. Marie. Only a thin, hard blackness in the wet that was like the color of Friendly uniforms.

I got to the church just as people were beginning to arrive. Under the dark, draining skies, the interior of the church was almost too dim to let me see my way about—for the Friendlies permit themselves no windows and no artificial lighting in their houses of worship. Gray light, cold wind and rain entered the doorless portal at the back of the church. Through the single rectangular opening in the roof watery sunlight filtered over Jamethon's body, on a platform set up on trestles. A transparent cover had been set up to protect the body from the rain, which was channeled off the open space and ran down a drain in the back wall. But the elder conducting the Death Service and anyone coming up to view the body was expected to stand exposed to sky and weather.

I got in line with the people moving slowly down the central aisle and past the body. To right and left of me the barriers at which the congregation would stand during the service were lost in gloom. The rafters of the steeply pitched roof were hidden in darkness. There was no music, but the low sound of voices individually praying to either side of me in the ranks of barriers and in the line blended into a sort of rhythmic undertone of sadness. Like Jamethon, the people were all very dark here, being of North African extraction. Dark into dark, they blended, and were lost about me in the gloom.

I came up and passed at last by Jamethon. He looked as I remembered him. Death had had no power to change him. He lay on his back, his hands at his side, and his lips were as firm and straight as ever. Only his eyes were closed.

I was limping noticably because of the dampness, and as I turned away from the body, I felt my elbow touched. I turned back sharply. I was not wearing my correspondent's uniform. I was in civilian clothes, so as to be inconspicuous.

I looked down into the face of the young girl in Jamethon's solidograph. In the gray rainy light her unlined face was like something from the stained glass window of an ancient cathedral back on Old Earth.

"You've been wounded," she said in a soft voice to me. "You must be one of the mercenaries who knew him on Newton, before he was ordered to Harmony. His parents, who are mine as well, would find solace in the Lord by meeting you."

The wind blew rain down through the overhead opening all about me, and its icy feel sent a chill suddenly shooting through me, freezing me to my very bones.

"No!" I said. "I'm not. I didn't know him." And I turned
247

sharply away from her and pushed my way into the crowd, back up the aisle.

After about fifteen feet, I realized what I was doing and slowed down. The girl was already lost in the darkness of the bodies behind me. I made my way more slowly toward the back of the church, where there was a little place to stand before the first ranks of the barriers began. I stood watching the people come in. They came and came, walking in in their black clothing with their heads down and talking or praying in low voices.

I stood where I was, a little back from the entrance, half numbed and dull-minded with the chill about me and the exhaustion I had brought with me from Earth. The voice droned about me. I almost dozed, standing there. I could not remember why I had come.

Then a girl's voice emerged from the jumble, bringing me back to full consciousness again.

"—he did deny it, but I am sure he is one of those mercenaries who was with Jamethon on Newton. He limps and can only be a soldier who hath been wounded."

It was the voice of Jamethon's sister, speaking with more of the Friendly cant on her tongue than she had used speaking to me, a stranger. I woke fully and saw her standing by the entrance only a few feet from me, half-facing two elder people who I recognized as the older couple in Jamethon's solidograph. A bolt of pure, freezing horror shot through me.

"No!" I nearly shouted at them. "I don't know him. I never knew him—I don't understand what you're talking about!" And I turned and bolted out through the entrance of the church into the concealing rain.

I all but ran for about thirty or forty feet. Then I heard no footsteps behind me; I stopped.

I was alone in the open. The day was even darker now and the rain suddenly came down harder. It obscured everything around me with a drumming, shimmering curtain. I could not even see the groundcars in the parking lot toward which I was facing; and for sure they could not see me from the church. I lifted my face up to the downpour and let it beat upon my cheeks and my closed eyelids.

"So," said a voice from behind me. "You did not know him?"

The words seemed to cut me down the middle, and I felt as a cornered wolf must feel. Like a wolf I turned.

"Yes, I knew him!" I said.

Facing me was Padma, in a blue robe the rain did not seem to dampen. His empty hands that had never held a weapon in their life were clasped together before him. But the wolf part of me knew that as far as I was concerned, he was armed and a hunter.

"You?" I said. "What are you doing here?"

"It was calculated you would be here," said Padma, softly. "So I am here, too. But why *are* you here, Tam? Among those people in there, there's sure to be at least a few fanatics who've heard the camp rumors of your responsibility in the matter of Jamethon's death and the Friendlies' surrender."

"Rumors!" I said. "Who started them?"

"You did," Padma said. "By your actions on St. Marie." He gazed at me. "Didn't you know you were risking your life, coming here today?"

I opened my mouth to deny it. Then I realized I had known.

"What if someone should call out to them," said Padma, "that Tam Olyn, the St. Marie campaign Newsman, is here incognito?"

I looked at him with my wolf-feeling, grimly.

"Can you square it with your Exotic principles if you do?"

"We are misunderstood," answered Padma calmly. "We hire soldiers to fight for us not because of some moral commandment, but because our emotional perspective is lost if we become involved."

There was no fear left in me. Only a hard, empty feeling.

"Then call them," I said.

Padma's strange, hazel eyes watched me through the rain. "If that was all that was needed," he said, "I could have sent word to them. I wouldn't have needed to come myself."

"Why did you come?" My voice tore at my throat. "What do you care about me, or the Exotics?"

"We care for every individual," said Padma. "But we care more for the race. And you remain dangerous to it. You're an idealist, Tam, warped to destructive purpose. There is a law of conservation of energy in the pattern of cause-and-effect as in other sciences. Your destructiveness was frustrated on St. Marie. Now it may turn inward to destroy you, or outward against the whole race of man."

I laughed, and heard the harshness of my laughter.

"What're you going to do about it?" I said.

"Show you how the knife you hold cuts the hand that holds it as well as what you turn it against. I have news for you, Tam. Kensie Graeme is dead."

"*Dead?*" The rain seemed to roar around me suddenly and the parking lot shifted unsubstantially under my feet.

"He was assassinated by three men of the Blue Front in Blauvain five days ago."

"Assassinated . . ." I whispered. "Why?"

"Because the war was over," said Padma. "Because Jamethon's death and the surrender of the Friendly troops without the preliminary of a war that would tear up the countryside left the civilian population favorably disposed toward our troops. Because the Blue Front found themselves farther from power than ever, as a result of this favorable feeling. They hoped by killing Graeme to provoke his troops into retaliation against the civilian population, so that the St. Marie government would have to order them home to our Exotics, and stand unprotected to face a Blue Front revolt."

I stared at him.

"All things are interrelated," said Padma. "Kensie was slated for a final promotion to a desk command back on Mara or Kultis. He and his brother Ian would have been out of the wars for the rest of their professional lives. Because of Jamethon's death, that allowed the surrender of his troops without fighting, a situation was set up which led the Blue Front to assassinate Kensie. If you and Jamethon had not come together on St. Marie, and Jamethon had won, Kensie would still be alive. So our calculations show."

"Jamethon and I?" The breath went dry in my throat without warning, and the rain came down harder.

"You were the factor," said Padma, "that helped Jamethon to his solution."

"I helped him!" I said. "*I* did?"

"He saw through you," said Padma. "He saw through the revenge-bitter, twisted surface you thought was yourself, to the idealistic core that was so deep in the bone of you that even your uncle hadn't been able to eradicate it."

The rain thundered between us. But Padma's every word came clearly through it to me.

"I don't believe you!" I shouted. "I don't believe he did anything like that!"

"I told you," said Padma, "you didn't fully appreciate the evolutionary advances of our Splinter Cultures. Jamethon's faith was not the kind that can be shaken by outer things. If you had been in fact like your uncle, he would not even have listened to you. He would have dismissed you as a soulless man. As it was, he thought of you instead as a man possessed. A man speaking with what he would have called Satan's voice."

"I don't believe it!" I yelled.

"You do believe it," said Padma. "You've got no choice except to believe it. Because only because of it could Jamethon find his solution."

"Solution!"

"He was a man ready to die for his faith. But as a commander he found it hard his men should go out to die for no other reasonable cause." Padma watched me, and the rain thinned for a moment. "But you offered him what he recognized as the devil's choice—his life in this world, if he would surrender his faith and his men, to avoid the conflict that would end in his death and theirs."

251

"What crazy thinking was that?" I said. Inside the church, the praying had stopped, and a single strong, deep voice was beginning the burial service.

"Not crazy," said Padma. "The moment he realized this, his answer became simple. All he had to do was begin by denying whatever the Satan offered. He must start with the absolute necessity of his own death."

"And that was a solution?" I tried to laugh but my throat hurt.

"It was the only solution," said Padma. "Once he decided that, he saw immediately that the one situation in which his men would permit themselves to surrender was if he was dead and they were in an untenable position for reasons only he had known."

I felt the words go through me with a soundless shock.

"But he didn't mean to die!" I said.

"He left it to his God," said Padma. "He arranged it so only a miracle could save him."

"What're you talking about?" I stared at him. "He set up a table with a flag of truce. He took four men—"

"There was no flag. The men were overage, martyrdom-seekers."

"He took four!" I shouted. "Four and one made five. The five of them against one man. I stood there by that table and saw. Five against—"

"Tam."

The single word stopped me. Suddenly I began to be afraid. I did not want to hear what he was about to say. I was afraid I knew what he was going to tell me. That I had known it for some time. And I did not want to hear it, I did not want to hear him say it. The rain grew even stronger, driving upon us both and mercilessly on the concrete, but I heard every word relentlessly through all its sound and noise.

Padma's voice began to roar in my ears like the rain, and a feeling came over me like the helpless floating sensation that comes in high fever. "Did you think that Jamethon for a minute fooled himself? He was a product of a Splinter Culture. He recognized another in Kensie. Did you think that for a minute he thought that barring a miracle he and four overage fanatics could kill an armed, alert and ready man of the Dorsai —*a man like Kensie Graeme?* Before they were gunned down and killed themselves?"

Themselves ... themselves ... themselves ...

I rode off a long way on that word from the dark day and the rain. Like the rain and the wind behind the clouds it lifted me and carried me away at last to that high, hard and stony land I had glimpsed when I had asked Kensie Graeme that question about his ever allowing Friendly prisoners to be killed. It was this land I had always avoided, but to it I was come at last.

And I remembered ...

From the beginning, I had known inside myself that the fanatic who had killed Dave and the others was not the image of all Friendlies. Jamethon was no casual killer. I had tried to make him into one in order to hide my own shame, my own self-destruction. For three years I had lied to myself. It had not been with me as I claimed, at Dave's death.

I had sat there under that tree watching Dave and the others die, watching the black-clad Groupman killing them with his machine rifle. And, in that moment, the thought in my mind had not been the one with which I justified three years of hunting for an opportunity to ruin someone like Jamethon and destroy the Friendly peoples.

It had not been me, thinking, *what is he doing there, what is he doing to those helpless, innocent men!* I had thought nothing so noble. Only one thought had filled all my mind and body in that instant. It had been simply—*after he's done, is he going to turn that gun on me?*

I came back to the day and to the rain. The rain was slackening and Padma was holding me upright. As with Jamethon, I was amazed at the strength of his hands.

"Let me go," I mumbled.

"Where would you go, Tam?" said Padma.

"Any place," I muttered. "I'll get out of it. I'll go hole up somewhere and get out of it. I'll give up."

"An action," said Padma, letting me go, "goes on reverberating for ever. Cause never ceases its effects. You can't let go now, Tam. You can only change sides."

"Sides!" I said. The rain was dwindling fast. "What sides?" I stared at him drunkenly.

"Your uncle's side which is one," said Padma. "And the opposing side, which is yours—which is ours as well." The rain was falling only lightly now, and the day was lightening. A little pale sunlight worked through thin clouds and illuminated the space between us. "In addition there are two strong influences besides we Exotics concerned with the attempt of man to evolve. We can't calculate or understand them yet, beyond the fact they act almost as single powerful individual wills. One seems to try to aid, one to frustrate, the evolutionary process; and their influences can be traced back at least as far as man's first venture into space from Earth."

I shook my head.

"I don't understand it," I muttered. "It's not my business."

"It is. It has been all your life." Padma's eyes caught light for a moment. "A force intruded on the pattern on St. Marie, in the shape of a unit warped by personal loss and oriented toward violence. That was you, Tam."

I tried to shake my head again, but I knew he was right.

"You are blocked in your effort," said Padma. "But the law of conservation of energies could not be denied. When you were frustrated by Jamethon, your force, transmuted, left the pattern in the unit of another individual, warped by personal loss and oriented toward violent effect on the fabric."

I stared at him and wet my lips. "What other individual?"

"Ian Graeme."

I stared at him.

"Ian found his brother's three assassins hiding in a hotel room in Blauvain. He killed them with his hands—and in

254

doing that he calmed the mercenaries and frustrated the Blue Front. But then he resigned and went home to the Dorsai. He's charged now with the sense of loss and bitterness you were charged with when you came to St. Marie." Padma paused and added softly, "Now he has great causal potential for some purpose we can't yet calculate."

"But—" I looked at Padma. "You mean I'm free!"

Padma shook his head.

"You're only charged with a different force instead," he said. "You received the full impact and charge of Jamethon's self-sacrifice."

He looked at me almost with sympathy, and in spite of the sunlight I began to shiver.

It was so. I could not deny it. Jamethon, in giving his life up for a belief, when I had thrown away all belief before the face of death, had melted and changed me as lightning melts and changes the uplifted sword-blade that it strikes. I could not deny what had happened to me.

"No," I said, shivering. "I can't do anything about it."

"You can," said Padma, calmly. "You will."

He unclasped his hands that he had held together earlier.

"The purpose for which we calculated I should meet you here is accomplished now," he said. "The idealism which was basic in you remains. Even your uncle couldn't take it from you. He could only attack it so that the threat of death on New Earth could twist it for a while against itself. Now you've been hammered straight in the forge of events on St. Marie."

I laughed, and the laugh hurt my throat still.

"I don't feel straight," I said.

"Give yourself time," said Padma. "Healing takes time. New growth has to harden, like muscle, before it becomes useful. Now you understand much more about the faith of the Friendlies, the courage of the Dorsai—and something of the philosophical strength for man we work toward on the Exotics."

He stopped and smiled at me. Almost an impish smile.

"It should have been clear to you a long while ago, Tam," he said. "Your job's the job of translator—between the old and the new. Your work will prepare the minds of the people on all the worlds—full-spectrum and Splinter Culture alike—for the day when the talents of the race will combine into the new breed." The smile softened, his face saddened. "You'll live to see more of it than I. Good-by, Tam."

He turned. Through the still misty, but brightening air, I saw him walking alone toward the church, from which came the voice of the speaker within, now announcing the number of the final hymn.

Dazedly, I turned away myself, went to my car and got in. Now the rain was almost over and the sky was brightening fast. The faint moisture fell, it seemed, more kindly; and the air was fresh and new.

I put the car windows open as I pulled out of the lot onto the long road back to the spaceport. And through the open window beside me I heard them beginning to sing the final hymn inside the church.

It was the Battle Hymn of the Friendly Soldiers that they sang. As I drove away down the road the voices seemed to follow me strongly. Not sounding slowly and mournfully as if in sadness and farewell, but strongly and triumphantly, as in a marching song on the lips of those taking up a route at the beginning of a new day.

> *Soldier, ask not—now, or ever,*
> *Where to war your banners go.*

The singing followed me as I drove away. And as I got farther into the distance, the voices seemed to blend until they sounded like one voice alone, powerfully singing. Ahead, the clouds were breaking. With the sun shining through, the patches of blue sky were like bright flags waving—like the banners of an army, marching forever forward into lands unknown.

I watched them, as I drove forward toward where they blended into open sky; and for a long time I heard the singing behind me, as I drove to the spaceport and the ship for Earth that waited in the sunlight.

Harlan is flamboyant. He's got the fastest, sharpest tongue in science fiction. What's more, he knows judo, karate, and foot-play, and packs a hundred eighty pounds of gristle, sinew, and muscle into a body that weighs a hundred twenty pounds altogether.

Don't ask me how, but he can get into a fight with three bruisers (non-science-fiction ones) each of whom is bigger than he is and come out the winner.

But he's a sport. He only picks on those science fiction personalities who have developed the reputation of being able to take care of themselves. Would he ever pick on Gordie Dickson whose chief weapon in wit-to-wit combat is a charming grin? Would he pick on Larry Niven whose slightly puzzled frown is his only defense against a grim world?

Never!

You know whom he picks on?

Me, that's whom.

From the other side of a huge ballroom, he sees me, and I can hear him coming all the way. Mercy? He doesn't know the meaning of the word.

He can ring every possible change on my waistline, for instance, just because it has a kind of sturdy expansiveness. I tell him over and over I need all that room to keep my spare brains in and he makes very ribald remarks about where I probably keep them. And you know the excuse he uses? He says I make fun of his height!

I *never!* Would I ever dream of mentioning that he is 62 inches tall? (Oh, he denies it, but if he stands on tippy-toe, he is.) Far from making jokes about his height, I've said a million times (and in public, too) that Harlan's height is no laughing matter.

Which reminds me that I remember Harlan when he was even younger than he is now, and just a fan, and a lot skinnier and more elfin. He used to scurry around the convention as quick as quicksilver and everyone else had to be careful not to trip over him.

Everyone knew he was special. Everyone knew he would go places. The question was what to do with him *meanwhile*.

We never found out then. But I think that, since then, we've learned.

Thus, at a convention just about a year ago as I write this, a young boy of sixteen showed up. He was skinny, sharp, self-confident, articulate, and had an IQ that sounded like two hundred.

A bunch of us looked at each other fearfully and one said, "He's another Harlan Ellison."

And someone, whose name I won't mention except to say that it was Robert Silverberg, said, "Let's kill him *now*."

4

"REPENT, HARLEQUIN!"
SAID THE TICKTOCKMAN

There are always those who ask, what is it all about? For those who need to ask, for those who need points sharply made, who need to know "where it's at," this:

"The mass of men serve the state thus, not as men mainly, but as machines, with their bodies. They are the standing army, and the militia, jailors, constables, posse comitatus, etc. In most cases there is no free exercise whatever of the judgment or of the moral sense; but they put themselves on a level with wood and earth and stones; and wooden men can perhaps be manufactured that will serve the purposes as well. Such command no more respect than men of straw or a lump of dirt. They have the same sort of worth only as horses and dogs. Yet such as these even are commonly esteemed good citizens. Others—as most legislators, politicians, lawyers, ministers, and office-holders—serve the state chiefly with their heads; and, as they rarely make any moral distinctions, they are as likely to serve the Devil, without intending it, as God. A very few, as heroes, patriots, martyrs, reformers in the great sense, and men, serve the state with their consciences also, and so necessarily resist it for the most part; and they are commonly treated as enemies by it."

> Henry David Thoreau,
> *"Civil Disobedience"*

That is the heart of it. Now begin in the middle, and later learn the beginning; the end will take care of itself.

But because it was the very world it was, the very world they had allowed it to *become*, for months his activities did not come to the alarmed attention of The Ones Who Kept The Machine Functioning Smoothly, the ones who poured the very best butter over the cams and mainsprings of the culture. Not until it had become obvious that somehow, someway, he had become a notoriety, a celebrity, perhaps even a hero for (what Officialdom inescapably tagged) "an emotionally disturbed segment of the populace," did they turn it over to the Ticktockman and his legal machinery. But by then, because it was the very world it was, and they had no way to predict he would happen—possibly a strain of disease long-defunct, now, suddenly, reborn in a system where immunity had been forgotten, had lapsed—he had been allowed to become too real. Now he had form and substance.

He had become a *personality*, something they had filtered out of the system many decades ago. But there it was, and there *he* was, a very definitely imposing personality. In certain circles—middle-class circles—it was thought disgusting. Vulgar ostentation. Anarchistic. Shameful. In others, there was only sniggering, those strata where thought is subjugated to form and ritual, niceties, proprieties. But down below, ah, down below, where the people always needed their saints and sinners, their bread and circuses, their heroes and villains, he was considered a Bolivar; a Napoleon; a Robin Hood; a Dick Bong (Ace of Aces); a Jesus; a Jomo Kenyatta.

And at the top—where, like socially-attuned Shipwreck Kellys, even tremor and vibration threatens to dislodge the wealthy, powerful and titled from their flagpoles—he was considered a menace; a heretic; a rebel; a disgrace; a peril. He was known down the line, to the very heartmeat core, but the important reactions were high above and far below. At the very top, at the very bottom.

So his file was turned over, along with his time-card and his cardioplate, to the office of the Ticktockman.

The Ticktockman: very much over six feet tall, often silent, a soft purring man when things went timewise. The Ticktockman.

Even in the cubicles of the hierarchy, where fear was generated, seldom suffered, he was called the Ticktockman. But no one called him that to his mask.

You don't call a man a hated name, not when that man, behind his mask, is capable of revoking the minutes, the hours, the days and nights, the years of your life. He was called the Master Timekeeper to his mask. It was safer that way.

"This is *what* he is," said the Ticktockman with genuine softness, "but not *who* he is? This time-card I'm holding in my left hand has a name on it, but it is the name of *what* he is, not *who* he is. This cardioplate here in my right hand is also named, but not whom named, merely what named. Before I can exercise proper revocation, I have to know who this what is."

To his staff, all the ferrets, all the loggers, all the finks, all the commex, even the mineez, he said, "Who is this Harlequin?"

He was not purring smoothly. Timewise, it was jangle.

However, it *was* the longest speech they had ever heard him utter at one time, the staff, the ferrets, the loggers, the finks, the commex, but not the mineez, who usually weren't around to know, in any case. But even they scurried to find out.

Who is the Harlequin?

High above the third level of the city, he crouched on the humming aluminum-frame platform of the air-boat (foof! airboat, indeed! swizzleskid is what it was, with a tow-rack jerryrigged) and stared down at the neat Mondrian arrangement of the buildings.

Somewhere nearby, he could hear the metronomic left-right-left of the 2:47 P.M. shift, entering the Timkin roller-bearing plant in their sneakers. A minute later, precisely, he heard the softer right-left-right of the 5:00 A.M. formation, going home.

An elfish grin spread across his tanned features, and his dimples appeared for a moment. Then, scratching at his thatch of auburn hair, he shrugged within his motley, as though girding himself for what came next, and threw the joystick forward, and bent into the wind as the air-boat dropped. He skimmed over a slidewalk, purposely dropping a few feet to crease the tassels of the ladies of fashion, and—inserting thumbs in large ears—he stuck out his tongue, rolled his eyes and went wugga-wugga-wugga. It was a minor diversion. One pedestrian skittered and tumbled, sending parcels everywhichway, another wet herself, a third keeled slantwise and the walk was stopped automatically by the servitors till she could be resuscitated. It was a minor diversion.

Then he swirled away on a vagrant breeze, and was gone. Hi-ho.

As he rounded the cornice of the Time-Motion Study Building, he saw the shift, just boarding the slidewalk. With practiced motion and an absolute conservation of movement, they side-stepped up onto the slowstrip and (in a chorus line reminiscent of a Busby Berkeley film of the antediluvian 1930's) advanced across the strips ostrich-walking till they were lined up on the expresstrip.

Once more, in anticipation, the elfin grin spread, and there was a tooth missing back there on the left side. He dipped, skimmed, and swooped over them; and then, scrunching about on the air-boat, he released the holding pins that fastened shut the ends of the home-made pouring troughs that kept his cargo from dumping prematurely. And as he pulled the trough-pins, the air-boat slid over the factory workers and one hundred and fifty thousand dollars worth of jelly beans cascaded down on the expresstrip.

Jelly beans! Millions and billions of purples and yellows and greens and licorice and grape and raspberry and mint and round and smooth and crunchy outside and soft-mealy inside and sugary and bouncing jouncing tumbling clittering clattering skittering fell on the heads and shoulders and hard-hats and carapaces of the Timkin workers, tinkling on the slidewalk and bouncing away and rolling about underfoot and filling the sky on their way down with all the colors of joy and childhood and holidays, coming down in a steady rain, a solid wash, a torrent of color and sweetness out of the sky from

263

above, and entering a universe of sanity and metronomic order with quite-mad coocoo newness. Jelly beans!

The shift workers howled and laughed and were pelted, and broke ranks, and the jelly beans managed to work their way into the mechanism of the slidewalks after which there was a hideous scraping as the sound of a million fingernails rasped down a quarter of a million blackboards, followed by a coughing and a sputtering, and then the slidewalks all stopped and everyone was dumped thisawayandthataway in a jackstraw tumble, and still laughing and popping little jelly bean eggs of childish color into their mouths. It was a holiday, and a jollity, an absolute insanity, a giggle. But . . .

The shift was delayed seven minutes.

They did not get home for seven minutes.

The master schedule was thrown off by seven minutes.

Quotas were delayed by inoperative slidewalks for seven minutes.

He had tapped the first domino in the line, and one after another, like chik chik chik, the others had fallen.

The System had been seven minutes worth of disrupted. It was a tiny matter, one hardly worthy of note, but in a society where the single driving force was order and unity and promptness and clocklike precision and attention to the clock, reverence of the gods of the passage of time, it was a disaster of major importance.

So he was ordered to appear before the Ticktockman. It was broadcast across every channel of the communications web. He was ordered to be *there* at 7:00 dammit on time. And they waited, and they waited, but he didn't show up till almost ten-thirty, at which time he merely sang a little song about moonlight in a place no one had ever heard of, called Vermont, and vanished again. But they had all been waiting since seven, and it wrecked *hell* with their schedules. So the question remained: Who is the Harlequin?

But the *unasked* question (more important of the two) was: how did we get *into* this position, where a laughing, irresponsible japer of jabberwocky and jive could disrupt our entire economic and cultural life with a hundred and fifty thousand dollars worth of jelly beans . . .

Jelly for God's sake beans! This is madness! Where did he get the money to buy a hundred and fifty thousand dollars worth of jelly beans? (They knew it would have cost that much, because they had a team of Situation Analysts pulled off another assignment, and rushed to the slidewalk scene to sweep up and count the candies, and produce findings, which disrupted *their* schedules and threw their entire branch at least a day behind.) Jelly beans! Jelly . . . *beans?* Now wait a second—a second accounted for—no one has manufactured jelly beans for over a hundred years. Where did he get jelly beans?

That's another good question. More than likely it will never be answered to your complete satisfaction. But then, how many questions ever are?

The middle you know. Here is the beginning. How it starts:

A desk pad. Day for day, and turn each day, 9:00—open the mail. 9:45—appointment with planning commission board. 10:30—discuss installation progress charts with J.L. 11:45—pray for rain. 12:00—lunch. *And so it goes.*

"I'm sorry, Miss Grant, but the time for interviews was set at 2:30, and it's almost five now. I'm sorry you're late, but those are the rules. You'll have to wait till next year to submit application for this college again." *And so it goes.*

The 10:10 local stops at Cresthaven, Galesville, Tonawanda Junction, Selby and Farnhurst, but not at Indiana City, Lucasville and Colton, except on Sunday. The 10:35 express stops at Galesville, Selby and Indiana City, except on Sundays & Holidays, at which time it stops at . . . *and so it goes.*

"I couldn't wait, Fred. I had to be at Pierre Cartain's by 3:00, and you said you'd meet me under the clock in the terminal at 2:45, and you weren't there, so I had to go on. You're always late, Fred. If you'd been there, we could have sewed it up together, but as it was, well I took the order alone . . ." *And so it goes.*

Dear Mr. and Mrs. Atterley: in reference to your son Gerold's constant tardiness, I am afraid we will have to suspend him from school unless some more reliable method can be instituted guaranteeing he will arrive at his classes on time. Granted he is an exemplary student, and his marks are high, his constant flouting of the schedules of this school makes it impractical to maintain him in a system where the other children seem capable of getting where they are supposed to be on time *and so it goes*.

YOU CANNOT VOTE UNLESS YOU APPEAR AT 8:45 A.M.

"I don't care if the script is *good*, I need it Thursday!"

CHECK-OUT TIME IS 2:00 P.M.

"You got here late. The job's taken. Sorry."

YOUR SALARY HAS BEEN DOCKED FOR TWENTY MINUTES TIME LOST.

"God, what time is it, I've gotta run!"

And so it goes. And so it goes. And so it goes. And so it goes goes goes goes goes tick tock tick tock tick tock and one day we no longer let time serve us, we serve time and we are slaves of the schedule, worshippers of the sun's passing, bound into a life predicted on restrictions because the system will not function if we don't keep the schedule tight.

Until it becomes more than a minor inconvenience to be late. It becomes a sin. Then a crime. Then a crime punishable by this:

EFFECTIVE 15 JULY 2389, 12:00:00 midnight, the office of the Master Timekeeper will require all citizens to submit their time-cards and cardioplates for processing. In accordance with Statute 555-7-SGH-999 governing the revocation of time per capita, all cardioplates will be keyed to the individual holder and—

What they had done, was devise a method of curtailing the amount of life a person could have. If he was ten minutes late, he lost ten minutes of his life. An hour was proportionately worth more revocation. If someone was consistently tardy, he might find himself, on a Sunday night, receiving a communique from the Master Timekeeper that his time had run out, and he would be "turned off" at high noon on Monday, please straighten your affairs, sir.

And so, by this simple scientific expedient (utilizing a scientific process held dearly secret by the Ticktockman's office) the System was maintained. It was the only expedient thing to do. It was, after all, patriotic. The schedules had to be met. After all, there *was* a war on!

But, wasn't there always?

"Now that is really disgusting," the Harlequin said, when pretty Alice showed him the wanted poster. "Disgusting and *highly* improbable. After all, this isn't the days of desperadoes. A *wanted* poster!"

"You know," Alice noted, "you speak with a great deal of inflection."

"I'm sorry," said the Harlequin, humbly.

"No need to be sorry. You're always saying 'I'm sorry.' You have such massive guilt, Everett, it's really very sad."

"I'm sorry," he repeated, then pursed his lips so the dimples appeared momentarily. He hadn't wanted to say that at all. "I have to go out again. I have to *do* something."

Alice slammed her coffee-bulb down on the counter. "Oh for God's *sake*, Everett, can't you stay home just *one* night! Must you always be out in that ghastly clown suit, running around *annoying* people?"

"I'm—" he stopped, and clapped the jester's hat onto his auburn thatch with a tiny tingling of bells. He rose, rinsed out his coffee-bulb at the tap, and put it into the drier for a moment. "I have to go."

She didn't answer. The faxbox was purring, and she pulled a sheet out, read it, threw it toward him on the counter. "It's about you. Of course. You're ridiculous."

He read it quickly. It said the Ticktockman was trying to locate him. He didn't care, he was going out to be late again. At the door, dredging for an exit line, he hurled back petulantly, "Well, *you* speak with inflection, *too!*"

Alice rolled her pretty eyes heavenward. "You're ridiculous."

The Harlequin stalked out, slamming the door, which sighed shut softly, and locked itself.

There was a gentle knock, and Alice got up with an exhalation of exasperated breath, and opened the door. He stood there. "I'll be back about ten-thirty, okay?"

She pulled a rueful face. "Why do you tell me that? Why? You *know* you'll be late! You *know it!* You're *always* late, so why do you tell me these dumb things?" She closed the door.

On the other side, the Harlequin nodded to himself. *She's right. She's always right. I'll be late. I'm always late. Why do I tell her these dumb things?*

He shrugged again, and went off to be late once more.

He had fired off the firecracker rockets that said: I will attend the 115th annual International Medical Association Invocation at 8:00 P.M. precisely. I do hope you will all be able to join me.

The words had burned in the sky, and of course the authorities were there, lying in wait for him. They assumed, naturally, that he would be late. He arrived twenty minutes early, while they were setting up the spiderwebs to trap and hold him, and blowing a large bullhorn, he frightened and unnerved them so, their own moisturized encirclement webs sucked closed, and they were hauled up, kicking and shrieking, high above the amphitheater's floor. The Harlequin laughed and laughed, and apologized profusely. The physicians, gathered in solemn conclave, roared with laughter, and accepted the Harlequin's apologies with exaggerated bowing and posturing, and a merry time was had by all, who thought the Harlequin was a regular foofaraw in fancy pants; all, that is, but the authorities, who had been sent out by the office of the Ticktockman, who hung there like so much dockside cargo, hauled up above the floor of the amphitheater in a most unseemly fashion.

(In another part of the same city where the Harlequin carried on his "activities," totally unrelated in every way to what concerns here, save that it illustrates the Ticktockman's power and import, a man named Marshall Delahanty received his turn-off notice from the Ticktockman's office. His wife received the notification from the grey-suited minee who delivered it, with the traditional "look of sorrow" plastered hideously across his face. She knew what it was, even without unsealing it. It was a billet-doux of immediate recognition to everyone these days. She gasped, and held it as though it were a glass slide tinged with botulism, and prayed it was not for her. Let it be for Marsh, she thought, brutally, realistically, or one of the kids, but not for me, please dear God, not for me. And then she opened it, and it *was* for Marsh, and she was at one and the same time horrified and relieved. The next trooper in the line had caught the bullet. "Marshall," she screamed, "Marshall! Termination, Marshall OhmiGod, Marshall, whattl we do, whattl we do, Marshall omigodmarshall . . ." and in their home that night was the sound of tearing paper and fear, and the stink of madness went up the flue and there was nothing, absolutely nothing they could do about it.)

(But Marshall Delahanty tried to run. And early the next day, when turn-off time came, he was deep in the forest two hundred miles away, and the office of the Ticktockman blanked his cardioplate, and Marshall Delahanty keeled over, running, and his heart stopped, and the blood dried up on its way to his brain, and he was dead that's all. One light went out on his sector map in the office of the Master Timekeeper, while notification was entered for fax reproduction, and Georgette Delahanty's name was entered on the dole roles till she could re-marry. Which is the end of the footnote, and all the point that need be made, except don't laugh, because that is what would happen to the Harlequin if ever the Ticktockman found out his real name. It isn't funny.)

The shopping level of the city was thronged with the Thursday-colors of the buyers. Women in canary yellow chitons and men in pseudo-Tyrolean outfits that were jade and leather and fit very tightly, save for the balloon pants.

When the Harlequin appeared on the still-being-constructed

shell of the new Efficiency Shopping Center, his bullhorn to his elfishly-laughing lips, everyone pointed and stared, and he berated them:

"Why let them order you about? Why let them tell you to hurry and scurry like ants or maggots? Take your time! Saunter a while! Enjoy the sunshine, enjoy the breeze, let life carry you at your own pace! Don't be slaves of time, it's a helluva way to die, slowly, by degrees . . . down with the Ticktockman!"

Who's the nut? most of the shoppers wanted to know. Who's the nut oh wow I'm gonna be late. I gotta run . . .

And the construction gang on the Shopping Center received an urgent order from the office of the Master Timekeeper that the dangerous criminal known as the Harlequin was atop their spire, and their aid was urgently needed in apprehending him. The work crew said no, they would lose time on their construction schedule, but the Ticktockman managed to pull the proper threads of governmental webbing, and they were told to cease work and catch that nitwit up there on the spire with the bullhorn. So a dozen and more burly workers began climbing into their construction platforms, releasing the a-grav plates, and rising toward the Harlequin.

After the debacle (in which, through the Harlequin's attention to personal safety, no one was seriously injured), the workers tried to reassemble, and assault him again, but it was too late. He had vanished. It had attracted quite a crowd, however, and the shopping cycle was thrown off by hours, simply hours. The purchasing needs of the system were therefore falling behind, and so measures were taken to accelerate the cycle for the rest of the day, but it got bogged down and speeded up and they sold too many float-valves and not nearly enough wegglers, which meant that the popli ratio was off, which made it necessary to rush cases and cases of spoiling Smash-O to stores that usually needed a case only every three or four hours. The shipments were bollixed, the trans-shipments were misrouted, and in the end, even the swizzleskid industries felt it.

"Don't come back till you have him!" the Ticktockman said, very quietly, very sincerely, extremely dangerously.

They used dogs. They used probes. They used cardioplate crossoffs. They used teepers. They used bribery. They used stiktytes. They used intimidation. They used torment. They used torture. They used finks. They used cops. They used search&seizure. They used fallaron. They used betterment incentive. They used fingerprints. They used Bertillon. They used cunning. They used guile. They used treachery. They used Raoul Mitgong, but he didn't help much. They used applied physics. They used techniques of criminology.

And what the hell: they caught him.

After all, his name was Everett C. Marm, and he wasn't much to begin with, except a man who had no sense of time.

"Repent, Harlequin!" said the Ticktockman.

"Get stuffed!" the Harlequin replied, sneering.

"You've been late a total of sixty-three years, five months, three weeks, two days, twelve hours, forty-one minutes, fifty-nine seconds, point oh three six one one one microseconds. You've used up everything you can, and more. I'm going to turn you off."

"Scare someone else. I'd rather be dead than live in a dumb world with a bogeyman like you."

"It's my job."

"You're full of it. You're a tyrant. You have no right to order people around and kill them if they show up late."

"You can't adjust. You can't fit in."

"Unstrap me, and I'll fit my fist into your mouth."

"You're a non-conformist."

"That didn't used to be a felony."

"It is now. Live in the world around you."

"I hate it. It's a terrible world."

"Not everyone thinks so. Most people enjoy order."

"I don't, and most of the people I know don't."

"That's not true. How do you think we caught you?"

"I'm not interested."

"A girl named pretty Alice told us who you were."

"That's a lie."

"It's true. You unnerve her. She wants to belong, she wants to conform, I'm going to turn you off."

"Then do it already, and stop arguing with me."

"I'm not going to turn you off."

"You're an idiot!"

"Repent, Harlequin!" said the Ticktockman.

"Get stuffed."

So they sent him to Coventry. And in Coventry they worked him over. It was just like what they did to Winston Smith in "1984" which was a book none of them knew about, but the techniques are really quite ancient, and so they did it to Everett C. Marm, and one day quite a long time later, the Harlequin appeared on the communications web, appearing elfish and dimpled and bright-eyed, and not at all brainwashed, and he said he had been wrong, that it was a good, a very good thing indeed, to belong, and be right on time hip-ho and away we go, and everyone stared up at him on the public screens that covered an entire city block, and they said to themselves, well, you see, he was just a nut after all, and if that's the way the system is run, then let's do it that way, because it doesn't pay to fight city hall, or in this case, the Ticktockman. So Everett C. Marm was destroyed, which was a loss, because of what Thoreau said earlier, but you can't make an omelet without breaking a few eggs, and in every revolution, a few die who shouldn't, but they have to, because that's the way it happens, and if you make only a little change, then it seems to be worthwhile. Or, to make the point lucidly:

"Uh, excuse me, sir, I, uh, don't know how to uh, to uh, tell you this, but you were three minutes late. The schedule is a little, uh, bit off."

He grinned sheepishly.

"That's ridiculous!" murmured the Ticktockman behind his mask. "Check your watch." And then he went into his office, going mrmee, mrmee, mrmee, mrmee.

Now I must deal with Jack again.

Knowing that I didn't know Jack Vance and that he would appear twice, I was in a terrible quandary. I had to find out something about him; something significant. It was no use determining that he lived in California; and that he was about my age and shape (which is very good in itself, of course). I wanted something more.

What to do? So I picked up the phone and called Robert Silverberg. It meant I would interrupt him at work since his schedule is something like mine but I would be doing him a favor because I understand he fights with his typewriter. (It keeps shrieking at him because it has sensitive keys and he has cold fingers.)

"Tell me about Jack Vance, Bob," I said.

So he did, and I listened and listened, and finally Bob said, "He's strangely uncommunicative in a way. That is, he loves to talk shop, but when I asked him whether he was influenced more by Kafka or by Dunsany, he changed the subject."

I was delighted, for right then I knew that Jack Vance was an all-right guy. I hate these writers who have been terribly influenced by Lord Kafka or Franz Dunsany—big show-offs. Personally, I was influenced by guys like Nat Schachner and Clifford Simak and John W. Campbell, Jr.

Back in the 1930s, you see, I was reading science fiction. A fellow with science fiction writing ambitions *should* read science fiction. I didn't waste my time reading Proust and Tolstoy and all them other highfalutin Greeks.

And neither, I'll bet, did Jack Vance. Good boy, Jack! It's you and I against the world.

5

THE LAST CASTLE

Toward the end of a stormy summer afternoon, with the sun finally breaking out under ragged black rain clouds, Castle Janeil was overwhelmed and its population destroyed.

Until almost the last moment the factions among the castle clans were squabbling as to how Destiny properly should be met. The gentlemen of most prestige and account elected to ignore the entire undignified circumstance and went about their normal pursuits, with neither more nor less punctilio than usual. A few cadets, desperate to the point of hysteria, took up weapons and prepared to resist the final assault. Others still, perhaps a quarter of the total population, waited passively, ready—almost happy—to expiate the sins of the human race.

In the end death came uniformly to all; and all extracted as much satisfaction in their dying as this essentially graceless process could afford. The proud sat turning the pages of their beautiful books, or discussing the qualities of a century-old essence, or fondling a favorite Phane. They died without deigning to heed the fact. The hot-heads raced up the muddy slope which, outraging all normal rationality, loomed above the parapets of Janeil. Most were buried under sliding rubble, but a few gained the ridge to gun, hack, stab, until they themselves were shot, crushed by the half-alive power-wagons, hacked or stabbed. The contrite waited in the classic posture of expiation, on their knees, heads bowed, and perished, so they believed, by a process in which the Meks were symbols and human sin the reality. In the end all were dead: gentlemen, ladies, Phanes in the pavilions; Peasants in the stables. Of all those who had inhabited Janeil, only the Birds survived, creatures awkward, gauche and raucous, oblivious to pride and faith, more concerned with the wholeness of their hides than the dignity of their castle.

As the Meks swarmed over the parapets, the Birds departed their cotes. They screamed strident insults as they flapped east toward Hagedorn, now the last castle of Earth.

Four months before, the Meks had appeared in the park before Janeil, fresh from the Sea Island massacre.

Climbing to the turrets and balconies, sauntering the Sunset Promenade, from ramparts and parapets, the gentlemen and ladies of Janeil, some two thousand in all, looked down at the brown-gold warriors. Their mood was complex: amused indifference, flippant disdain, over a substratum of doubt and foreboding. All these moods were the product of three basic circumstances: their own exquisitely subtle civilization, the security provided by Janeil's wall and the fact that they could think of nothing to do to alter the circumstances.

The Janeil Meks had long since departed to join the revolt. There only remained Phanes, Peasants and Birds from which to fashion what would have been the travesty of a punitive force.

At the moment there seemed no need for such a force. Janeil was deemed impregnable. The walls, two hundred feet tall, were black rock-melt contained in the meshes of a silver-blue steel alloy. Solar cells provided energy for all the needs of the castle, and in the event of emergency food could be synthesized from carbon dioxide and water vapor, as well as syrup for Phanes, Peasants and Birds. Such a need was not envisaged. Janeil was self-sufficient and secure, though inconveniences might arise when machinery broke down and there were no Meks to repair it. The situation, then, was disturbing but hardly desperate. During the day the gentlemen so inclined brought forth energy-guns and sport-rifles and killed as many Meks as the extreme range allowed.

After dark the Meks brought forward power-wagons and earth-movers, and began to raise a dike around Janeil.

The folk of the castle watched without comprehension until the dike reached a height of fifty feet and dirt began to spill down against the walls. Then the dire purpose of the Meks became apparent, and insouciance gave way to dismal foreboding.

All the gentlemen of Janeil were erudite in at least one realm of knowledge. Certain were mathematical theoreticians, others had made a profound study of the physical sciences. Some of these, with a detail of Peasants to perform the sheer physical exertion, attempted to restore the energy-cannon to functioning condition. Unluckily, the cannon had not been maintained in good order. Various components were obviously corroded or damaged. Conceivably these components might have been replaced from the Mek shops on the second sub-level, but none of the group had any knowledge of the Mek nomenclature or warehousing system. Warrick Madency Arban (which is to say, Arban of the Madency family on the Warrick clan) suggested that a work-force of Peasants search the warehouse. But in view of the limited mental capacity of the Peasants, nothing was done and the whole plan to restore the energy-cannon came to naught.

The gentlefolk of Janeil watched in fascination as the dirt piled higher and higher around them, in a circular mound like a crater. Summer neared its end, and on one stormy day dirt and rubble rose above the parapets, and began to spill over into the courts and piazzas. Janeil must soon be buried and all within suffocated.

It was then that a group of impulsive young cadets, with more elan than dignity, took up weapons and charged up the slope. The Meks dumped dirt and stone upon them, but a handful gained the ridge where they fought in a kind of dreadful exaltation.

Fifteen minutes the fight raged and the earth became sodden with rain and blood. For one glorious moment the cadets swept the ridge clean. Had not most of their fellows been lost under the rubble anything might have occurred. But the Meks regrouped, thrust forward. Ten men were left, then six, then four, then one, then none. The Meks marched down the slope, swarmed over the battlements, and with somber intensity

277

killed all within. Janeil, for seven hundred years the abode of gallant gentlemen and gracious ladies, had become a lifeless hulk.

The Mek, standing as if a specimen in a museum case, was a man-like creature native, in his original version, to a planet of Etamin. His tough rusty-bronze hide glistened metallically as if oiled or waxed. The spines thrusting back from scalp and neck shone like gold, and indeed they were coated with a conductive copper-chrome film. His sense organs were gathered in clusters at the site of a man's ears; his visage—it was often a shock, walking the lower corridors, to come suddenly upon a Mek—was corrugated muscle, not dissimilar to the look of an uncovered human brain. His maw, a vertical irregular cleft at the base of this 'face', was an obsolete organ by reason of the syrup sac which had been introduced under the skin of the shoulders, and the digestive organs, originally used to extract nutrition from decayed swamp vegitation and coelenterates, had atrophied. The Mek typically wore no garment except possibly a work apron or a tool-belt, and in the sunlight his rust-bronze skin made a handsome display. This was the Mek solitary, a creature intrinsically as effective as man— perhaps more by virtue of his superb brain which also functioned as a radio transceiver. Working in the mass, by the teeming thousands, he seemed less admirable, less competent: a hybrid of sub-man and cockroach.

Certain savants, notably Morninglight's D. R. Jardine and Salonson of Tuang, considered the Mek bland and phlegmatic, but the profound Claghorn of Castle Hagedorn asserted otherwise. The emotions of the Mek, said Claghorn, were different from human emotions, and only vaguely comprehensible to man. After deligent research Claghorn isolated over a dozen Mek emotions.

In spite of such research, the Mek revolt came as an utter surprise, no less to Claghorn, D. R. Jardine and Salonson than to anyone else. Why? asked everyone. How could a group so long submissive have contrived so murderous a plot?

The most reasonable conjecture was also the simplest: the Mek resented servitude and hated the Earthmen who had removed him from his natural environment. Those who argued against this theory claimed that it projected human emotions and attitudes into a non-human organism, that the Mek had every reason to feel gratitude toward the gentlemen who had liberated him from the conditions of Etamin Nine. To this, the first group would inquire, "Who projects human attitudes now?" And the retort of their opponents was often: "Since no one knows for certain, one projection is no more absurd than another."

II

Castle Hagedorn occupied the crest of a black diorite crag overlooking a wide valley to the south. Larger, more majestic than Janeil, Hagedorn was protected by walls a mile in circumference, three hundred feet tall. The parapets stood a full nine hundred feet above the valley, with towers, turrets and observation eyries raising even higher. Two sides of the crag, at east and west, dropped sheer to the valley. The north and south slopes, a trifle less steep, were terraced and planted with vines, artichokes, pears and pomegranates. An avenue rising from the valley circled the crag and passed through a portal into the central plaza. Opposite stood the great Rotunda, with at either side the tall Houses of the twenty-eight families.

The original castle, constructed immediately after the return of men to Earth, stood on the site now occupied by the plaza. The tenth Hagedorn had assembled an enormous force of Peasants and Meks to build the new walls, after he demolished the old castle. The twenty-eight Houses dated from this time, five hundred years before.

Below the plaza were three service levels: the stables and garages at the bottom, next the Mek shops and Mek living quarters, then the various storerooms, warehouses and special shops: bakery, brewery, lapidary, arsenal, repository, and the like.

The current Hagedorn, twenty-sixth of the line, was a Claghorn of the Overwheles. His selection had occasioned general surprise, because O. C. Charle, as he had been before his elevation, was a gentleman of no remarkable presence. His elegance, flair, and erudition were only ordinary; he had never been notable for any significant originality of thought. His physical proportions were good; his face was square and bony, with a short straight nose, a benign brow, narrow gray eyes. His expression was normally a trifle abstracted—his detractors used the word 'vacant'. But by a simple lowering of the eyelids, a downward twitch of the coarse blond eyebrows, it at once became stubborn and surly, a fact of which O. C. Charle, or Hagedorn, was unaware.

The office, while exerting little or no formal authority, exerted a pervasive influence, and the style of the gentleman who was Hagedorn affected everyone. For this reason the selection of Hagedorn was a matter of no small importance, subject to hundreds of considerations, and it was the rare candidate who failed to have some old solecism or gaucherie discussed with embarrassing candor. While the candidate might never take overt umbrage, friendships were inevitably sundered, rancors augmented, reputations blasted. O. C. Charle's elevation represented a compromise between two factions among the Overwheles, to which clan the privilege of selection had fallen.

The gentlemen between whom O. C. Charle represented a compromise were both highly respected, but distinguished by basically different attitudes toward existence. The first was the talented Garr of the Zumbeld family. He exemplified the traditional virtues of Castle Hagedorn: he was a notable connoisseur of essences, he dressed with absolute savoir, with never so much as a pleat nor a twist of the characteristic Overwhele rosette awry. He combined insouciance and flair with dignity. His repartee coruscated with brilliant allusions and turns of phrase. When aroused his wit was utterly mordant. He could quote every literary work of consequence; he performed expertly upon the nine-stringed lute, and was thus in constant

demand at the Viewing of Antique Tabards. He was an antiquarian of unchallengeable erudition and knew the locale of
every major city of Old Earth, and could discourse for hours
upon the history of the ancient times. His military expertise
was unparalleled at Hagedorn, and challenged only by D. K.
Magdah of Castle Delora and perhaps Brusham of Tuang.
Faults? Flaws? Few could be cited: over-punctilio which might
be construed as waspishness; an intrepid pertinacity which
could be considered ruthless.

O. Z. Garr could never be dismissed as insipid or indecisive,
and his personal courage was beyond dispute. Two years before a stray band of Nomads had ventured into Lucerne Valley,
slaughtering Peasants, stealing cattle, and going so far as to
fire an arrow into the chest of an Isseth cadet. O. Z. Garr
instantly assembled a punitive company of Meks, loaded them
aboard a dozen power-wagons and set forth in pursuit of the
Nomads, finally overtaking them near Drene River, by the
ruins of Worster Cathedral. The Nomads were unexpectedly
strong, unexpectedly crafty, and were not content to turn tail
and flee. During the fighting O. Z. Garr displayed the most
exemplary demeanor, directing the attack from the seat of
his power-wagon, a pair of Meks standing by with shields to
ward away arrows.

The conflict ended in a rout of the Nomads. They left
twenty-seven lean black-cloaked corpses strewn on the field,
while only twenty Meks lost their lives.

O. Z. Garr's opponent in the election was Claghorn, elder of
the Claghorn family. As with O. Z. Garr, the exquisite discriminations of Hagedorn society came to Claghorn as easily
as swimming to a fish.

He was no less erudite than O. Z. Garr, though hardly so
versatile, his principal field of study being the Meks, their
physiology, linguistic modes, and social patterns. Claghorn's
conversation was more profound, but less entertaining and not
so trenchant as that of O. Z. Garr. He seldom employed the
extravagant tropes and allusions which characterized Garr's

discussions, preferring a style of speech which was almost unadorned. Claghorn kept no Phanes; O. Z. Garr's four matched Gossamer Dainties were marvels of delight, and at the viewing of Antique Tabards Garr's presentations were seldom outshone. The important contrast between the two men lay in their philosophic outlook. O. Z. Garr, a traditionalist, a fervent exemplar of his society, subscribed to its tenets without reservation. He was beset by neither doubt nor guilt; he felt no desire to alter the conditions which afforded more than two thousand gentlemen and ladies lives of great richness. Claghorn, while by no means an Expiationist, was known to feel dissatisfaction with the general tenor of life at Castle Hagedorn, and argued so plausibly that many folk refused to listen to him, on the grounds that they became uncomfortable. But an indefinable malaise ran deep, and Claghorn had many influential supporters.

When the time came for ballots to be cast, neither O. Z. Garr nor Claghorn could muster sufficient support. The office finally was conferred upon a gentleman who never in his most optimistic reckonings had expected it: a gentleman of decorum and dignity but no great depth; without flippancy, but likewise without vivacity; affable but disinclined to force an issue to a disagreeable conclusion: O. C. Charle, the new Hagedorn.

Six months later, during the dark hours before dawn, the Hagedorn Meks evacuated their quarters and departed, taking with them power-wagons, tools, weapons and electrical equipment. The act had clearly been long in the planning, for simultaneously the Meks at each of the eight other castles made a similar departure.

The initial reaction at Castle Hagedorn, as elsewhere, was incredulity, then shocked anger, then—when the implications of the act were pondered—a sense of foreboding and calamity.

The new Hagedorn, the clan chiefs, and certain other notables appointed by Hagedorn met in the formal council chamber to consider the matter. They sat around a great table covered with red velvet: Hagedorn at the head; Xanten and

Isseth at his left; Overwhele, Aure and Beaudry at his right; then the others, including O. Z. Garr, I. K. Linus, A. G. Bernal, a mathematical theoretician of great ability, B. F. Wyas, an equally sagacious antiquarian who had identified the sites of many ancient cities: Palmyra, Lubeck, Eridu, Zanesville, Burton-on-Trent, Massilia among others. Certain family elders filled out the council: Marune and Baudune of Aure; Quay, Roseth and Idelsea of Xanten; Uegus of Isseth, Claghorn of Overwhele.

All sat silent for a period of ten minutes, arranging their minds and performing the silent act of psychic accommodation known as 'intression'.

At last Hagedorn spoke. "The castle suddenly is bereft of its Meks. Needless to say, this is an inconvenient condition to be adjusted as swiftly as possible. Here, I am sure, we find ourselves of one mind."

He looked around the table. All thrust forward ivory tablets to signify assent—all save Claghorn, who however did not stand it on end to signify dissent.

Isseth, a stern white-haired gentleman magnificently handsome in spite of his seventy years, spoke in a grim voice. "I see no point in cogitation or delay. What we must do is clear. Admittedly the Peasants are poor material from which to recruit an armed force. Nonetheless, we must assemble them, equip them with sandals, smocks and weapons so that they do not discredit us, and put them under good leadership: O. Z. Garr or Xanten. Birds can locate the vagrants, whereupon we will track them down, order the Peasants to give them a good drubbing and herd them home on the double."

Xanten, thirty-five years old, extraordinarily young to be a clan chief, and a notorious firebrand, shook his head. "The idea is appealing but impractical. Peasants simply could not stand up to the Meks, no matter how we trained them."

The statement was manifestly accurate. The Peasants, small andromorphs originally of Spica Ten, were not so much timid as incapable of performing a vicious act.

A dour silence held the table. O. Z. Garr finally spoke. "The dogs have stolen our power-wagons, otherwise I'd be tempted to ride out and chivvy the rascals home with a whip." *

"A matter of perplexity," said Hagedorn, "is syrup. Naturally they carried away what they could. When this is exhausted —what then? Will they starve? Impossible for them to return to their original diet—what was it, swamp mud? Eh, Claghorn, you're the expert in these matters. Can the Meks return to a diet of mud?"

"No," said Claghorn. "The organs of the adult are atrophied. If a cub were started on the diet, he'd probably survive."

"Just as I assumed." Hagedorn scowled portentously down at his clasped hands to conceal his total lack of any constructive proposal.

A gentleman in the dark blue of the Beaudrys appeared in the doorway: he poised himself, held high his right arm, bowed.

Hagedorn rose to his feet. "Come forward, B. F. Robarth; what is your news?" For this was the significance of the newcomer's genuflection.

"The news is a message broadcast from Halcyon. The Meks have attacked; they have fired the structure and are slaughtering all. The radio went dead one minute ago."

All swung around, some jumped to their feet. "Slaughter?" croaked Claghorn.

"I am certain that by now Halcyon is no more."

* This is only an approximate translation and fails to capture the pungency of the language. Several words have no contemporary equivalents. 'Skirkling', as in 'to send skirkling', denotes a frantic pell-mell flight in all directions accompanied by a vibration or twinkling or a jerking motion. To 'volith' is to toy idly with a matter, the implication being that the person involved is of such Jovian potency that all difficulties dwindle to contemptible triviality. 'Raudelbogs' are the semi-intelligent beings of Etamin Four, who were brought to Earth, trained first as gardeners, and then construction laborers, then sent home in disgrace because of certain repulsive habits they refused to forgo.

The statement of O. Z. Garr, therefore, becomes something like this: "Were power-wagons at hand, I'd volith riding forth with a whip to send the raudelbogs skirkling home."

Claghorn sat staring with eyes unfocused. The others discussed the dire news in voices heavy with horror.

Hagedorn once more brought the council back to order. "This is clearly an extreme situation; the gravest, perhaps, of our entire history. I am frank to state that I can suggest no decisive counteract."

Overwhele inquired, "What of the other castles? Are they secure?"

Hagedorn turned to B. F. Robarth: "Will you be good enough to make general radio contact with all other castles, and inquire as to their condition?"

Xanten said, "Others are as vulnerable as Halcyon: Sea Island and Delora, in particular, and Maraval as well."

Claghorn emerged from his reverie. "The gentlemen and ladies of these places, in my opinion, should consider taking refuge at Janeil or here until the uprising is quelled."

Others around the table looked at him in surprise and puzzlement. O. Z. Garr inquired in the silkiest of voices: "You envision the gentlefolk of these castles scampering to refuge at the cock-a-hoop swaggering of the lower orders?"

"Indeed I do, should they wish to survive," responded Claghorn politely. A gentleman of late middle-age, Claghorn was stocky, strong, with black-gray hair, magnificent green eyes, a manner which suggests great internal force under stern control. "Flight by definition entails a certain diminution of dignity," he went on to say. "If O. Z. Garr can propound an elegant manner of taking to one's heels, I will be glad to learn it, and everyone else should likewise heed, because in the days to come the capability may be of comfort to all."

Hagedorn interposed before O. Z. Garr could reply. "Let us keep to the issues. I confess I cannot see to the end of all this. The Meks have demonstrated themselves to be murderers. How can we take murderers back into our service? But if we don't—well, to say the least, conditions will be austere until we can locate and train a new force of technicians."

"The spaceships!" exclaimed Xanten. "We must see to them at once!"

"What's this?" inquired Beaudry, a gentleman of rock-hard face. "How do you mean: 'see to them'?"

"They must be protected from damage! What else? They are our link to the Home Worlds. The maintenance Meks probably have not deserted the hangars, since, if they propose to exterminate us, they will want to deny us the spaceships."

"Perhaps you care to march with a levy of Peasants to take the hangars under firm control?" suggested O. Z. Garr in a somewhat supercilious voice. A long history of rivalry and mutual detestation existed between himself and Xanten.

"It may be our only hope," said Xanten. "Still—how does one fight with a levy of Peasants? Better that I fly to the hangars and reconnoiter. Meanwhile, perhaps you, and others with military expertise, will take in hand the recruitment and training of a Peasant militia."

"In this regard," stated O. Z. Garr, "I await the outcome of our current deliberations. If it develops that here lies the optimum course, I naturally will apply my competences to the fullest degree. If your own capabilities are best fulfilled by spying out the activities of the Meks, I hope you will be large-hearted enough to do the same."

The two gentlemen glared at each other.

A year previously their enmity had almost culminated in a duel. Xanten, a gentleman tall, clean-limbed, nervously active, was gifted with great natural flair, but likewise evinced a disposition too easy for absolute elegance. The traditionalists considered him 'sthross', indicating a manner flawed by an almost imperceptible slackness and lack of punctilio: not the best possible choice for clan chief.

Xanten's response to O. Z. Garr was blandly polite. "I shall be glad to take this task upon myself. Since haste is of the essence I will risk the accusation of precipitousness and leave at once. Hopefully I return to report tomorrow." He rose, performed a ceremonious bow to Hagedorn, another all-inclusive salute to the council and departed.

He crossed to Esledune House where he maintained an apartment on the thirteenth level: four rooms furnished in the style known as Fifth Dynasty, after an epoch in the history of the Altair Home Planets, from which the human race had returned to Earth.

His current consort, Araminta, a lady of the Onwane family, was absent on affairs of her own, which suited Xanten well enough. After plying him with questions she would have discredited his simple explanation, preferring to suspect an assignation at his country place. Truth to tell, he had become bored with Araminta and had reason to believe that she felt similarly —or perhaps his exalted rank had provided her less opportunity to preside at glittering social functions than she had expected. They had bred no children. Araminta's daughter by a previous connection had been tallied to her. Her second child must be tallied to Xanten, preventing him from siring another child.*

Xanten doffed his yellow council vestments. Assisted by a young Peasant buck, he donned dark yellow hunting-breeches with black trim, a black jacket, black boots. He drew a cap of soft black leather over his head, slung a pouch over his shoulder, into which he loaded weapons: a coiled blade, an energy-gun.

Leaving the apartment he summoned the lift and descended to the first level armory, where normally a Mek clerk would have served him. Now Xanten, to his vast disgust, was forced to take himself behind the counter, and rummage here and there. The Meks had removed most of the sporting rifles, all the pellet ejectors and heavy energy-guns. An ominous circumstance, thought Xanten. At last he found a steel sling-

---

* The population of Castle Hagedorn was fixed; each gentleman and each lady was permitted a single child. If by chance another were born he must either find someone who had not yet sired to sponsor it, or dispose of it another way. The usual procedure was to give the child into the care of the Expiationists.

whip, spare power-slugs for his gun, a brace of fire grenades, a high-powered monocular.

He returned to the lift, rode to the top level, ruefully considering the long climb when eventually the mechanism broke down, with no Meks at hand to make repairs. He thought of the apoplectic furies of rigid traditionalists such as Beaudry and chuckled. Eventful days lay ahead!

Stopping at the top level he crossed to the parapets, proceeded around to the radio room. Customarily three Mek specialists connected into the apparatus by wires clipped to their quills sat typing messages as they arrived. Now B. F. Robarth stood before the mechanism, uncertainly twisting the dials, his mouth wry with deprecation and distaste for the job.

"Any further news?" Xanten asked.

B. F. Robarth gave him a sour grin. "The folk at the other end seem no more familiar with this cursed tangle than I. I hear occasional voices. I believe that the Meks are attacking Castle Delora."

Claghorn had entered the room behind Xanten. "Did I hear you correctly? Delora Castle is gone?"

"Not gone yet, Claghorn. But as good as gone. The Delora walls are little better than a picturesque crumble."

"Sickening situation!" muttered Xanten. "How can sentient creatures perform such evil? After all these centuries, how little we actually knew of them!" As he spoke he recognized the tactlessness of his remarks; Claghorn had devoted much time to a study of the Meks.

"The act itself is not astounding," said Claghorn shortly. "It has occurred a thousand times in human history."

Mildly surprised that Claghorn should use human history as referent to a case involving the sub-orders, Xanten asked: "You were never aware of this vicious aspect to the Mek nature?"

"No. Never. Never indeed."

Claghorn seemed unduly sensitive, thought Xanten. Understandable, all in all. Claghorn's basic doctrine as set forth during the Hagedorn selection was by no means simple, and

288

Xanten neither understood it nor completely endorsed what he conceived to be its goals; but it was plain that the revolt of the Meks had cut the ground out from under Claghorn's feet. Probably to the somewhat bitter satisfaction of O. Z. Garr, who must feel vindicated in his traditionalist doctrines.

Claghorn said tersely, "The life we've been leading couldn't last forever. It's a wonder it lasted as long as it did."

"Perhaps so," said Xanten in a soothing voice. "Well, no matter. All things change. Who knows? The Peasants may be planning to poison our food . . . I must go." He bowed to Claghorn, who returned him a crisp nod, and to B. F. Robarth, then departed the room.

He climbed the spiral staircase—almost a ladder—to the cotes, where the Birds lived in an invincible disorder, occupying themselves with gambling at the game of quarrels, a version of chess, with rules incomprehensible to every gentleman who had tried to understand it.

Castle Hagedorn maintained a hundred Birds, tended by a gang of long-suffering Peasants, whom the Birds held in vast disesteem. They were garish garrulous creatures, pigmented red, yellow, blue, with long necks, jerking inquisitive heads, an inherent irreverence which no amount of discipline or tutelage could overcome. Spying Xanten, they emitted a chorus of rude jeers: "Somebody wants a ride! Heavy thing!" "Why don't the self-anointed two-footers grow wings for themselves?" "My friend, never trust a Bird! We'll sky you, then fling you down on your fundament!"

"Quiet!" called Xanten. "I need six fast, silent Birds, upon an important mission. Are any capable of such a task?"

"Are any capable, he asks!" "*A ros ros ros!* When none of us have flown for a week!" "Silence? We'll give you silence, yellow and black!"

"Come then. You. You. You of the wise eye. You there. You with the cocked shoulder. You with the green pompon. To the basket."

The Birds designated, jeering, grumbling, reviling the Peasants, allowed their syrup sacs to be filled, then flapped to the wicker seat where Xanten waited. "To the space depot at Vincenne," he told them. "Fly high and silently. Enemies are abroad. We must learn what harm if any has been done to the spaceships."

"To the depot then!" Each Bird seized a length of rope tied to an overhead framework; the chair was yanked up with a jerk calculated to rattle Xanten's teeth, and off they flew, laughing, cursing each other for not supporting more of the load, but eventually all accommodating themselves to the task and flying with a coordinated flapping of the thirty-six sets of wings. To Xanten's relief, their garrulity lessened; silently they flew south, at a speed fifty or sixty miles per hour.

The afternoon was already waning. The ancient countryside, scene to so many comings and goings, so much triumph and so much disaster, was laced with long black shadows. Looking down, Xanten reflected that though the human stock was native to this soil, and though his immediate ancestors had maintained their holdings for seven hundred years, Earth still seemed an alien world.

The reason of course was by no means mysterious or rooted in paradox. After the Six-Star War, Earth had lain fallow for three thousand years, unpopulated save for a handful of anguished wretches who somehow had survived the cataclysm and who had become semi-barbaric Nomads. Then seven hundred years ago certain rich lords of Altair, motivated to some extent by political disaffection, but no less by caprice, had decided to return to Earth. Such was the origin of the nine great strongholds, the resident gentlefolk and the staffs of specialized andromorphs.

Xanten flew over an area where an antiquarian had directed excavations, revealing a plaza flagged with white stone, a broken obelisk, a tumbled statue. The sight, by some trick of association, stimulated Xanten's mind to an astonishing vision, so simple and yet so grand that he looked around, in all directions, with new eyes. The vision was Earth re-populated with men, the land cultivated, Nomads driven back into the wilderness.

At the moment the image was far-fetched. And Xanten, watching the soft contours of old Earth slide below, pondered the Mek revolt which had altered his life with such startling abruptness.

Claghorn had long insisted that no human condition endured forever, with the corollary that the more complicated such a condition, the greater its susceptibility to change.

In that case the seven hundred year continuity at Castle Hagedorn—as artificial, extravagant and intricate as life could be—became an astonishing circumstance in itself. Claghorn had pushed his thesis further. Since change was inevitable, he argued that the gentlefolk should soften the impact by anticipating and controlling the changes—a doctrine which had been attacked with great fervor. The traditionalists labeled all of Claghorn's ideas demonstrable fallacy, and cited the very stability of castle life as proof of its viability. Xanten had inclined first one way, then the other, emotionally involved with neither cause. If anything, the fact of O. Z. Garr's traditionalism had nudged him toward Claghorn's views.

Now it seemed as if events had vindicated Claghorn. Change had come, with an impact of the maximum harshness and violence.

There were still questions to be answered, of course. Why had the Meks chosen this particular time to revolt? Conditions had not altered appreciably for five hundred years, and the Meks had never previously hinted dissatisfaction. In fact, they had revealed nothing of their feelings—though no one had ever troubled to ask them—save Claghorn.

The Birds were veering east to avoid the Ballarat Mountains, to the west of which were the ruins of a great city, never satisfactorily identified. Below lay the Lucerne Valley, at one time a fertile farm land. If one looked with great concentration the outline of the various holdings could sometimes be distinguished. Ahead, the spaceship hangars were visible, where Mek technicians maintained four spaceships that were jointly the property of Hagedorn, Janeil, Tuang, Morninglight and

Maraval, though, for a variety of reasons, the ships were never used.

The sun was setting. Orange light twinkled and flickered on the metal walls. Xanten called instructions up to the Birds: "Circle down; alight behind that line of trees, but fly low so that none will see."

Down on stiff wings curved the Birds, six ungainly necks stretched toward the ground. Xanten was ready for the impact. The Birds never seemed able to alight easily when they carried a gentleman. When the cargo was something in which they felt a personal concern, dandelion fluff would never have been disturbed by the jar.

Xanten expertly kept his balance, instead of tumbling and rolling in the manner preferred by the Birds. "You all have syrup," he told them. "Rest: make no noise; do not quarrel. By tomorrow's sunset, if I am not here, return to Castle Hagedorn and say that Xanten was killed."

"Never fear!" cried the Birds. "We will wait forever!" "At any rate till tomorrow's sunset!" "If danger threatens, if you are pressed—*a ros ros ros!* Call for the Birds!" "*A ros!* We are ferocious when aroused!"

"I wish it were true," said Xanten. "The Birds are arrant cowards, this is well known. Still I value the sentiment. Remember my instructions, and be quiet above all! I do not wish to be set upon and stabbed because of your clamor."

The Birds made indignant sounds. "Injustice, injustice! We are quiet as the dew!"

"Good." Xanten hurriedly moved away lest they should bellow new advice or reassurances after him.

IV

Passing through the forest, he came to an open meadow at the far edge of which, perhaps a hundred yards distant, was the rear of the first hangar. He stopped to consider.

Several factors were involved. First, the maintenance Meks, with the metal structure shielding them from radio contact, might still be unaware of the revolt. Hardly likely, he decided, in view of the otherwise careful planning. Second, the Meks, in continuous communication with their fellows, acted as a collective organism. The aggregate functioned more completely than its parts, and the individual was not prone to initiative. Hence, vigilance was not likely to be extreme. Third, if they expected anyone to attempt a discreet approach, they would necessarily scrutinize most closely the route which he proposed to take.

Xanten decided to wait in the shadows another ten minutes, until the setting sun shining over his shoulder should most effectively blind any who might watch.

Ten minutes passed. The hangars, burnished by the dying sunlight, bulked long, tall, completely quiet. In the intervening meadow long golden grass waved and rippled in a cool breeze.

Xanten took a deep breath, hefted his pouch, arranged his weapons, strode forth. It did not occur to him to crawl through the grass.

He reached the back of the nearest hangar without challenge. Pressing his ear to the metal he heard nothing. He walked to the corner, looked down the side: no sign of life. Xanten shrugged. Very well then; to the door.

He walked beside the hangar, the setting sun casting a long black shadow ahead of him. He came to a door opening into the hangar administrative office. Since there was nothing to be gained by trepidation, Xanten thrust the door aside and entered.

The offices were empty. The desks, where centuries before underlings had sat, calculating invoices and bills of lading, were bare, polished, free of dust. The computers and information banks, black enamel, glass, white and red switches, looked as if they had been installed only the day before.

Xanten crossed to the glass pane overlooking the hangar floor, shadowed under the bulk of the ship.

He saw no Meks. But on the floor of the hangar, arranged in neat rows and heaps, were elements and assemblies of the ship's control mechanism. Service panels gaped wide into the hull to show where the devices had been detached.

Xanten stepped from the office out into the hangar. The spaceship had been disabled, put out of commission. Xanten looked along the neat rows of parts. Certain savants of various castles were expert in the theory of space-time transfer; S. X. Rosenhox of Maraval had even derived a set of equations which, if translated into machinery, eliminated the troublesome Hamus Effect. But not one gentleman, even were he so oblivious to personal honor as to touch a hand to a tool, would know how to replace, connect and tune the mechanisms heaped upon the hangar floor.

When had the malicious work been done? Impossible to say.

Xanten returned to the office, stepped back out into the twilight, walked to the next hangar. Again no Meks; again the spaceship had been gutted of its control mechanisms. Xanten proceeded to the third hangar, where conditions were the same.

At the fourth hangar he discerned the faint sounds of activity. Stepping into the office, looking through the glass wall into the hangar, he found Meks working with their usual economy of motion, in a near silence which was uncanny.

Xanten, already uncomfortable because of skulking through the forest, became enraged by the cool destruction of his property. He strode forth into the hangar. Slapping his thigh to attract attention he called in a harsh voice: "Return the components to place! How dare you vermin act in such a manner?"

The Meks turned about their blank countenances, studied him through black beaded lensclusters at each side of their heads.

"What?" Xanten bellowed. "You hesitate?" He brought forth his steel whip usually more of a symbolic adjunct than a punitive instrument, and slashed it against the ground. "Obey! This ridiculous revolt is at its end!"

The Meks still hesitated, and events wavered in the balance. None made a sound, though messages were passing among

294

them, appraising the circumstances, establishing a consensus. Xanten could allow them no such leisure. He marched forward, wielding the whip, striking at the only area where the Meks felt pain: the ropy face. "To your duties," he roared. "A fine maintenance crew are you! A destruction crew is more like it!"

The Meks made their soft blowing sound which might mean anything. They fell back, and now Xanten noted one standing at the head of the companionway leading into the ship: a Mek larger than any he had seen before and one in some fashion different. This Mek was aiming a pellet-gun at his head. With an unhurried flourish Xanten whipped away a Mek who had leapt forward with a knife, and without deigning to aim fired at and destroyed the Mek who stood on the companionway, even as the slug sang past his head.

The other Meks were nevertheless committed to an attack. All surged forward. Lounging disdainfully against the hull, Xanten shot them as they came, moving his head once to avoid a chunk of metal, again reaching to catch a throw-knife and hurl it into the face of him who had thrown it.

The Meks drew back, and Xanten guessed that they had agreed on a new tactic: either to withdraw for weapons or perhaps to confine him within the hangar. In any event no more could be accomplished here. He made play with the whip and cleared an avenue to the office. With tools, metal bars and forgings striking the glass behind him, he sauntered through the office and out into the night. He did not look behind.

The full moon was rising, a great yellow globe casting a smoky saffron glow, like an antique lamp. Mek eyes were not well adapted for night seeing, and Xanten waited by the door. Presently Meks began to pour forth, and Xanten hacked at their necks as they came.

The Meks drew back inside the hangar. Wiping his blade Xanten strode off the way he had come, looking neither right nor left. He stopped short. The night was young. Something tickled his mind: the recollection of the Mek who had fired the pellet-gun. He had been larger, possibly a darker bronze, but, more significantly, he had displayed an indefinable poise, almost authority—though such a word, when used in connection with the Meks, was anomalous. On the other hand, some-one must have planned the revolt, or at least originated the concept of a revolt in the first place.

It might be worthwhile to extend the reconnaissance, though his primary information had been secured.

Xanten turned back and crossed the landing area to the barracks and garages. Once more, frowning in discomfort, he felt the need for discretion. What times these were when a gentleman must skulk to avoid such as the Meks! He stole up behind the garages, where a half-dozen power-wagons* lay dozing.

Xanten looked them over. All were of the same sort, a metal frame with four wheels and an earth-moving blade at the front. Nearby must be the syrup stock.

Xanten presently found a bin containing a number of containers. He loaded a dozen on a nearby wagon and slashed the rest with his knife, so that the syrup gushed across the ground. The Meks used a somewhat different formulation; their syrup would be stocked at a different locale, presumably inside the barracks.

Xanten mounted a power-wagon, twisted the 'awake' key, tapped the 'Go' button, pulled a lever which set the wheels into reverse motion. The power-wagon lurched back. Xanten halted it and turned it so that it faced the barracks. He did likewise with three others, then set them all in motion, one after the other.

* Power-wagons, like the Meks, were originally swamp-creatures from Etamin Nine. They were great rectangular slabs of muscle, slung into a rectangular frame and protected from sunlight, insects and rodents by a synthetic pelt. Syrup sacs communicated with their digestive apparatus, wires led to motor nodes in the rudimentary brain. The muscles were clamped to rocker arms which actuated rotors and drive-wheels. The power-wagons were economical, long-lived and docile, and so they were principally used for heavy cartage, earth-moving, heavy-tillage, and other arduous jobs.

They trundled forward. The blades cut open the metal wall of the barracks, the roof sagged. The power-wagons continued, pushing the length of the interior, crushing all in their way.

Xanten nodded in profound satisfaction, returned to the power-wagon he had reserved for his own use. Mounting to the seat, he waited. No Meks issued from the barracks. Apparently they were deserted, with the entire crew busy at the hangars. Still, hopefully, the syrup stocks had been destroyed. Many might perish by starvation.

From the direction of the hangars came a single Mek, evidently attracted by the sounds of destruction. Xanten crouched on the seat and as it passed, coiled his whip around the stocky neck. He heaved; the Mek spun to the ground.

Xanten leapt down, seized its pellet-gun. Here was another of the larger Meks, and now Xanten saw it to be without a syrup sac, a Mek in the original state. Astounding! How did the creature survive? Suddenly there were many new questions to be asked; hopefully a few to be answered. Standing on the creature's head, Xanten hacked away the long antenna quills which protruded from the back of the Mek's scalp. It was now insulated, alone, on its own resources; a situation certain to reduce the most stalwart Mek to apathy.

"Up!" ordered Xanten. "Into the back of the wagon!" He cracked the whip for emphasis.

The Mek at first seemed disposed to defy him, but after a blow or two obeyed. Xanten climbed into the seat, started the power-wagon, directed it to the north. The Birds would be unable to carry both himself and the Mek—or in any event they would cry and complain so raucously that they might as well be believed at first. They might or might not wait until the specified hour of tomorrow's sunset. As likely as not they would sleep the night in a tree, awake in a surly mood and return at once to Castle Hagedorn.

All through the night the power-wagon trundled, with Xanten on the seat and his captive huddled in the rear.

V

The gentlefolk of the castles, for all their assurance, disliked to wander the countryside by night, by reason of what some derided as superstitious fear. Others cited travelers benighted beside mouldering ruins and their subsequent visions: the eldritch music they had heard, or the whimper of moon-mirkins, or the far horns of spectral huntsmen. Others had seen pale lavender and green lights, and wraiths which ran with long strides through the forest; and Hode Abbey, now a dank tumble, was notorious for the White Hag and the alarming toll she exacted.

A hundred such cases were known. While the hard-headed scoffed, none needlessly traveled the countryside by night. Indeed, if truly ghosts haunt the scenes of tragedy and heart-break, then the landscape of Old Earth must be home to ghosts and specters beyond all numbering; especially that region across which Xanten rolled in the power-wagon, where every rock, every meadow, every vale and swale was crusted thick with human experience.

The moon rose high. The wagon trundled north along an ancient road, the cracked concrete slabs shining pale in the moonlight. Twice Xanten saw flickering orange lights off to the side, and once, standing in the shade of a cypress tree, he thought to see a tall quiet shape, silently watching him pass. The captive Mek sat plotting mischief, Xanten well knew. Without its quills it must feel depersonified, bewildered, but Xanten told himself that it would not do to doze.

The road led through a town, certain structures of which yet stood. Not even the Nomads took refuge in these old towns, fearing either miasma or perhaps the redolence of grief.

The moon reached the zenith. The landscape spread away in a hundred tones of silver, black and gray. Looking about, Xanten thought that for all the notable pleasures of civilized life, there was yet something to be said for the spaciousness and simplicity of Nomadland . . . The Mek made a stealthy movement. Xanten did not so much as turn his head. He cracked his whip in the air. The Mek became quiet.

All through the night the power-wagon rolled along the old road, with the moon sinking into the west. The eastern horizon glowed green and lemon-yellow, and presently, as the pallid moon disappeared over the distant line of the mountains the sun came up.

At this moment, Xanten spied a drift of smoke off to the right.

He halted the wagon. Standing up on the seat he craned his neck to spy a Nomad encampment about a quarter-mile distant. He could distinguish three or four dozen tents of various sizes, a dozen dilapidated power-wagons. On the hetman's tall tent he thought to see a black ideogram which he thought he recognized. If so, this would be the tribe which not long before had trespassed on the Hagedorn domain, and which O. Z. Garr had repulsed.

Xanten settled himself upon the seat, composed his garments, set the power-wagon in motion and guided it toward the camp.

A hundred black-cloaked men, tall and lean as ferrets, watched his approach. A dozen sprang forward and whipping arrows to bows aimed them at his heart. Xanten turned them a glance of supercilious inquiry, drove the wagon up to the hetman's tent, halted. He rose to his feet. "Hetman," he called. "Are you awake?"

The hetman parted the canvas which closed off his tent, peered out and after a moment came forth. Like the others he wore a garment of limp black cloth, swathing head and body alike. His face thrust through a square opening: narrow blue eyes, a grotesquely long nose, a chin long, skewed and sharp.

Xanten gave him a curt nod. "Observe this." He jerked his thumb toward the Mek in the back of the wagon. The hetman flicked aside his eyes, studied the Mek a tenth-second, returned to a scrutiny of Xanten. "His kind have revolted against the gentlemen," said Xanten. "In fact they massacre all the men of Earth. Hence we of Castle Hagedorn make this offer to the Nomads. Come to Castle Hagedorn! We will feed, clothe and arm you. We will train you to discipline and the arts of formal warfare. We will provide the most expert leadership within our power. We will then annihilate the Meks, expunge them from Earth. After the campaign, we will train you to technical skills, and you may pursue profitable and interesting careers in the service of the castles."

The hetman made no reply for a moment. Then his weathered face split into a ferocious grin and he spoke in a voice which Xanten found surprisingly well-modulated. "So your beasts have finally risen up to rend you! A pity they forebore so long! Well, it is all one to us. You are both alien folk and sooner or later your bones must bleach together."

Xanten pretended incomprehension. "If I understand you aright, you assert that in the face of alien assault, all men must fight a common battle; and then, after the victory, cooperate still to their mutual advantage; am I correct?"

The hetman's grin never wavered. "You are not men. Only we of Earth soil and Earth water are men. You and your weird slaves are strangers together. We wish you success in your mutual slaughter."

"Well then," declared Xanten, "I heard you aright after all. Appeals to your loyalty are ineffectual, so much is clear. What of self-interest then? The Meks, failing to expunge the gentlefolk of the castles, will turn upon the Nomads and kill them as if they were so many ants."

"If they attack us, we will war on them," said the hetman. "Otherwise let them do as they will."

Xanten glanced thoughtfully at the sky. "We might be willing, even now, to accept a contingent of Nomads into the service of Castle Hagedorn, this to form a cadre from which a larger and more versatile group may be formed."

From the side another Nomad called in an offensively jeering voice: "You will sew a sac on our backs where you can pour your syrup, hey?"

Xanten replied in an even voice. "The syrup is highly nutritious and supplies all bodily needs."

"Why then do you not consume it yourself?"

Xanten disdained reply.

The hetman spoke. "If you wish to supply us weapons, we will take them, and use them against whomever threatens us. But do not expect us to defend you. If you fear for your lives, desert your castles and become Nomads."

"Fear for our lives?" exclaimed Xanten. "What nonsense! Never! Castle Hagedorn is impregnable, as is Janeil, and most of the other castles as well."

The hetman shook his head. "Any time we choose we could take Hagedorn, and kill all you popinjays in your sleep."

"What?" cried Xanten in outrage. "Are you serious?"

"Certainly. On a black night we would send a man aloft on a great kite and drop him down on the parapets. He would lower a line, haul up ladders and in fifteen minutes the castle is taken."

Xanten pulled at his chin. "Ingenious, but impractical. The Birds would detect such a kite. Or the wind would fail at a critical moment . . . All this is beside the point. The Meks fly no kites. They plan to make a display against Janeil and Hagedorn and then, in their frustration, they will go forth and hunt Nomads."

The hetman moved back a step. "What then? We have survived similar attempts by the men of Hagedorn. Cowards all! Hand to hand, with equal weapons, we would make you eat the dirt like the contemptible dogs you are."

Xanten raised his eyebrows in elegant disdain. "I fear that you forget yourself. You address a clan chief of Castle Hagedorn. Only fatigue and boredom restrain me from punishing you with this whip."

"Bah," said the hetman. He crooked a finger to one of his archers. "Spit this insolent lordling."

The archer discharged his arrow, but Xanten had been expecting some such act. He fired his energy-gun, destroying arrow, bow, and the archer's hands. He said, "I see I must teach you common respect for your betters; so it means the whip after all." Seizing the hetman by the scalp, he coiled the whip smartly once, twice, thrice around the narrow shoulders. "Let this suffice. I cannot compel you to fight, but at least I can demand decent respect from scuttling dung beetles." He leapt to the ground and, seizing the hetman, pitched him into the back of the wagon alongside the Mek. Then, backing the power-wagon around, he departed the camp without so much as a glance over his shoulder, the thwart of the seat protecting his back from the arrows of the hetman's stunned subjects.

The hetman scrambled erect, drew his dagger. Xanten turned his head slightly. "Take care! Or I will tie you to the wagon, and you shall run behind in the dust."

The hetman hesitated, made a spitting sound between his teeth, drew back. He looked down at his blade, turned it over, sheathed it with a grunt. "Where do you take me?"

Xanten halted the wagon. "No farther. I merely wished to leave your camp with dignity, without dodging and ducking a hail of arrows. You may alight. I take it you still refuse to bring your men into the service of Castle Hagedorn?"

The hetman once more made the spitting sound between his teeth. "When the Meks have destroyed the castles, we shall destroy the Meks. Then Earth will be cleared of star-things for all time!"

"You are a gang of intractable savages. Very well, alight, return to your encampment. Reflect well before you again show disrespect to a Castle Hagedorn clan chief."

"Bah," muttered the hetman. Leaping down from the wagon, he stalked back down the track toward his camp. He did not look back.

VI

About noon Xanten came to Far Valley, at the edge of the Hagedorn lands.

Nearby was a village of Expiationists: malcontents and neurasthenics in the opinion of castle gentlefolk, and a curious group by any standards. A few had held enviable rank; certain others were savants of recognized erudition; but others yet were persons of neither dignity nor reputation, subscribing to the most bizarre and extreme of philosophies. All now performed toil, no different from that relegated to the Peasants, and all seemed to take a perverse satisfaction in what by castle standards was filth, poverty and degradation.

As might be expected, their creed was by no means homogeneous. Some might better have been described as 'nonconformists', and others still, a minority, argued for a dynamic program.

Between castle and village was little intercourse. Occasionally the Expiationists bartered fruit or polished wood for tools, nails, medicaments, or the gentlefolk might make up a party to watch the Expiationists at their dancing and singing. Xanten had visited the village on many such occasions and had been attracted by the artless charm and informality of the folk at their play. Now, passing near the village, Xanten turned aside and followed a lane which wound between tall blackberry hedges and out upon a little common, where goats and cattle grazed. Xanten halted the wagon in the shade, saw that the syrup sac was full. He looked back at his captive. "What of you? If you need syrup, pour yourself full. But no, you have no sac. What then do you feed upon? Mud? Unsavory fare. I fear none here is rank enough for your taste. Ingest syrup or munch grass, as you will; only do not stray overfar from the wagon, for I watch with an intent eye."

The Mek, sitting hunched in a corner, gave no signal that it comprehended. Nor did it move to take advantage of Xanten's offer.

Xanten went to a watering trough. Holding his hands under the trickle which issued from a lead pipe, he rinsed his face, then drank a swallow or two from his cupped hand.

Turning, he found that a dozen folk of the village had approached. One he knew well, a man who might have become Godalming, or even Aure, had he not become infected with expiationism.

Xanten performed a polite salute. "A. G. Philidor. It is I, Xanten."

"Xanten, of course. But here I am A. G. Philidor no longer; merely Philidor."

Xanten bowed. "My apologies. I have neglected the full rigor of your informality."

"Spare me your wit," said Philidor. "Why do you bring us a shorn Mek? For adoption, perhaps?" This last alluded to the gentlefolk practice of bringing over-tally babies to the village.

"Now who flaunts his wit? But you have not heard the news?"

"News arrives here last of all. The Nomads are better informed."

"Prepare yourself for surprise. The Meks have revolted against the castles. Halcyon and Delora are demolished, and all killed; perhaps others by this time."

Philidor shook his head. "I am not surprised."

"Well, then, are you not concerned?"

Philidor considered. "To this extent. Our own plans, never very feasible, become more far-fetched than ever."

"It appears to me," said Xanten, "that you face grave and immediate danger. The Meks surely intend to wipe out every vestige of humanity. You will not escape."

Philidor shrugged. "Conceivably the danger exists . . . We will take counsel and decide what to do."

"I can put forward a proposal which you may find attractive," said Xanten. "Our first concern, of course, is to suppress the revolt. There are at least a dozen Expiationist communities, with an aggregate population of two or three thousand—perhaps more. I propose that we recruit and train a corps of highly disciplined troops, supplied from the Castle Hagedorn armory, led by Hagedorn's most expert military theoreticians."

Philidor stared at him incredulously. "You expect us, the Expiationists, to become your soldiers?"

"Why not?" asked Xanten ingeniously. "Your life is at stake no less than ours."

"No one dies more than once."

Xanten in his turn evinced shock. "What? Can this be a former gentleman of Hagedorn speaking? Is this the face a man of pride and courage turns to danger? Is this the lesson of history? Of course not! I need not instruct you in this; you are as knowledgeable as I."

Philidor nodded. "I know that the history of man is not his technical triumphs, his kills, his victories. It is a composite: a mosaic of a trillion pieces, the account of each man's accommodation with his conscience. This is the true history of the race."

Xanten made an airy gesture. "A. G. Philidor, you oversimplify grieviously. Do you consider me obtuse? There are many kinds of history. They interact. You emphasize morality. But the ultimate basis of morality is survival. What promotes survival is good, what induces mortefaction is bad."

"Well spoken!" declared Philidor. "But let me propound a parable. May a nation of a million beings destroy a creature who otherwise will infect all with a fatal disease? Yes, you will say. Once more. Ten starving beasts hunt you, that they may eat. Will you kill them to save your life? Yes, you will say again, though here you destroy more than you save. Once more: a man inhabits a hut in a lonely valley. A hundred spaceships descend from the sky, and attempt to destroy him. May he destroy these ships in self-defense, even though he is one and they are a hundred thousand? Perhaps you say yes. What then if a whole world, a whole race of beings, pits itself against this single man? May he kill all? What if the attackers are as human as himself? What if he were the creature of the first instance, who otherwise will infect a world with disease? You see, there is no area where a simple touchstone avails. We have searched and found none. Hence, at the risk of sinning against Survival, we—I, at least; I can only speak for myself—have chosen a morality that at least allows me calm. I kill—*nothing*. I destroy *nothing*."

"Bah," said Xanten contemptuously. "If a Mek platoon entered this valley and began to kill your children, you would not defend them?"

Philidor compressed his lips, turned away. Another man spoke. "Philidor has defined morality. But who is absolutely moral? Philidor—or I, or you—might in such a case desert his morality."

Philidor said, "Look about you. Is anyone here you recognize?"

Xanten scanned the group. Nearby stood a girl of extraordinary beauty. She wore a white smock and in the dark hair curling to her shoulders she wore a red flower. Xanten nodded. "I see the maiden O. Z. Garr wished to introduce into his menage at the castle."

"Exactly," said Philidor. "Do you recall the circumstances?"

"Very well indeed," said Xanten. "There was vigorous objection from the Council of Notables—if for no other reason than the threat to our laws of population control. O. Z. Garr attempted to sidestep the law in this fashion. 'I keep Phanes,' he said. 'At times I maintain as many as six, or even eight, and no one utters a word of protest. I will call this girl a Phane and keep her among the rest.' I and others protested. There was almost a duel on this matter. O. Z. Garr was forced to relinquish the girl. She was given into my custody and I conveyed her to Far Valley."

Philidor nodded. "All this is correct. Well—we attempted to dissuade Garr. He refused to be dissuaded, and threatened us with his hunting force of perhaps thirty Meks. We stood aside. Are we moral? Are we strong or weak?"

"Sometimes it is better," said Xanten, "to ignore morality. Even though O. Z. Garr is a gentleman and you are but Expiationists . . . Likewise in the case of the Meks. They are destroying the castles, and all the men of earth. If morality means supine acceptance, then morality must be abandoned!"

Philidor gave a sour chuckle. "What a remarkable situation! The Meks are here, likewise Peasants and Birds and Phanes, all altered, transported and enslaved for human pleasure. Indeed, it is this fact that occasions our guilt, for which we must expiate. And now you want us to compound this guilt!"

"It is a mistake to brood overmuch about the past," said

Xanten. "Still, if you wish to preserve your option to brood, I suggest that you fight Meks now, or at the very least take refuge in the castle."

"Not I," said Philidor. "Perhaps others may choose to do so."

"You will wait to be killed?"

"No. I and no doubt others will take refuge in the remote mountains."

Xanten clambered back aboard the power-wagon. "If you change your mind, come to Castle Hagedorn."

He departed.

The road continued along the valley, wound up a hillside, crossed a ridge. Far ahead, silhouetted against the sky, stood Castle Hagedorn.

VII

Xanten reported to the council.

"The spaceships cannot be used. The Meks have rendered them inoperative. Any plan to solicit assistance from the Home Worlds is pointless."

"This is sorry news," said Hagedorn with a grimace. "Well then—so much for that."

Xanten continued. "Returning by power-wagon I encountered a tribe of Nomads. I summoned the hetman and explained to him the advantages of serving Castle Hagedorn. The Nomads, I fear, lack both grace and docility. The hetman gave so surly a response that I departed in disgust.

"At Far Valley I visited the Expiationist village, and made a similar proposal, but with no great success. They are as idealistic as the Nomads are churlish. Both are of a fugitive tendency. The Expiationists spoke of taking refuge in the mountains. The Nomads presumably will retreat into the steppes."

Beaudry snorted. "How will flight help them? Perhaps they gain a few years—but eventually the Meks will find every last one of them; such is their methodicity."

"In the meantime," O. Z. Garr declared peevishly, "we might

307

have organized them into an efficient combat corps, to the benefit of all. Well, then, let them perish! We are secure."

"Secure yes," said Hagedorn gloomily. "But what when the power fails? When the lifts break down? When air circulation cuts off so that we either stifle or freeze? What then?"

O. Z. Garr gave his head a grim shake. "We must steel ourselves to undignified expedients, with as good a grace as possible. But the machinery of the castle is sound, and I expect small deterioration or failure for conceivably five or ten years. By that time anything may occur."

Claghorn, who had been leaning indolently back in his seat, spoke at last: "Essentially this is a passive program. Like the defection of the Nomads and Expiationists, it looks very little beyond the immediate moment."

O. Z. Garr spoke in a voice carefully polite. "Claghorn is well aware that I yield to none in courteous candor, as well as optimism and directness: in short, the reverse of passivity. But I refuse to dignify a stupid little inconvenience by extending it serious attention. How can he label this procedure 'passivity'? Does the worthy and honourable head of the Claghorns have a proposal which more effectively maintains our status, our standards, our self-respect?"

Claghorn nodded slowly, with a faint half-smile which O. Z. Garr found odiously complacent. "There is a simple and effective method by which the Meks might be defeated."

"Well then!" cried Hagedorn. "Why hesitate? Let us hear it!"

Claghorn looked around the red velvet-colored table, considered the faces of all: the dispassionate Xanten; Beaudry, with his burly, rigid face muscles clenched in an habitual expression unpleasantly like a sneer; old Isseth, handsome, erect and vital as the most dashing cadet; Hagedorn troubled, glum, his inward perplexity all too evident; the elegant Garr; Overwhele, thinking savagely of the inconveniences of the future; Aure, toying with his ivory tablet, either bored, morose or defeated; the others displaying various aspects of doubt, foreboding, hauteur, dark resentment, impatience; and in the case of Floy, a quiet smile—or as Isseth later characterized it, an imbecilic smirk—intended to convey his total disassociation from the entire irksome matter.

Claghorn took stock of the faces, and shook his head. "I will not at the moment broach this plan, as I fear it is unworkable. But I must point out that under no circumstances can Castle Hagedorn be as before, even should we survive the Mek attack."

"Bah!" exclaimed Beaudry. "We lose dignity, we become ridiculous, by even so much as discussing the beasts."

Xanten stirred himself. "A distasteful subject, but remember! Halcyon is destroyed, and Delora and who knows what others? Let us not thrust our heads in the sand! The Meks will not waft away merely because we ignore them."

"In any event," said O. Z. Garr, "Janeil is secure and we are secure. The other folk, unless they are already slaughtered, might do well to visit us during the inconvenience, if they can justify the humiliation of flight to themselves. I myself believe that the Meks will soon come to heel, anxious to return to their posts."

Hagedorn shook his head gloomly. "I find this hard to believe. Very well then, we shall adjourn."

The radio communications system was the first of the castle's vast array of electrical and mechanical devices to break down.

The failure occurred so soon and so decisively that certain of the theoreticians, notably I. K. Harde and Uegus, postulated sabotage by the departing Meks. Others remarked that the system had never been absolutely dependable, that the Meks themselves had been forced to tinker continuously with the circuits, that the failure was simply a result of bad engineering. Harde and Uegus inspected the unwieldy apparatus, but the cause of failure was not obvious. After a half-hour of consultation they agreed that any attempt to restore the system would necessitate complete re-design and re-engineering, with consequent contruction of testing and calibration devices, and the fabrication of a complete new family of components. "This is manifestly impossible," stated Uegus in his report to the council. "Even the simplest useful system would require several technician-years. There is not even one single technician to hand. We must therefore await the availability of trained and willing labor."

"In retrospect," stated Isseth, the oldest of the clan chiefs, "it is clear that in many ways we have been less than provident. No matter that the men of the Home Worlds are vulgarians! Men of shrewder calculation than our own would have maintained inter-world connection."

"Lack of 'shrewdness' and 'providence' were not the deterring factors," stated Claghorn. "Communication was discouraged simply because the early lords were unwilling that Earth should be overrun with Home-World parvenus. It is as simple as that."

Isseth grunted, and started to make a rejoinder, but Hagedorn said hastily, "Unluckily, as Xanten tells us, the spaceships have been rendered useless. While certain of our number have a profound knowledge of the theoretical considerations, again who is there to perform the toil? Even were the hangars and spaceships themselves under our control."

O. Z. Garr declared, "Give me six platoons of Peasants and six power-wagons equipped with high-energy-cannons, and I'll regain the hangars. No difficulties there!"

Beaudry said, "Well, here's a start, at least. I'll assist in the training of the Peasants, and though I know nothing of cannon operation, rely on me for any advice I can give."

Hagedorn looked around the group, frowned, pulled at his chin. "There are difficulties to this program. First, we have at hand only the single power-wagon in which Xanten returned from his reconnaissance. Then what of our energy-cannons? Has anyone inspected them? The Meks were entrusted with maintenance, but it is possible, even likely, that they wrought mischief here as well. O. Z. Garr, you are reckoned an expert military theoretician. What can you tell us in this regard?"

"I have made no inspection to date," stated O. Z. Garr.

"Today the 'Display of Antique Tabards' will occupy us all until the 'Hour of Sundown Appraisal'." * He looked at his watch. "Perhaps now is as good a time as any to adjourn, until I am able to provide detailed information in regard to the cannons."

Hagedorn nodded his heavy head. "The time indeed grows late. Your Phanes appear today?"

"Only two," replied O. Z. Garr. "The Lazule and the Eleventh Mystery. I can find nothing suitable for the Gossamer Delights nor my little Blue Fay, and the Gloriana still requires tutelage. Today B. Z. Maxelwane's Variflors should repay the most attention."

"Yes," said Hagedorn. "I have heard other remarks to this effect. Very well then, until tomorrow. Eh, Claghorn, you have something to say?"

"Yes, indeed," said Claghorn mildly. "We have all too little time at our disposal. Best that we make the most of it. I seriously doubt the efficacy of Peasant troops; they are like rabbits against wolves. What we need, rather than rabbits, are panthers."

"Ah, yes," said Hagedorn vaguely. "Yes indeed."

"Where, then, are panthers to be found?" Claghorn looked inquiringly around the table. "Can no one suggest a source? A pity. Well then, if panthers fail to appear, I suppose rabbits must do. Let us go about the business of converting rabbits into panthers, and instantly. I suggest that we postpone all fetes and spectacles until the shape of our future is more certain."

Hagedorn raised his eyebrows, opened his mouth to speak, closed it again. He looked intently at Claghorn to ascertain

* 'Display of Antique Tabards'; 'Hour of Sundown Appraisal'; the literal sense of the first term was yet relevant; that of the second had become lost and the phrase was a mere formalism, connoting that hour of late afternoon when visits were exchanged, wines, liqueurs and essences tasted: in short, a time of relaxation and small talk before the more formal convivialities of dining.

whether or not he joked. Then he looked dubiously around the table.

Beaudry gave a rather brassy laugh. "It seems that erudite Claghorn cries panic."

O. Z. Garr stated: "Surely, in all dignity, we cannot allow the impertinence of our servants to cause us such eye-rolling alarm. I am embarrassed even to bring the matter forward."

"I am not embarrassed," said Claghorn, with the full-faced complacence which so exasperated O. Z. Garr. "I see no reason why you should be. Our lives are threatened, in which case a trifle of embarrassment, or anything else, becomes of secondary importance."

O. Z. Garr rose to his feet, performed a brusque salute in Claghorn's direction, of such a nature as to constitute a calculated affront. Claghorn, rising, performed a similar salute, this so grave and overly complicated as to invest Garr's insult with burlesque overtones. Xanten, who detested O. Z. Garr, laughed aloud.

O. Z. Garr hesitated, then, sensing that under the circumstances taking the matter further would be regarded as poor form, strode from the chamber.

The Viewing of Antique Tabards, an annual pageant of Phanes wearing sumptuous garments took place in the Great Rotunda to the north of the central plaza.

Possibly half of the gentlemen, but less than a quarter of the ladies, kept Phanes. These were creatures native to the caverns of Albireo Seven's moon: a docile race, both playful and affectionate, which after several thousand years of selective breeding had become sylphs of piquant beauty. Clad in a delicate gauze which issued from pores behind their ears, along their upper arms, down their backs, they were the most inoffensive of creatures, anxious always to please, innocently vain. Most gentlemen regarded them with affection, but rumors sometimes told of ladies drenching an especially hated Phane in tincture of ammonia, which matted her pelt and destroyed her gauze forever.

A gentleman besotted by a Phane was considered a figure of fun. The Phane, though so carefully bred as to seem a delicate girl, if used sexually became crumpled and haggard, with gauzes drooping and discolored, and everyone would know that such and such a gentleman had misused his Phane. In this regard, at least, the women of the castles might exert their superiority. They did so by conducting themselves with such extravagant provocation that the Phanes in contrast seemed the most ingenious and fragile of nature sprites. Their life-span was perhaps thirty years, during the last ten of which, after they had lost their beauty, they encased themselves in mantles of gray gauze and performed menial tasks in boudoirs, kitchens, pantries, nurseries and dressing rooms.

The Viewing of Antique Tabards was an occasion more for the viewing of Phanes than the tabards, though these, woven of Phane-gauze, were of intricate beauty in themselves.

The Phane owners sat in a lower tier, tense with hope and pride, exulting when one made an especially splendid display, plunged into black depths when the ritual postures were performed with other than grace and elegance. During each display highly formal music was plucked from a lute by a gentleman from a clan different to that of the Phane owner. The owner never played the lute to the performance of his own Phane. The display was never overtly a competition and no formal acclamation was allowed, but all watching made up their minds as to which was the most entrancing and graceful of the Phanes, and the repute of the owner was thereby exalted.

The current Viewing was delayed almost half an hour by reason of the defection of the Meks, and certain hasty improvisations had been made necessary. But the gentlefolk of Castle Hagedorn were in no mood to be critical and took no heed of the occasional lapses as a dozen young Peasant bucks struggled to perform unfamiliar tasks. The Phanes were as entrancing as ever, bending, twisting, swaying to plangent chords of the lute, fluttering their fingers as if feeling for rain-drops, crouching suddenly, gliding, then springing upright straight as wands, finally bowing and skipping from the platform.

Halfway through the program a Peasant sidled awkwardly into the Rotunda, and mumbled in an urgent manner to the cadet who came to inquire his business. The cadet at once made his way to Hagedorn's polished jet booth. Hagedorn listened, nodded, spoke a few terse words and settled calmly back in his seat as if the message had been of no consequence, and the gentlefolk of the audience were reassured.

The entertainment proceeded. O. Z. Garr's delectable pair made a fine show, but it was generally felt that Lirlin, a young Phane belonging to Isseth Floy Gazuneth, for the first time at a formal showing, made the most captivating display.

The Phanes appeared for a last time, moving all together through a half-improvised minuet. Then they performed a final half-gay, half-regretful salute and departed the rotunda. For a few moments more the gentlemen and ladies would remain in their booths, sipping essences, discussing the display, arranging affairs and assignations. Hagedorn sat frowning, twisting his hands.

Suddenly he rose to his feet. The rotunda instantly became silent.

"I dislike intruding an unhappy note at so pleasant an occasion," said Hagedorn. "But news has just been given to me, and it is fitting that all should know. Janeil Castle is under attack. The Meks are there in great force, with hundreds of power-wagons. They have circled the castle with a dike which prevents any effective use of the Janeil energy-cannon.

"There is no immediate danger to Janeil, and it is difficult to comprehend what the Meks hope to achieve, the Janeil walls being all of two hundred feet high.

"The news nevertheless is somber, and it means that eventually we must expect a similar investment—thought it is even more difficult to comprehend how Meks could hope to inconvenience us. Our water derives from four wells sunk deep into the earth. We have great stocks of food. Our energy is derived from the sun. If necessary, we could condense water and synthesize food from the air—at least I have been so assured by our great biochemical theoretician X. B. Ladisname. Still—this is the news. Make of it what you will. Tomorrow the Council of Notables will meet."

VIII

"Well, then," said Hagedorn to the council, "for once let us dispense with formality. O. Z. Garr: what of our cannon?"

O. Z. Garr, wearing the magnificent gray and green uniform of the Overwhele Dragoons, carefully placed his morion on the table, so that the panache stood erect. "Of twelve cannon, four appear to be functioning correctly. Four have been sabotaged by excision of the power-leads. Four have been sabotaged by some means undetectable to careful investigation. I have commandeered a half-dozen Peasants who demonstrate a modicum of mechanical ability, and have instructed them in detail. They are currently engaged in splicing the leads. This is the extent of my current information in regard to the cannon."

"Moderately good news," said Hagedorn. "What of the proposed corps of armed Peasants?"

"The project is under way. A. F. Mull and I. A. Berzelius are now inspecting Peasants with a view to recruitment and training. I can make no sanguine projection as to the military effectiveness of such a corps, even if trained and led by such as A. F. Mull, I. A. Berzelius and myself. The Peasants are a mild ineffectual race, admirably suited to the grubbing of weeds, but with no stomach whatever for fighting."

Hagedorn glanced around the council. "Are there any other suggestions?"

Beaudry spoke in a harsh angry voice. "Had the villains but left us our power-wagons, we might have mounted the cannon aboard! The Peasants are equal to this, at least. Then we could roll to Janeil and blast the dogs from the rear."

"These Meks seem utter fiends!" declared Aure. "What conceivably do they have in mind? Why, after these centuries, must they suddenly go mad?"

315

"We all ask ourselves the same," said Hagedorn. "Xanten, you returned from reconnaissance with a captive: have you attempted to question him?"

"No," said Xanten. "Truth to tell, I haven't thought of him since."

"Why not attempt to question him? Perhaps he can provide a clue or two."

Xanten nodded assent. "I can try. Candidly I expect to learn nothing."

"Claghorn, you are the Mek expert," said Beaudry. "Would you have thought the creatures capable of so intricate a plot? What do they hope to gain? Our castles?"

"They are certainly capable of precise and meticulous planning," said Claghorn. "Their ruthlessness surprises me—more, possibly, than it should. I have never known them to covet our material possessions, and they show no tendency toward what we consider the concomitants of civilization: fine discriminations of sensation and the like. I have often speculated—I won't dignify the conceit with the status of a theory—that the structural logic of a brain is of rather more consequence than we reckon with. Our own brains are remarkable for their utter lack of rational structure. Considering the haphazard manner in which our thoughts are formed, registered, indexed and recalled, any single rational act becomes a miracle. Perhaps we are incapable of rationality. Perhaps all thought is a set of impulses generated by one emotion, monitored by another, ratified by a third. In contrast the Mek brain is a marvel of what seems careful engineering. It is roughly cubical and consists of microscopic cells interconnected by organic fibrils, each a monofilament molecule of negligible electrical resistance. Within each cell is a film of silica, a fluid of variable conductivity and dielectic properties, a cusp of a complex mixture of metallic oxides. The brain is capable of storing great quantities of information in an orderly pattern. No fact is lost, unless it is purposely forgotten, a capacity which the Meks possess. The brain also functions as a radio transceiver, possibly as a radar transmitter and detector, though this again is speculation.

"Where the Mek brain falls short is in its lack of emotional color. One Mek is precisely like another, without any personality differentiation perceptible to us. This, clearly, is a function of their communicative system. It would be unthinkable for a unique personality to develop under these conditions. They served us efficiently and—so we thought—loyally, because they felt nothing about their condition, neither pride in achievement, nor resentment, nor shame. Nothing whatever. They neither loved us nor hated us. Nor do they now. It is hard for us to conceive this emotional vacuum, when each of us feels something about everything. We live in a welter of emotions. They are as devoid of emotion as an ice-cube. They were fed, housed, maintained in a manner they found satisfactory. Why did they revolt? I have speculated at length, but the single reason which I can formulate seems so grotesque and unreasonable that I refuse to take it seriously. If this after all is the correct explanation . . ." His voice drifted away.

"Well?" demanded O. Z. Garr peremptorily. "What then?"

"Then—it is all the same. They are committed to the destruction of the human race. My speculation alters nothing."

Hagedorn turned to Xanten. "All this should assist you in your inquiries."

"I was about to suggest that Claghorn assist me, if he is so inclined," said Xanten.

"As you like," said Claghorn, "though in my opinion the information, no matter what, is irrelevant. Our single concern should be a means to repel them and to save our lives."

"And—save the force of 'panthers' you mentioned at our previous session—you can conceive of no subtle weapon?" asked Hagedorn wistfully. "A device to set up electrical resonances in their brains, or something similar?"

"Not feasible," said Claghorn. "Certain organs in the creatures' brains function as overload switches. Though it is true that during this time they might not be able to communicate." After a moment's reflection he added thoughtfully:

317

"Who knows? A. G. Bernal and Uegus are theoreticians with a profound knowledge of such projections. Perhaps they might construct such a device, or several, against a possible need."

Hagedorn nodded dubiously, and looked toward Uegus. "Is this possible?"

Uegus frowned. " 'Construct'? I can certainly design such an instrument. But the components—where? Scattered through the storerooms helter-skelter, some functioning, others not. To achieve anything meaningful I must become no better than an apprentice, a Mek." He became incensed, and his voice hardened. "I find it hard to believe that I should be forced to point out this fact! Do you hold me and my talents then of such small worth?"

Hagedorn hastened to reassure him. "Of course not! I for one would never think of impugning your dignity."

"Never!" agreed Claghorn. "Nevertheless, during this present emergency, we will find indignities imposed upon us by events, unless now we impose them upon ourselves."

"Very well," said Uegus, a humorless smile trembling at his lips. "You shall come with me to the storeroom. I will point out the components to be brought forth and assembled, you shall perform the toil. What do you say to that?"

"I say yes, gladly, if it will be of real utility. However, I can hardly perform the labor for a dozen different theoreticians. Will any others serve beside myself?"

No one responded. Silence was absolute, as if every gentleman present held his breath.

Hagedorn started to speak, but Claghorn interrupted. "Pardon, Hagedorn, but here, finally, we are stuck upon a basic principle, and it must be settled now."

Hagedorn looked desperately around the council. "Has anyone relevant comment?"

"Claghorn must do as his innate nature compels," declared O. Z. Garr in the silkiest of voices. "I cannot dictate to him. As for myself, I can never demean my status as a gentleman of Hagedorn. This creed is as natural to me as drawing breath; if ever it is compromised I become a travesty of a gentleman,

318

a grotesque mask of myself. This is Castle Hagedorn, and we represent the culmination of human civilization. Any compromise therefore becomes degradation; any expedient diminution of our standards becomes dishonor. I have heard the word 'emergency' used. What a deplorable sentiment! To dignify the rat-like snappings and gnashings of such as the Meks with the word 'emergency' is to my mind unworthy of a gentleman of Hagedorn!"

A murmur of approval went around the council table.

Claghorn leaned far back in his seat, chin on his chest, as if in relaxation. His clear blue eyes went from face to face, then returned to O. Z. Garr whom he studied with dispassionate interest. "Obviously you direct your words to me," he said. "I appreciate their malice. But this is a small matter." He looked away from O. Z. Garr, to stare up at the massive diamond and emerald chandelier. "More important is the fact that the council as a whole, in spite of my earnest persuasion, seems to endorse your viewpoint. I can urge, expostulate, insinuate no longer, and I will now leave Castle Hagedorn. I find the atmosphere stifling. I trust that you survive the attack of the Meks, though I doubt that you will. They are a clever resourceful race, untroubled by qualms or preconceptions, and we have long underestimated their quality."

Claghorn rose from his seat, inserted the ivory tablet into its socket. "I bid you all farewell." Hagedorn hastily jumped to his feet, held forth his arms imploringly. "Do not depart in anger, Claghorn! Reconsider! We need your wisdom, your expertise."

"Assuredly you do," said Claghorn. "But even more you need to act upon the advice I have already extended. Until then we have no common ground, and any further interchange is futile and tiresome." He made a brief all-inclusive salute and departed the chamber.

Hagedorn slowly resumed his seat. The others made uneasy motions, coughed, looked up at the chandelier, studied their ivory tablets. O. Z. Garr muttered something to B. F. Wyas who sat beside him, who nodded solemnly. Hagedorn spoke in a subdued voice: "We will miss the presence of Claghorn, his penetrating if unorthodox insights . . . We have accomplished little. Uegus, perhaps you will give thought to the projector under discussion. Xanten, you were to question the captive Mek. O. Z. Garr, you undoubtedly will see to the repair of the energy-cannon . . . Aside from these small matters, it appears that we have evolved no general plan of action, to help either ourselves or Janeil."

Marune spoke. "What of the other castles? Are they still extant? We have had no news. I suggest that we send Birds to each castle, to learn their condition."

Hagedorn nodded. "Yes, this is a wise motion. Perhaps you will see to this, Marune?"

"I will do so."

"Good. We will now adjourn for a time."

The Birds were dispatched by Marune of Aure and one by one returned. Their reports were similar:

"Sea Island is deserted. Marble columns are tumbled along the beach. Pearl Dome is collapsed. Corpses float in the Water Garden."

"Maraval reeks of death. Gentlemen, Peasants, Phane—all dead. Alas! Even the Birds have departed!"

"Delora: *a ros ros ros!* A dismal scene! No sign of life to be found!"

"Alume is desolate. The great wooden door is smashed. The eternal Green Flame is extinguished."

"There is nothing at Halcyon. The Peasants were driven into a pit."

"Tuang: silence."

"Morninglight: death."

IX

Three days later, Xanten constrained six Birds to a lift chair. He directed them first on a wide sweep around the castle, then south to Far Valley.

The Birds aired their usual complaints, then bounded down the deck in great ungainly hops which threatened to throw Xanten immediately to the pavement. At last gaining the air, they flew up in a spiral. Castle Hagedorn became an intricate miniature far below, each House marked by its unique cluster of turrets and eyries, its own eccentric roof line, its long streaming pennon.

The Birds performed the prescribed circle, skimming the crags and pines of North Ridge. Then, setting wings aslant the upstream, they coasted away toward Far Valley.

Over the pleasant Hagedorn domain flew the Birds and Xanten: over orchards, fields, vineyards, Peasant villages. They crossed Lake Maude with its pavilions and docks, the meadows beyond where the Hagedorn cattle and sheep grazed, and presently came to Far Valley, at the limit of Hagedorn lands.

Xanten indicated where he wished to alight. The Birds, who would have preferred a site closer to the village where they could have watched all that transpired, grumbled and cried out in wrath and set Xanten down so roughly that had he not been alert the shock would have pitched him head over heels.

Xanten alighted without elegance but at least remained on his feet. "Await me here!" he ordered. "Do not stray; attempt no flamboyant tricks among the lift-straps. When I return I wish to see six quiet Birds, in neat formation, lift-straps untwisted and untangled. No bickering, mind you! No loud caterwauling, to attract unfavorable comment! Let all be as I have ordered!"

The Birds sulked, stamped their feet, ducked aside their necks, made insulting comments just under the level of Xanten's hearing. Xanten turned with a final glare of admonition and walked down the lane which led to the village.

The vines were heavy with ripe blackberries and a number of the girls of the village filled baskets. Among them was the girl O. Z. Garr had thought to pre-empt for his personal use. As Xanten passed, he halted and performed a courteous salute. "We have met before, if my recollection is correct."

The girl smiled, a half-rueful, half-whimsical smile. "Your

recollection serves you well. We met at Hagedorn, where I was taken a captive. And later, when you conveyed me here, after dark, though I could not see your face." She extended her basket. "Are you hungry? Will you eat?"

Xanten took several berries. In the course of the conversation he learned that the girl's name was Glys Meadowsweet, that her parents were not known to her, but were presumably gentlefolk of Castle Hagedorn who had exceeded their birth tally. Xanten examined her even more carefully than before but could see resemblance to none of the Hagedorn families. "You might derive from Castle Delora. If there is any family resemblance I can detect, it is to the Cosanzas of Delora—a family noted for the beauty of its ladies."

"You are not married?" she asked artlessly.

"No," said Xanten, and indeed he had dissolved his relationship with Araminta only the day before. "What of you?"

She shook her head. "I would never be gathering blackberries if I were. It is work reserved for maidens. Why do you come to Far Valley?"

"For two reasons. The first to see you." Xanten heard himself say this with surprise. But it was true, he realized with another small shock of surprise. "I have never spoken with you properly and I have always wondered if you were as charming and gay as you are beautiful."

The girl shrugged and Xanten could not be sure whether she were pleased or not, compliments from gentlemen sometimes setting the stage for a sorry aftermath. "Well, no matter. I came also to speak to Claghorn."

"He is yonder," she said in a voice toneless, even cool, and pointed. "He occupies that cottage." She returned to her blackberry picking. Xanten bowed, proceeded to that cottage the girl had indicated.

Claghorn, wearing loose knee-length breeches of gray homespun, worked with an axe chopping faggots into stove-lengths. At the sight of Xanten he halted his toil, leaned on the axe, mopped his forehead. "Ah, Xanten. I am pleased to see you. How are the folk of Castle Hagedorn?"

"As before. There is little to report, even had I come to bring you news."

"Indeed, indeed?" Claghorn leaned on the axe handle, surveyed Xanten with a bright blue gaze.

"At our last meeting," went on Xanten, "I agreed to question the captive Mek. After doing so I am distressed that you were not at hand to assist, so that you might have resolved certain ambiguities in the responses."

"Speak on," said Claghorn. "Perhaps I shall be able to do so now."

"After the council meeting I descended immediately to the storeroom where the Mek was confined. It lacked nutriment; I gave it syrup and a pail of water, which it sipped sparingly, then evinced a desire for minced clams. I summoned kitchen help and sent them for this commodity and the Mek ingested several pints. As I have indicated, it was an unusual Mek, standing as tall as myself and lacking a syrup sac. I conveyed it to a different chamber, a storeroom for brown plush furniture, and ordered it to a seat.

"I looked at the Mek and it looked at me. The quills which I removed were growing back; probably it could at least receive from Meks elsewhere. It seemed a superior beast, showing neither obsequiousness nor respect, and answered my questions without hesitation.

"First I remarked: 'The gentlefolk of the castles are astounded by the revolt of the Meks. We had assumed that your life was satisfactory. Were we wrong?'

"'Evidently.' I am sure that this was the word signaled, though never had I suspected the Meks of wit of any sort.

"'Very well then,' I said. 'In what manner?'

"'Surely it is obvious. We no longer wished to toil at your behest. We wished to conduct our lives by our own traditional standards.'

"The response surprised me. I was unaware that the Meks

323

possessed standards of any kind, much less traditional standards."

Claghorn nodded. "I have been similarly surprised by the scope of the Mek mentality."

"I reproached the Mek: 'Why kill? Why destroy our lives in order to augment your own?' As soon as I had put the question I realized that it had been unhappily phrased. The Mek, I believe, realized the same; however, in reply he signaled something very rapidly which I believe was: 'We knew we must act with decisiveness. Your own protocol made this necessary. We might have returned to Etamin Nine, but we prefer this world Earth, and will make it our own, with our own great slipways, tubs and basking ramps.'

"This seemed clear enough, but I sensed an adumbration extending yet beyond. I said, 'Comprehensible. But why kill, why destroy? You might have taken yourself to a different region. We could not have molested you.'

"'Infeasible, by your own thinking. A world is too small for two competing races. You intended to send us back to Etamin Nine.'

"'Ridiculous!' I said. 'Fantasy, absurdity. Do you take me for a mooncalf?'

"'No,' the creature insisted. 'Two of Castle Hagedorn's notables were seeking the highest post. One assured us that, if elected, this would become his life's aim.'

"'A grotesque misunderstanding,' I told him. 'One man, a lunatic, can not speak for all men!'

"'No? One Mek speaks for all Meks. We think with one mind. Are not men of a like sort?'

"'Each thinks for himself. The lunatic who assured you of this tomfoolery is an evil man. But at least matters are clear. We do not propose to send you to Etamin Nine. Will you withdraw from Janeil, take yourselves to a far land and leave us in peace?'

"'No. Affairs have proceeded too far. We will now destroy all men. The truth of the statement is clear: one world is too small for two races.'

" 'Unluckily then, I must kill you,' I told him. 'Such acts are not to my liking, but, with opportunity, you would kill as many gentlemen as possible.' At this the creature sprang upon me, and I killed it with an easier mind than had it sat staring.

"Now you know all. It seems that either you or O. Z. Garr stimulated the cataclysm. O. Z. Garr? Unlikely. Impossible. Hence, you, Claghorn, you! have this weight upon your soul!"

Claghorn frowned down at the axe. "Weight, yes. Guilt, no. Ingenuousness, yes; wickedness, no."

Xanten stood back. "Claghorn, your coolness astounds me! Before, when rancorous folk like O. Z. Garr conceived you a lunatic—"

"Peace, Xanten!" exclaimed Claghorn irritably. "This extravagant breast-beating becomes maladroit. What have I done wrong? My fault is that I tried too much. Failure is tragic, but a phthisic face hanging over the cup of the future is worse. I meant to become Hagedorn, I would have sent the slaves home. I failed, the slaves revolted. So do not speak another word. I am bored with the subject. You cannot imagine how your bulging eyes and your concave spine oppress me."

"Bored you may be," cried Xanten. "You decry my eyes, my spine—but what of the thousands dead?"

"How long would they live in any event? Lives are as cheap as fish in the sea. I suggest that you put by your reproaches and devote a similar energy to saving yourself. Do you realize that a means exists? You stare at me blankly. I assure you that what I say is true, but you will never learn the means from me."

"Claghorn," said Xanten, "I flew to this spot intending to blow your arrogant head from your body—" But Claghorn, no longer heeding, had returned to his wood-chopping.

"Claghorn!" cried Xanten.

"Xanten, take your outcries elsewhere, if you please. Remonstrate with your Birds."

Xanten swung on his heel, marched back down the lane. The girls picking berries looked at him questioningly and moved aside. Xanten halted, looked up and down the lane. Glys

Meadowsweet was nowhere to be seen. In a new fury he continued. He stopped short. On a fallen tree a hundred feet from the Birds sat Glys Meadowsweet, examining a blade of grass as if it had been an astonishing artifact of the past. The Birds for a marvel had actually obeyed him and waited in a fair semblance of order.

Xanten looked up toward the heavens, kicked at the turf. He drew a deep breath and approached to Glys Meadowsweet. He noted that she had tucked a flower into her long loose hair.

After a second or two she looked up and searched his face. "Why are you so angry?"

Xanten slapped his thigh, seated himself beside her. " 'Angry'? No. I am out of my mind with frustration. Claghorn is as obstreperous as a sharp rock. He knows how Castle Hagedorn can be saved but he will not divulge his secret."

Glys Meadowsweet laughed—an easy merry sound, like nothing Xanten had ever heard at Castle Hagedorn. "Secret? When even I know it?"

"It must be a secret," said Xanten. "He will not tell me."

"Listen. If you fear the Birds will hear it, I will whisper." She spoke a few words into his ear.

Perhaps the sweet breath befuddled Xanten's mind. But the explicit essence of the revelation failed to strike home into his consciousness. He made a sound of sour amusement. "No secret there. Only what the prehistoric Scythians termed 'bathos'. Dishonor to the gentlemen! Do we dance with the Peasants? Do we serve the Birds essences and discuss with them the sheen of our Phanes?"

" 'Dishonor' then?" She jumped to her feet. "Then it is also dishonor for you to talk to me, to sit here with me, to make ridiculous suggestions!"

"I made no suggestions!" protested Xanten. "I sit here in all decorum—"

"Too much decorum, too much honor!" With a display of passion which astounded Xanten, Glys Meadowsweet tore the flower from her hair, hurled it at the ground. "There. Hence!"

"No," said Xanten in sudden humility. He bent, picked up

326

the flower, kissed it, replaced it in her hair. "I am not over-honorable. I will try my best." He put his arms on her shoulders, but she held him away.

"Tell me," she inquired with a very mature severity, "do you own any of those peculiar insect-women?"

"I? Phanes? I own no Phanes."

With this Glys Meadowsweet relaxed and allowed Xanten to embrace her, while the Birds clucked, guffawed and made vulgar scratching sounds with their wings.

X

The summer waned. On June 30 Janeil and Hagedorn celebrated the Fete of Flowers, even though the dike was rising high around Janeil.

Shortly after, Xanten flew six select Birds into Castle Janeil by night and proposed to the council that the population be evacuated by Bird-lift—as many as possible, as many who wished to leave. The council listened with stony faces and without comment passed on.

Xanten returned to Castle Hagedorn. Using the most careful methods, speaking only to trusted comrades, Xanten enlisted thirty or forty cadets and gentlemen to his persuasion, though inevitably he could not keep the doctrinal thesis of his program secret.

The first reaction of the traditionalists was mockery and charges of poltroonery. At Xanten's insistence, challenges were neither issued nor accepted by his hot-blooded associates.

On the evening of September 9 Castle Janeil fell. The news was brought to Castle Hagedorn by excited Birds who told the grim tale again and again in voices ever more hysterical.

Hagedorn, now gaunt and weary, automatically called a council meeting; it took note of the gloomy circumstances. "We then are the last castle! The Meks cannot conceivably do us harm; they can build dikes around our castle walls for twenty years and only work themselves to distraction. We are secure; but yet it is a strange and portentous thought to

327

realize that at last, here at Castle Hagedorn, live the last gentlemen of the race!"

Xanten spoke in a voice strained with earnest conviction: "Twenty years—fifty years—what difference to the Meks? Once they surround us, once they deploy, we are trapped. Do you comprehend that now is our last opportunity to escape the great cage that Castle Hagedorn is to become?"

" 'Escape', Xanten? What a word! For shame!" hooted O. Z. Garr. "Take your wretched band, escape! To steppe or swamp or tundra! Go as you like, with your poltroons, but be good enough to give over these incessant alarms!"

"Garr, I have found conviction since I became a 'poltroon'. Survival is good morality: I have this from the mouth of a noted savant."

"Bah! Such as whom?"

"A. G. Philidor, if you must be informed of every detail."

O. Z. Garr clapped his hand to his forehead. "Do you refer to Philidor the Expiationist? He is of the most extreme stripe, an Expiationist to out-expiate all the rest! Xanten, be sensible, if you please!"

"There are years ahead for all of us," said Xanten in a wooden voice, "if we free ourselves from the castle."

"But the castle is our life!" declared Hagedorn. "In essence, Xanten, what would we be without the castle? Wild animals? Nomads?"

"We would be alive."

O. Z. Garr gave a snort of disgust, turned away to inspect a wall-hanging. Hagedorn shook his head in doubt and perplexity. Beaudry threw his hands up into the air. "Xanten, you have the effect of unnerving us all. You come in here, inflict this dreadful sense of urgency, but why? In Castle Hagedorn we are as safe as in our mother's arms. What do we gain by throwing aside all—honor, dignity, comfort, civilized niceties —for no other reason than to slink through the wilderness?"

"Janeil was safe," said Xanten. "Today where is Janeil? Death, mildewed cloth, sour wine. What we gain by 'slinking' is the assurance of survival. And I plan much more than simple 'slinking'."

"I can conceive of a hundred occasions when death is better than life!" snapped Isseth. "Must I die in dishonor and disgrace? Why may my last years not be passed in dignity?"

Into the room came B. F. Robarth. "Councilmen, the Meks approach Castle Hagedorn."

Hagedorn cast a wild look around the chamber. "Is there a consensus? What must we do?"

Xanten threw up his hands. "Everyone must do as he thinks best! I argue no more: I am done. Hagedorn, will you adjourn the council so that we may be about our affairs? I to my 'slinking'?"

"Council is adjourned," said Hagedorn, and all went up to stand on the ramparts.

Up the avenue into the castle trooped Peasants from the surrounding countryside, packets slung over their shoulders. Across the valley, at the edge of Bartholomew Forest, was a clot of power-wagons and an amorphous brown-gold mass: Meks.

Aure pointed west. "Look—there they come, up the Long Swale." He turned, peered east. "And look, there at Bambridge: Meks!"

By common consent, all swung about to scan North Ridge. O. Z. Garr pointed to a quiet line of brown-gold shapes. "There they wait, the vermin! They have penned us in! Well then, let them wait!" He swung away, rode the lift down to the plaza, crossed swiftly to Zumbeld House, where he worked the rest of the afternoon with his Gloriana, of whom he expected great things.

The following day the Meks formalized the investment. Around Castle Hagedorn a great circle of Mek activity made itself apparent: sheds, warehouses, barracks. Within this periphery, just beyond the range of the energy-cannon, power-wagons thrust up mounds of dirt.

During the night these mounds lengthened toward the

castle; similarly the night after. At last the purpose of the mounds became clear: they were a protective cover above passages or tunnels leading toward the crag on which Castle Hagedorn rested.

The following day several of the mounds reached the base of the crag. Presently from the far end began to flow a succession of power-wagons loaded with rubble. They issued, dumped their loads and once again entered the tunnels.

Eight of these above-ground tunnels had been established. From each trundled endless loads of dirt and rock, gnawed from the crag on which Castle Hagedorn sat. To the gentlefolk who crowded the parapets the meaning of the work at last became clear.

"They make no attempt to bury us," said Hagedorn. "They merely mine out the crag from below us!"

On the sixth day of the siege, a great segment of the hillside shuddered, slumped, and a tall pinnacle of rock reaching almost up to the base of the walls collapsed.

"If this continues," muttered Beaudry, "our time will be less than that of Janeil."

"Come then," called O. Z. Garr in sudden energy. "Let us try our energy-cannon. We'll blast open their wretched tunnels, and what will the rascals do then?" He went to the nearest emplacement, shouted down for Peasants to remove the tarpaulin.

Xanten, who happened to stand nearby, said, "Allow me to assist you." He jerked away the tarpaulin. "Shoot now, if you will."

O. Z. Garr stared at him uncomprehendingly, then leapt forward, swiveled the great projector about so that it aimed at a mound. He pulled the switch; the air crackled in front of the ringed snout, rippled, flickered with purple sparks. The target area steamed, became black, then dark red, then slumped into an incandescent crater. But the underlying earth, twenty feet in thickness, afforded too much insulation; the molten puddle became white-hot but failed to spread or deepen. The energy-cannon gave a sudden chatter, as electricity short-circuited through corroded insulation. The cannon went dead.

O. Z. Garr inspected the mechanism in anger and disappointment. Then, with a gesture of repugnance, he turned away. The cannons were clearly of limited effectiveness.

Two hours later, on the east side of the crag, another great sheet of rock collapsed, and just before sunset, a similar mass sheared from the western face, where the wall of the castle rose almost in an uninterrupted line from the cliff below.

At midnight Xanten and those of his persuasion, with their children and consorts, departed Castle Hagedorn. Six teams of Birds shuttled from the flight deck to a meadow near Far Valley, and long before dawn had transported the entire group.

There were none to bid them farewell.

XI

A week later another section of the east cliff fell away, taking a length of rock-melt buttress with it. At the tunnel mouths the piles of excavated rubble had become alarmingly large.

The terraced south face of the crag was the least disturbed; the most spectacular damage having occurred to east and west. Suddenly, a month after the initial assault, a great section of the terraces slumped forward, leaving an irregular crevasse which interrupted the avenue and hurled down the statues of former notables emplaced at intervals along the avenue's balustrade.

Hagedorn called a council meeting. "Circumstances," he said in a wan attempt at facetiousness, "have not bettered themselves. Our most pessimistic expectations have been exceeded. A dismal situation! I confess that I do not relish the prospect of toppling to my death among all my smashed belongings."

Aure made a desperate gesture. "A similar thought haunts me! Death—what of that? All must die! But when I think of my precious belongings I become sick. My books trampled!

331

My fragile vases smashed! My tabards ripped! My rugs buried! My Phanes strangled! My heirloom chandeliers flung aside! These are my nightmares."

"Your possessions are no less precious than any others," said Beudry shortly. "Still they have no life of their own; when we are gone, who cares what happens to them?"

Marune winced. "A year ago I put down eighteen dozen flasks of prime essence; twelve dozen Green Rain; three each of Balthazar and Faidor. Think of these, if you would contemplate tragedy!"

"Had we only known!" groaned Aure. "I would have—I would have . . ." His voice trailed away.

O. Z. Garr stamped his foot in impatience. "Let us avoid lamentation at all costs! We had a choice, remember? Xanten beseeched us to flee; now he and his like go skulking and foraging through the north mountains with the Expiationists. We chose to remain, for better or worse, and unluckily the 'worse' is occurring. We must accept the fact like gentlemen."

To this the council gave melancholy assent. Hagedorn brought forth a flask of priceless Rhadamanth, and poured with a prodigality which previously would have been unthinkable. "Since we have no future—to our glorious past!"

That night disturbances were noted here and there around the ring of Mek investment: flames at four separate points, a faint sound of hoarse shouting. On the following day it seemed that the tempo of activity had lessened a trifle.

But during the afternoon a vast segment of the east cliff fell away. A moment later, as if after majestic deliberation, the tall east wall split off, toppled, leaving the backs of six great houses exposed to the open sky.

An hour after sunset a team of Birds settled to the flight-deck. Xanten jumped from the seat. He ran down the circular staircase to the ramparts, came down to the plaza by Hagedorn's palace.

Hagedorn, summoned by a kinsman, came forth to stare at

Xanten in surprise. "What do you do here? We expected you to be safely north with the Expiationists!"

"The Expiationists are not safely north," said Xanten. "They have joined the rest of us. We are fighting."

Hagedorn's jaw dropped. "Fighting? The gentlemen are fighting Meks?"

"As vigorously as possible."

Hagedorn shook his head in wonder. "The Expiationists too? I understood that they had planned to flee north."

"Some have done so, including A. G. Philidor. There are factions among the Expiationists just as here. Most are not ten miles distant. The same with the Nomads. Some have taken their power-wagons and fled. The rest kill Meks with fanatic fervor. Last night you saw our work. We fired four storage warehouses, destroyed syrup tanks, killed a hundred or more Meks, as well as a dozen power-wagons. We suffered losses, which hurt us, because there are few of us and many Meks. This is why I am here. We need more men. Come fight beside us!"

Hagedorn turned, motioned to the great central plaza. "I will call forth the folk from their Houses. Talk to everyone."

The Birds, complaining bitterly at the unprecedented toil, worked all night, transporting gentlemen, who, sobered by the imminent destruction of Castle Hagedorn, were now willing to abandon all scruples and fight for their lives. The staunch traditionalists still refused to compromise their honor, but Xanten gave them cheerful assurance: "Remain here then, prowling the castle like so many furtive rats. Take what comfort you can in the fact that you are being protected; the future holds little else for you."

And many who heard him stalked away in disgust.

Xanten turned to Hagedorn. "What of you? Do you come or do you stay?"

Hagedorn heaved a deep sigh, almost a groan. "Castle Hagedorn is at an end. No matter what the eventuality. I will come with you."

The situation suddenly had altered. The Meks, established in a loose ring around Castle Hagedorn, had calculated upon no resistance from the countryside and little from the castle. They had established their barracks and syrup depots with thought only for convenience and none for defense; raiding parties, consequently, were able to approach, inflict damages and withdraw before sustaining serious losses of their own. Those Meks posted along North Ridge were harassed almost continuously and finally were driven down with many losses. The circle around Castle Hagedorn became a cusp; then two days later, after the destruction of five more syrup depots, the Meks drew back even farther. Throwing up earthworks before the two tunnels leading under the south face of the crag, they established a more or less tenable defensive position, but now instead of beleaguering, they became the beleaguered, though still fighting.

Within the area thus defended the Meks concentrated their remaining syrup stocks, tools, weapons, ammunition. The area outside the earthworks was floodlit after dark and guarded by Meks armed with pellet-guns, making any frontal assault impractical.

For a day the raiders kept to the shelter of the surrounding orchards, appraising the new situation. Then a tactic was attempted. Six light carriages were improvised and loaded with bladders of a light inflammable oil, with a fire grenade attached. To each of these carriages ten Birds were harnessed, and at midnight sent aloft, with a man for each carriage. Flying high, the Birds then glided down through the darkness over the Mek position, where the fire bombs were dropped.

The area instantly seethed with flame. The syrup depot burnt; the power-wagons, awakened by the flames, rolled frantically back and forth, crushing Meks and stores, colliding with each other, adding vastly to the terror of the flames. The Meks who survived took shelter in the tunnels. Certain of the floodlights were extinguished and, taking advantage of the confusion, the men attacked the earthworks.

After a short bitter battle, the men killed all the sentinels and took up positions commanding the mouths of the tunnels, which now contained all that remained of the Mek army. It seemed as if the Mek uprising had been put down.

XII

The flames died. The human warriors—three hundred men from the castle, two hundred Expiationists and about three hundred Nomads—gathered about the tunnel mouth and, during the balance of the night, considered methods to deal with the immured Meks.

At sunrise those men of Castle Hagedorn whose children and consorts were yet within the castle went to bring them forth. With them, upon their return, came a group of castle gentlemen: among them Beaudry, O. Z. Garr, Isseth, and Aure. They greeted their one-time peers, Hagedorn, Xanten, Claghorn and others, crisply, but with a certain austere detachment, which recognized that loss of prestige incurred by those who fought Meks as if they were equals.

"Now what is to happen?" Beaudry inquired of Hagedorn. "The Meks are trapped but you can't bring them forth. Not impossibly they have syrup stored within for the power-wagons. They may well survive for months."

O. Z. Garr, assessing the situation from the standpoint of a military theoretician, came forward with a plan of action. "Fetch down the cannon—or have your underlings do so—and mount them on power-wagons. When the vermin are sufficiently weak, roll the cannon in and wipe out all but a labor force for the castle. We formerly worked four hundred, and this should suffice."

"Ha!" exclaimed Xanten. "It gives me great pleasure to inform you that this will never be. If any Meks survive they will repair the spaceships and instruct us in the maintenance and we will then transport them and Peasants back to their native worlds."

"How then do you expect us to maintain our lives?" demanded Garr coldly.

335

"You have the syrup generator. Fit yourself with sacs and drink syrup."

Garr tilted back his head, stared coldly down his nose. "This is your voice, yours alone, and your insolent opinion. Others are to be heard from. Hagedorn, is this your philosophy, that civilization should wither?"

"It need not wither," said Hagedorn, "provided that all of us—you as well as we—toil for it. There can be no more slaves. I have become convinced of this."

O. Z. Garr turned on his heel, swept back up the avenue into the castle, followed by the most traditional-minded of his comrades. A few moved aside and talked among themselves in low tones, with one or two black looks for Xanten and Hagedorn.

From the ramparts of the castle came a sudden outcry: "The Meks! They are taking the castle! They swarm up the lower passages! Attack, save us!"

The men below stared up in consternation. Even as they looked the castle portals swung shut.

"How is this possible?" demanded Hagedorn. "I swear all entered the tunnels!"

"It is only too clear," said Xanten bitterly. "While they undermined, they drove a tunnel up to the lower levels!"

Hagedorn started forward as if he would charge up the crag alone, then halted. "We must drive them out! Unthinkable that they pillage our castle!"

"Unfortunately," said Claghorn, "the walls bar us as effectually as they did the Meks."

"We can send up a force by Bird-car! Once we consolidate, we can exterminate them!"

Claghorn shook his head. "They can wait on the ramparts and flight-deck and shoot down the Birds as they approach. Even if we secured a foothold there would be great bloodshed: one of us killed for every one of them. And they still outnumber us three or four to one."

Hagedorn groaned. "The thought of them revelling among

my possessions, strutting about in my clothes, swilling my essences—it sickens me!"

"Listen!" said Claghorn. From on high they heard the hoarse yells of men, the crackle of energy-cannon. "Some of them, at least, hold out on the ramparts!"

Xanten went to a nearby group of Birds who were for once awed and subdued by events. "Lift me up above the castle, out of range of the pellets, but where I can see what the Meks do!"

"Care, take care!" croaked one of the Birds. "Ill things occur at the castle."

"Never mind! Convey me up, above the ramparts!"

The Birds lifted him, swung in a great circle around the crag and above the castle, sufficiently distant to be safe from the Mek pellet-guns.

Beside those cannon which yet operated stood thirty men and women. Between the great Houses, the rotunda and the palace, everywhere the cannon could not be brought to bear, swarmed Meks. The plaza was littered with corpses: gentlemen, ladies and their children—all those who had elected to remain at Castle Hagedorn.

At one of the cannon stood O. Z. Garr. Spying Xanten he gave a shout of hysterical rage, swung up the cannon, fired a bolt. The Birds, screaming, tried to swerve aside, but the bolt smashed two. Birds, car, Xanten, fell in a great tangle. By some miracle, the four yet alive caught their balance and a hundred feet from the ground, with a frenzied groaning effort, they slowed their fall, steadied, hovered an instant, sank to the ground.

Xantern staggered free of the tangle. Men came running. "Are you safe?" called Claghorn.

"Safe, yes. Frightened as well!" Xanten took a deep breath, went to sit on an outcrop of rock.

"What's happening up there?" asked Claghorn.

"All dead," said Xanten, "all but a score. Garr has gone mad. He fired on me."

"Look! Meks on the ramparts!" cried A. L. Morgan.

"There!" cried someone else. "Men! They jump! . . . No, they are flung!"

Some were men, some were Meks whom they had dragged with them; with awful slowness they toppled to their deaths. No more fell. Castle Hagedorn was in the hands of the Meks.

Xanten considered the complex silhouette, at once so familiar and so strange. "They can't hope to hold out. We need only destroy the sun-cells, and they can synthesize no syrup."

"Let us do it now," said Claghorn, "before they think of this and man the cannon! Birds!"

He went off to give the orders, and forty Birds, each clutching two rocks the size of a man's head, flapped up, circled the castle and presently returned to report the sun-cells had been destroyed.

Xanten said, "All that remains is to seal the tunnel entrances against a sudden eruption, which might catch us off guard—then patience."

"What of the Peasants in the stables—and the Phanes?" asked Hagedorn in a forlorn voice.

Xanten gave his head a slow shake. "He who was not an Expiationist before must become one now."

Claghorn muttered, "They can survive two months at most —no more."

But two months passed, and three months, and four months. Then one morning the great portals opened, a haggard Mek stumbled forth.

He signaled: "Men: we starve. We have maintained your treasures. Give us our lives or we destroy all before we die."

Claghorn responded: "These are our terms. We give you your lives. You must clean the castle, remove and bury the corpses. You must repair the spaceships and teach us all you know regarding them. We will then transport you to Etamin Nine."

"The terms you offer are accepted."

Five years later Xanten and Glys Meadowsweet, with their two children, had reason to travel north from their home near

338

Sande River. They took occasion to visit Castle Hagedorn, where now lived only two or three dozen folk, among them Hagedorn.

He had aged, so it seemed to Xanten. His hair was white; his face, once bluff and hearty, had become thin, almost waxen. Xanten could not determine his mood.

They stood in the shade of a walnut tree, with castle and crag looming above them. "This is now a great museum," said Hagedorn. "I am curator, and this will be the function of all the Hagedorns who come after me, for there is incalculable treasure to guard and maintain. Already the feeling of antiquity has come to the castle. The Houses are alive with ghosts. I see them often, especially on the nights of the fetes. . . . Ah, those were the times, were they not, Xanten?"

"Yes, indeed," said Xanten. He touched the heads of his two children. "Still, I have no wish to return to them. We are men now, on our own world, as we never were before."

Hagedorn gave a somewhat regretful assent. He looked up at the vast structure, as if now were the first occasion he had laid eyes on it. "The folk of the future—what will they think of Castle Hagedorn? Its treasures, its books, its tabards?"

"They will come, they will marvel," said Xanten. "Almost as I do today."

"There is much at which to marvel. Will you come within, Xanten? There are still flasks of noble essence laid by."

"Thank you no," said Xanten. "There is too much to stir old memories. We will go our way, and I think that we will do so immediately."

Hagedorn nodded sadly. "I understand very well. I myself am often given to reverie these days. Well then, good-by, and journey home with pleasure."

"We will do so, Hagedorn. Thank you and good-by," said Xanten, and turned away from Castle Hagedorn, toward the world of men.

For the last dozen years or so, what we might call "hard science fiction" has receded somewhat into the background. By hard science fiction, I mean those stories in which the details of science play an important role and in which the author is accurate about those details, too, and takes the trouble to explain them clearly.

In its place, there has moved into the forefront the emotional story in which science is relegated to the background. Literary style, not physical theory, is what counts; experimentation in form, not in the laboratory; the wrenching of souls, rather than of minds.

As for myself (for I will conceal nothing from you) I'm a hard science fiction man myself. For instance, in the same issue of the same magazine in which Harlan Ellison published "I Have No Mouth and I Must Scream" which was all emotion and which won a Hugo, I published "Billiard Ball" which was all thought and which didn't win a Hugo.

Naturally, miscarriages of justice like this cause me to brood, but I feel better when it turns out that there are still hard science fiction writers among the younger generation. Ben Bova, for instance, writes hard science fiction, and so does Larry Niven.

What's more, Larry Niven made it big and won a Hugo with his excellent story, "Neutron Star."

The only trouble with the victory was that when I read his story I was overwhelmed with grief. I don't mean merely the grief that overcomes me whenever someone else wins a Hugo. I mean a highly special grief over the nature of the plot.

You see, I write a science article in every issue of *The Magazine of Fantasy and Science Fiction* (and have just completed my 151st article as I write this). In the May 1966 issue I wrote an article called "Time and Tide" and as I thought back on that particular article I was overwhelmed with poignant sorrow. The plot of "Neutron Star" was implicit in my article and if I had only thought fiction-wise instead of article-wise, I might have written the story.

Eventually, of course, I met Larry Niven, a remarkably quiet fellow, who dresses most neatly and conservatively, has a clean-shaven square countenance, a soft voice, and a penchant for speculating on the sex life of Superman.

"Listen, Larry," I said, shaking my head sadly, "I once wrote an article entitled 'Time and Tide' which dealt with—"

"I know," said Larry calmly. "It was when I read that article that I got the idea for 'Neutron Star.' "

It is a tribute to the essential sweetness of my character, that the man still lives!

6

NEUTRON STAR

I

The Skydiver dropped out of hyperspace an even million miles above the neutron star. I needed a minute to place myself against the stellar background and another to find the distortion Sonya Laskin had mentioned before she died. It was to my left, an area the apparent size of the Earth's moon. I swung the ship around to face it.

Curdled stars, muddled stars, stars that had been stirred with a spoon.

The neutron star was in the center, of course, though I couldn't see it and hadn't expected to. It was only eleven miles across, and cool. A billion years had passed since BVS-1 burned by fusion fire. Millions of years, at least, since the cataclysmic two weeks during which BVS-1 was an X-ray star, burning at a temperature of five billion degrees Kelvin. Now it showed only by its mass.

The ship began to turn by itself. I felt the pressure of the fusion drive. Without help from me, my faithful metal watchdog was putting me in hyperbolic orbit that would take me within one mile of the neutron star's surface. Twenty-four hours to fall, twenty-four hours to rise . . . and during that time, something would try to kill me. As something had killed the Laskins.

The same type of autopilot, with the same program, had chosen the Laskin's orbit. It had not caused their ship to collide with the star. I could trust the autopilot. I could even change its program.

I really ought to.

How did I get myself into this hole?

The drive went off after ten minutes of maneuvering. My

orbit was established, in more ways than one. I knew what would happen if I tried to back out now.

All I'd done was walk into a drugstore to get a new battery for my lighter!

Right in the middle of the store, surrounded by three floors of sales counters, was the new 2603 Sinclair intrasystem yacht. I'd come for a battery, but I stayed to admire. It was a beautiful job, small and sleek and streamlined and blatantly different from anything that's ever been built. I wouldn't have flown it for anything, but I had to admit it was pretty. I ducked my head through the door to look at the control panel. You never saw so many dials. When I pulled my head out, all the customers were looking in the same direction. The place had gone startlingly quiet.

I can't blame them for staring. A number of aliens were in the store, mainly shopping for souvenirs, but they were staring too. A puppeteer is unique. Imagine a headless, three-legged centaur wearing two Cecil the Seasick Sea Serpent puppets on his arms, and you'll have something like the right picture. But the arms are weaving necks, and the puppets are real heads, flat and brainless, with wide flexible lips. The brain is under a bony hump set between the bases of the necks. This puppeteer wore only its own coat of brown hair, with a mane that extended all the way up its spine to form a thick mat over the brain. I'm told that the way they wear the mane indicates their status in society, but to me it could have been anything from a dock worker to a jeweler to the president of General Products.

I watched with the rest as it came across the floor, not because I'd never seen a puppeteer, but because there is something beautiful about the dainty way they move on those slender legs and tiny hooves. I watched it come straight toward me, closer and closer. It stopped a foot away, looked me over and said, "You are Beowulf Shaeffer, former chief pilot for Nakamura Lines."

Its voice was a beautiful contralto with not a trace of accent. A puppeteer's mouths are not only the most flexible speech

343

organs around, but also the most sensitive hands. The tongues are forked and pointed, the wide, thick lips have little finger-like knobs along the rims. Imagine a watchmaker with a sense of taste in his fingertips.

I cleared my throat. "That's right."

It considered me from two directions. "You would be interested in a high-paying job?"

"I'd be fascinated in a high-paying job."

"I am our equivalent of the regional president of General Products. Please come with me, and we will discuss this elsewhere."

I followed it into a displacement booth. Eyes followed me all the way. It was embarrassing, being accosted in a public drugstore by a two-headed monster. Maybe the puppeteer knew it. Maybe it was testing me to see how badly I needed money.

My need was great. Eight months had passed since Naka-mura Lines folded. For some time before that, I had been living very high on the hog, knowing that my back pay would cover my debts. I never saw that back pay. It was quite a crash, Naka-mura Lines. Respectable middle-aged businessmen took to leaving their hotel windows without their lift belts. Me, I kept spending. If I'd started living frugally, my creditors would have done some checking . . . and I'd have ended in debtor's prison.

The puppeteer dialed thirteen fast digits with its tongue. A moment later we were elsewhere. Air puffed out when I opened the booth door, and I swallowed to pop my ears.

"We are on the roof of the General Products building." The rich contralto voice thrilled along my nerves, and I had to remind myself that it was an alien speaking, not a lovely woman. "You must examine this spacecraft while we discuss your assignment."

I stepped outside a little cautiously, but it wasn't the windy season. The roof was at ground level. That's the way we build on We Made It. Maybe it has something to do with the fifteen-hundred-mile-an-hour winds we get in summer and winter.

344

hind it was a windowless reflective silver. From the back wall of the relaxation room an access tube ran aft, opening on various instruments and the hyperdrive motors.

There were two acceleration couches in the control cabin. Both had been torn loose from their mountings and wadded into the nose like so much tissue paper, crushing the instrument panel. The backs of the crumpled couches were splashed with rust brown. Flecks of the same color were all over everything, the walls, the windows, the viewscreens. It was as if something had hit the couches from behind: something like a dozen paint-filled toy balloons, striking with tremendous force.

"That's blood," I said.

"That is correct. Human circulatory fluid."

II

Twenty-four hours to fall.

I spent most of the first twelve hours in the relaxation room, trying to read. Nothing significant was happening, except that a few times I saw the phenomenon Sonya Laskin had mentioned in her last report. When a star went directly behind the invisible BVS-1, a halo formed. BVS-1 was heavy enough to bend light around it, displacing most stars to the sides; but when a star went directly behind the neutron star, its light was displaced to all sides at once. Result: a tiny circle which flashed once and was gone almost before the eye could catch it.

I'd known next to nothing about neutron stars the day the puppeteer picked me up. Now I was an expert. But I still had no idea what was waiting for me when I got down there.

All the matter you're ever likely to meet will be normal matter, composed of a nucleus of protons and neutrons, surrounded by electrons in quantum energy states. In the heart of any star there is a second kind of matter: for there, the tremendous pressure is enough to smash the electron shells. The result is degenerate matter: nuclei forced together by pressure and gravity, but held apart by the mutual repulsion of the more or less continuous electron 'gas' around them. The right circumstances may create a third type of matter.

Given: a burnt-out white dwarf with a mass greater than 1·44 times the mass of the Sun—Chandrasekhar's Limit, named for an Indian-American astronomer of the nineteen hundreds. In such a mass the electron pressure alone would not be able to hold the electrons back from the nuclei. Electrons would be forced against protons—to make neutrons. In one blazing explosion most of the star would change from a compressed mass of degenerate matter to a closely packed lump of neutrons: neutronium, theoretically the densest matter possible in this universe. Most of the remaining normal and degenerate matter would be blown away by the liberated heat.

For two weeks the star would give off X-rays, as its core temperature dropped from five billion degrees Kelvin to five hundred million. After that it would be a light-emitting body perhaps ten to twelve miles across: the next best thing to invisible. It was not strange that BVS-1 was the first neutron star ever found.

Neither is it strange that the Institute of Knowledge on Jinx would have spent a good deal of time and trouble looking. Until BVS-1 was found, neutronium and neutron stars were only theories. The examination of an actual neutron star could be of tremendous importance. Neutron stars could give us the key to true gravity control.

Mass of BVS-1: 1·3 times the mass of Sol, approximately.

Diameter of BVS-1 (estimated): eleven miles of neutronium, covered by half a mile of degenerate matter, covered by maybe twelve feet of ordinary matter.

Escape velocity: 130,000 mps, approximately.

Nothing else was known of the tiny black star until the Laskins went in to look. Now the Institute knew one thing more. The star's spin.

"A mass that large can distort space by its rotation," said the puppeteer. "The Institute ship's projected hyperbola was twisted across itself in such a way that we can deduce the star's period of rotation to be two minutes, twenty-seven seconds."

The bar was somewhere in the General Products building. I don't know just where, and with the transfer booths it doesn't matter. I kept staring at the puppeteer bartender. Naturally only a puppeteer would be served by a puppeteer bartender, since any biped would resent knowing that somebody made his drink with his mouth. I had already decided to get dinner somewhere else.

"I see your problem," I said. "Your sales will suffer if it gets out that something can reach through one of your hulls and smash a crew to bloody smears. But where do I fit in?"

"We wish to repeat the experiment of Sonya Laskin and Peter Laskin. We must find—"

"With me?"

"Yes. We must find out what it is that our hulls cannot stop. Naturally you may—"

"But I won't."

"We are prepared to offer one million stars."

I was temped, but only for a moment. "Forget it."

"Naturally you will be allowed to build your own ship, starting with a #2 General Products hull."

"Thanks, but I'd like to go on living."

"You would dislike being confined. I find that We Made It has re-established the debtor's prison. If General Products made public your accounts . . ."

"Now, *just* a—"

"You owe money in the close order of five hundred thousand stars. We will pay your creditors before you leave. If you re-turn"—I had to admire the creature's honesty in not saying *when*—"we will pay you the remainder. You may be asked to speak to news commentators concerning the voyage, in which case there will be more stars."

"You say I can build my own ship?"

"Naturally. This is not a voyage of exploration. We want you to return safely."

"It's a deal," I said.

After all, the puppeteer had tried to blackmail me. What happened next would be its own fault.

They built my ship in two weeks flat. They started with a #2 General Products hull, just like the one around the Institute of Knowledge ship, and the lifesystem was practically a duplicate of the Laskin's, but there the resemblance ended. There were no instruments to observe neutron stars. Instead, there was a fusion motor big enough for a Jinx warliner. In my ship, which I now called Skydiver, the drive would produce thirty gees at the safety limit. There was a laser cannon big enough to punch a hole through We Made It's moon. The puppeteer wanted me to feel safe, and now I did, for I could fight and I could run. Especially I could run.

I heard the Laskins' last broadcast through half a dozen times. Their unnamed ship had dropped out of hyperspace a million miles above BVS-1. Gravity warp would have prevented their getting closer in hyperspace. While her husband was crawling through the access tube for an instrument check, Sonya Laskin had called the Institute of Knowledge ". . . we can't see it yet, not with the naked eye. But we can see where it is. Every time some star or other goes behind it, there's a little ring of light. Just a minute. Peter's ready to use the telescope . . ."

Then the star's mass had cut the hyperspacial link. It was expected, and nobody had worried—then. Later, the same effect must have stopped them from escaping whatever attacked them, into hyperspace.

When would-be rescuers found the ship, only the radar and the cameras were still running. They didn't tell us much. There had been no camera in the cabin. But the forward camera gave us, for one instant, a speed-blurred view of the neutron star. It was a featureless disc the orange color of perfect barbecue coals, if you know someone who can afford to burn wood. This object had been a neutron star a long time.

"There'll be no need to paint the ship," I told the president.

"You should not make such a trip with the walls transparent. You would go insane."

"I'm no flatlander. The mind-wrenching sight of naked space fills me with mild, but waning interest. I want to know nothing's sneaking up behind me."

The day before I left, I sat alone in the General Products bar letting the puppeteer bartender make me drinks with his mouth. He did it well. Puppeteers were scattered around the bar in twos and threes, with a couple of men for variety; but the drinking hour had not yet arrived. The place felt empty.

I was pleased with myself. My debts were all paid, not that that would matter where I was going. I would leave with not a mini-credit to my name; with nothing but the ship . . .

All told, I was well out of a sticky situation. I hoped I'd like being a rich exile.

I jumped when the newcomer sat down across from me. He was a foreigner, a middle-aged man wearing an expensive night-black business suit and a snow-white asymmetric beard. I let my face freeze and started to get up.

"Sit down, Mr. Shaeffer."

"Why?"

He told me by showing me a blue disc. An Earth-government ident. I looked it over to show I was alert, not because I'd know an ersatz from the real thing.

"My name is Sigmund Ausfaller," said the government man. "I wish to say a few words concerning your assignment on behalf of General Products."

I nodded, not saying anything.

"A record of your verbal contract was sent to us as a matter of course. I noticed some peculiar things about it. Mr. Shaeffer, will you really take such a risk for only five hundred thousand stars?"

"I'm getting twice that."

"But you only keep half of it. The rest goes to pay debts. Then there are taxes. But never mind. What occurred to me was that a spaceship is a spaceship, and yours is very well armed and has powerful legs. An admirable fighting ship, if you were moved to sell it."

"But it isn't mine."

"There are those who would not ask. On Canyon, for example, or the Isolationist party of Wonderland."

I said nothing.

"Or, you might be planning a career of piracy. A risky business, piracy, and I don't take the notion seriously."

I hadn't even thought about piracy. But I'd have to give up on Wonderland . . .

"What I would like to say is this, Mr. Shaeffer. A single entrepreneur, if he were sufficiently dishonest, could do terrible damage to the reputation of all human beings everywhere. Most species find it necessary to police the ethics of their own members, and we are no exception. It occurred to me that you might not take your ship to the neutron star at all; that you would take it elsewhere and sell it. The puppeteers do not make invulnerable war vessels. They are pacifists. Your Skydiver is unique.

"Hence I have asked General Products to allow me to install a remote control bomb in the Skydiver. Since it is inside the hull, the hull cannot protect you. I had it installed this afternoon.

"Now, notice! If you have not reported within a week I will set off the bomb. There are several worlds within a week's hyperspace flight of here, but all recognize the dominion of Earth. If you flee, you must leave your ship within a week, so I hardly think you will land on a nonhabitable world. Clear?"

"Clear."

"If I am wrong, you may take a lie-detector test and prove it. Then you may punch me in the nose, and I will apologize handsomely."

I shook my head. He stood up, bowed and left me sitting there cold sober.

Four films had been taken from the Laskins' cameras. In the time left to me, I ran through them several times, without seeing anything out of the way. If the ship had run through a gas cloud, the impact could have killed the Laskins. At perihelion they were moving at better than half the speed of light. But there would have been friction, and I saw no sign of heating in the films. If something alive had attacked them, the beast was invisible to radar and to an enormous range of light frequencies. If the attitude jets had fired accidentally—I was clutching at straws—the light showed on none of the films.

There would be savage magnetic forces near BVS-1, but that couldn't have done any damage. No such force could penetrate a General Products hull. Neither could heat, except in special bands of radiated light, bands visible to at least one of the puppeteers' alien customers. I hold adverse opinions on the General Products hull, but they all concern the dull anonymity of the design. Or maybe I resent the fact that General Products holds a near-monopoly on spacecraft hulls and isn't owned by human beings. But if I'd had to trust my life to, say, the Sinclair yacht I'd seen in the drugstore, I'd have chosen jail.

Jail was one of my three choices. But I'd be there for life. Ausfaller would see to that.

Or I could run for it in the Skydiver. But no world within reach would have me, that is. Of course, if I could find an undiscovered Earthlike world within a week of We Made It . . .

Fat chance, I preferred BVS-1 to that any day.

III

I thought that flashing circle of light was getting bigger, but it flashed so seldom I couldn't be sure. BVS-1 wouldn't show even in my telescope. I gave that up and settled for just waiting.

Waiting, I remembered a long-ago summer I spent on Jinx. There were days when, unable to go outside because a derth of clouds had spread the land with raw blue-white sunlight, we amused ourselves by filling party balloons with tap water and dropping them on the sidewalk from three stories up. They made lovely splash patterns—which dried out too fast. So we put a little ink in each balloon before filling it. Then the patterns stayed.

Sonya Laskin had been in her chair when the chairs collapsed. Blood samples showed that it was Peter, who had struck them from behind, like a water balloon dropped from a great height.

What could get through a General Products hull?

Ten hours to fall.

I unfastened the safety net and went for an inspection tour. The access tunnel was three feet wide, just right to push through in free fall. Below me was the length of the fusion tube; to the left, the laser cannon; to the right, a set of curved side tubes leading to inspection points for the gyros, the batteries and generator, the air plant, the hyperspace shunt motors. All was in order—except me. I was clumsy. My jumps were always too short or too long. There was no room to turn at the stern end, so I had to back fifty feet to a side tube.

Six hours to go, and still I couldn't find the neutron star. Probably I would see it only for an instant, passing at better than half the speed of light. Already my speed must be enormous.

Were the stars turning blue?

Two hours to go, I was sure they were turning blue. Was my speed that high? Then the stars behind should be red. Machinery blocked the view behind me, so I used the gyros. The ship turned with peculiar sluggishness. And the stars behind were blue, not red. All around me were blue-white stars.

Imagine light falling into a savagely steep gravitational well. It won't accelerate. Light can't move faster than light. But it can gain in energy, in frequency. The light was falling on me, harder and harder as I dropped.

I told the dictaphone about it. That dictaphone was probably the best protected item on the ship. I had already decided to earn my money by using it, just as if I expected to collect. Privately I wondered just how intense the light would get.

Skydiver had drifted back to vertical, with its axis through the neutron star, but now it faced outward. I'd thought I had

354

the ship stopped horizontally. More clumsiness. I used the gyros. Again the ship moved mushily, until it was halfway through the swing. Then it seemed to fall automatically into place. It was as if the Skydiver preferred to have its axis through the neutron star.

I didn't like that in the least.

I tried the maneuver again, and again the Skydiver fought back. But this time there was something else. Something was pulling at me.

So I unfastened my safety net and fell headfirst into the nose.

The pull was light, about a tenth of a gee. It felt more like sinking through honey than falling. I climbed back into my chair, tied myself in with the net, now hanging face down, turned on the dictaphone. I told my story in such nitpicking detail that my hypothetical listeners could not but doubt my hypothetical sanity. "I think this is what happened to the Laskins," I finished. "If the pull increases, I'll call back."

Think? I never doubted it. This strange, gentle pull was inexplicable. Something inexplicable had killed Peter and Sonya Laskin. Q.E.D.

Around the point where the neutron star must be, the stars were like smeared dots of oilpaint, smeared radially. They glared with an angry, painful light. I hung face down in the net and tried to think.

It was an hour before I was sure. The pull was increasing. And I still had an hour to fall.

Something was pulling on me, but not on the ship.

No, that was nonsense. What could reach out to me through a General Products hull? It must be the other way around. Something was pushing on the ship, pushing it off course.

If it got worse I could use the drive to compensate. Meanwhile, the ship was being pushed *away* from BVS-1, which was fine by me.

But if I was wrong, if the ship were not somehow being pushed away from BVS-1, the rocket motor would send the Skydiver crashing into eleven miles of neutronium.

And why wasn't the rocket already firing? If the ship was being pushed off course, the autopilot should be fighting back. The accelerometer was in good order. It had looked fine when I made my inspection tour down the access tube.

Could something be pushing on the ship *and* on the accelerometer, but not on me?

It came down to the same impossibility. Something that could reach through a General Products hull.

To hell with theory, said I to myself, said I. I'm getting out of here. To the dictaphone I said, "The pull has increased dangerously. I'm going to try to alter my orbit."

Of course, once I turned the ship outward and used the rocket, I'd be adding my own acceleration to the X force. It would be a strain, but I could stand it for a while. If I came within a mile of BVS-1, I'd end like Sonya Laskin.

She must have waited face down in a net like mine, waited without a drive unit, waited while the pressure rose and the net cut into her flesh, waited until the net snapped and dropped her into the nose, to lie crushed and broken until the X force tore the very chairs loose and dropped them on her.

I hit the gyros.

The gyros weren't strong enough to turn me. I tried it three times. Each time the ship rotated about fifty degrees and hung there, motionless, while the whine of the gyros went up and up. Released, the ship immediately swung back to position. I was nose down to the neutron star, and I was going to stay that way.

Half an hour to fall, and the X force was over a gee. My sinuses were in agony. My eyes were ripe and ready to fall out. I don't know if I could have stood a cigarette, but I didn't get the chance. My pack of Fortunados had fallen out of my pocket, when I dropped into the nose. There it was, four feet beyond my fingers, proof that the X force acted on other objects besides me. Fascinating.

I couldn't take any more. If it dropped me shrieking into the neutron star, I had to use the drive. And I did. I ran the thrust up until I was approximately in free fall. The blood which had pooled in my extremities went back where it belonged. The gee dial registered one point two gee. I cursed it for a lying robot.

The soft-pack was bobbing around in the nose, and it occurred to me that a little extra nudge on the throttle would bring it to me. I tried it. The pack drifted toward me, and I reached, and like a sentient thing it speeded up to avoid my clutching hand. I snatched at it again as it went past my ear, but again it was moving too fast. That pack was going at a hell of a clip, considering that here I was, practically in free fall. It dropped through the door to the relaxation room, still picking up speed, blurred and vanished as it entered the access tube. Seconds later I heard a solid Thump.

But that was *crazy*. Already the X force was pulling blood into my face. I pulled my lighter out, held it at arm's length and let go. It fell gently into the nose. But the pack of Fortunados had hit like I'd dropped it from a *building*.

Well.

I nudged the throttle again. The mutter of fusing hydrogen reminded me that if I tried to keep this up all the way, I might well put the General Products hull to its toughest test yet: smashing it into a neutron star at half lightspeed. I could see it now: a transparent hull containing only a few cubic inches of dwarf star matter wedged into the tip of the nose.

At one point four gee, according to that lying gee dial, the lighter came loose and drifted towards me. I let it go. It was clearly falling when it reached the doorway. I pulled the throttle back. The loss of power jerked me violently forward, but I kept my face turned. The lighter slowed and hesitated at the entrance to the access tube. Decided to go through. I cocked my ears for the sound, then jumped as the whole ship rang like a gong.

And the accelerometer was right at the ship's center of mass. Otherwise the ship's mass would have thrown the needle off. The puppeteers were fiends for ten-decimal-point accuracy.

I favored the dictaphone with a few fast comments, then got

to work reprogramming the autopilot. Luckily what I wanted was simple. The X force was but an X force to me, but now I knew how it behaved. I might actually live through this.

The stars were fiercely blue, warped to streaked lines near that special point. I thought I could see it now, very small and dim and red; but it might have been imagination. In twenty minutes, I'd be rounding the neutron star. The drive grumbled behind me. In effective free fall, I unfastened the safety net and pushed myself out of the chair.

A gentle push aft—and ghostly hands grasped my legs. Ten pounds of weight hung by my fingers from the back of the chair. The pressure should drop fast. I'd programmed the autopilot to reduce the thrust from two gees to zero during the next two minutes. All I had to do was be at the center of mass, in the access tube, when the thrust went to zero.

Something gripped the ship through a General Products hull. A psychokinetic life form stranded on a sun twelve miles in diameter? But how could anything alive stand such gravity?

Something might be stranded in orbit. There is life in space: outsiders and sailseeds and maybe others we haven't found yet. For all I knew or cared, BVS-1 itself might be alive. It didn't matter. I knew what the X force was trying to do. It was trying to pull the ship apart.

There was no pull on my fingers. I pushed aft and landed on the back wall, on bent legs. I knelt over the door, looking aft/down. When free fall came, I pulled myself through and was in the relaxation room looking down/forward into the nose.

Gravity was changing faster than I liked. The X force was growing as zero hour approached, while the compensating rocket thrust dropped. The X force tended to pull the ship apart; it was two gee forward at the nose, two gee backward at the tail and diminished to zero at the center of mass. Or so I hoped. The pack and lighter had behaved as if the force pulling them had increased for every inch they moved stern-ward.

The dictaphone was fifty feet below, utterly unreachable. If I had anything more to say to General Products, I'd have to say it in person. Maybe I'd get the chance. Because I knew what force was trying to tear the ship apart.

It was the tide.

The motor was off, and I was at the ship's midpoint. My spread-eagled position was getting uncomfortable. It was four minutes to perihelion.

Something creaked in the cabin below me. I couldn't see what it was, but I could clearly see a red point glaring among blue radial lines, like a lantern at the bottom of a well. To the sides, between the fusion tube and the tanks and other equipment, the blue stars glared at me with a light that was almost violet. I was afraid to look too long. I actually thought they might blind me.

There must have been hundreds of gravities in the cabin. I could even feel the pressure change. The air was thin at this height, one hundred and fifty feet above the control room.

And now, almost suddenly, the red dot was more than a dot. My time was up. A red disc leapt up at me; the ship swung around me; and I gasped and shut my eyes tight. Giants' hands gripped my arms and legs and head, gently but with great firmness, and tried to pull me in two. In that moment it came to me that Peter Laskin had died like this. He'd made the same guesses I had, and he'd tried to hide in the access tube. But he'd slipped. As I was slipping . . .

When I got my eyes open the red dot was shrinking into nothing.

IV

The puppeteer president insisted I be put in a hospital for observation. I didn't fight the idea. My face and hands were flaming red, with blisters rising, and I ached like I'd been beaten. Rest and tender loving care, that's what I wanted.

I was floating between a pair of sleeping plates, hideously

uncomfortable, when the nurse came to announce a visitor. I knew who it was from her peculiar expression.

"What can get through a General Products hull?" I asked it.

"I hoped you would tell me." The president rested on its single back leg, holding a stick that gave off green, incense-smelling smoke.

"And so I will. Gravity."

"Do not play with me, Beowulf Shaeffer. This matter is vital."

"I'm not playing. Does your world have a moon?"

"That information is classified." The puppeteers are cowards. Nobody knows where they come from, and nobody is likely to find out.

"Do you know what happens when a moon gets too close to its primary?"

"It falls apart."

"Why?"

"I do not know."

"Tides."

"What is a tide?"

Oho, said I to myself, said I. "I'm going to try to tell you. The Earth's moon is almost two thousand miles in diameter and does not rotate with respect to Earth. I want you to pick two rocks on the Moon, one at the point nearest the Earth, one at the point furthest away."

"Very well."

"Now, isn't it obvious that if those rocks were left to themselves they'd fall away from each other? They're in two different orbits, mind you, concentric orbits, one almost two thousand miles outside the other. Yet those rocks are forced to move at the same orbital speed."

"The one outside is moving faster."

"Good point. So there *is* a force trying to pull the Moon apart. Gravity holds it together. Bring the Moon close enough to Earth, and those two rocks would simply float away."

"I see. Then this *tide* tried to pull your ship apart. It was

360

powerful enough in the lifesystem of the Institute ship to pull the acceleration chairs out of their mounts."

"And to crush a human being. Picture it. The ship's nose was just seven miles from the center of BVS-1. The tail was three hundred feet further out. Left to themselves they'd have gone in completely different orbits. My head and feet tried to do the same thing, when I got close enough."

"I see. Are you moulting?"

"What?"

"I noticed you are losing your outer integument in spots."

"Oh, *that*. I got a bad sunburn from exposure to starlight."

Two heads stared at each other for an eyeblink. A shrug? The puppeteer said, "We have deposited the remainder of your pay with the Bank of We Made It. One Sigmund Ausfaller, human, has frozen the account until your taxes are computed."

"Figures."

"If you will talk to reporters now, explaining what happened to the Institute ship, we will pay you ten thousand stars. We will pay cash so that you may use it immediately. It is urgent. There have been rumors."

"Bring 'em in." As an afterthought I added, "I can also tell them that your world is moonless. That should be good for a footnote somewhere."

"I do not understand." But two long necks had drawn back, and the puppeteer was watching me like a pair of pythons.

"You'd know what a tide was if you had a moon. You couldn't avoid it."

"Would you be interested in . . ."

". . . a million stars? I'd be fascinated. I'll even sign a contract if it includes what we're hiding. How do *you* like being blackmailed?"

HUGO AWARDS 1962–1967

1962: 20th Convention—Chicago
Novel—STRANGER IN A STRANGE LAND by Robert A. Heinlein
Short Fiction—The Hothouse Series by Brian W. Aldiss
Professional Magazine—*Analog*
Amateur Magazine—*Warhoon*, Richard Bergeron, ed.
Professional Artist—Ed Emshwiller
Dramatic Presentation—"The Twilight Zone" by Rod Serling
1963: 21st Convention—Washington, D.C.
Novel—THE MAN IN THE HIGH CASTLE by Philip K. Dick
Short Fiction—"The Dragon Masters" by Jack Vance
Dramatic Award—No Award
Professional Magazine—*The Magazine of Fantasy and Science Fiction*
Amateur Magazine—*Zero*, Dick Lupoff, ed.
Professional Artist—Roy Krenkel
Special Awards—P. Schuyler Miller (For Best Book Reviews)
Isaac Asimov (For Distinguished Contributions to the Field)
1964: 22nd Convention—Oakland
Novel—WAY STATION by Clifford Simak
Short Fiction—"No Truce With Kings" by Poul Anderson
Professional Magazine—*Analog*
Professional Artist—Ed Emsh
Book Publisher—Ace Books
Amateur Publication—*Amra*, George Scithers, ed.
1965: 23rd Convention—London
Novel—THE WANDERER by Fritz Leiber
Short Fiction—"Soldier, Ask Not" by Gordon R. Dickson
Professional Magazine—*Analog*
Book Publisher—Ballantine Books

Amateur Publication—*Yandro*, Robert & Juanita Coulson, eds.

Dramatic Presentation—"Dr. Strangelove"

1966: 24th Convention—Cleveland

Novel (tie)—AND CALL ME CONRAD by Roger Zelazny and DUNE by Frank Herbert

Short Fiction—" 'Repent, Harlequin!' said the Ticktockman" by Harlan Ellison

Professional Magazine—*IF*

Professional Artist—Frank Frazetta

Amateur Magazine—*ERB-dom*, Camille Cazeddessus, Jr., ed.

Best All-time Series—Foundation Series by Isaac Asimov

1967: 25th Convention—New York

Novel—THE MOON IS A HARSH MISTRESS by Robert A. Heinlein

Novelette—"The Last Castle" by Jack Vance

Short Story—"Neutron Star" by Larry Niven

Professional Magazine—*IF*

Professional Artist—Jack Gaughan

Dramatic Presentation—"The Menagerie" (Star Trek)

Amateur Publication—*Niekas*, Ed. Meskys and Felice Rolfe, eds.

Fan Artist—Jack Gaughan

Fan Writer—Alexei Panshin

Science Against Man

Edited by ANTHONY CHEETHAM

"A very good collection of 11 short stories taking the theme that science has stopped being a good servant and is becoming a hard master.

"THE LOST CONTINENT by Norman Spinrad . . . is brilliant. So is HAROLD WILSON AT THE COSMIC COCKTAIL PARTY . . . by Bob Shaw. Notable contributions come from Harry Harrison, James Blish and Robert Silverberg."
– Edmund Cooper, *The Sunday Times*

Other contributors include:

Brian Aldiss

Andrew Travers

John Brunner

Piers Anthony

Paul Ableman

Michael Moorcock

Sphere   30p

Out of the Mouth of the Dragon

MARK S. GESTON

Amon VanRoark heard the prophet speaking in the market place of the decayed city. He called men to the wars, to the fabled Meadows where the armies of Good would meet the forces of Evil, in one final Armageddon that would decide the fate of a world already doomed and dying.

VanRoark followed the prophet to the Meadows and there he witnessed the last cataclismic battle between humanity and the dark powers of Salasar.

Sphere   30p

The Year's Best Science Fiction No. 5

Edited by HARRY HARRISON
& BRIAN ALDISS

The best SF shorts of 1971

Including stories by

ROBERT SCHECKLEY

ARTHUR C. CLARKE

JAMES BLISH

DONALD BARTHELME

NORMAN SPINRAD

KINGSLEY AMIS

THOMAS M. DISCH

and 11 other writers whose stories
represent the finest sf of 1971

Sphere   35p

Science Fiction Hall of Fame

Edited by ROBERT SILVERBERG

This superb anthology contains the finest SF stories published before 1965.

Volume 1 includes stories by Clifford Simak, Robert Heinlein, Isaac Asimov, A. E. van Vogt.

Volume 2 includes such writers as Cordwainer Smith, James Blish, Ray Bradbury, Anthony Boucher and Arthur C. Clarke.

"Something for the connoisseur to gloat over, a magnificent line-up" – *Evening Standard*

Sphere   40p each